ED JAMES is the author of the bestselling DI Simon
Fenchurch novels, Seattle-based FBI thrillers starring Max
Carter, and the self-published Detective Scott Cullen series and
its Craig Hunter spin-off books. During his time in IT project
management, Ed spent every moment he could writing and
has now traded in his weekly commute to London in order
to write full-time. He lives in the Scottish Borders with
far too many rescued animals.

## Praise for *Senseless*:

'*Senseless* is a stand-out crime novel in a genre where the bar
has never been higher. Taking us into the dark heart of a missing
person investigation, Ed James skilfully ratchets up the tension
and the pace never drops for a second. Some great wry humour
too! Chilling, highly original, and highly recommended'
Caz Frear

'I can't remember the last time I read a book in one sitting, but
with ingenious plotting, clever pacing and a hold-your-breath
race against the clock, I couldn't stop myself. It's the
best police procedural I've read in ages'
Michelle Davies

'Just when your heart rate is getting back to normal, *Senseless*
smacks you in the face with another twist. Compelling stuff'
Jenny Blackhurst

# SENSELESS

## ED JAMES

HEADLINE

First published in 2020 by
HEADLINE PUBLISHING GROUP

2

Cataloguing in Publication Data is available from the British Library

ISBN 978 1 4722 6806 8

Typeset in 11/14.85 pt Sabon by Jouve (UK), Milton Keynes

Printed and bound in Great Britain by Clays Ltd, Elcograf S.p.A.

Headline's policy is to use papers that are natural, renewable and recyclable
products and made from wood grown in well-managed forests and other
controlled sources. The logging and manufacturing processes are expected
to conform to the environmental regulations of the country of origin.

HEADLINE PUBLISHING GROUP
An Hachette UK Company
Carmelite House
50 Victoria Embankment
London
EC4Y 0DZ

www.headline.co.uk
www.hachette.co.uk

*To Kat*

# Day one

# One

*[Bob, 11:10]*

Bob Rutherford stepped back and took one last look at his handiwork. Aside from the slate wall missing some ivy, nobody could tell which part he'd spent the past couple of hours patching up. Thin slices, neatly stacked, following the path of the road weaving towards the village.

A car rumbled behind him, going way too fast along the single-track lane.

Bob pushed himself face first against his van. The dark SUV shot past in a blur of kicked-up leaves and diesel fumes, then disappeared round the bend, lost to the canopy of trees.

*Missed me by inches!*

*Berk.*

Bob hopped in the cabin and twisted the key in the ignition. The engine spluttered into life and he set off. His phone rang through the dashboard.

'You on your way home, then?' Shirley's voice boomed out of the speaker.

Bob turned it down as he eased round the bend. 'Got my tax return to do, haven't I? Absolutely starving, I am. Magnificent job, though, even if I do say so myself.' No sign of the pillock in the SUV up ahead. He took another bend, the trees darker and thicker here, blocking out the morning sun. More slate walls on both sides, a gap on the right for Proudfoot Farm. He caught sight of the SUV, idling on the right. Then it shot off away from Bob at a rate he couldn't hope to catch.

But he also spotted a shape on the ground, almost white against the lush green.

Bob slammed on the brakes and let out an almighty screech. He jerked forward, the belt digging into his ribs.

'What's up, Bob?'

Flat, low, and resting on a bed of nettles, almost hidden by the thick bush encroaching on the road.

A body.

A human body.

'Bob?'

'Shirley, I think I've just seen a dead body.'

Her gasp rattled out of the speakers. 'Call the police!'

'Yeah, of course.' Bob snapped out of his daze with a vigorous nod, as though she could see him. 'I'll phone you back.' He jabbed the red button, then tapped 999 into the keypad, keeping his focus on the motionless shape, leg jigging up and down, the phone ringing and ringing and—

'Emergency. What service?'

'Police, please.' Bob cracked open the door and stepped out of the van. A gentle breeze rustled down the lane, carrying the cloying smell of honeysuckle through the whispering leaves.

He took another look at the body. Definitely a woman. Young, too. And naked as the day she was born . . .

'You're through to the police.' A male voice, high and

bright as a summer's day. 'What's the address or location of your emergency?'

Bob tightened his grip on the mobile, staying exactly where he was. He looked up and down the lane. 'I don't know the exact postcode or map co-ordinates, but I'm just outside Minster Lovell. Little place near Witney in Oxfordshire. It's . . . It's the top road coming into the village.'

'Just a second. And what's your name, sir?'

'Bob Rutherford.' He watched both ways for any other cars, listening closely, then took another step across the road.

'Hi, Bob, would that be the Leafield Road?'

'Sounds about right. Mate, I'm fixing a wall for this old couple. The Maitlands. Live a few hundred yards past the village sign.'

'Okay, I've got you.' Sounded like the guy was smiling. 'Now, Bob, what's happened?'

'I've found a girl's body.' Bob looked over again. She was painfully skinny. He groaned. 'Listen, she's like a sack of bones. I think she might be a druggy.'

'Is she breathing?'

'Mate, you need to send someone out to sort this—'

The woman rolled over onto her side.

'Christ!' Bob jumped back, pressing himself against his van.

The woman's eyes were shut, but her chest was moving, like she was sipping shallow breaths.

'She's alive.'

'Thanks, Bob. That's . . . That's good.'

Heart racing, Bob approached her, keeping low. 'You okay there, love?'

The woman didn't react.

'I made a mistake. I said police to the operator. You need to send an ambulance and pronto.'

'They're both on their way, Bob.'

The girl's eyes opened and her head swivelled towards him, her gaze wild and lost to something. Maybe drugs, but maybe not. Maybe something else.

'It's okay, love.' Bob held out his free hand, smiling at her. 'I'm Bob. What's your name?'

Her fingers twitched, then bunched up around the weed bed she lay on, screwing up the nettles and dock. Like she was trying to get up, but just didn't have the energy.

Bob took another step forward, widening his smile. 'Hey, it's okay.'

'Sir, I advise you to—'

She started blinking, hard and fast. Then she squinted at Bob and let out a moan, low and loud. Like that feral cat who'd made a nest under their decking, protecting her kittens as the Cats Protection woman caught them for rehoming.

He took another step and the woman screamed.

# Two

*[Corcoran, 11:55]*

Detective Sergeant Aidan Corcoran shifted on the passenger seat, trying to get comfortable as they bombed down the country lane. He straightened his leg out into the footwell. His right hip was in spasm, not excruciating, but—

Something clicked and he let out a shallow sigh. Almost panting with relief.

DI Alana Thompson drove the pool Volvo like an idiot, battering across the bridge, and something metallic crunched underneath. The cricket ground and its car park passed in a blur, then she swerved out to overtake a cyclist, bumping onto the grass verge. A weeping willow caressed the windscreen with its leaves.

Corcoran gave her a look. 'Ma'am, can you slow down?'

'Don't ma'am me, Sergeant. You're not in the Met any more.' Thompson rounded the bend onto another road that looked like the right one, but you never knew out here in the sticks. They tore through a picture postcard village. Country pub, a hodgepodge of stone cottages, some with thatched roofs, then the density thinned out in that middle England way, the village not quite ready to give up its grip as it gradually turned into countryside. A car park on the right had no sign what it was for, just a warning of a single-track road without passing places. Neat slate walls lined the lane on both sides.

Thompson jerked to a halt, the tyres screeching.

A young lad in uniform leaned against a wall, clutching a clipboard, half a roll of police tape flapping in the breeze as it blocked the lane beyond. He set off towards them, eager and keen.

Thompson lowered the window and held out her warrant card. 'This strictly necessary, Constable?'

The uniform stood up tall like he was meeting the Queen. 'Sorry, ma'am, but I thought there might be forensics?'

She twisted the key and the engine rattled. 'She's dead?'

'No, ma'am, but—'

'Stop ma'aming me. It's Alana.' Thompson got out and slammed the door.

Corcoran let his seatbelt ride up slowly, opened the door and stepped out onto the lane, taking his time to analyse the scene.

An ambulance idled up ahead, the lights pulsing in the bright sunshine. Another two uniforms stood by it, chatting to a green-clad paramedic. In the distance, a female uniform blocked off the lane from that end.

Thompson stuffed her hands in her pockets. 'Any idea who she is?'

'Afraid not. Bloke found her naked. I've searched the vicinity but no clothes, no phone, no wallet, nothing.'

'And what stopped you searching?'

'Your colleague told me to take over down here.' The uniform pointed at a female plainclothes officer halfway up the lane.

Not someone Corcoran recognised, but that didn't narrow it down much. She was taking a statement from a ruddy-faced man standing by a van. Stonemason's overalls. Heavy-set, like so many round here. Farming stock. Tinge of red in the cheeks, meaning a drinker, his belly indicating beer.

The uniform nodded up the lane. 'That's the bloke who found her. Bob Rutherford. Had a little chat with him. Bore the arse off you, mate.' He smirked at Corcoran, then scratched at his neck. 'Reckons he saw an SUV going pretty fast not long before. Chased after it, but saw her lying there so stopped. Could be a VW or a Vauxhall. Black, maybe dark grey.'

Corcoran looked back at Bob giving his statement, assessing him. He'd already listened to the 999 call on the way out and he'd read the statement later, then take a view. And if this guy was a hell of a bore, he'd just repeat his story, but each new version would increase his role in the mystery.

Corcoran gave the uniform a conspiratorial nod. 'I'll take your advice, then.' He scanned the immediate area. No tracks, no footprints, not even the imprint of a human body. Just a bed of weeds under a bush. 'Do me a favour and call in the SUV sighting, okay?'

'Sarge.'

Thompson patted the uniform on the arm. 'Call Control and tell them *I* want forensics here, okay?'

He gave a nervous nod as he tapped his Airwave police radio. 'Ma'am.'

Thompson blundered through the tape and made her way down the winding road, her round shoulders drooping low, head forward, beady eyes scanning the lane.

Corcoran followed, but struggled to match her pace. 'Alana, wait up.'

She stopped, frowning back the way. 'You know, that just sounds weird.'

'Shall we just stick with "ma'am"?'

'No, apparently I need to develop a better rapport with my subordinates, so let's go with Alana.' Thompson slowed as they closed on the ambulance, the engine still rumbling. Two uniforms let Thompson through to the paramedic. 'Where is she?'

The paramedic stopped folding up the ramp. 'Neil Hart' was stamped on his uniform. He pointed inside the ambulance with his left thumb. 'In here.'

'Okay, get out of my way.' Thompson nudged him to the side.

Inside, Neil's colleague crouched by a gurney, holding out a giant silver sheet. 'Come on, I need you to—'

'No!' A voice, female, weak but still a shout. 'No!'

But the paramedic got his way, wrapping the blanket around the woman. She was flat on her back on the gurney, her legs raised up. Her head peeped out of a hole in the silver, wild-eyed, her mouth open like she was in constant pain. Hair curled and matted thick like badly done dreadlocks. Her skin was pale, almost white, with a tinge of blue. And she was skeletally thin, no fat or muscle to cushion the bones in her skull and jaw.

The paramedic wrapped a woolly blanket round her shoulders and didn't seem to get any resistance.

Corcoran smiled back at Neil the paramedic. 'Any chance we can speak to her?'

'We really need to get her to hospital.' A sharp shake of

10

the head. 'Her body's in starvation mode, so we need to get her stabilised. Those blankets will get her body temperature up, but we're limited with what we're able to do here. I've called ahead and they're prepping a room for her.'

'The Radcliffe?'

'Afraid so.' Neil checked his watch. 'Oxford traffic is a nightmare at the best of times, and this is the worst.'

'I'll see what I can do to ease your way.' Thompson got out her mobile and set off.

'Kind of lucky we got here so fast. Responding to a prank call in Witney. First time I've ever been thankful.' Neil shook his head again. 'She wouldn't have lasted much longer if we hadn't got here.'

Corcoran took another look at the woman, now shivering uncontrollably as her body started to heat up. Weird how it worked like that.

'Druggies in Oxfordshire!' Down the lane, the stonemason was shouting, arms wide. 'What's the world coming to, I ask you?'

Corcoran played that through as a possibility. Heroin user with a deep debt, maybe a prostitute. Taken out to the country-side and released, kept alive to send a message to her and her fellow streetwalkers. Not killed so she could repay that debt.

Or was that his brain still being stuck in London? Out in Oxfordshire, sure they had their problems, but this?

He frowned at Neil. 'Any evidence that she's a drug user?'

'You mean heroin?' The paramedic stopped what he was doing and sucked in a deep breath. 'No track marks on her arms.' He looked back inside with a frown. 'Her ankles, though . . .'

'Injection marks?'

'No.' Neil clicked his tongue a few times. 'Thing is, her skin's worn, like she'd been tied up, and not like it was her boyfriend's birthday, if you catch my drift.' He gave a crafty wink.

Corcoran weighed up the evidence.

Signs of being tied up. Starvation. Panic, but nowhere near enough energy to fight off even a friendly paramedic putting a blanket on her.

What did it mean? Abduction? Prolonged captivity? His drug-prostitute-revenge theory felt less likely. Leaving him with nothing much to go on.

He fixed a hard stare on the paramedic. 'I need to speak to her.'

'We've got to—'

'Someone's done this to her. I need to find them. And besides, you've got to finish packing up here, right? Thirty seconds, that's all I ask.'

Neil clicked his tongue again, then nodded. 'Not a second longer.'

'Appreciate it.' Corcoran smiled as he stepped up into the back of the ambulance, his hip twinging.

The other paramedic kept tending to the victim, wrapping a second woolly blanket around her legs and waist.

The woman lay flat on her back, scanning the interior, her gaze landing on everything. Except Corcoran. Half-crazed, starved and deeply unwell.

Corcoran's theory of imprisonment was looking more likely. He gave her a smile and waited for full eye contact. Not a glance, but her full attention.

There. He smiled. 'My name is Aidan. I'm a detective.

I want to help find out who did this to you.' Her blue eyes seemed to swell as tears filled them. 'Let's start with your name, shall we?'

But he lost her. Her head wobbled back and stayed there, looking up. Harsh breathing, her nostrils flaring.

The other paramedic grabbed Corcoran's arm. 'I need to get her on a drip, so can you . . .?'

Corcoran stepped away and let him work.

But the woman's gasps were forming into four equal sounds, like she was playing an instrument.

One. Two. Three. Four.

Say. Rah. Lang. Ton.

Sarah Langton.

Corcoran crouched down low and looked up at her. 'Sarah Langton?'

She nodded, slight and fleeting but definitely a nod.

'Thanks, Sarah. You're in great hands now, okay?' Corcoran jumped down onto the asphalt as the back door slammed.

Thompson yanked it open again, a uniform hanging around next to her.

The paramedic scowled out at her. 'We need to—'

'I want her to get a rape kit, okay?' She pushed the uniform towards the door. 'And I need an officer in the ambulance with her for continuity of evidence. Okay?'

'Fine.' The paramedic helped the uniform up into the back, then slammed the door in her face.

Thompson made a face at Corcoran. 'Honestly, Aidan, you'd think we were on different sides or something.'

The ambulance set off with a pulse of siren. Ahead, the uniforms cleared the tape from the path to let it past.

Corcoran reached into his pocket for his radio and put it to his ear.

'Control receiving, over.'

'Safe to talk. It's DS Aidan Corcoran. Need you to run a PNC search for one Sarah Langton. IC1 female, mid-twenties, over.'

'You got an address?'

Corcoran gritted his teeth. 'Afraid not.'

'One second.'

Corcoran stood there, the breeze kicking up a sweet smell.

'Okay, I've found a missing person. One Sarah Kimberley Langton, aged twenty-six. Reported missing six weeks ago from Cambridge.'

# Three

## *[12:40]*

'Come on, come on, come on.' DI Thompson hurtled through the roundabout, chasing an ambulance almost bumper to bumper. 'What's the hold-up?'

Corcoran looked across at the hospital, the least Oxford-looking building in the world. Eight or nine storeys of sixties' concrete and glass catching the afternoon sun, feeling a world away from the ancient colleges just down the road. 'Please don't beep them.'

'I'll beep who I like.' Thompson stopped at another roundabout, where they seemed to be constantly losing out to the traffic coming from the right. She looked over at him, eyebrows raised. 'You getting anywhere with her?'

Corcoran put away his phone. 'Got hold of the investigating officer. A DC based in Cambridge.' He pointed up at the hospital. 'Said he'll meet us here.'

'And what about her?'

Corcoran showed her his smartphone, the screen filled with the photo from Sarah's MisPer file. Happy with round cheeks and a slight tan. 'This look like the woman in the ambulance to you?'

Thompson took the device, studying the image carefully.

'Could be anyone.' She handed it back, then cut across the roundabout into the hospital car park, pulling straight into a disabled bay. 'Could even be me if I lost a couple of stone.' She killed the engine.

'Hence me asking our friend in Cambridgeshire to bring her husband here to confirm we've found his Sarah Langton and not someone else.' Corcoran stared at the face again, then tapped back into the MisPer report. 'Reported missing from Cambridge, then six weeks later she's in a ditch in Oxfordshire, at least two hours' drive away. Long way to take someone.'

Thompson opened her door. 'You got any theories?'

'Too many, and all of them make me sick to the stomach.'

## [12:57]

'Inspector?' A female doctor joined them at the Accident & Emergency reception. Medium height, mid-grey hair, her face filled with laughter lines, widening as she gave a broad grin. 'Dr Tamar Yadin. Can we have a word?'

Thompson thumbed at Corcoran. 'You mind if the boy wonder here joins us?'

'Be my guest.' Dr Yadin marched off through the bleak hellscape that was the Accident & Emergency waiting area. Six rows of chairs facing each other in pairs, almost all filled with the walking wounded or relatives of the sick and dying. Yadin opened a door and held it for them.

Thompson didn't give Corcoran the option of letting her go first. He let Yadin go, then followed her.

Into a cupboard. Shelved walls filled with cleaning materials and medical supplies. A mop was stuffed into a bucket that stank of harsh chemicals and something worse.

'I'm sorry, but we're stretched for space today so I'll make this brief.' Dr Yadin leaned back against the door, arms folded. 'Sarah's being rehydrated just now. That's our first priority. Her body isn't critically dehydrated, but we need to get her on a D5W solution in order to—'

'A what?'

Yadin sighed at Thompson. 'A saline solution mixed with five percent dextrose. We are commencing refeeding, supplementing the solution with vitamins to restore her electrolyte levels and with potassium to prevent any cardiac issues. Refeeding syndrome is our biggest risk over the next twenty-four hours. The body will generate glycogen, protein and fat to the detriment of blood, so we have to constantly monitor her condition and make micro-adjustments.' She clenched her jaw. 'I will warn you now, this isn't going to be quick. Days, even weeks before we get a prognosis.'

Thompson rolled her eyes. 'You mean we won't get to speak to her?'

'You're welcome to try. I won't stand here trying to stop you, you know that, but she's in an incredibly weakened state and her care should be both of our primary concerns.'

'This state she's in, is it starvation?'

'Absolutely.' Yadin inspected a tablet computer, perched in the crook of her elbow. 'Sarah's showing all the symptoms: skin rashes, hair loss, ulcers, bleeding gums, cramps. And she's as weak as a day-old kitten.' She looked up from her machine. 'I've dealt with a great number of eating disorders in adult patients and . . .' She drifted off, her expression darkening.

Thompson gave her a few seconds. 'Bottom line, doc?'

'Like I say, this is going to be days and weeks, rather than hours. Sorry. And that's if she even pulls through.'

## *[14:38]*

A knock at the door.

Thompson opened it and peered out. Then she opened it wide. 'Come into our grotto.'

A lumbering giant ducked under the doorway and meandered in. Early forties, bald, cheap suit hanging off wide shoulders. He held out a hand to Corcoran. 'DC Will Butcher, Cambridgeshire police. We spoke on the phone?'

'That was quick.' Corcoran shook his hand, gesturing at his boss. 'This is DI Alana Thompson.'

She kept her hands in her pockets. 'You brought the husband?'

'I did.' Butcher thumbed behind him. 'Waiting out there. Funny old world, eh?'

'What's so funny about it?' Thompson opened the door again and stepped past him.

'What's her problem?' Butcher scowled at the closing door. 'You try doing a hundred on *that* road with a member of the public in the back . . .'

'She's like that with everyone, Constable. Don't take it personally.'

Butcher gave Corcoran a narrow-eyed stare. 'Haven't got

hold of Sarah's parents yet. Left voicemails and sent a text to each of them.' He rubbed a hand across his pale lips. 'And it's *definitely* Sarah?'

'That's what we want to find out.'

# *[14:50]*

Christopher Langton stood in another doorway, fingers twitching as he listened to Dr Yadin. The words didn't seem to be going in. Medium height, mid-brown hair, and slim like he ran a lot. No distinguishing features – the sort of bloke who'd be a nightmare to find if he ever went missing. He looked completely destroyed, exhausted from worry that had long since turned to grief. Deep bags under his eyes, shrouding a vacant stare. But hope had started twinkling in his eyes. He nodded and followed Dr Yadin through to a room, the small whiteboard outside earmarking it for Sarah Langton.

Butcher's breath misted the window's glass as he muttered, 'The *state* of her . . .'

Sarah lay on the bed, asleep now. She looked even older than back at the roadside, her face hardened.

Her husband stood over her like a statue. Then he crouched, squinting, tears glistening in his eyes. He said something, then reached for Sarah.

Dr Yadin grabbed his wrist and spoke into his ear.

Langton covered his eyes with his hand and gave a slight nod. He came back out into the corridor, rubbing at his eyes, breathing hard and fast. 'It's her. That's my Sarah.' He made a noise, half sigh, half groan. Not quite at the stage of relief. Still weeks of worry ahead of him, but on the road away from abject despair. 'She's lost so much weight. I barely recognised her. Can't believe someone's done this to her.'

Dr Yadin led him away.

Thompson stepped between the two cops. 'Lads, I need you to interview him while I brief the powers that be.' She shook her head. 'Two forces . . . That's going to be *so* much fun.'

# Four

## [15:12]

'Through here, sir.' Corcoran opened the door and let Langton into a family room. Tastefully decorated in shades of beige, with three sofas around a square coffee table. A box of tissues rested on top beside some fresh flowers, whites, pinks and purples.

Corcoran put a hand across the door frame to stop Butcher entering. He had to look up at him – the guy must be six or seven inches taller, but they probably weighed about the same. 'I'm leading here, okay?'

'Okay, Sarge.' Butcher entered and sat opposite the husband, his long legs blocking the path between them.

Corcoran had to go round the back of Langton's to sit on the third settee. 'Thanks for identifying your wife, sir. I understand how difficult this is, but we're determined to find whoever did this to her.' He waved at Butcher. 'I appreciate you've been over this with my colleague here, but—'

'Let me get this straight, you're interested now she's been found?' Langton barked out a humourless laugh. 'The time for this was when the trail was warm. She—'

'I understand how—'

'Don't give me that!' Langton stabbed a finger towards the

door. 'You've seen the state of her! You've seen how broken she is!' Another jab with the finger, but his head sunk low. 'You should've found her before now.'

'I understand your frustration, sir.' Corcoran shifted forward on his seat. 'I wish we could devote more resources to cases such as your wife's, but DC Butcher here—'

'Bollocks.' Langton couldn't bring himself to look at Butcher. 'Absolute bollocks. *He* could've done a *lot* more six weeks ago.' He swallowed the words, then screwed his eyes shut. 'I'm sorry.' He looked over at Butcher. 'I'm all over the place, I . . .'

'I understand, sir. But you're right.' Butcher flashed him a smile. 'There's always more that can be done, and I'm sorry we didn't find Sarah before. But now we've got her, we know something untoward has happened to her. Before, well, it could've—'

Corcoran caught Butcher's attention and his glare got him to shut up. He looked over at Langton. 'Until we can speak to Sarah, I'm treating this as malicious. Assuming someone has done this to her, I want to find them and, with luck and time, bring them to justice.'

Langton sat there, drilling his gaze into Corcoran. 'Someone just dumped her? How can . . .?' Langton reached for a tissue and dabbed his eyes. 'How can I help?'

'It would be extremely useful if you could take us through everything from the start. I know it's—'

'Fine.' Langton stared hard at Corcoran. He must've rehearsed this speech so many times, given it to friends, family, colleagues, even the police. 'That night, a Friday, I'd been out playing squash. Had a few beers after with the guys, then got home, but Sarah wasn't in. The house was cold and she'd usually have the heating on. She likes it warm. And poor Milhouse hadn't been fed. He's our cat. Sarah loves him to pieces.' He shut his eyes. 'He's missed her . . .'

'You never received any messages?'

'None. And believe me, I was looking.' Langton gestured at Butcher. 'There aren't many people who I'd show my phone to, but he's been through it.'

'Fine-tooth comb.' Butcher nodded. 'We haven't managed to recover Sarah's phone, either. Last location was outside her house.'

Corcoran looked at Langton. 'Cambridge, correct?'

'Quiet village on the outskirts.' Langton sighed. 'Can't help but think if we lived in a town, it would've been much harder for them to take her.'

'Living in a city isn't much protection from abduction, sir.'

Langton nodded, like it had closed off some avenue of worry. 'What else can I say? She loves photography. Got her a new Sony camera at Christmas, not that she . . .' His nostrils quivered. 'We both run. Do the London and Paris marathons each year. We'd been talking of doing Boston and New York next.'

Corcoran glanced at Butcher. 'Was she into fitness tracking?'

'She got a smartwatch last summer to track her running and so on. Weighed herself on these fitness scales every morning. One of those fancy ones that measures body fat and . . .' Langton's lip quivered. 'She was obsessed about getting it below fifteen percent. Now she's . . .' He reached for another tissue and masked fresh tears with blowing his nose.

A shadow passed over the door's glass just before it opened. Dr Yadin stood there, smiling. 'Mr Langton, Sarah's parents have arrived. Can I ask you to assist them?'

'Sure thing.' Langton got up, then stopped, frowning at Corcoran. 'Do you need anything else from me?'

'I'm sure there'll be other things, sir, but you should spend time with them.'

'Okay.' Head low, Langton followed Yadin out of the room.

Butcher got up and started pacing the room. 'Poor guy.'

'One way of looking at it.' Corcoran leaned back, arms folded. 'What was all that animosity?'

'Guy's angry at everyone for what's happened. You must've seen that yourself, yeah?'

'Sure that's all it is?'

'I know what you're thinking. I'm not some local idiot cop messing up here.' Butcher's shoulders slumped. Not the joy of a man whose missing person had been found, but the fear of a man about to get his backside kicked for not being the one to recover her. He slouched in the seat Langton had sat in. 'Trouble is, Sarah was just another MisPer. You must get loads in Thames Valley, right? Students under so much pressure to succeed at Oxford University. Same as with Cambridge. The ones who don't try to kill themselves, some just up and leave. Then there are all the little towns and villages, where people run away from home every day . . .'

'Did you have any suspects?'

'Funny you should ask.' Butcher leaned forward and looked at the door. 'I thought it was possible he'd murdered her.'

Most murder victims knew their killer. Starting with the family was the obvious strategy.

'What made you think that?'

'My first thought was she'd run off with someone.' A darkness twisted Butcher's features. 'But we never found any big withdrawals or any other telltale signs she'd been planning to scarper. And him . . . he kept phoning me up. Never anything new, but it felt like he was fishing, seeing if he was a suspect.'

'You get any evidence to support that theory?'

'Thing is, his story checked out. He was out with his mates from squash. Pub CCTV, bus CCTV, street CCTV.' Butcher gripped his thighs. 'Doesn't mean he didn't have help.'

The door opened again. Thompson thundered in and collapsed next to Corcoran, nudging his shin with her shoe. 'Budge.' She reached into her pocket for a mint and crunched it without offering the packet round. 'I've spoken to my boss and our opposite numbers in Cambridgeshire police. This is now a major inquiry and I'm Deputy SIO, for my sins. Means it's my arse on the line here. Means we'll get more bodies in to help us out.' She gave Butcher a frosty look. 'I appreciate all your efforts so far, Constable. You're seconded to my team, so you can thank me later. We're based at Thames Valley Force HQ, okay?' She popped another mint in, sucking this time. 'Initially we're keeping a media blackout. Then we'll release as few details as possible. Last thing we want is to scare the public.' She raised her eyebrows. 'Unless you think they should be scared?'

Butcher kept his gaze neutral. 'I don't know what you're getting at.'

'It looks very much like someone's abducted a woman, Constable. Held her somewhere for six weeks.' Thompson tossed a photo of Sarah Langton onto the table. A further-away shot of her clad in Lycra, warming up for a run. Her athletic physique was nothing like the skeleton found by the side of the road. 'I'm asking if there's someone out there who will be terrified by news of us being onto them? Will they do this again?'

Butcher bristled. 'What do—'

'Alana.' Corcoran shot a look at Butcher to keep him quiet. 'Look, we still don't know yet that she was abducted. She could've had a psychotic break and decided to starve herself.' He picked up the photo. 'DC Butcher drew a blank before, but now we've recovered her, alive, we can start a detailed investigation and with adequate resourcing. We've already discussed the possibility of it being her husband. I want to investigate that further.'

'Okay.' Thompson crunched another mint. 'Usual drill. Husband, family, neighbours, co-workers, ex-boyfriends, ex-girlfriends, criminal contacts, bank accounts. Then any leads on drugs, mental illness, medical problems. Right now, we're throwing *all* the bodies at it.'

Corcoran looked to Butcher. 'Anything else we should be focusing on, Constable?'

Butcher cleared his throat. 'The other possibility is her job. She worked as a research assistant in a pharmaceutical lab, doing statistical analysis. There's a load of them round Cambridge, but this one was on the radar of some animal rights nutters. Received a good number of threats over the years.'

'But?'

'Sarah didn't do experiments herself. And she hadn't received any threats directly.'

Corcoran played it through. 'I still think it's a possibility, Alana.'

'You have my blessing.' Thompson got up with a fresh crunch of mint. 'Okay, so while I'm setting up an Incident Room and all that good stuff, can you two get back to first principles? Just so we're clear, Butcher, I'm not criticising you.' She winked at Corcoran. 'Get up to Cambridge and chase down any and all leads. Find out if this is an abduction and, if so, find whoever did this to that poor woman. Okay?'

# Five

## [17:42]

Corcoran pulled up at the gate and waited. The Cambridge-shire Police HQ sprawled around him, a lump of bulging concrete surrounding a car park dominated by a sprawling oak. He wound down his window.

A hut sat to the side, the tinny sounds of opera leaking out. The door opened and a security guard limped over to his car, each lopsided step looking like it cost him greatly.

Corcoran held up his warrant card. 'Here to see DC Butcher.'

'Little Will?' The guard frowned, twisting his face tight, then nodded over at a grey Mondeo sandwiched between two squad cars. 'Good luck finding him, he's a slippery bugger at the best of times.' He tapped a button on a remote and the barrier lifted, almost in sync with Corcoran's rising window as he trundled over.

A car pulled out of a space under the giant tree and Corcoran grabbed it. His aching hip made him take his time getting out. A dull throb had settled in as he weaved around Oxford's infernal bypass, and right now he'd give a good few years of his life for a deep-tissue massage. He shut the door, pleased to avoid any fresh stabs of pain.

28

'There you are.'

Corcoran jerked round and got that sharp twinge in his side.

Butcher sucked on a cigarette, hunching low to fit his giant frame under the smoking shelter. He held out a pack for Corcoran, but got a shake of the head. 'Trying to quit?'

Corcoran stayed outside, but still got coils of blue smoke heading his way. 'Tried starting six times, just couldn't get into it.'

Butcher barked out a laugh. Then took another deep suck. 'Everything these days is either cancer or vaping. Or both.' He exhaled through his nostrils, slowly, eyes closed like it was his sole surviving pleasure. 'Just give me a good, honest cigarette any day of the week.'

Corcoran tried to stand upwind of him. 'So, where do you suggest we start?'

Butcher stared at the ground, still avoiding eye contact. 'You're the boss.'

'Case file would be a good place. Then witness statements, CCTV and wherever else the night takes us.'

Butcher stamped his butt out on the bin and dropped it in. 'Don't ask for much, do you?'

## [17:47]

Corcoran followed him along the corridor. 'You got a problem with me?'

Butcher finally looked at him as he swiped through a security reader. 'Not with you.'

'Thompson?'

'Got it in two.' Butcher set off down a long corridor, without waiting for Corcoran, his rubber-soled shoes squeaking over the lino. 'What's her deal?'

'She's a DI.' Corcoran managed to catch up, but he was out of breath. 'Sure you've got them here, right?'

'Mate, don't get smart with me. I was asking if she was a direct entry or something.'

'I'm new to her team, so I don't know. But you'll know the way the force is going. They've got so much pressure heaped on their shoulders. It's bad enough being a sergeant these days.'

Butcher shook his head.

Corcoran knew his argument wasn't cutting any mustard with him. 'Look, she wasn't being a dick to you because you've made a mess of anything, she's just—'

'A mess?' Butcher opened a door and held it for him. 'You honestly think—'

'No, but I know that you think that she thinks . . .' Corcoran caught himself and sighed. 'She's stressed, okay? We've found Sarah Langton and there's a possibility that someone's abducted her and tortured her. Meaning a big investigation. Thompson is Deputy SIO, so she's got all the day-to-day management. All the stress, all the hassle, all the pressure. Dealing with people like me.' That got a smile. 'Right now, our priority isn't arguing about stupid stuff, it's determining whether someone's done something to Sarah and finding them. And if there's something you have made a mess of, now's the time to tell me.'

Butcher stared at him for a few seconds, lips twitching like he was going to say something, but instead set off up the staircase, clenched fists in his trouser pockets.

Cops and their precious egos . . .

# [17:52]

Corcoran walked into the open-plan office space and stopped, taking in the usual display of idle cops trying to look busy. A pair of older officers bantered over by the water filter, voices low. Another two female officers looked up from their computers, following Corcoran's path. Butcher was farting around in a kitchen area near the window, shrouded by the caramel smell of Colombian medium roast, a filter machine bubbling and hissing away next to him.

The view was mostly blocked by the sprawling oak, but the squad cars' acid yellow cut through the foliage.

Butcher stretched out, his shirt popping out of his trousers. 'You must be knackered from that drive. Know I am.' He held up the jug of dark liquid and let out a yawn. 'I brew a mean coffee.'

'I'd rather look at the case file?'

'Over there.' Butcher nodded at a desk in the corner. A bonsai apple tree sat next to the monitor. 'Sure you don't want—'

'Just milk, cheers.' Corcoran walked across and pulled over a spare seat. The case file sat on the desk, looking frustratingly thin. He opened it and gave it a quick scan. Standard fare – everything in the right place, just . . . hardly any of it. Modern-day resource constraints were one thing, but this just smacked of a lack of care.

The second time, he sifted through it, aware of at least five officers' prying eyes on him. That familiar sixth sense that could pinpoint eyes feasting on the new guy in the room. Corcoran got nothing new from his second pass, but there were a couple of names to speak to again, now that a Missing Person was a Found Person. But sod all otherwise.

Butcher was still over by the filter machine, sniffing a milk carton. A man in a suit was bending his ear about something, no doubt his DI on arse-covering activities. With a final nod, Butcher picked up both mugs and walked back over, his boss's narrow-eyed gaze locked on Corcoran.

'Here you go.' Butcher clunked a mug down on the table and slurped from his own. 'So, did I give you enough rope to hang me with?'

Corcoran put the coffee to his lips and savoured the smell. Surprisingly good for a police station. Then a sip, full of deep tones, and that sweet caramel smell turned into flavour. 'This is good coffee.'

'I'm in charge of the machine.' Butcher took another drink, now sitting on the edge of the desk despite his chair being free. 'Got to watch these buggers or they'll top up the jug with *instant*.'

Corcoran laughed, loud enough to bring all the attention back to him. When you're in the lion's den, act like you own the place. 'It's good. If this police malarkey goes to shit, you've got a promising career as a barista.' He nudged the case file over the desk. 'Okay, so let's start with anyone you couldn't speak to in January.'

Butcher set his mug down and picked up the file. 'I was as

thorough as the time would allow me. Spoke to all of her neighbours and her boss.'

'Nicely caveated.'

Butcher shrugged. 'My DI deprioritised the case.'

Corcoran caught the suit walking over from the side of his eye. 'Anyone see anything?'

'Nada.'

'CCTV?'

Before Butcher could get out another word, the suit thrust out his hand in front of Corcoran, all smiles. Mid-forties, but the bags under his eyes and slack skin around his neck could push it higher. His thinning hair was a few shades too dark for his complexion. 'DI Thomas Hinshelwood. It's Corcoran, right?'

'That's right.' Corcoran gave his hand a nice, tight squeeze. Didn't get anything other than a raised eyebrow. 'Take it you've been briefed, sir?'

'Call me Tom.' Hinshelwood stood there, arms folded. 'And yes, Will called me on his way over. Is he playing nice?'

'He's a sweetie.'

Hinshelwood laughed hard, clearly enjoying Butcher's blush. 'Can we have a quick chat?'

'Sure.' Corcoran followed him over to a glass-walled office, filled on three sides by filing cabinets, the external window blocked by a desk stacked high with paper files. He left the door open.

Hinshelwood didn't sit, instead pacing around what little of the space he could. 'Look, Sergeant, I'll be frank. Your presence here concerns me.' He sighed. 'In my experience, when people like you dig up leads we might've dropped, well, I'm sure you understand how it looks . . .'

'And how will it look?'

Another sigh. 'The day after Will caught the case, literally the next day, we landed a major murder investigation. A young couple found in the Cam just outside of the city. Strangled, naked. Case was all over the news. I had no choice but to reallocate Will. No choice whatsoever.'

'I understand, sir. I'm not here to investigate your incompetence.' Corcoran got a bristle instead of a smile. 'But the fact is, Sarah Langton has turned up in a lane in Oxfordshire. She's been starved. And we're going to find out why and catch who did it.'

'Assuming someone did.'

'Quite.'

Hinshelwood adjusted his cufflinks, making them catch the spotlights. 'The thing is, given my pressing resource constraint, I reviewed the case personally and I deemed it to be a standard "runaway". Does it appear to be anything else?'

'Hard to say just yet.'

'Well, if it is, I'll struggle to sleep, believe me.' Hinshelwood cleared a path round to his chair and sat, hands clamped on his knees. 'We were unable to progress the case any further due to operational constraints, so go easy on us, okay?'

'Did you catch the killer? In the Cam strangling.'

Hinshelwood picked up a file and stared at it absently. 'Killers.'

'That's a positive thing, then.'

'Mm.' Hinshelwood put the file down and fixed a hard glare on Corcoran. 'Whatever you're thinking right now, it's not malice or incompetence. We just don't have enough skulls to do our jobs properly. Sure it's the same over in Thames Valley?'

Corcoran smiled, letting the frost melt a touch. 'We don't even get the luxury of detectives investigating Missing Persons cases.'

'Time was . . .' Hinshelwood shook his head, a bitter expression on his face. 'I'll let you get on with things, okay? I'm glad Sarah has turned up. Genuinely . . . I just wish it was safe and sound, not . . . This. What's happened to her.'

'Thanks, sir.' Corcoran gave him a broad smile, then left him to his dark thoughts and darker regrets.

Back at Butcher's desk, he picked up his lukewarm coffee and finished it in one go. 'Anything?'

'Perfect timing.' Butcher nodded at the screen, black and empty. 'Just pulled up the CCTV footage from the night Sarah went missing. Waiting on you to finish your . . .' He raised an eyebrow. 'What did he—'

'Just play it.'

Butcher smacked his thumb off the space-bar on his keyboard and sat back, arms crossed.

The black screen transitioned to a dark street, a generic English village, older stone cottages muddled up with modern brick houses. Raindrops dotted deep puddles, wind battering them into a fine spray. A woman pounded along the street, splashing through the puddles, checking her watch, a bright white headphone cable dangling from a strap on her arm.

Sarah Langton, a healthy and fit young woman. Before the

trauma, before the torment. Then she was gone, lost between cameras.

'What about the other side of that building?'

Butcher crunched back in his chair. 'That's it. No more CCTV around her home.'

Corcoran stared out of the window, getting a partial view across the car park, leaves dappling the fading sunlight. Seeing her like that hit him hard. The before picture. Healthy and strong, not a sack of bones and skin. The coffee sat heavy in his gut. 'Replay it.'

Another crunch of the space-bar.

This time, Corcoran ignored Sarah, instead focusing on her surroundings. In the mouth of a side street, a silver Audi idled, the exhaust pluming in the night air. He reached over to pause it, then tapped the screen. 'Who's that?'

'I saw it.' Butcher cleared his throat. 'Of course I saw it.' He scratched his neck. 'Trouble was, I couldn't get plates off it.'

Corcoran squinted at the screen, trying to decipher the hieroglyphs. Butcher was right – the plates were unreadable. Whether by malice or fortune was another thing. He knew which way he'd bet if he had to.

'I even checked the nearby CCTV cameras, not that there's that many. There's a Sainsbury's half a mile away that's covered in them. A B&Q and a cash and carry next door. Long and short of it is, there's just way too many Audi A4s driving at that time in that area.'

'Take it you—'

'Yep. All the drivers I spoke to had alibis for where they went next and where they'd been.'

'And the ones you didn't?'

'Spoke to them all, mate.' Butcher looked away towards Hinshelwood's office. 'Didn't get the chance to actually check the alibis, mind.'

Cursing his luck, Corcoran checked the screen again. Something wasn't quite right with the picture. He tapped the glass again. 'That's not an A4. It's an S4.'

Butcher blushed. 'You some sort of car dick, or something?'

'I just know my cars.' Corcoran traced the outline of the car on the screen. 'Biggest difference is the engine, but it's got a sports trim. This model's more expensive than the vanilla, and much rarer. Meaning easier to find.' He stood up tall. 'Can you grant me access to the CCTV? I'll need your—'

Butcher gasped out a sigh. 'Fine. I'll pass it all over.'

'No need to be like that.' Corcoran hit play again and rewatched the footage. Nothing else jumped out at him. 'But you should already be rechecking your sources for any S4s.'

'Right.' Butcher took his seat with a grunt and started taking it out on the keyboard.

Corcoran stood up to stretch out. 'You want a top-up?'

Butcher nudged his mug with an elbow.

Corcoran walked over to the coffee machine and splashed out two fresh cups. The milk smelled sour, so he just added it to Butcher's.

'Sergeant.' Hinshelwood had decided this was the perfect moment to start rooting around in the cupboard for a mug. 'How goes it?'

'Getting somewhere, maybe.'

Corcoran toasted him with his mug and headed back to Butcher. 'Anything?'

'Cheers.' Butcher took a sip then smacked his lips. 'Okay, so I've found three Audi S4s. All of them were caught by the ANPR camera as that road entered the M11.' He looked at Corcoran with pleading eyes. 'Want to head out and speak to them?'

Corcoran sat back in his chair, drinking his coffee and thinking. Hinshelwood was pouring himself a cup, looking straight at them. Each move would be under close scrutiny, so it had to be careful and precise.

He leaned forward, closer to Butcher and his computer, then replayed the footage again, but in half speed this time. Each step made Sarah look like she was running on the moon. Towards the end, she checked her watch a second time, then slightly raised her hand. Was she waving at someone?

He wound it back and played it again.

'You're thinking this is news to me, right?' Butcher rolled his eyes. 'She's waving at another runner.'

'Someone she knew?'

Butcher held open the case file. 'Andy Murphy, a neighbour. In the same WhatsApp running group as Sarah and Christopher. They check who's up for a run that night, all that jazz. Andy ran with Sarah and Christopher regularly, got to know them pretty well.'

'So why was Sarah running alone that night?'

Butcher snorted as he rested the file on his desk. 'Christopher told me that Sarah ran home from work fairly often. Eight miles door to door.'

Corcoran finished his coffee, the taste turning bitter. 'Regularly?'

'Like clockwork, mate. Every Monday, Wednesday, Friday.'

Corcoran felt a stabbing pain in his gut, that familiar realisation that someone could know her movements inside out, could know precisely where she'd be at what time. Someone who'd followed her for a couple of weeks and established a pattern.

Or someone who knew her.

# Six

*[18:17]*

Sarah Langton lived in a two-storey stone cottage, the low-maintenance front garden filled with pebbles and mature shrubs. It looked empty and dark. Had to be rented – no way a young couple could afford to own a house here. Inside, a cat mewed, pawing at the door.

'Someone needs to feed him.'

Butcher was leaning back against his car, arms folded, lips pressed tight. 'Better remind Christopher.'

Corcoran took another scan of the house. 'So, this Andy?'

'Three doors down.' Butcher set off, leaving the stone end of the street for the more modern brick incursion, post-war and still way out of a cop's price range. He opened a squeaking garden gate and walked up the short path, giving the door a sharp policeman's knock.

Over by a small shed, an angle grinder hid under a navy tarpaulin. Sawdust heaped in a sagging pile, rain-free, unlike the rest of the garden. Meaning freshly used.

The door clunked open and the reek of fresh paint burst out, slightly masking the smell of cooking garlic. A man stood there, his topless torso splashed with emulsion, his running shorts somehow escaping it. Late twenties, but his

40

thick beard was streaked white with paint, giving him the look of an ancient mariner. A few seconds of staring at Butcher, then he frowned. 'Is there some news about Sarah?'

'Can we come in, Andy?'

'It's bad? Shit.' Andy collapsed back against the wall. Stayed standing, but it looked touch and go.

'We've found her. Alive. She's not in a good way, but she's alive.'

Worry eased off Andy's face. Then it tightened again. 'How bad a way are we talking?'

Corcoran stepped in front of Butcher and cleared his throat. 'Sir, I need to speak to you. Can we do this inside?'

'It's an absolute pigsty, mate.' Andy stepped out onto the path and pulled the door behind him. 'How can I help?'

Corcoran stood there, arms folded. Not letting the cops in was never a good sign, even if you were mid-decoration. 'She was found in rural Oxfordshire, starved almost to death. On the CCTV from the night Sarah disappeared, she waved at you, correct?'

Andy blew out garlicky breath. 'That's right.' He swallowed hard. 'I've been over it so many times in my head, you know? I didn't see anything. Wish I had.'

'It's possible you were the last person to see her.'

Another breath. 'That night, I was going through some personal stuff and . . .' He leaned back against his front door. 'I had to get out and pound the pavements.' He kneaded his beard like it was bread dough. 'My father-in-law had a stroke at Christmas time, so Kate's back in Australia, helping her stepmother cope with everything. I'm doing this place up while she's away, and every night when I'm working all I can think of is Sarah waving at me. I wish I could've stopped her there and then. Saved her from whatever's happened. But I was so caught up in my own *bullshit*.'

'This isn't your fault, sir.' Corcoran pulled out a sheet of paper, a grainy screen grab of the Audi. 'Do you recognise this car?'

Andy took it off him and nodded. 'DC Butcher here asked me about it, but I don't remember seeing it.'

'Ever see that car back round here?'

'No, sorry.' Andy handed the page back. 'I'm so sorry.'

Corcoran folded it carefully and put it away. 'You were close to Sarah, right?'

'Running alone is great thinking time. With someone else, you get to know them. Most of your brain focuses on the mechanics of running, so there's no bullshit or subterfuge or games, just who you are. I went out with Sarah a few times, just the two of us, and we put the world to rights.'

Just the two of them on a run. Could be innocent, but could be something. And Andy would know her running patterns.

'She ever talk about her job?'

'Not that kind of chat, mate.'

'What about her husband?'

'Chris is a good guy. No issues there, least not that I'm aware of.'

'She ever mention any threats?'

'*Threats?*' Andy's mouth hung open. 'You think some-one's . . .?' He swallowed again. 'Never mentioned a threat to me, no.'

Corcoran waited for him to make eye contact again. There.

'Now that Sarah's been found, is there anything that sticks out?'

Butcher gritted his teeth. 'Now wait a minute . . .'

Corcoran shut him up with a glare. He refocused on Andy. 'Any conversations that take on a different light?'

'None.' Andy frowned, though. 'Well . . . There's something Sarah said. To Kate, actually, not me.' His frown deepened. 'Just before Christmas, she told Kate about this work colleague. A man.'

Corcoran clocked Butcher's surprise. 'What about him?'

'She got the distinct impression this guy might've been stalking Sarah.'

## *[18:45]*

Butcher drove out of the far side of Cambridge, the elegant houses giving way to twenty-first-century office buildings, all glass and chrome catching the evening sun. Some Cambridge University science buildings nestled in amongst big-name tech firms and some lesser-known names. He looked over at Corcoran. 'You seriously think this colleague could've taken her?'

Surely if this guy had been a sufficiently credible threat, Butcher's investigation – no matter how scant – would've got some sniff of it. Wouldn't it?

Then again, a work colleague would know her daily movements. Wouldn't even have to follow her to find the most opportune moment in her day.

Butcher muttered something as he pulled up at a security

barrier. A sign was filled with a logo that might've read 'Lens Lock'. Behind, a giant building loomed, two-storey on three sides, the fourth at least ten high. He wound down the window and let in the motorway rumble. Must be close, maybe a few hundred metres away.

A security guard stepped out, big and strong and carrying a hell of a lot more threat than the police station's guard. He looked at Butcher, his expression emotionless. 'Can I help you, sir?'

Butcher flashed his warrant card. 'Here to see Wendy Templeton-Smith.'

'You got a prior appointment?'

'Afraid not.'

The guard gestured with his fingers, like he wanted them to turn around. 'You'll just have to come back when you do. This is a secure site, sir.'

Corcoran got out his warrant card. 'DS Aidan Corcoran of Thames Valley Police. We're investigating the disappearance of one of your employees.'

'I can't change the directors' calendars, sir. Now, I need you to—'

'She's been found in a lane in Oxfordshire.' Corcoran left out any facts of her appearance, instead motioning at the building. 'Now, I don't know what the hell you lot are up to in there, but I gather some people might strongly disagree with it. I'd hate to be the one having to explain to your boss how you refused two friendly cops entry before some animal rights terrorists claimed credit for an attack on an employee. You know how PR works, right? Getting ahead of the story and all that?'

The guard looked round at the building, his gaze sweeping up the tower. 'Ask for her at reception. I'll approve your access.'

# [19:02]

The office was near the top of the tower, with a view across Cambridge towards the University colleges, lit up in the night sky in all their opulence.

Corcoran perched on a stool at a glass desk. No chairs lower than that in the whole room. 'So what exactly is it you do here?'

Wendy Templeton-Smith ran a hand through her deep-red hair, sipping iced water from a glass, tall and thin like it'd been modelled on her figure. 'Lens Lock are committed to ending childhood blindness. That's our mission, Sergeant.'

Corcoran mixed a good amount of frown into his smile. 'So you experiment on animals?'

'This is a research company.' She gave a frosty look as she crunched an ice cube between her teeth. 'We operate within the legal guidelines of several jurisdictions.'

'But you do receive threats, right?'

'Frequently.' She waved at the window. 'Hence the extreme security. You'll notice there's no car park? All of our employees get a ride-share car into work. It's the only way to protect them.' She rested her glass on the table next to Butcher. 'But I'm relieved to learn that Sarah's been found.'

'She's very far from being out of the woods, but at least she's alive.' Corcoran scanned Wendy's face for any signs of malice or foreknowledge. Nothing, but someone who had an office like this would have a few tricks up their sleeve. 'Did Sarah personally receive any threats?'

'Not to my knowledge.' Wendy walked over to her desk and stood behind a giant aluminium computer, raised up so she could work standing. 'While some of our employees have been named online and targeted by some groups, Sarah is a project manager and isn't responsible for any of our, uh, day-to-day operations.'

'But sometimes employees try to be heroes and hide threats, right?'

Wendy looked over the screen with an arched eyebrow. 'That has happened, despite the extensive training and monitoring we have in place.' She took a slow breath. 'But that sort of thing usually affects their job performance and Sarah's was consistently excellent. She was going places.' She stared into space, like Sarah's destination was this very office.

Corcoran pulled out his notebook and rested it on the glass next to his untouched water. 'I notice from the file that we've asked for the CCTV from the night of the twenty-seventh of January. DC Butcher, have you received it?'

Butcher cleared his throat. 'Not as of yet.'

'I'll arrange to send it on.' Wendy looked over at Butcher. 'I've got your contact details on file.'

Butcher grunted. 'You weren't so compliant back in January.'

'Things have moved on.' Wendy gave him a wolf grin. 'We have to prioritise our activities.'

Corcoran let her stew for a few seconds, watching for any tells. An overhead air freshener hissed out a pine scent. 'Were you aware of any issues between Sarah and any work colleagues?'

Wendy licked her lips. 'I assure you there's nothing in whatever you've heard.'

'And what might that be?'

She laughed, but said nothing.

Corcoran got up and walked over to her desk, resting his palms on the perfect glass as he faced her, eye to eye. 'This isn't a Missing Persons case any more. It looks very much like someone abducted Sarah, starved her for weeks and let her go.'

She took a halting breath, but didn't say anything.

'I need any help I can get, especially from you.' He waited for a nod, and got only a small one. 'Now, we've heard that someone who worked with Sarah was stalking her.'

'*Stalking?*' Wendy shook her head. 'God, no.'

'If I find that you're lying to—'

'That's not what I meant.' Wendy combed her fingers through her perfect hair. 'The someone you've heard about did indeed work for Sarah, but they were having an affair.'

# Seven

## *[19:27]*

Butcher pulled up on a suburban cul-de-sac on the outskirts of Cambridge, the lights on inside most of the houses now. 'Whatever you're thinking, I—'

Corcoran got out of the car and walked up the drive, past a shiny Nissan Leaf. He stopped dead.

A silver Audi sat inside a garage, the same sports trim as the one on the CCTV.

Corcoran shifted his focus from the car to the house. Low-slung, new build. Expensive windows and doors. Snazzy lighting more focused on mood than security. Tasteful jazz bleeding out of the nearest room. He looked round at Butcher and thumbed at the car. 'Run the plates. Check ANPR. Whatever it takes, your job is placing this car at the scene of the disappearance.'

'Sarge.' Butcher got out his phone with a sigh and walked off.

Corcoran took it slowly as he approached the house door. He pressed the button on the high-tech ringer mounted in the mushroom door.

A rising chime blasted out. The door opened and a woman

peered out. 'Can I help?' Western European accent – German, Swiss, Austrian, maybe even Dutch.

'DS Corcoran.' He flipped out his warrant card. 'Looking for a Klaus Werner.'

'At this time of night?'

Corcoran checked his watch. Seven twenty-eight was nobody's 'this time of night'. 'Mrs Werner?'

'Podolski, Lena Podolski. But I am the wife of Klaus, yes.'

'I need a word with your husband.'

'Do you have a warrant? Does he need a lawyer?'

A flash of movement behind her. A tall man, hiding behind his wife.

'Just a quick—'

She shut the door.

Corcoran raised his hand, ready to knock this time.

'Sarge.' Butcher crunched up the gravel drive towards him, waving his phone around. 'That's our car. ANPR has it getting on the M11 at the Madingley Road ten minutes after that sighting. Then off at the A14, which is how you'd get to Sarah's. Still, it didn't show up on the CCTV in Sarah's street because of whatever they'd done to the plates.'

Corcoran tried to figure out what it meant. The night she was taken, Werner had left Sarah's work, then visited her home. He'd masked the number plates, but that's all they had. Was it enough to bring him in? Hell yeah. He thumped the door this time, hard and insistent. Then waited.

Nothing.

He knelt and flipped open the letterbox. 'Klaus, this is

about Sarah Langton. I think you know what happened to her.'

The door opened and Klaus Werner stood there, head slumping. An elaborate goatee beard covered his chin and the surrounding flesh. Smooth skin led up to an even smoother haircut. Quite the looker, though he maybe didn't know it. 'You've found Sarah's body?' No trace of a German accent, but it certainly sounded like he'd lived in East Anglia for a good few years.

Corcoran stepped over the threshold and patted the man's sleeve, ready to grab tight if needed. 'We need to speak to you down at the station.'

Lena appeared again, punching Klaus on the arm, hard. 'What the hell is going on?'

'Just need a quiet word with—'

Lena slapped Klaus, sounding like a body hitting the sea from a great height. 'Who is this Sarah?'

'Stop!' Corcoran got between them, deflecting her attacks until her blunt forearm barely touched her husband's shoulder. He tightened his grip on Klaus and led him away.

## [20:22]

The Cambridge police station interview rooms weren't up to the same standard as Thames Valley's, especially the Kidlington HQ. The walls were several years past needing a new coat of paint and every slight movement echoed around the cramped space.

Klaus sat opposite Corcoran, scratching at his beard.

A machine coffee smouldered in front of him, the acrid tang a world away from the wonders of Butcher's filter, two fresh cups of which sat on Corcoran's side of the table.

Butcher took a delicate sip. 'We gather you worked for Sarah Langton?'

Klaus looked at his lawyer, a grey suit where a human being should be, then just shook his head. Still hadn't said anything.

Corcoran focused on the lawyer, eyebrows raised. 'You might want to get your client to speak to us. A woman's been found and—'

'Sarah?' Klaus looked up, eyes wide. 'You *have* found Sarah's body?'

'In Oxfordshire.'

Klaus's mouth hung open. 'My god.'

Corcoran sat back and watched his reaction unfold. His eyes widening, his mouth closing, his jaw clenching. Nothing that showed he knew her fate. Or that he was acting. 'We know you were sleeping with Sarah.'

'That's . . .' Klaus sucked in a deep breath. 'I . . . Where did you . . .?'

Corcoran pulled out the CCTV still and took his time unfolding it, then slid it across the scarred wood. 'That's your car outside Sarah's house, isn't it?'

No reply from Klaus.

'Mr Werner, this doesn't look good.' Corcoran gave a long pause before pulling out the ANPR extract. 'You followed Sarah home from work the night she went missing.'

'That isn't what happened!'

Corcoran took a long drink of his coffee and let him stew for a moment. 'What did happen, then?'

Klaus traced a finger across the bottom of his left eye. 'My wife can't learn any of this.'

Corcoran gave a slight nod. Left nothing on the record.

'Okay, so I work *with* Sarah.' Klaus held up a finger. 'With, not for. She's the project manager and I'm the research lead. Technically, she should work for me.' He looked at his lawyer, long enough to get a nod. 'And I was sleeping with Sarah.' His shoulders deflated with the release of the long-held truth coming out. 'It started at a conference back home in Germany. We were both drunk and . . . We agreed it was a one-off thing.' More rustling as he scratched at his beard. 'But she kept wanting to see me. So we . . . We embarked on an affair.' He leaned back in his chair and stared up at the ceiling, seeming to relax for the first time in months. 'To avoid detection from our . . . from our spouses, Sarah would run home and I'd meet her in a lane and we'd . . . in my car. I'd give her a lift home and it'd look like she'd run all the way.'

'That must've been a lot of guilt to hold on to for the six weeks she's been missing.'

'You don't know the half of it.'

'Of course, this is what you told my colleague here?'

'I didn't speak to him.'

'Which is very curious. This was in the news, correct?'

Klaus sat back, stroking his beard.

A slight flicker of guilt, but was it enough?

Corcoran showed him the CCTV still again. 'What happened that night?'

'As usual, I left work not long after Sarah, and drove to the meeting place.' Klaus swallowed. 'But Sarah didn't turn up. I waited for about fifteen minutes, then followed the route she would've taken.' He picked up the photo and ran his finger over Sarah, mid-run. 'I was worried she might've been in an accident, so I went to her house, but there was no sign of her.'

'And that's what you were doing in that photo?'

'Of course. This was not far from her home.'

'You saw her, though?'

'We spoke.' Tears filled his eyes. 'She still had one earbud in, music still playing.' He tossed the sheet back to Corcoran. 'She told me it was over. She was worried about her husband finding out. I told her we could delete the messages; we could have a system that . . .' He sighed. 'But she said she wanted to save her marriage.'

'You didn't see it that way?'

'I wanted to keep it going. I can't leave my wife, but . . . But Sarah *insisted* it was over.'

'How did you leave it that night?'

'I drove off.' Klaus snarled. He looked like he was going to add something, but he kept his peace.

Something left unsaid. Was it trivial or crucial?

'But?'

'But nothing.' Klaus sighed. 'I gather her husband has a furious temper.'

'You know him?'

'Christopher Langton.' Klaus took a sip of his coffee. 'We met at a work function a few years ago. I didn't like the man.'

'None of this explains why you didn't come forward.'

Klaus took another drink of coffee, looking at Butcher then back at Corcoran. 'Because I thought if I spoke to the police, I'd become a suspect.'

'You are a suspect now. And your omission makes you look guilty.'

'I didn't want my wife to find out.' His voice was small now, like a chided schoolboy. 'I didn't see anything happen to Sarah, I swear.'

Corcoran sat back in his chair and stared at him for a few seconds, weighing up his innocence in his mind. 'She's alive.'

Klaus's eyes bulged. 'What?' He blinked hard, fighting confusion, relief, grief. 'I thought . . . I thought . . .'

'You thought she was dead. Well, she was found today. Alive, but very, very unwell.' And Corcoran had seen enough to know that this was news to him.

Whatever transgressions the guy was responsible for, he didn't look like an abductor, just a man guilty of adultery and living a lie.

Besides, they had no evidence against him.

Corcoran nudged Butcher and nodded at the door. He walked over and sipped coffee in the corridor until the door shut. 'What's your read on him?'

Butcher slumped against the wall, letting a pair of uniformed officers walk past while he gathered his thoughts. Couldn't look at Corcoran. 'I feel really bad about not getting these leads.'

'Forget about your feelings.' Corcoran arched his neck until he got eye contact. 'I understand your situation, believe me, and I wish you'd been luckier with the timing. Maybe you would've found her with a few more days.'

'I tried, mate. I just . . . kept drawing blanks.'

'It happens.' Corcoran swallowed down bile. 'Do you think he kidnapped her?'

Butcher seemed to consider his words for the first time since they'd met. 'We've got nothing to say he did.'

'But his movements aren't accounted for.' Corcoran finished his coffee and handed the empty cup to Butcher. 'Can you get an alibi from him and check it?'

Butcher looked down the corridor at a huddle of uniforms chatting about football or *EastEnders* or whatever. 'Sure.'

'Thanks.' Corcoran slapped his back. 'Call me. However it plays out, okay?'

'You're going?'

'Let him go once you've got his statement. His wife's going to give him worse hell than being held here. Maybe something will slip.'

# Eight

## [22:40]

Corcoran stepped into the whirlwind of the main Incident Room, still in the process of being set up, and stepped back out again. Their office space was dead, all the major players out hunting down whoever took Sarah. And no sign of Thompson in her office.

But he could smell coffee, meaning she was likely still around, so he walked over to the swanky silver machine. Thompson wasn't there either. He hit the button, but got a bleeping noise. The pod tray was empty. Maybe he had a use for Butcher after all – get him to man a filter machine when he came over. He rooted around in the drawer, finding an Ethiopian pod at the back, the foil only slightly torn at one side, and he slid it in and hit the button for Americano. This time, the machine hissed and whirred.

Through the window, the car park was almost empty, dotted with regularly spaced trees, the thin wood just beyond giving way to a large field. Rural Oxfordshire, so far away from the grit of Corcoran's home.

He reached into the fridge for the pint of semi-skimmed and shook it, then tipped it into his mug. He sipped the strong drink and played it all through in his head, but nothing stood out to him.

'The boys are back in town.' Thompson was standing behind him, hands on hips. 'When did you get back to civilisation?'

'Just now and this is hardly . . .' Corcoran gave up, but waved around the desolate space. 'Looks like the square root of—'

'They're all out.' Thompson set off, beckoning him to follow. 'Getting absolutely nowhere here.'

'Which makes sense.'

Thompson stopped outside an interview room. 'How?'

'As far as we know, Sarah's life is over in Cambridge, not Minster Lovell or anywhere in Oxfordshire. Did you listen to the voicemail I left?'

She grunted. 'You seem to have made some good progress over there, no thanks to that beanpole knuckle-dragger.'

'Butcher's okay.' Corcoran held her gaze, staring deep into the dark pits of her eyes. 'Sure the same thing has happened many times over on similar cases in this force.'

'Maybe in the Met, but you need to accept that this is your home now and act accordingly.' Thompson opened the interview room door a crack, letting Corcoran see Sarah's husband, Christopher Langton. 'You got anything on him?'

'Let's just see.' Corcoran followed her in and settled for the seat opposite Langton. No lawyer, which made for a nice change.

Langton shifted his gaze between them. 'What's happened?'

Thompson eased off her suit jacket and carefully rested it on the back of her chair. 'Sounds like there's something you should be telling us?'

'You're treating me like a suspect.' Spoken into his hand, rather than directly at either of them.

'Of course we are. It's our job to look at all the stories we get, put them together, tear them apart, then find out who's been hiding things from us. More often than you'd think, it leads us to who did it.'

Langton glared at Corcoran, then switched his ire to Thompson. 'There is *no way* I could've done this to Sarah.'

'By "this", you mean abducting her, starving her, keeping her locked up for six weeks?' Thompson snorted. 'No way? Really? See, where I'm sat, I can see a really strong motive.' She left an artful pause, her lips curling up at the edges. 'Your wife had an affair.'

Langton just shook his head.

'What she did made you hate her, made you want her to suffer. Right? You did this to her, didn't you? Kidnapped her, starved her, kept her locked up.'

The shaking increased in speed as she spoke.

A flash of eyebrows instructed Corcoran to lead.

Corcoran leaned forward, resting his elbows on the wood. 'You could've saved me the trip, you know? Two hours there, two hours back, plus three hours in Cambridge. Just to find out your wife had been sleeping with a colleague.'

Langton looked away.

'Why didn't you mention Klaus Werner to DC Butcher?'

Langton let out a deep sigh. Not the look of a vengeful kidnapper, but the resignation of a man clinging on to a failing marriage.

'So you knew about their affair?'

'I had a suspicion.' Langton frowned. 'But it was only a

suspicion. I didn't want the police to waste time on my theories . . . I mean, I had no proof and it might've made me look guilty, like I was trying to point blame elsewhere.'

Corcoran shared a look with Thompson, then doubled down on Langton. 'You care to air this theory now?'

'I thought it might've been Andy she was seeing. I don't know.' He gasped, all of his restraint and control snapping out in one motion. 'It'd been going on for months. Over a year, at least.' Eyes shut, he let out a long breath. Probably the first people he'd spoken to about this, including Sarah. He opened his eyes again, blinking slowly. 'The worst part was I felt so guilty. I'd let Sarah down so badly that she was looking for someone else. We've been together since we were fourteen. *Fourteen*. We were just kids. And now we're twenty-six and married and . . . it's felt like it's just hanging together by a thread for a long time now.'

'And when you found out, the thread snapped. Right?'

Langton looked over, eyes pleading with Corcoran. 'Right. I swear I didn't know his name. Who is he?'

'He knows you.'

'That doesn't help me.'

Corcoran held his gaze, but caught Thompson's strange look at him in his peripheral vision. 'Do you think it's possible Klaus did this to your wife?'

Langton flinched at the last word. 'It's possible . . . I mean, I don't know the man.' He stared hard at Corcoran, fire burning in his eyes, his jaw clenched tight. Then he looked away, shaking his head.

They'd lost him.

# [23:21]

Thompson shut her office door with a clatter and stomped over to her desk chair. 'So is Butcher just inept or is it something much worse?'

'Are you asking me if he's corrupt?' Corcoran stayed near the door. 'I doubt it. I spoke to his boss over there and I totally understand the situation they were in when Sarah went missing. And based on what I've seen, I don't think Butcher's inept or corrupt. He's just way too busy and they're short-staffed.'

Thompson slid into her chair and ran a hand through her hair. 'I need to speak to his DI over in Cambridge. You meet them?'

'DI Thomas "Call me Tom" Hinshelwood. But I don't think scoring points is a good use of our time.' Corcoran caught her glare, warning him he should tread carefully. But he ignored it anyway. 'I mean, by all means grab some of their lads to progress things at that end, but my take is Butcher's a good cop caught in a shitty situation.'

She huffed out a laugh, harsh and short. 'So, we've got two suspects. Klaus Werner and Christopher Langton, right?'

'Both are possible.' Corcoran got out his notebook and flicked through it. 'Her neighbour too. Guy called Andy, used to run with Sarah, wife's back in Australia for family stuff. I always get a bit itchy when someone shuts their door behind them.' He shut his notebook. 'None of them offer a decent explanation for the starvation. And why drop her in Oxfordshire? That doesn't seem to mean anything to them.'

'You're thinking there's something else going on here?'

'That makes me think you've got evidence there is.'

'Touché.' Thompson reached into a drawer and pulled out a document. 'Initial stab at forensics shows no evidence of rape, but the ligature marks are old and sustained. Indicating someone's held her.'

Now Corcoran saw it for what it was, and cast aside what it wasn't. Forget a suicide attempt, or someone running away, or a breakdown caused by drugs, or just failing health. Someone had abducted Sarah and held her captive.

He refocused all the information but still came up short.

'We've got precious little in the way of leads. Sure, an affair is juicy, but does it explain what they did to Sarah?' He got a flash of the living skeleton in the hospital. 'What happened to her was brutal. And premeditated. Calculated. But also completely senseless.'

'It makes sense to someone.'

Corcoran had to blink away the image of Sarah again. 'And that someone has contended with the logistics of keeping Sarah hostage for six weeks. That requires an isolated space, regular supervision, and some means of restraining her. It'd take a lot of effort and determination. And letting Sarah go would surely be self-defeating, too. If she recognised them, she could identify them to us.'

'But she didn't, Aidan. When you spoke to her in the ambulance, she gave her name, not Christopher or Klaus. Even this Andy.'

'Well, until we've spoken to Sarah, we need to keep our options open.' Corcoran slid the report back across to her, but she didn't take it. 'Have you made any progress here?'

'Nothing.' Her sigh gave away just how little. 'Absolutely nothing. Only crumb I'm clinging to is that stonemason told us he spotted an SUV hurtling down the lane just before he found Sarah. If we can pin it to one of their suspects, then we'll be golden.'

'That's a long shot.'

'Aidan, I could do with some positivity here.' She unlocked her computer and winced as she scanned the screen, probably her email inbox bursting at the seams. 'Get yourself home, get some shut eye. This is a major inquiry now. Seven o'clock briefing, all that jazz.'

Corcoran's late-evening coffee wasn't battling through four hours of driving on top of a full shift. 'I've still not spoken to Sarah's parents yet.'

'No need.' Thompson grabbed her car keys and got up with a yawn. 'I'm heading to the hospital right now.'

# Nine

## [Thompson, 23:36]

The car park's lights caught them perfectly, huddling in the smoking shelter like they were still at school, bunking off third-period French. He held her hand while she sucked deep from her cigarette, letting it out in a fine mist.

Thompson got her notebook out of the glovebox and flicked through the pages. There. Sally and Richard Norton. She looked up and their breaths misted in the bitter air as they came to terms with the shock of their daughter's return. She turned to a fresh page, just blank lines waiting for the time, the date and their names. Sally and Richard. Remember them. She scribbled a loose to-do list, all the standard activities she needed to complete, in a completely non-standard case. She got out into the cold night and scanned the car park. Hospitals were never empty, even at this time.

A Volkswagen SUV was between them, a grieving man sitting with his head pressed back, tears streaming down his face. No time to ask if he was okay, even if it was her place.

She sloped over to Sally and Richard, and stopped with a friendly smile.

Red lines spidered the whites of their eyes. The extra grey

hairs. The frown lines. The doubt. The fear. The toll Sarah's disappearance had taken on them.

Her father more hopeful, standing there with his chest puffed out, but even he couldn't cope with the sheer terror of having Sarah back in that state, teetering on the brink of death.

Sally lit a second cigarette and took a deep drag. Her eyes looked like she'd put used teabags underneath them. Probably drinking so many cups to help her through the long nights she could barely sleep. Her silvery-brown roots pushed through the blonde and she clearly hadn't had time to dye her hair in six weeks of terminal worry.

'Alana Thompson.' She held out her warrant card with a comforting smile, leaving it long enough for them to scan the front and memorise everything, enough time to gain their trust. 'I'm the Deputy Senior Investigating Officer on the investigation into your daughter's disappearance.'

Smoke clouds rounded Sally's face. 'Abduction.'

'We're trying to establish whether your daughter went missing by her own—'

'Someone took my daughter.' Sally took another drag on her cigarette. 'I want you to find out who.'

The VW's engine started up, then it pulled away, trundling through the empty car park. A Tiguan, 65 plates. Dark grey.

Thompson gave Sally another smile, firmer and making it clear she wasn't going to take no for an answer, but still with a trace of sympathy. 'We should do this inside.' She held out a hand and gestured into the cloying warmth of the hospital.

Richard looked like he was going to follow her lead.

But Sally didn't. She just stood there. 'All this time, you're arguing about whether someone's taken her. I know they have.'

Maybe she'd held something back. Probably not, but Thompson nodded, letting her get it out of her system.

'And it's not just about my Sarah. That's bad enough. But I can't help but think there's someone else going through what I have, their child suffering through this horrific, horrific ordeal.'

So there wasn't anything. Concern and empathy, though. And the forensics only gave part of Sarah's story. Thompson smiled, knowing she needed to get Sally and Richard Norton's part next. 'I appreciate your concern, Mrs Norton, but we've no concrete evidence to confirm Sarah was abducted, let alone that there's anyone else going through this.' Again, she gestured inside. 'Now, shall we?'

# Ten

## *Howard*

His chest moves up and down, his eyelids fluttering as he comes up from the dream like a diver from the ocean depths. Howard has no recognition of anyone else in the room, just himself, lying on the bed, the chains rattling as he moves.

Then the speakers crackle into life. A deep thud of bass erupts, the noise jolting him upright.

'He's Charlie the Seahorse and there's nothing he can't do!' Shrill children's singing, twisted and distorted by the sheer volume.

Breathing hard, Howard takes in his immediate surroundings. The same place as ever. Harsh brick walls, burnt and blackened, dull in the pale overhead light. The door, locked as it always is, metal bars preventing any attempt at an escape, any consideration of it. The bed he lies on. The desk mounted to the wall, the office chair in front of it, bolted down.

No signs his captor has been back in.

'He's Charlie the Seahorse and he makes everything okay!'

The sound is deafening. Howard puts his head down on the bare mattress, but he hears it even when it's not playing now. He's no idea how long he's been here.

But it must've stopped playing because he falls asleep. And he is dreaming of surfing, flying across the waves, faster than ever, outrunning another surfer, but as he closes on the shore, big arms drag him and pull him under.

'He's Charlie the Seahorse and he's here for you!'

He's groggy, his eyes struggling to stay open and he—

'—lie! Isn't life a dream?'

He jolts awake again. The music's louder, like it's been turned up, and he just wants to sleep. Just wants death now. But sleep will do.

'Charlie! Oh, Charlie! Isn't this your sea?'

He lies flat on his back and keeps his eyes shut, then counts the in breaths and out breaths.

The music loops back round to the start again, the plinky-plonk piano sounding the size of a football stadium. 'He's Charlie the Seahorse and there's nothing he can't do!'

Over the noise of the music, he hears movement at the door.

Howard doesn't dare look. He wants to stare at him, but he wants him to come over too. So he can take him down.

'—the Seahorse and he makes everything okay!'

Something grips his ankles like a vice and pulls Howard off the bed, dragging him across the flagstone floor, out of the room into a cellar. Wide and long, with a low ceiling. A wheelchair sits in the middle, straps resting on the arms.

'He's Charlie the Seahorse and he's here for you!' The music is a muted din from behind him, still loud and rasping at his ears. Then the door shuts and the wood sucks all the treble from the childish singing, leaving a chilling lower version that sounds like a choir of devils, accompanied by a thudding drumbeat. 'He's Charlie the Seahorse and it's time to play!'

Strong fingers grip his armpits and lift him up to a sitting position, facing back to his cell. The door on the left is lit up, the naked bulb catching the white sign printed with 'HOWARD'. Two crosshead screws at either side, the metal twinkling in the pale glow.

'Charlie! Oh, Charlie! Isn't this—'

The music dies but the white noise still lingers in Howard's ears. He still hears the piano and drums and satanic kids' choir.

But there's another sound. Dulled groans come from the door on the right, sitting in shadow. A lightbulb hangs down, giving an occasional flicker, but he doesn't know if he can read the sign. Four letters, beginning with M, but it's just too dark.

Something grips his hair and jerks his head forward. He lets out a confused scream, his arms shooting out, and he tries to stand but he's trapped. Those strong fingers under his armpits, pulling him up to sitting now, like he's on a chair. He tries to twist his neck, but he can't get round far enough to see properly. Just a black leather biker jacket. And a smell of smoke, not cigarettes but a burnt tyre or burnt plastic.

He tries wriggling but he can't move. All that planning, all that waiting, and he can't move when he needs to!

Then he is moving, propelled from behind. Over in the corner, a spiral staircase leads up, the concrete flat and smooth. He looks down and sees the wheels spinning round.

The last thing he sees of his prison is the middle door, the nameplate marked 'Sarah'.

# Day two

# Eleven

## [Corcoran, 05:55]

The sun still wasn't up as Corcoran pulled off the main road, his headlights tracing across the dark tarmac, picking out potholes and fallen branches from last night's wind. His dashboard blasted out that ringtone, the one he really should change. DI Thompson calling . . .

He sighed as he hit the green button. 'Alana, I'm almost there.'

'Taking your time, aren't you?'

He checked the dashboard clock. 'It's not even six. I wouldn't normally be up yet and I was—'

'Be thankful for the sleep you have had.'

He swallowed another sigh. 'Let me check this out and get back to you. Okay?'

'Fine.' And she was gone.

A glow up ahead, three squad cars pointing away from the road, their beams lighting up the trees.

Corcoran pulled up, taking a final hit from his Thermos mug as the engine rattled off.

One of the uniforms clocked him and raced over. 'Sir, this is a private—'

'DS Corcoran.' He got out with a flourish of his warrant

card. 'DI Thompson sent me. You based in Amersham nick?'

'Yes, Sarge.' The local cop stood his ground. Tall and bulky, thick arms folded across his chest. 'Got a call two hours ago. Local farmer spotted a fire, thought it was someone ruining his crops. Turns out it was a motor. Get the occasional joyrider out this way, but . . .'

'But?'

'I saw that message last night. DI Thompson's communication to the entire Thames Valley police?'

Corcoran's turn to sigh. Be nice to be told about these things before they happened for once. 'Come on, show me the car.' He followed the uniform into the woods, stepping across decaying branches towards a huddle of cops. Quite why it needed six of them was anyone's guess. They broke apart at Corcoran's approach, four of them heading back to their cars and getting back to where the hell they were supposed to be.

The frame of a car smouldered in a pile of ash. Slightly taller than a normal car, so it fit their request for an SUV.

Corcoran snapped on a nitrile glove and stepped closer. Still warm at a distance, meaning the metal was way too hot to touch. He kicked at the ash round the front. A VW badge lay there, charred, buckled and now completely unsuitable for hanging on a chain round your neck. He rounded the car, the pile of ash spreading in a wide circle, and crouched at the back. And there we go. TIGUAN in silver letters on the left, 0 TDI on the right, all scored with the heat but still attached to the boot. He stepped back and spotted the 2 and decimal point missing from the boot. 'Have the fire service been out?'

His local minder was crouched low, using a stick to sift through the ash. 'They've been made aware, but a factory fire in the Fairview industrial estate and a couple of houses down in Chalfont St Giles mean they're—'

'Okay, well make sure I get both interim and full reports from them.'

'Will do.' The uniform was still sifting away. 'Er, this might help.' He reached down and snatched his hand away. 'Bugger me hard and fast, that's hot that is.'

Corcoran snatched his stick and flipped what he was going for. The licence plate, a 65 too. He got out his phone and snapped it, then texted it to Thompson: 'Run this for me?' He stood there, taking in the scene.

Four miles from Amersham, two from Chalfont St Giles. If you looked up 'the middle of nowhere' in the dictionary, it would show a map of this wood. Perfect place to dump a car. Siphon the petrol and set it—

But it was a TDI. Diesel didn't ignite with a naked flame. Meaning a jerrycan of petrol in the boot. Meaning someone really wanted rid of this car.

Christopher Langton or Klaus Werner? Too soon to tell, and nothing pointing at either of them.

Corcoran got out his phone and opened the map app. Yesterday's route from Minster Lovell to Cambridge was still there. This place was about twenty miles too far south.

He searched over to his current location. Looked like an hour's walk to Amersham, so whoever it was could've taken a cab from there. But that was a hell of a risk to take.

Hang on. He tapped on the other route, the one that

took the M40 south, then the M1 north up towards Cambridge. An extra half an hour, but motorways, so more anonymous roads. But roads with automated number plate tracking.

His phone danced in his hands. *DI Thompson calling . . .* Again.

He put it to his ear. 'Alana.'

'Still sounds weird to me.' She laughed. 'Anyway, my little cherub, we've run that plate. Graphite Tiguan. Two-litre turbo diesel. Graphite is dark grey, right?'

'Yep. Have you got anything on it?'

'Reported stolen from High Wycombe last week.'

Corcoran let out a sigh. 'So, not belonging to—'

'Nope. Doesn't mean Klaus or Christopher didn't steal it, or buy it off someone who did.'

'Or it's unconnected to this.'

'Indeed.' Thompson clicked her tongue. 'When he found Sarah, Bob Rutherford said he saw a car hurtling down the lane, right? A Volkswagen or a Vauxhall. This could be it. This could be our perp covering his tracks. Whoever it was, they knew we were onto them. They've panicked and burnt the car.'

'But we're not onto them, are we?'

Thompson paused. 'I saw a 65 Tiguan at the hospital last night.'

'The same one?'

'I don't know. I'll check.' She clicked her tongue again. 'Okay, I'll get a local cop to speak to the owner. You're running late for my briefing.'

# *[07:00]*

Corcoran stopped outside the Incident Room and let out a yawn. One of those ones that just kept on going. He swallowed a glug of coffee and opened the door.

The room was crowded, a mix of thirty or so plainclothes and uniformed officers, standing and sitting. He hovered near the back, getting a nod from a couple of colleagues as he tried to keep a low profile.

Butcher was by the swanky new TV at the front, frowning at the laptop he cradled in his arms, the three cables stretched tight. 'Should be playing. I don't—'

Thompson snatched the remote from him and hit a button. The screen filled with a CCTV still. 'There you go.'

Butcher stood back with a smile. 'Thanks.'

Onscreen and in full colour, Sarah Langton stood by a bike shelter in the Lens Lock courtyard, stretching out her hamstrings. White earbuds dangled to the phone case strapped around her bicep. Looked like she was talking to someone on the phone, though she wasn't laughing. She pressed a button on her watch and set off, powering away at a fast pace.

The screen flipped to a greyscale view of the long road in Cambridge they'd visited the previous night, with the Lens Lock front entrance and its aggressive security guard. Sarah shot through, her pace more a sprint than a light jog, a woman burning some demons.

Butcher hit a key on the laptop and the image froze. He pointed at the screen, indicating a silver Audi parked by the side of the road. 'This is an Audi S4. Sports trim.' He looked around the room, like that was his own knowledge. 'This car belongs to Klaus Werner, a colleague of Sarah's who she was having an affair with.' He hit a key again.

After Sarah shot past, the car set off, following her.

Corcoran didn't know what to make of it. Klaus said he'd set off after Sarah. Now it looked like he'd stalked her route home.

'That's the last footage we've found until she turned up in her street, just before she went missing.'

'Thank you, Constable.' Thompson stepped over to Butcher and rested the remote on the laptop. 'I need you back in Cambridge confirming the movements of Messrs Werner and Langton, okay?'

Butcher's shoulders slumped like a stroppy teenager. 'But I've just driven here?'

'And I thank you for that.' Thompson fiddled with the laptop and the screen switched to the Thames Valley logo. 'Now, this case is live on HOLMES, thanks to DS Sortwell, and you should all have actions allocated with corresponding notifications in your inboxes. If you don't, then please please please please speak to DS Sortwell. Do not speak to me. I cannot help you and can barely remember my own password. Pete can and will help you.'

A ripple of laughter ran around the room.

'Now, the initial forensics analysis has found only the discoverer's DNA on Sarah. Nobody else's.' Thompson scanned around the room, her gaze settling on Corcoran. She gave a welcoming wink, then continued her sweep. 'No shoe prints or anything that'd help us, except . . . Well, we found some tyre tracks just off the road past where Sarah was dropped. Forensics are going to try to match that with the burnt-out Tiguan that DS Corcoran has just visited. Could be entirely innocent, or it could be precisely what we need to crack the case wide open.' She looked back at him. 'Anything to add, Sergeant?'

'You mean, did Sarah's husband or Klaus Werner drive that car?'

'Either.'

'Then, no. But we should try to pin either one to burning that SUV. Both are credible suspects, so if we can map their movements to those of the vehicle, then—'

'Agreed.' Thompson picked up the TV remote and pointed it at DS Sortwell, like she could control the big lump with it. 'Pete, can you add it to the actions log for DC Butcher?'

He gave a huffed nod.

Thompson looked around, a wry smile on her lips. 'Now, any other questions?'

Butcher raised a hand like he was still at school. 'Just wondering if there's any update on the pharma angle?'

'You mean, was Sarah targeted because she worked for a known vivisectionist?'

Butcher cleared his throat. 'Yeah, that.'

'We've found nothing to indicate that's a motive. Usually if some group or other abducts someone, they try to spread their message via the media or, these days, social media. They usually take the credit for it before we even know about it. Remember that case in Scotland a couple of—'

'Maybe they've starved her to show what happens to animals in a lab?'

Thompson's mouth hung open. Corcoran couldn't tell if it was shock at being interrupted mid-sentence or at the daftness of Butcher's question. 'Like I said, Constable, it's a possibility. We're monitoring matters in conjunction with the media offices of four forces. Okay?'

It seemed to placate Butcher.

Thompson tossed the remote onto the table with a clatter. 'I've got the dubious honour of hosting a press conference at eight-thirty. We're hoping to be live on Radio 4 for all of those commuters who can still bring themselves to listen to the *Today* show. We'll also catch the nine o'clock TV and radio news.' She looked around the room again, nodding slowly. 'Now, I trust each and every one of you. You're all top officers and we're a good team. You've all seen what's happened to Sarah. Yesterday, we treated it like she could've done this to herself, but it's looking increasingly likely that she was abducted. I can't let that lie and won't. We will catch this individual and bring them to justice for Sarah and her family. Okay?' Another sweep, then she gave a thumbs up. 'Dismissed.'

Corcoran let the scrum settle, with most of the squad heading for the canteen or the vending machine, before walking over.

Thompson was in Butcher's face. '—rupt me during a briefing, okay?'

'Sorry, ma'am.'

'Now, I need you to head back to Cambridge and do your job. Can you do that for me?'

Butcher stood there, head bowed, jaw clenched in silent fury. 'Will do, ma'am.'

Thompson gave Corcoran a bitter look, then stomped

towards DS Sortwell and the queue of cops who hadn't been allocated actions.

'You okay, Will?'

Butcher looked up at Corcoran, nostrils flaring. 'I've driven from Cambridge to bloody Kidlington and now I've got to head back?' He snarled. 'And that's . . .' A sigh. 'The thing that gets me is I failed. I was supposed to find Sarah and I didn't.'

Corcoran gave him a smile. 'Listen, I have experience of things going wrong in a case. The law of unintended consequences is a complete bastard. It'll twist your melon until you can only see blame in yourself for not saving everyone. But this isn't on you, okay? You did everything you were told to. Nothing less. Then you were hauled off by your boss, shoved onto something shiny and new. Us guys at the bottom, that's all we're here for. Doing. Not leading. It's not our responsibility. This isn't your fault.'

'Still stings.' Butcher shook his head. 'The skeleton in that hospital bed.' He swallowed. 'I couldn't sleep last night. Just kept seeing her like that, thinking I could've done more. *Knowing* I could.'

'You can do more *now*. You can help us catch this guy. Get back to Cambridge, go through the CCTV and log their movements. Sarah's, Christopher's, Klaus's. Times leaving, arriving at work, when they ran, who with. Whoever did this probably knew Sarah's movements over a week, so either they're really close to her or they've been watching her. If it's Christopher or Klaus, then catching them at it would be a good feeling. If it's someone else, you might spot them watching her. And if you log every licence plate and speak to the owners, maybe we'll find who's been following her.'

Butcher sucked in a deep breath. 'You're right.' He gave a tight nod. 'Thanks, mate.'

'And on your way home, go to Wycombe and speak to the owner of the Tiguan.'

'Bloody hell . . .' Butcher sloped off towards the door.

Corcoran found a desk and sat down. Wanted someone above to save him from fragile egos . . .

'Aidan!' Thompson was by the window, mobile to her head, beckoning him over with her hand. She covered the phone. 'Sarah's awake. There's a criminal psychologist heading to the hospital to speak to her. Go there. And play nice.'

# Twelve

## [Harry, 07:20]

Harry scrunched down in his beanbag and almost went flying. So he got up and scrunched down again and this time he did, rolling backwards onto the floor in a heap of giggles. He got up onto his elbows and lay on the floorboards, his head bobbing in time to the theme tune.

'He's Charlie the Seahorse and there's nothing he can't do!' The television glowed in the dark family room and Charlie the Seahorse jumped onto the screen, grinning wide. He sang along to his tune, dancing in the waves. 'He's Charlie the Seahorse and he makes everything okay!'

Singing along, Harry pushed himself up to standing and raced over to the window, sliding on his socks for the second half, catching himself on the table in the window. He put his knee down on the chair and pulled himself up so he could get the second one up, then he was there.

'He's Charlie the Seahorse and he's here for you!'

His dolls lay on the tabletop, perfectly arranged. Charlie the Seahorse, Octopus Robert, Sharky Keith and Dominic the Dolphin. Harry picked up Charlie and moved him in time with the action on the screen, first dancing around Dominic, then running away from Sharky Keith as he snapped his teeth.

The programme froze on the title page, Charlie standing there, beaming wide. Then it cut to Sharky Keith in his hut under the waves.

And Harry let out a snort. He hated Sharky Keith. Kept giving him nightmares, even made him piddle the bed once at Nana's, which made her cross. He kept watching the episode, but it was mostly Keith. So he looked out of the window instead.

Oh, there was that fox that Daddy didn't believe him about! Then it was gone and the paperboy wheeled past, his bright-red footballer headphones catching the light. He stopped at their house and strutted up the path, reading the front page of Daddy's paper, then slotted it through. Harry heard the thump by the front door and his father's thumping footsteps.

'Daddy?'

But he wasn't listening. He had his own headphones in, listening to his podcast, soaked with sweat from his exercise in the garage. Harry knew not to interrupt him when he was like that.

Outside, the paperboy walked back to his BMX, dancing in time to his music, strutting like he was in a video on You-Tube. He stopped and waved his arm in a circle, mouthing 'oh yeah', then hopped on the bike and scooted off back to the main road, his long arm indicating left.

Across the road, the church's front door cracked open and the vicar stepped out. Harry waved at him, but the vicar shut his eyes and sucked in the fresh morning air, listening to the few birds tweeting this early in the year, feeling the light rain on his cheeks, the gust of wind blowing his greying hair. He opened his eyes again and scanned the street, a broad grin on his face, but still didn't see Harry's waving arm, and he went back inside the church.

Harry looked at the screen and it was *still* Sharky Keith, though he was now chasing Octopus Robert, all eight of his legs flailing. But *still* no sign of Charlie the Seahorse. Harry picked up his Sharky Keith doll and flung it across the room, the plastic skidding along the floor and hitting his beanbag.

'Harry, can you get yourself ready for nursery?' Daddy's voice was a shout, his headphones too loud.

And now all Harry wanted was to watch Sharky Keith as he schemed with Dominic the Dolphin.

'Harry? Come on!'

He pouted, but there was nobody around to see it. So he got up. But outside, a van had parked in the exact spot Daddy hated people parking in. 'Daddy!'

A man got out onto the street and pulled up the collar of his black leather jacket. He looked around like a baddie, then opened the back of the van and kicked out a ramp.

'Daddy, there's a man!'

But Daddy *still* wasn't listening, instead thumping up the stairs towards his shower.

The man pulled out a wheelchair holding another man, easing it down to the street. The ramp bent as it took his weight. The bad man took another look around the street but it was still quiet, still dead.

'Daddy! Mummy!'

The man removed a gag on the other man's face and let it go, stuffing it in his pocket and looking round *again*, then he loosened the ropes around the other man's wrists and let the ropes dangle free on both sides, but the man was awake now and he was looking right at the bad man and he shouted but Harry couldn't hear it. The other man lashed out with his head – just like when Sharky Keith tried to headbutt Charlie the Seahorse – but he missed!

'Daaaadddddyyyyy!'

The bad man grabbed the other man's shoulder and pulled him out of the chair. It tipped up and the other man fell flat on his face! But the wheelchair hit the bad man in the knees and he fell over too! Then the other man grabbed his arm and the wheelchair landed on the bad man's leg, but the other man punched his arm over and over again!

'Mummy! Daddy!'

But the good man might be a bad man too because he tried biting the bad man just like Sharky Keith would and just missed his ear. The bad man hit him on the neck and pushed him away and the wheelchair rolled into the middle of the road where Mrs McAllister told them never to cycle. They got up at the same time, but the bad man was quicker. He hit the other man in the tummy with an elbow. The other man doubled over like at nursery when Lewis hit Alfie in the naughty place and he had to go to the doctor and was away for *ages*. Then the bad man kicked the back of the man's head and pushed him face first into the ground.

'Daddy!'

The bad man ran towards his van and pushed his wheelchair in the back. He slammed the door and ran to the driver's side and drove off.

'Mummy!'

The other man got up like his naughty place was really

sore. He stood there, staring into space, but he was muttering something.

'Daddy!'

The vicar came back out again, clutching a teacup, a wide smile filling his face. He frowned when he saw the other man storming towards him, jabbing his finger and pointing.

'Harry!' Daddy stood in the doorway, shaking his head like he was *really* angry. 'Are you still not ready yet? I told you—'

'Look!' Harry pointed at the window. 'A man got attacked!'

Daddy stomped over the floorboards. 'You don't half talk a lot of nonsense, my boy.' He tried to scoop Harry up, but stopped. 'Oh my Christ!'

# Thirteen

## *[Palmer, 08:45]*

'You can't blame yourselves for what's happened to your daughter.' Dr Marie Palmer perched forward in her chair, giving an open gesture with her hands, tilting her head to the side in sympathy. 'This isn't your fault or responsibility, okay?'

Sally Norton was athletic and healthy, looking a lot like her daughter's 'before' photo. Lines around her mouth, and a few stray greys in her long blonde hair, the roots starting to bleed through. She reached over to the table for a fresh tissue and blew her nose, already bright red. 'That's easy for you to say.'

'I know it is. But it's actually quite hard for me to mean it.' Palmer let the words settle in. 'And I do, I mean every single word. In situations like this, people will say things all the time, nice little homilies to get you to think in a positive way and handle the situation. Facebook memes. Condolence cards. But based on everything I know, what's happened to Sarah is neither of your faults.'

Richard Norton sat forward, mirroring Palmer's body language. 'We always did the best for Sarah.' A bear of a man, but with the softest voice. Scottish islands, maybe. He grabbed hold of his wife's hand. 'I like to think that Sarah had a happy upbringing.'

Palmer smiled again. 'Well, I'm sure she'd agree, Mr Norton.'

'I keep thinking if she'd not stuck with . . . with Christopher Langton . . .'

Palmer settled back in her chair, eyebrow arched. 'Oh?'

'Ach, he's a good lad.' Richard ran a hand down his face. 'I play golf with Chris's father. When he's not cheating, he's . . .' He sighed. 'Thing is, Sarah and Chris were childhood sweethearts. And that never ends well, does it?'

Sally stared into space, eyes wide, nibbling her bottom lip. 'I should've got her to end it. Should've insisted she went to a different university, instead of following him to Cambridge like a lost puppy.'

Palmer reached down to her rucksack and liberated her notebook. 'Do you think Sarah's husband is involved in her abduction?'

'Do you?'

Palmer held up her hands. 'I'm just asking. You seem to be inferring that he might be.'

'Don't listen to us . . .' Richard crossed his left leg over his right. Becoming at ease with Palmer now. 'Chris is a good guy and I just want my daughter to be happy. Please, catch the animal who's done this to our wee girl.'

A knock on the door behind Palmer. A man with dark hair and a scientifically precise amount of stubble on his chin. Overweight but tall and with an intense look in his eyes. The holy trinity – tall, dark and handsome. And with a slight limp as he walked over to whisper, 'DS Aidan Corcoran. Need a word.' London accent, gruff like he smoked forty a day.

Palmer clapped her thighs and got up with a polite smile. 'I'll give you some space.' She grabbed her rucksack and joined Corcoran in the corridor, offering her hand. 'Dr Marie Palmer, but you can call me Marie if you want.'

'Sure.' Corcoran shook her hand, but he seemed on edge. 'Look, I've been asked to accompany you when you speak to Sarah.'

'Oh, a shadow. Superb.' Palmer's turn to frown. 'She's awake?'

'Isn't that why you're here?' Corcoran set off down the long corridor, forcing her to follow his lopsided walk.

'Well, yes, but I was told to keep myself busy until I was formally notified.' Palmer had to hurry to keep up with him, limp or not. 'What's your take on what's happened?'

'My take?' Corcoran chuckled as he rounded a corner into another long corridor, doors leading off on both sides. An orderly pushed a trolley, head bobbing to the beat from his headphones. 'You've just spent fifty minutes with her parents, so you tell me.'

'Do you think Christopher Langton could've done this to his wife?'

'Do you?'

'Stop playing games with me.' Palmer stopped and waited, resting her backpack at her feet. 'Are you treating him as a suspect?'

'We are.' Corcoran stood there, a dark look on his face as the orderly weaved past. 'Same as the German guy Sarah was sleeping with. Klaus Werner. We've interviewed them both.'

'Oh.'

Corcoran folded his arms. 'Sounds like you think this isn't either of them.'

'It's not my place to say either way.'

'You're a criminal psychologist, right?'

'Well, yes, but—'

'If you think I'm barking up the wrong tree with those, then please say. That way I can apply my resources more intelligently than having them combing through CCTV for months.'

'I see.'

'So?'

'So what?'

'What's your professional take on this?'

'You say that with such enthusiasm.' Palmer grabbed her bag and walked on. 'In my opinion, and that's with having seen little in the way of hard evidence, starving someone to the point of death before releasing them is a very calculated method of torture.'

'Meaning her husband could've done it?'

'You honestly think that being cuckolded is sufficient motive for this?' Her shoes squelched as they walked along the drying floor. 'Were that the case, isn't it more likely her husband would've committed a crime of passion? Something rash like a stabbing or pushing her off a cliff?'

'Is that you officially ruling him out?'

'If he did this to his wife, then he probably would've done it to both Sarah and the man involved with his wife, this Klaus Werner, and not just to her.'

Corcoran looked at her, his forehead creasing slightly. 'Interesting.' He stopped at the station, waving his hands in front of a male nurse's face to wake him. 'Here to see Dr Yadin?'

The nurse came to and stood up in instalments. 'I'll see where she is.' He waddled off.

Corcoran focused on Palmer, his bright blue eyes dazzling under the light. 'Okay, so what about Klaus? Could he have done it?'

Palmer looked away, drumming her fingers on the laminated wood. 'I think he's a more likely suspect, given the circumstances. But I think the probability is third-level decimal places different, not first.'

'And in words a mere police officer could understand?'

'Well, I mean neither is likely to be your guy.'

'So I should stop our investigation into them?'

'Well, no. You asked me and I'm validating your hypotheses against an incredibly limited data set. I know how police investigations work. This is your decision, not mine.'

Corcoran stared at her again, running a hand across his stubble.

'Sergeant.' Dr Yadin stood in the doorway, smiling. Silver hair with an elfin look. Green scrubs, creased. 'Ah, I see you've met.' She opened a door behind her. 'I've got a slightly better office this time, if you'll just follow me?'

Corcoran let Palmer go first, into a consulting room with a broad white desk. Walls stacked with filing cabinets, a narrow window overlooking the car park.

Palmer took the chair nearer the window and rested her bag on the floor. She fished out her notebook and pen from the side pockets, then turned to a fresh page.

'Okay, so I've got an update on Sarah's condition.' Yadin sat behind the desk and focused on her tablet computer. 'I spoke to a starvation specialist this morning and, coupled with the health data we've obtained from Sarah's smartwatch and Wi-Fi scales,' – she looked up to smile at Corcoran – 'we can determine that Sarah's weight when she was abducted was seven stone, seven pounds. Which is one hundred and five pounds, or forty-seven point six kilos, depending on what floats your boat. And she had just under fifteen percent body fat.'

Corcoran folded his arms across his chest, rasping at his stubble with his free hand. 'Is that healthy?'

'It's borderline healthy. Any lower and you're at risk of not being able to fight off infections, colds and so on. Athletes are obsessed with minimising it, but Sarah went maybe a bit too low.' Yadin tapped something on the tablet's screen. 'Given her height of five foot three, her BMI was eighteen point five. Again, that's on the lower borderline, but it's still healthy.' She looked up, a grave expression on her face. 'Now she's four stone twelve.'

'My god.' Palmer's mouth was dry.

'That's sixty-eight pounds, or thirty point eight kilos, giving a BMI of just twelve. My expert said that's the same level he saw in famine victims in Somalia and Ethiopia.'

Palmer sat back, her gut doing somersaults. She looked over at Corcoran and saw her revulsion reflected. 'Like I said, Sergeant, Sarah's been starved, and carefully. This is almost like torture.'

Corcoran gave a tight nod. 'What else have you got, doc?'

Yadin tapped her fingers on her tablet. 'We know that Sarah's been missing for over forty days and that she's lost a third of her bodyweight. By our reckoning, she's had no calories in the last three weeks.'

'You mean not many?'

'No, I mean zero. Zilch, nada. Absolutely no nutrition. The rule of thumb is three days without water, three weeks without food. She was at that hard limit.' Yadin shifted her focus between them. 'And given that she didn't have much body fat to begin with, Sarah's body has converted all of her muscle into energy instead. And I mean all of it.'

Corcoran swallowed hard. 'Her body's eaten itself?'

'That's one way of phrasing it, yes.'

Palmer looked down at the blank page, too stunned to write any of it down. She forced herself to, noting data points that might lead somewhere.

*Someone's done this to her. Someone who wants her to suffer. Someone with . . .*

She stopped writing.

Then, *Why?*

She couldn't think of a single example of something similar. Starving someone almost to death was one thing, but then releasing them? She added '*Release*', underlined it twice, then looked up.

Corcoran was frowning. 'And in plain English?'

Dr Yadin locked her machine and set it to the side, then smiled like she was humouring a small child. 'Sergeant, Sarah is going to take many months to get back to her previous weight, and it's going to be weeks until we can assess her chances of a full recovery. We'll monitor her throughout, but this level of starvation will have placed extreme stress on her liver and other organs.'

Corcoran looked like he'd swallowed something down. 'But Sarah is awake, yes?'

# *[09:00]*

Palmer followed Yadin into the room, leaving Corcoran standing by the door.

Sarah lay on the bed, barely moving, a skeleton with skin. Tubes and wires hung out of her arms, attached to four separate drip bags. Her heart rate on the machine was dangerously low, her blood pressure even worse. She frowned at them, but her eyes were intense and full of life, fear and hope mixing in a toxic blend. She reached over to them, struggling with the effort. 'Find him.'

Palmer sat next to the bed and took Sarah's hand. Bony and long, her thin skin stretched too tight. Just like Palmer's nana before she died, the cancer eating away at everything. 'Sarah, my name is Dr Marie Palmer and I'm working with the police to help find who did this to you. I know you've suffered a horrendous ordeal, but the worst is over. You're safe and no further harm will come to you. Dr Yadin will try to help you back to full health, but I've been tasked with helping your mental journey. I want to—'

'*Find* him.'

Palmer stroked Sarah's palm, deciding to toss out the rest of her script and just play it by ear, letting Sarah guide them. At least for a bit. 'It was definitely a man?'

'I think so. He . . .' Sarah shut her eyes and her body started to rock. It was like she was crying, but there were no tears.

'Sarah, how about you tell us everything you remember?'

She took an exhausting breath, then opened her eyes again. 'Where do you want me to start?'

Palmer smiled at her. 'Wherever you like.'

# Fourteen

## *Sarah*

'Yeah, okay.' I pull the headphone cord tight, pushing the mic to my lips, so Christopher can hear me better. 'I won't be long.' I squat down low, my quads and hamstrings stretching hard, the Lycra rucking around the knees of these old leggings. Definitely need new ones. 'I need to let off steam, you know how it is.'

'Okay, well I worry about you, that's all.' Christopher's voice is as cold as the winter air. Like he doesn't even mean the words.

'I'll be home in an hour. Love you.'

A pause. 'Okay.' And he is gone.

My breath mists in the air and I rub away the fresh tears from my eyes. I'd thought I was all cried out but . . . Jesus.

The music resumes after the call, Maroon 5 blasting in my ears, way too loud. I turn it down, then start my watch on the setting for running. And I shoot off through the cold night air, like they all say, putting one foot after another, my shoes thumping off the pavement, splashing through the puddles. My breath locks into the music's beat and the running becomes a blur. My footsteps join in the shared rhythm and my brain flies free, my troubles slipping away, my head clearing of project schedules and milestones and risks and issues and all this shit with Christopher and—

*His* silver Audi trundles past me, the window down low, slowing to a halt. Klaus gets out of his car and walks over, hands in pockets, *that* impish grin on his face. 'There you are.'

I stop and suck in deep breaths, pausing my watch and the music. Four miles in, decent pace. 'No, Klaus.'

He reaches for me, frowning. 'What?'

I bat his hungry paws away. 'I said, *no.*' I can't even look him in the eye. 'We can't do this any more. It's over.'

He looks absolutely destroyed. 'But we—'

'Chris . . .' I suck in another breath and love swells in my chest, making my heart flutter. 'I need to make it work with him, Klaus. And as much as I like you, I don't love you.'

'But I love you, Sarah.'

His words sting my heart. And just seeing him there, being in his presence . . . It feels so different from how I played it out in my head. Intellectualising my feelings, sticking them in a box and locking them away. Being here, with him, those feelings come back with a vengeance.

I shut my eyes. 'You tell yourself you love me, Klaus, but if you really did we'd have been discussing how we're going to leave Chris and Lena, not meeting in your car for sex. Because sex is all it is. This isn't love.'

I almost convince myself. Still can't look at him, at those gorgeous eyes, his beautiful lips.

'This is going to be so difficult at work, Sarah. I mean, we—'

'We should've thought of that when you got me drunk in Hamburg.' I push past him and set off again. 'I'll see you on Monday, okay?'

But he grabs my arm as I pass. 'Sarah, please!'

'Klaus!' I try to shake him off, but he's way stronger than me. That thing I love about him turned against me. He lets me go, but he's still blocking my path. 'Look, we can be friends, okay? You just need time to accept it, but it's over. Then we can discuss how to be friends again and how we can still work together.'

He grabs my arm again, his grip tighter than before. 'Sarah, please!'

'If *this* is how you're going to be—?'

'Sorry.' Klaus lets go and shuts his eyes, thinking it all through, then opens them with a nod. 'You're correct, of course. This is now hurting others. We need it to stop.'

It's hurting me like a knife in the guts, but this is the right thing to do. The only thing we can do. Seeing him there, he's somebody else's. He's not mine. This isn't right. I made a mistake – *we* made a mistake – a one-night thing that became twenty nights, thirty nights, and it's over.

'Klaus, what we had wasn't real. We shouldn't have started it. The right thing is to end it now. Okay?'

He still can't look at me. Then he nods. 'Come here.' He opens his arms.

And I hug him, tight. And he doesn't try to kiss me, like part of me thinks. Like part of me still hopes. 'You're a good guy, Klaus.' I peck his cheek and run off.

Definitely the right thing to do.

Isn't it?

Of course it is.

So why do I feel so raw inside, even if it's the right thing to do?

Half a mile away and I've not restarted my run or my music. But I can see our house, at the end of the road, lit up in the night. Chris will be inside, maybe sipping wine while the dinner cooks in the oven. Maybe even have a bath running for me. I speed up, running *to* him for the first time in years.

But, of course, he's out playing squash, choosing to spend his Friday with old university friends rather than me. Those lights are just Milhouse triggering those fancy ones Chris bought.

Then I see *his* car sitting there, the engine running. Klaus doesn't get out this time, just gives a tame wave.

I approach, my guts churning, and dip my head as I speed up, trying to put that last distance between us.

Don't look back. Never look back.

But of course I do. Klaus is leaning forward, like he's crying. He's got the message at least.

I run on, fresh tears welling, my heart thudding.

Someone runs towards me.

Andy!

I wave at him, but he has the look of someone who just wants to get out of their own way. I know that feeling.

So I speed on, heading for home and at least Milhouse still loves me and—

Someone steps out in front of me, a blur of black leather, and I bump into them and fly through the air. I land on the ground, hard, slabs slicing through my leggings and cutting my hands to ribbons.

An arm comes from behind, grabbing across my throat. I wriggle but something sticks into my neck and . . .

\*   \*   \*

I wake up and it's pitch dark. My head's thumping. Fabric kisses my lips as I breathe, rubs against my ears. I try to move but I'm tied down, rope biting into my wrists. My hands and knees burn.

The rope eases off around my wrists and I can move. Feels like I'm underwater, everything's delayed and slow and I feel so heavy.

Something tears at the skin on my cheeks and bright light attacks my eyes, making me close them. I try to keep them open.

Someone stands there, a man, facing away. Tall and broad-shouldered. Black leather jacket.

'Help!'

But he walks away and the door shuts with a clunk. Then a key turns in a lock. There's a wide slot on the door and an eye looks in at me. Then even the slot shuts.

I look around the room. Bare concrete walls. No windows. A bed with plain white sheets. And a desk in the corner. I limp over and shake it, but it's bolted into the wall, just a lamp and a stack of books on top. All moral philosophy, by the looks of it, the sort of shit Christopher had to read at university.

An empty bucket sits by the door.

A cell.

A prison cell.

And Christ, I'm naked. Where are my clothes? My knees are raw, dried blood caking on the right, the left swollen to twice the normal size. After eight miles of running on an empty stomach, I'm thirsty and so, so hungry.

It takes me a minute to get over to the door, my knee

stabbing with bitter pain, each step aching like it's torn the skin right off. I try the hatch, but it's stuck. 'Let me out!'

My voice reverberates around the room, followed by deadly silence.

All I can do is sit on the bed. 'Klaus? I won't tell anyone. It's okay!'

Silence.

Wait, there's a sound, a deep rumble, like someone moving chairs about upstairs.

'Let me out! Help!'

The hatch opens and a bottle of water pops through, landing with a thud.

I let out a scream and just keep going and going and . . .

My brain is whirring when I wake up. I look around and I'm still here. Six scores on the wall above the desk, tally bars marking the days. Not that there's any daylight. Six sleeps. Who knows if that translates into real days. But either way, it's been close to a week now and no sign of the man who took me. At all. No contact, no conversation, no messages, no notes. Nothing. All I know is it's probably a man.

Is it Klaus, angry after I let him go?

Or has Chris found out and . . .?

Could he? Could he really do this to me?

My stomach's way past hunger, just giving me that giddy lightness. But I'm so thirsty that it feels like I can't open my mouth.

Wait.

There's something on my face. I can taste moist leather.

I reach up and touch a mask. I tear at it, but I can't get it off. It's locked on. I can breathe through my nostrils, but there's just a thin slot over my mouth.

He's gagged me!

What have I done to deserve this?

But the sound coming out isn't fury, it's just a whimper.

By the door, there's a stack of water bottles. Supermarket mineral water. Own brand, bottled in Buxton. A hundred of them, maybe more.

I go over and crack open a bottle. The lid just about fits through the slot in my mask. I gulp down the water, but I can't scream.

I need to scream. It's all that's kept me going so far.

I sit at the desk and make the fourteenth scratch on the wall.

Two weeks. Is that right? Have I missed a day?

My fingers ache and I'm so hungry that I just don't know how long I've been here. I don't know anything. My arms are thin, I can see my ribs, and my legs look more like arms. I stand up, but I'm so dizzy that I have to sit again.

I can't even focus on the books. Why has he put them here?

What does he want from me? He hasn't asked anything, hasn't even spoken to me. Aside from the bottles of water, I've no proof there's anyone there. It's possible a machine could drop bottles in, but . . .

I pick up the first book. Immanuel Kant, *Metaphysics of Morals*. I tear out a page and push the paper through the hole in my mask, taking it in my mouth, trying to chew but it's—

I vomit. Bile and water fill the mask and flood the desk.

Some strange metallic taste. He's done something to the book.

I can't even eat the paper.

I shuffle over to the bed and lie on the dirty sheets, stinking of sweat. A putrid smell comes from the bucket that hasn't been emptied in days, not that I can pass anything now. My kidneys ache.

I lie there, staring at the ceiling. This is all I have the energy for. My mouth aches from the mask, itching from the constant contact with the leather.

I'd rather die than go through this any more.

I can't think that.

But I do.

I get up and stand tall. The room spins as I shuffle over to the door. I brace against the metal as I try to breathe through this fucking mask.

I try to scream, but I'm empty.

I have nothing left.

Wait.

I pick up a water bottle and open it. I tip the contents onto the floor and throw the bottle in the bucket. Then I open another one and pour it over my head.

'How do you like this?'

Another one over my head.

'How do you like this?'

And more and more and more, dowsing myself in his water like it's petrol and I can set myself on fire.

'How do you like this?'

I'm speaking to my captor but I don't hear the words.

Am I even saying them out loud? Am I even here? Do I still exist?

I pour the last bottle over my head and collapse onto the bed, soaking and exhausted. I let myself close my eyes.

I wake up to fourteen tallies, my head thudding, my mouth dry.

I can't remember anything now. Did I miss a day? Wasn't it fourteen yesterday?

What happened?

I look around. The cell's clean, no empty bottles, no bucket, no books on the table now.

Just a fresh stack of water bottles by the door. The plastic wrapping's been torn open. I'm too weak to do it myself.

'Why are you doing this to me?'

As always, there's no answer.

He wants me to suffer, but the fucking coward won't face me.

So I push up to standing. Then fall to my scabby knees. They won't heal properly. I shuffle over to the door. And sit there, breathing hard and heavy.

I get out the first bottle, feels so heavy in my hands. With great effort, I manage to open it, then tip it over my head.

'How do you like this?'

I'm ready to die.

Three days without drinking and I'll die of dehydration. I reach for another bottle and—

I open my eyes and gag. Water fills my throat and I feel like I'm drowning. Something's covering my eyes.

There's a hand around my throat, another pinning my chest to the bed. Then the pressure's gone and the door shuts.

The gag is still on but there's a strange taste in my mouth, not the usual iron-y taste. It's wet. He's forced water down my throat, trying to keep me alive.

I reach up and claw at my eyes. A sleep mask, the kind they sell on airplanes, flops back so I can see the room again, but I don't have the strength to hold it up.

So I lie there, head thumping. Dizzy. Heart racing. So, so hungry.

He's just left. Fifteen tallies on the wall. But I've missed two days, at least. And the days don't mean anything, anyway.

Over by the door, the water hasn't been restocked, just an empty space where the pile was.


Still fifteen tallies and my mouth is so dry. Headache, dizzy. There's another three marks above the bed. I can't even move over to the desk now. So I reach up and scratch another mark. Each inch I move my hand up aches like someone's twisting my arm up my back.

I hope I'll be dead soon. The only way this will all be over soon. I have to stop him starting the clock again by forcing me to drink.

Thump, different to the usual thumping from the wall, like music. This is like—

A bottle lies on the floor by the door.

Christ. He's taunting me now.

I'm so thirsty.

I need this to be over. Let nature take its course and this will all be over soon.

But he'll get away with it. I don't know how, but he'll get rid of my body, so the police will never find me.

What if that thumping rhythm isn't just noise in my head? What if it's someone else? What if he's doing this to them, or worse? What if they're trying to tell me they're there? That they're suffering the same pain as me?

I need to help the police find him.

I need to do all I can to stay alive.

So I try to move. Putting my bony foot on the freezing cold floor, trying to put my weight down, but I tumble over and my hip cracks off the hard concrete.

I lie there, gasping, pain searing up my side. I'm so thin now I doubt I'll even bruise. It feels like I've snapped something.

But I can't give up. I can't let this end.

I snake over to the door and grab the water bottle. Takes ages for my damaged fingers to open the bottle. I hold it in front of my mouth.

Drinking this means restarting the clock. Letting him win. For now. But I need to stay alive. To stop him, I need to stay alive, give myself the chance to win.

I slurp down a mouthful, feeling it trickle down my gullet. I might be imagining it, but I'm sure I hear someone whispering thank you.

Forty-two tallies on the wall.

I think.

Twenty-seven above the bed. Fifteen over by the desk. Does that . . . Does that even add up? I can't think.

Wait, where is the desk? When did that go?

My legs are sticks, my arms like knitting needles. I can barely move. I'm just trapped here, waiting to die.

The hatch opens but no water drops through.

Or does it?

I can't tell.

I can only lie here. But I'm so thirsty. And I need to stay awake.

My finger brushes against something on the bed. A bottle, resting against the wall. I try to pick it up but . . .

Come on. You've got to get through this. Stay alive. Get him. Take him down.

I grab the bottle and try to open the lid. My thumbnail tears down the middle, sliced right to the quick. I try to scream but I can barely open my parched lips.

I lie there. Can't open my eyes. Can't move. Can't think.

No idea when this is. Even *if* it is. Have I died? I can't move. Can't . . .

Moving. Someone's picked me up? Or I'm going to heaven. Am I . . .?

Someone's carrying me, then they rest me down on something. I'm sitting up, my back against something hard. A seat? And I'm moving? Is he pushing me? Something's squeaking. Am I on a wheelchair?

He opens the door and I can make it out but I can't even move. I hear music and—

\* \* \*

Wind hits my skin. Air. Fresh air. I can open my mouth. Just. I can't move. I'm so tired. So hungry.

'You okay there, love?' A man is standing over me, concern etched on his face.

Did he do this to me?

# Fifteen

## *[Corcoran, 09:30]*

Corcoran perched on the plastic chair.

Sarah's shallow breaths came faster now she'd finished telling her story. The life-support machine beeped and fluid trickled out from the drip into her arm.

An abduction now. Officially. No doubt about it.

His toes clenched. Someone had done all of that to Sarah. To another human being.

Corcoran couldn't stay still. He got up and paced around the room, his gut foaming, bitter bile building in his throat. He wanted to speak, but just didn't have the vocabulary.

'Thanks for telling us that, Sarah.' Dr Palmer leaned forward, kicking the back legs of her chair up, cradling Sarah's stick fingers in her hand. Her dark hair was plaited, hanging down her neck in a ponytail, twisted round and round like that Jewish bread Corcoran's mother used to make. Her designer glasses reflected the pulse from the machines, the white pinstripes on her suit catching the harsh overhead lights. 'I know how hard it was for you to share that with us.'

'You've got no idea.' Sarah looked over at Corcoran, looking like she had barely enough muscle control to frown, though her bony face did most of the work for her. 'Was that the man who took me?'

'That was who found you.' Corcoran moved over, squatting in front of the bed. 'He was fixing a wall nearby. Called 999 and—'

'Where?'

'Just outside a village called Minster Lovell.'

Sarah gave him a blank look.

'It's in Oxfordshire, Sarah.' Palmer pulsed her hands. 'Near Witney.'

'Was I held there?'

'I wanted to ask you that.' Corcoran stood up tall again. 'You said you were in a cell. Did you see anything to indicate where you were?'

'You don't know?' Sarah's voice was a weak rasp. Her expression suggested she wanted to shout but couldn't. 'You have no idea where he is?' Her breathing was speeding up, her heart rate pulsing that bit quicker.

'Hey, hey, hey.' Palmer smiled and squeezed her fingers again. 'It's okay, Sarah. You're safe now.'

'But he could come back, he could—'

'Nobody's doing anything, Sarah. Okay? You're safe in here. There are guards posted outside this room. Whoever did this to you can't get at you any more.'

Sarah's breathing slowed a touch, but her eyes still scanned the room for threats.

Corcoran stayed back, giving her space and distance. 'Can you describe him for me?'

'I told you it was a man.' Sarah pursed her lips, still frowning. 'I didn't see much of him.'

'You said he was big. Broad-shouldered. Strong.'

'Right. That's all I saw. He wore a leather jacket. Black. Like a biker's jacket.'

'Have you seen him before in your life?'

Sarah's eyes stopped their manic dance and locked onto Corcoran. 'I don't think so.'

'Did you hear his voice?'

'No.'

'Was it someone you knew?'

Sarah pulled her hands away from Palmer and her breathing spiked. She gasped, her face twisting, then let out a deep moan.

Dr Palmer shot over to the door, her glare suggesting that Corcoran should leave.

But instead he gave Sarah a smile. 'Was it Christopher or Klaus?'

Eyes shut now, lips twitching. 'I thought it might be Klaus. I thought it could be Chris. But I couldn't say if it was either of them.'

Dr Yadin stormed into the room. 'What's happened?'

Palmer raised her eyebrows at Corcoran. '*Leave.*'

'Okay.' He held up his hands and left the room. He pulled the door shut and sucked in the bitter tang of cleaning chemicals.

Palmer could try and make him look like an idiot for that. But all he'd done was ask a basic question, and Sarah's reaction was telling. In her head, the affair with Klaus was still secret. She'd been locked in a room for over six weeks, starved and tortured, with nothing but her thoughts for company. She didn't know there was a police investigation into her disappearance, didn't know there were cops prying into her private life, didn't know her husband and Klaus were now prime suspects.

Did any of it shed any new light on her ordeal?

Not really.

Corcoran shifted out of the way of a passing gurney. He ran his hand through his hair, down his face, across the sandpaper stubble that badly needed trimming.

'Aidan?' DI Thompson was thundering along the corridor, scowling at anyone and everything. 'What's happened? Is she—'

'God, no.' Corcoran held up his hands. 'No, she's fine. Well, not fine fine, it's just . . .' He let out a deep breath. 'How was the news conference?'

'Waste of time, as per usual.' Thompson stared into her phone, tutting at texts and emails. 'But you know the drill, Aidan, we've got to go through the motions, make it look blah blah blah. The calls have started already, the usual nutters trying to take credit for it, curtain twitchers trying to get their neighbours into trouble.' She flashed her eyebrows, then nodded at Sarah's door. 'Did you get *anything* out of her?'

'We—'

The door opened and Palmer stomped out, tossing her rucksack over her shoulder with a violence she probably wanted to inflict on Corcoran. 'Inspector, I need a word.'

'Okay.' Thompson smiled at her and held out her hand. 'I presume you're Dr Palmer?'

She gave a withering look. 'In private. Please.'

'I'm kind of short of time here, so if you could cut to the chase?'

Palmer couldn't look at the source of her irritation. She just stood there, nostrils twitching.

Thompson wasn't giving any ground, just folded her arms. 'Okay, so what's going on here?'

Palmer looked at him now, strong lenses distorting her dark eyes, and snorted. 'I managed to coax some information out of Sarah.'

'Doc, we need to find who did this to Sarah. What have you got for me?'

'This is far too early to tell and—'

'I need to know what kind of person we should be looking for.'

Palmer let her bag slip to the floor and leaned back against the wall, pressing her head against the white paint, eyes closed, forehead twitching.

Thompson cleared her throat. 'Doc?'

Palmer opened her eyes with another withering look. 'It appears likely that whoever did this designed this whole experience for Sarah's suffering. The gag, no food, the water bottles . . .' She seemed to shiver. 'Someone has starved Sarah, both nutritionally and emotionally.' She frowned again, at Corcoran this time. 'Though not intellectually, curiously enough. The books on philosophy were . . . Hmm. An interesting touch, would you say?'

'Someone's forcing a *university degree* on her?' Thompson folded her arms. 'What the hell is she talking about?'

Corcoran nodded. 'There were some moral philosophy books on the desk, presumably for Sarah to read and mull over something she'd done.'

Palmer locked eyes with Corcoran and he could see they were on the same page. 'Philosophy textbooks – and moral philosophy at that – would imply there's a message here, something he wants her to digest and understand and reflect on and admit and potentially make reparations towards.'

'Meaning her husband?'

'I'm not sure.'

'We discussed this earlier and I don't think we've heard anything that changes it.' Corcoran got a nod from Palmer. 'Alana, it's unlikely Christopher is our guy.'

'I need *more* suspects, not less . . .'

'Fewer.' Palmer picked up her rucksack. 'And I agree with DS Corcoran's statement. I don't think her husband has done this.' She fiddled with the zip, making the metal rattle. 'My initial read of the perpetrator clashes with what I've seen and heard of Christopher Langton.' She stopped fiddling. 'Wouldn't her husband want Sarah to know who was torturing her? Wouldn't he want her to die? And why would he release her?'

Thompson didn't have an answer.

Palmer dumped her bag again. 'Whoever did this is someone who knows Sarah's life intimately. Someone who followed her home and trapped her like that. It's possible they've been torturing Christopher as much as Sarah. All the worry and concern and fear and hope of a missing spouse. I've seen the toll it's taken on him from photos.'

Thompson inhaled. 'Aidan, do you agree? Is he in the clear?'

'This isn't about being in the clear or not.' Corcoran noticed another twitch on Palmer's forehead. 'It's about probability. What Dr Palmer's saying is, I think, that we're close to eliminating him.'

Thompson's phone rang. She checked the display but didn't answer it.

Palmer gave Corcoran another look. 'When your colleague here asked about who could do this, Sarah visibly panicked.'

'So, is it Klaus?'

'It's possible. She mentioned him and her husband.' Palmer shut her eyes. 'But, as with her husband, Klaus would likely want Sarah to know who was doing this and, having gone to all the hassle of abducting her, he'd probably kill her as well. He wouldn't want the risk of discovery, either, meaning that after he'd punished Sarah, he'd hide the body somewhere.' She opened her eyes and scanned both of them. 'From what Sarah told us, whoever did this took great pains to avoid any interactions with her. Any time he was in her room, she was asleep, probably drugged. He imparted no message to her, didn't even say read X page of Y book. There was nothing for her to learn from this experience.'

Palmer sighed. 'And letting Sarah go is a colossal risk. There's a care and precision in everything around her abduction, but they're not omniscient. Someone could've witnessed her abduction. There could be something Sarah saw or heard or even smelled in her cell that could lead us to them. Some tiny detail, maybe some forensic trace, but something that would give us an edge over him. Releasing her is a huge gamble and I'm not sure what the pay-off is.'

Thompson stood there, hands on hips, tapping her fingers. 'I need results.'

'Fine. I need space to work and think.' Palmer glanced at Corcoran. 'And I need him kept at arm's reach. He was far too aggressive in there.'

'Aidan?'

Corcoran shook his head. 'I simply asked Sarah a question. She reacted badly.'

'I've not got time for this.' Thompson pointed at Corcoran. 'He's an experienced officer. You're an experienced criminal psychologist. You're on the same side, okay? Now, if I need to bang your heads together, I will. Work together on this. We need to find who did this to Sarah, not get into petty arguments.'

'Petty?' Palmer snorted again. 'Inspector, I've been doing this for ten years and—'

'Do we have a problem here?'

Another snort. 'I need some space and time to pull together a profile on the attacker.'

'Fine by me.' Thompson clapped Corcoran on the shoulder. 'But I need you to help us find who did this to that poor woman. I don't care how many assumptions and caveats you need to cover your arse, but I'd like something by the close of play today. Okay?'

Palmer threw up her hands. '*Fine.*'

'Good. Now, Aidan, I'm absolutely Hank Marvin so I'll see you in the cafeteria.' Another clap on his shoulder and she waddled off, staring at her phone.

Corcoran didn't follow, instead focusing on Palmer. She couldn't look at him. 'I want to clear the air.'

Palmer raised her thin eyebrows. 'Why, because your boss hauled you over the coals?'

'You haven't seen anything.' Corcoran couldn't help but laugh. 'If we're working together, we need to trust each other. If you think I went over the score there, then I'm sorry. I'll let you take the lead in these situations.'

'I'm not getting into any more of these situations, Sergeant. I was here to help assess Sarah and now I've got to pull together a profile based on scant information. *Police*.' The word was a snarl.

'I sympathise, doc, I really do, but—'

His phone rang. Unknown number.

'Should that be on in here?'

'I need to be contactable.' Corcoran put it to his ear. 'Hello?' He walked off with a wave, ignoring her glower.

'Is that DS Corcoran?'

'Speaking.'

'Okay. It's Sergeant Nigel Haverford, Warwickshire police.'

Corcoran stopped in the corridor. Thompson was up ahead, hammering something out on her mobile. 'How can I help?'

'Listen, I saw the news conference this morning on that Witney woman case? Just tried calling DI Thompson but she's not picking up. You're listed as the secondary contact on HOLMES.'

'Am I?'

'I think I might have another case related to yours.'

Which was police code for palming off a foul-smelling case on to a major investigation with a budget and resources.

Corcoran spun round and saw Palmer scribbling in a notebook. 'Okay . . .'

Haverford coughed. 'Couple of my lads were called to a church in Rugby this morning. Young lad stumbled in, delirious and violent. Tried arresting him, but he's hostile, incoherent, you name it. We've got him in hospital.'

Corcoran sighed. 'I'm very pleased for you.'

'No need to be like that, mate. I'm trying to help you here.'

'So get to the punchline. I need a good laugh.'

'This guy said someone kidnapped him and locked him in a cell.'

# Sixteen

## [Palmer, 11:28]

Corcoran hugged the tail of a bus, swearing under his breath, then shot out into the oncoming lane, only to jerk the wheel back for another car to whiz past. 'Come on, come on, come on.'

'Can you just—' Palmer grabbed the handle above the door, jaw clamped tight. 'You don't need to—'

Corcoran hared past the bus, pushing Palmer back into her seat. The speedo hit seventy, eighty, then ninety. Up ahead, a car hurtled towards them, flashing its lights.

'Aidan!'

He yanked the wheel and pulled back into his lane. Calm and collected.

'Jesus Christ!' Palmer punched the dashboard. 'You almost got us killed!'

'Of course I didn't.' Corcoran slowed back to sixty. 'You've been quiet.'

Palmer picked up her bag, hugging it tight like it would protect her from a head-on collision. 'I've been *terrified*, actually.'

'I'd rather you thought about the case.'

'Given half a chance . . .' Palmer looked down at the

notebook splayed on her lap, both pages covered in scribbles even she'd struggle to decipher. 'I've been praying your phone call has nothing to do with Sarah's abduction.'

The briefest glance from him. 'Me too.'

'Back at the hospital, you said you wanted to clear the air?'

'Right.' He focused on the road, eyes locked tight like he did this sort of manic driving all the time. 'We haven't got off on the right foot and I don't want any bad blood between us.'

'You're acting like I'm harming your case. But I'm here to help, that's it. We've got different approaches, that's all. Let me do my job, Aidan.'

Corcoran flinched at the mention of his name. He indicated right, signposted for Hospital of St Cross, and slowed to a halt. The car idled, the traffic still passing in a flurry. 'I know your type, all theoretical and *scientific*.' He almost spat the word. 'And you don't like being in the line of fire.'

She tried to laugh it off, but he could probably see doubt in her eyes. 'You're a piece of— SHIIIIIT!'

Corcoran shot across the front of a work van into the hospital car park.

Palmer slammed her hands against the dashboard.

The van just cleared the back of Corcoran's car and he kept on through the car park. He pulled into a space and reached onto the back seat for something. 'Let's just see what's what, shall we?' He placed a 'Police' sign on the dashboard and opened his door. It took a good few seconds for him to get out of the car, manoeuvring his body through some weird angles.

Palmer got out much quicker. 'Should you be on duty with a damaged hip?'

Corcoran marched off without a reply.

119

# [11:45]

Palmer found Corcoran speaking to a tallish man with a bushy moustache in full police uniform, and a coffee-skinned doctor in a business suit cut from a similar cloth to her own.

'This is Dr Marie Palmer, our criminal psychologist. This is the consultant, Ms Isobel Hayden.'

Hayden shook Palmer's hand with a broad smile. 'A pleasure.' A warm, smoky voice. 'Let's walk and talk.' She set off at a brisk pace, fast enough to make Corcoran grimace. 'I'll be frank here. There are no clear signs as to what's wrong with Howard.'

'Just Howard?' Corcoran was struggling to breathe as he kept up with her. 'You've not got a surname?'

'Listen, all we know is he's called Howard. He kept shouting it at the police and the paramedics who brought him in. The emotional trauma he seems to have suffered . . . He's . . . broken, that's all I can say.'

Palmer kept pace with Hayden, even with those heels biting her ankles. 'What do you know about him?'

'That's it. A name. He won't speak.'

'Won't or can't?'

'Wish I knew.' Hayden's mouth twitched as she walked. 'Physically he's in good shape. Muscular. Army fit.' She stormed through a door marked 'Accident and Emergency' and set off along a wide corridor. Through a side door, a male nurse bandaged a female patient's arm. Hayden stopped outside another room. 'Here he is.'

Corcoran stepped forward.

'Aidan.' Palmer blocked his path and spoke in a whisper. 'I'm trained for this. Like we agreed, let me do my job, you can do yours. And this is probably not connected. Right?'

'Right.' Corcoran ran a hand across his stubbly chin. 'I'll just watch.'

Hayden showed Palmer into the room. 'Jane, give us a minute?'

The nurse slipped off, letting Palmer get a view of the patient.

Howard looked worse than Hayden had suggested. Physically he did seem okay, buff even, but he looked tired and confused, deep bags around his eyes. Mouth twitching, nostrils flaring. Then he barked out a loud laugh, scattering round the room like machine-gun fire. Short, percussive, but absolutely no humour in it. His head sank low against his chest and he started rocking slightly. He was crying now.

Palmer stayed standing but kept a distance. 'Howard?'

He looked up, eyes swivelling in his head. 'Isn't life a dream?'

A chill crawled up Palmer's spine. 'What?'

But she'd lost him. Howard stared into his lap again, lips twitching, head nodding.

'Howard, my name is Dr Marie Palmer.'

His lips kept moving and spat out some noise. Maybe words, or maybe just more gibberish.

'You told the officers who found you that you were in a cell?'

'Cell, cage.' Howard was breathing faster, just like Sarah had been. 'He makes everything okay.'

'Who does?'

Veins bulged in Howard's thick neck. 'It's time to play!'

121

He screwed his face tight, then drilled his gaze into her skull like she should know what he meant.

'It's going to be okay.' Palmer stepped closer, hands raised to placate him. 'Howard, you said you were in a cell?'

He looked her up and down, his breathing settling. 'A prison cell.' He shook his head. 'How can everything be okay when you're locked up like that?'

'I want to help find who did this, Howard. We'll find who put you in that cell, okay?'

He nodded.

Palmer let out a shallow breath. 'What's your full name, Howard?'

'What's the date?'

'It's Tuesday the tenth of March.'

'Isn't life a dream?' Howard slumped back in the bed. 'Howard.' He looked over at Hayden by the door. 'My name is Howard!'

'Have you got a surname, Howard?'

'Howard Ritchie.' He spoke like a child in primary school learning to repeat his name over and over. Had his ordeal reduced him to this, or did he have a learning disorder? 'Howard Ritchie. I'm Howard Ritchie. Isn't life a dream?'

'That's good, Howard. Thanks.' Palmer gave him her warmest smile. 'And how old are you, Howard?'

He frowned. 'There's nothing he can't do.'

Palmer was starting to think a learning disability was more likely. 'When were you born, Howard?'

'Ninety. June. Eighteenth.'

'Thanks, Howard.' She gave him a broad smile. 'You're doing great.' Another smile. 'Where do you live, Howard?'

He mumbled something that sounded like 'Devon'.

'Did you say Devon?'

He nodded. 'Ax. Ax. Ax.'

Devon could mean Axminster, or Axmouth. Maybe Exeter. Try them one at a time. 'Do you mean Axminster?'

Howard was still nodding, furiously now. 'Ax. Ax. Ax.'

'Back in a sec.' Corcoran walked out to the corridor.

Hayden stood there, hands in pockets, concern etched on her face.

Palmer gave her a curt nod, then focused on the twitching figure in the bed. 'What do you do for a living, Howard?'

'I'm a chef.' He smiled at her, some humanity filling his face. 'I cook. Love my job, love it. It makes everything okay!' He laughed, joy filling his face. 'Cooking, waves, drinking.' He said it like it was a set phrase. 'Charlie! Oh, Charlie! Isn't this your sea?' He was singing now.

Palmer stepped closer, gripping her hands into fists. 'Howard, who's Charlie?'

He stared at her like she should know.

'Did Charlie take you, Howard?'

He sang again: 'He's Charlie the Seahorse and there's nothing he can't do!'

'Is that a nickname?'

'He's Charlie the Seahorse and he makes everything okay!' Tears streamed down his cheeks.

'Do you like surfing, Howard?'

'Surfing?' He scowled at her through teary eyes. Something of the human being underneath crept back into his expression and an adult looked out at her. A mature intellect, someone to be reasoned with. Someone with awareness of his surroundings and his company. He punched his thigh. 'Why would someone do this to me?'

Palmer raised her hands, palms out. 'Howard, Ms Hayden and I are going to help you get through this, okay?'

He nodded, barely noticeable.

'Now, you said someone put you in some sort of prison cell?'

'Are you calling me a liar?'

'No, Howard, I'm—'

'Because they did!' Howard jerked himself upright, his meaty fists pressing the bed. 'Was it you?' He grabbed Palmer by the arm and pulled her close to him, his fingers digging into her flesh. 'Did you do this to me?!'

'Stop!' In a flash, Corcoran darted across the room, pushing himself between Howard and Palmer. 'Stop!' He grabbed Howard's wrist and twisted, pressing him down to the bed, face first.

Palmer pushed herself away from them, rubbing at the biting pain in her forearm. She rolled up her sleeve and the skin already looked bruised.

'You bastard! You fucking bastard . . .' Howard was crying. 'He's Charlie the Seahorse and he's here for you. He's Charlie the Seahorse and it's time to play.'

An orderly steamed into the room, six foot plus of fat, muscle and training, and took over from Corcoran. 'Okay, mate, are you going to play it cool?'

Corcoran held tight as he let the orderly take over, eyebrows raised and focused on Palmer. 'You okay?'

She stared into his baby-blue eyes. 'I'll live.' Her voice sounded thin and vague.

'Okay, guys.' Hayden nudged Palmer and Corcoran, pushing them out of the room. 'No amount of information is worth that.' She closed the door as the orderly pierced a syringe into Howard's arm.

'Thanks for letting us in there.' Palmer nodded at Corcoran and collapsed against the wall. 'That was . . .' She exhaled and tried to rub away the goosebumps puckering her arms. She set off down the corridor, determined to put as much space between herself and Howard as possible.

Corcoran followed. 'Charlie the bloody Seahorse . . .'

'Who the hell is he?'

'You don't know it?'

Palmer just shrugged. 'Should I?'

'Doc, doc, doc.' Corcoran got out his smartphone. 'It's a kids' cartoon. Pretty big with the three to five age group.'

He held up the screen, showing a video of a smiling seahorse dancing in the surf at a beach, shimmying past an octopus, a shark and a dolphin. The theme tune played low, a ghoulish kids' choir, saccharine sweet: 'He's Charlie the Seahorse and there's nothing he can't do! He's Charlie the Seahorse and he makes everything okay!'

Corcoran jabbed a finger on his phone and stopped the cacophony. 'As to what it means? I wish I knew . . .' He frowned. 'But the good news is I think I've found him on the system. Howard John Ritchie, went missing from Axminster in Devon on the twenty-seventh of February.'

'Twelve days ago . . .' Something caught in Palmer's throat. 'That means – assuming this is related – that someone held Howard and Sarah simultaneously for twelve days?'

'Let's not get ahead of ourselves.' Corcoran put his phone

away. 'All I know is this guy left at dawn to go surfing at a beach about an hour away but didn't come home. I've got a call out with the investigating officer.'

'In Devon? You want to head down there now?'

'No, doc. Let's see where he was released first.'

# Seventeen

## *[Corcoran, 12:11]*

Corcoran kept it much slower than when they'd driven to the hospital, mainly because of Palmer's overreaction. He pulled left onto a quiet street. A cat crossed the road in a hurry. Further up, a squad car sat outside a church hiding in the trees. He parked and let the engine die slowly. 'I'm leading here, okay?' He winched himself out onto the street.

No sign of the owners of the squad car.

A vicar stood in the doorway, staring into space, sucking on a cigarette with the look of a man who desperately needed a nicotine hit. He didn't even glance up at Corcoran's approach or his warrant card.

'DS Aidan Corcoran, are you—?'

'That's me.' The vicar stamped out his cigarette and put it in the bin. 'I was here when he came over.' He shook his head. 'Poor, poor man. I can only imagine what he's going through.'

Palmer was resting against the car, taking yet more notes.

Corcoran focused on the vicar again. 'Did he attack you?'

'Quite the opposite. He . . . I was just having my morning tea and running through Sunday's sermon, when he raced up to me, wild-eyed and in a fury. Gave me the fright of my life,

I swear.' The vicar frowned. 'And he was crying. Then . . .' His frown deepened. 'It's hard to explain, but he was *singing*. The theme tune to that infernal programme. *Charlie the Seahorse*.' His frown was now a scowl.

'Did he say anything else?'

'There was some mention of a prison cell, of course.' The vicar screwed up his eyes. 'I'm thankful to my friend up there' – his eyes shifted to the heavens – 'for sending those police officers in my time of direst need.' He waved behind Corcoran.

Two local cops walked over from a nearby house, big lumps looking like two-thirds of the front row of a rugby scrum.

'Thanks.' Corcoran flashed a smile at the vicar and walked over. 'I expected you to be here when I arrived.'

'Sorry.' The sergeant held out a hand for Corcoran to shake. 'Nigel Haverford.' Slightly smaller than his mate, and heavily balding without his cap. One of those hairlines that were a couple of years past the point you should just shave it all off. 'My lads have just finished taking the statement from the neighbour who called it in.' He thumbed over the road. 'Joe?'

The constable took over, reading from his flip-open notebook like it was a hymn book. 'Bloke said his kid was getting ready for nursery when he noticed someone shouting at the vicar over there.' He nodded at the church, but no sign of the rector. 'Didn't recognise the assailant, so he called it in. We were just round the corner, so we shot round and subdued the guy, and . . . mate, he was in a *state*, so—'

'You mean a drunken state?'

Haverford gave a curt nod to let Joe know he was taking over. 'We restrained him and got the paramedics to take him to the hospital instead.'

'You did the right thing.' Corcoran was aware of Palmer listening to them, still writing away. 'Anything else?'

Haverford stepped in close, dipping his head. 'There's maybe something. Joe?'

'I don't believe it, Nige.'

Corcoran put up a hand. 'Don't believe what?'

'Just tell him.'

'Right.' Joe closed his notebook. 'So this kid, Harry, he's four or five, but he *might've* seen this Howard bloke attacking a man.'

Palmer was between Corcoran and Joe now. 'The vicar?'

'No, love, before.' Joe frowned. 'Look, most of the stuff my youngest says is utter bollocks, some of—'

'But not all of it is nonsense, Constable.' Corcoran folded his arms. 'What exactly did Harry see?'

'Said this Howard was in a wheelchair and . . . There was this guy pushing him and Howard attacked him. Got into a scrape, rolled around on the floor. I mean, it sounds like WWE to me, but you never know.' Joe shrugged.

The house was a post-war job, but set back in a generous garden. Thick foliage blocked their view of the road, even in March. Two big windows looked onto the street, so someone could probably see the road from inside.

Corcoran nodded at Haverford. 'I want you to find this man, okay? If Howard attacked him, he might be injured, might be getting treated right now. Check with local hospitals, and get people speaking to the other neighbours.'

Haverford stood there, hands tucked into his belt. 'Sure, sure.'

'Any time you like.'

'Oh, okay.' Haverford and Joe cleared off towards the car. Corcoran watched them go. 'Pair of plonkers.'

Palmer was still making notes. 'You think that's important?'

'Not sure, but unless we find this strange guy with the wheelchair, assuming he even exists, then we're no further forward.' Corcoran scratched at his chin. 'What are you thinking?'

'Well, primarily I'm trying to match the MO with Sarah in Minster Lovell. While Sarah and Howard were both dumped at the side of the road, Sarah's was an isolated location in the countryside, whereas here . . .' She looked up and waved around the leafy street. 'There are houses and it's overlooked on all sides. And I can't get out of my head the feeling it's like Howard was *aimed* at that church.'

'You think someone targeted the vicar?'

'Or the church.' Palmer put her notebook away. 'It could be to get police attention. But you saw the state Howard was in.' She grabbed her forearm. 'When he tried to attack me. Whoever had him, maybe they could predict what would happen when they released him. Focus the anger and rage.'

'I see your point.'

'Reluctantly?'

Corcoran grinned at her. 'Always.'

'So what's the plan?'

Corcoran thought it through. So many options, none of them particularly promising. 'I'm thinking I should head down to Devon. Spend a few hours speaking to Howard's friends and family, maybe see if there's any connection between Howard and Sarah.'

'You don't need me?'

'Reckon it's nearly four hours each way, plus you're dealing with rural cops. Not to be recommended. I mean, it's bad enough here and in Oxfordshire. You really think eight hours in a car with me is a good use of your time?'

She raised her eyebrows at him. 'I suspect it'll be much less than four hours given your idiotic driving.'

'You could interview this child, see if his story matches up?'

'I'm sure Thames Valley or Warwickshire constabularies have other advanced interviewers, someone trained in mining information from a child?'

'Fair enough.'

'Aidan, I'd really like to see where Howard was taken from with my own eyes.'

'You're the boss.' Corcoran got his keys out of his pocket. 'How about you spend that four hours talking me through all the scribbles in your notebook?'

# Eighteen

## [14:03]

'Coming up, police still have no solid leads in the Witney woman case.' The radio crackled as Corcoran pulled up at a roundabout, a queue of six cars ahead. The muppet at the front didn't seem to know what they were doing. 'We'll be speaking to the lead detective just after these—'

Corcoran snapped off the radio and looked over to Palmer. She was talking but the words just floated over the engine, more background noise. He reached into the middle for his half-eaten burger and unwrapped it. Another hungry bite, swallowed down with cola, the ice all but melted.

'You shouldn't be eating behind the wheel, Aidan.'

'My stomach's devouring itself.' He took another bite and slipped forward in the queue, chewing this time. He got another flash of the skeleton in the hospital bed. 'Sarah . . . I shouldn't joke about it.'

'You shouldn't. But I don't think you were.'

'You think these could be connected?'

'Well.' Palmer already had her eyebrows raised when he looked over. 'Howard's abduction has a similar MO to Sarah's, but is it close enough? Are they actually connected? I know

132

you're hoping it's just a coincidence, but two people who just so happen to have been caged, then released?'

Corcoran finished his burger, barely tasting it. His hands were clammy on the wheel.

'I mean, this is all speculation, Aidan. Pre-scientific, naturally, but these two cases *could* be linked.' Palmer was staring at her notebook, covered in ink like a footballer's sleeve tattoos, her basic theories of how someone could abduct two people looking like a confusing mess of words and lines. 'I just don't know yet. I mean, it could be, but Howard's too disoriented and confused to be sure. And what if his brain hasn't recorded events correctly?'

Corcoran pulled forward in the queue. 'What do you mean?'

'Extreme disorientation can prevent the brain from recording. It's what happens when people black out from alcohol – they experience it at the time, but their brain doesn't record it for later.' She flipped the page and started writing, sketching a diagram. Then stopped with a sigh. 'You know what the trouble is, Aidan?'

He slipped forward another car length and looked over, meeting her stern gaze. 'Trouble with what?'

'This. This *whole* thing.' She waved her pen around, indicating the whole world was in on it. '*If* these are connected, then someone has abducted *two* people, not just Sarah, and held them at the same time. That means we're in a different territory, meaning my expertise comes to the fore.' She looked at him, her eyes showing how much the thought terrified her. 'Do you think they're connected?'

'All I know is it's all over the news, against my better

judgement. When you go out to the public, people want to crawl over a famous case, including cops. They see connections that don't exist. Other forces see an opportunity to shove a line on a spreadsheet over to someone else's spreadsheet.'

'But the cells, Aidan?'

'I know of at least one serial offender who locked people up in cages.' Corcoran couldn't look at her. 'Worked a case back in London where this murderer kept his victims for a while before he killed them.' He gave her a glance. 'But you're the expert here. You've spoken to the people who do this, and in great detail. How do we find this guy before he starts killing people?'

'As I was saying, the trouble with shifting from explanation to prediction, i.e. knowing where they'll strike next – who, when, or how – is we need more data to go on. Three cases is the start of a pattern, but two? While tragic, it's not enough.'

Corcoran nudged forward in the queue again. 'Is assuming they're connected the best move here?'

She stared out of the window. 'I just don't know.'

Corcoran inched forward again.

'I need to be honest with you.' Palmer was fiddling with the ends of her plait, unravelling and retying. 'I realise I'm panicking about the pressure of being in an operational scenario. With you. Seeing my worst fears come to life, being out in the field with a serial offender.'

'Come on, I've only offended you once.'

She laughed hard at that and the ice maybe started to melt a little.

# [16:03]

'Perfect timing.' Corcoran pulled into the car park, with the sun a couple of hours above the horizon, almost due south-west. Over the low tidal wall, Exmouth beach spread out, wide and flat.

In the passenger seat, Palmer looked up from her note-book. 'Not exactly great for surfing, is it?' She went back to writing.

She had a point. The sea was about half a mile out and no sign of any surfers, just a middle-aged couple walking a grey-hound, the poor thing shivering in its maroon coat.

'I see what you mean.' Corcoran got out onto the bitumen and stretched out. The cold air was bliss on his skin, burning from the heater Palmer had insisted on having up high. Three-and-a-half-hour straight drive, and his entire left side was numb. No pain, just a vague tingling. He swallowed down another pair of high-strength ibuprofen with the second half of the giant energy drink can. His phone was still locked on the driving mode, but he somehow got it to speak to him.

No messages from anyone.

He felt his shoulders deflate along with any lingering hope that Thompson would've solved the case while they drove down.

Aside from a brief chat at a roundabout, Palmer had spent the journey doodling in her notebook, while he played the case through all the filters in his brain. And when he'd lis-tened to the radio, it was either terrible music or speculation about the case. His case. Their case, maybe.

Palmer stepped out of her side and took in their surroundings. 'It's beautiful, isn't it?'

'One way of looking at it.' Corcoran crushed his can and looked around for a recycling bin. Nothing, so he dropped it in the door pocket. 'You got any fresh insights?'

Palmer's grin slipped away. 'No matter how hard I push, I just keep drawing blanks. I need more data.'

'Meaning more kidnappings?'

'Maybe not.' She gritted her teeth. 'But I keep replaying the traumas Sarah and Howard endured. Can you imagine what it must've been like?'

Corcoran looked away from the beach, following the gradual slope up to some sheer cliffs. 'I can't begin to imagine.'

'It's all I can do, Aidan.' Palmer splayed her notebook on the roof, her forehead tightening as she stared at it.

Was he being too hard on her? She seemed tough, with experience and expertise as tightly knitted as her plaited hair, but that could just be a front.

Corcoran could spot a masochist at a hundred paces. She seemed the sort to push herself too hard, to punish herself just as badly as he would. And she needed the result as badly as he did, or just an insight, a lead, anything, something to give them hope.

Behind her, the car park was busy with cars and vans, a few covered with adverts for local dog-walking companies – Exmouth Doggie Heaven, Derek's Dogs, WalkYrDogs – covering the full range from hip frippery to professional to aggressive canine keep-fit. Up on the cliffs, a young woman took charge of eight dogs, including a few Jack Russells and a pair of hulking ridgebacks. A few hundred metres behind her, a man pulled his own pack.

'They must have a good view out to sea up there.' Palmer was following his gaze. 'Meaning that if they . . . Hmm.' She walked over to a van, Derek's Dogs, advertising 'four walks a day, dawn to dusk', and frowned. 'Meaning someone could've been here when Howard was taken. Meaning this isn't a perfect abduction site.'

Corcoran joined her by the van. 'Sarah was taken from a back street, sure, but it was still a street. People in houses who could oversee what happened to her. Same with where Howard was released. My point is it doesn't need to be perfect, just needs to be the best spot to take them in their daily or weekly routine.'

A Mondeo swerved into the car park and shot over to them, missing Corcoran by inches. The door opened with a blast of death metal roar and thrash. A short woman got out, scabby suit, dyed-silver hair tied back in a severe ponytail. 'You're early.'

Corcoran held out his hand, but she didn't shake it. 'DC Pritzakis?'

'Right.' She leaned back against her car, arms folded across her chest. 'You can call me Kathy if I can call you Aidan.'

Corcoran smiled. 'I didn't say you could call me that. This is . . .' He looked over at Palmer, but she was wandering between the dog-walking vans, scribbling away. 'Fine, you can call me Aidan.'

'Just so you know, I've briefed Howard's father. My partner's taking him up to the hospital. I've never been to Rugby.'

'You're not missing much.' Corcoran motioned around the beach. 'It's beautiful here.'

'Is it?' Kathy walked over to the wall and hopped up in one bound. 'What do you want to know?'

'Everything. Start with his disappearance.'

'Well, I got a call almost two weeks ago.' She walked along the wall, hands in pockets like she didn't mind the prospect of smacking teeth-first onto the tarmac below. 'Howard Ritchie. He lives in Axminster, where I'm based now. It's about an hour away from here, kind of inland, but kind of along the coast too. It's practically *Dorset*.' She spat out the word. Clearly their own 'them and us' thing going on down here. 'Anyway, Howard's a chef at a hotel in Ax. Nice enough place, if you like posh food.'

Corcoran kept up with her slow progress along the wall, like he was walking with a small child. Up ahead, a dad was doing the same with his kid. No sign of Palmer now, but her thoughts resonated in his head. 'This doesn't look like a great place to abduct someone. Way too busy.'

'Howard came here first thing. We think, anyway.' Kathy skipped down off the wall and sped up, pushing Corcoran to keep up with her. 'All I've pieced together is he left his flat really early and drove here to be in the water for the first surf at dawn.' She gave him a sly look. 'Shared flat, and yes, we've interviewed his housemate.'

'This doesn't exactly strike me as a great spot for surfing.'

'You an expert?' Kathy held his gaze, an impish grin on her face, and pointed out to sea, to the couple with the grey-hound, now walking back to the dry sand. 'According to

Howard's housemate, this is a hidden gem and Howard drove here every morning to surf.'

Corcoran felt a jab in his neck. Another repeating pattern. 'Every morning?'

'Pretty much. I checked the charts and so on. I mean, tides being what they are, this place is weird. Most of the week, you can get good surf until nine o'clock. Some strange riptide further out causes it. I don't know.'

'Every single day?'

'Well, not quite. Sometimes Howard had to cover breakfast at the hotel, and he'd get out after his shift ended. There are another couple of places nearer Ax.' She pointed away towards Axminster and shrugged again. 'So, that's you up to speed, I guess.'

'He definitely arrived here?' Palmer was standing next to Corcoran.

Kathy scowled at her. 'Eh, who the hell are you?'

'Dr Marie Palmer.' She tucked her notebook under her arm and shook Kathy's hand. 'I'm working with DS Corcoran.'

'Right. Well, he definitely arrived.' Kathy pointed at a black Tesla shining in the dusk glow. 'His van was in that very space. Local cops called it in and we hotfooted it over here. No sign of him. His wetsuit and board were inside and bone dry.' She looked out to sea again. 'I mean, we combed the area, the better half of Devon and Cornwall police, plus some idiots from Dorset. Walked right out at low tide, along the coast in both directions. Inland for a mile-by-six search grid. Coastguards were out too. And we found nothing. So we stopped. I'm sure you get missing persons up in Thames Valley?'

Corcoran examined the parking space, like the Tesla hid some missed clue. 'The colleges bring students and enough stress to break some of them. And the rest of our area isn't as affluent as you'd think. That brings different pressures.'

'So you'll know that we just have to give up on them, then.'

'Right.' Just like in Cambridge. Corcoran caught Palmer making notes, like she was keeping a record of the chat. He focused on Kathy again. 'So what was your take on it?'

'My take?' She laughed. 'I'm not paid enough to have a take. My bosses, though, they thought it was either a suicide or he died out there.' She looked out to sea, eyes misting over.

Palmer looked up from her notes. 'But?'

Kathy's gaze snapped back to focus on her. 'People think Devon's this lovely place, all cream teas and seaside walks and real ale. A few years back, Exmouth High School was the biggest in Europe. Place was huge. Thousands of kids, and that brings problems. Drugs, violence, rape, you name it. They've sorted it out a bit now, but it takes a long time for the tail to fade away, if you catch my drift.'

'Assuming I do, your theory is some locals killed him?'

'Why, I don't know.' Another shrug. 'That, or he killed himself.'

'I can see that.' Corcoran's turn to shrug. 'But he came here every day?'

'Maybe plucking up the courage?'

Palmer twisted her face into a scowl. 'Anything specific to make you think this was a random attack from some locals?'

Kathy shifted her gaze between them. 'Is this where you tell me it was something else?'

'A local gang wouldn't cage someone and—'

140

'*Cage?*' Kathy's cool mask slipped. 'What the hell?'

'It was more of a cell, but . . .'

Kathy looked over at Corcoran, eyes full of fury. 'You should've told me!'

'I'm sorry, I—'

'You think this is funny?' Kathy got in Corcoran's face, jabbing her finger against his chest. 'Giving me enough rope to hang myself? Having a laugh at my expense, yeah?'

'It's nothing like that.' Corcoran fought to keep his expression neutral. 'I wanted your opinion untainted.' He glanced at Palmer, then back into Kathy's ire. 'We think this case might be connected to another. I just wanted to know what you thought, uncoloured by that.' He flashed her a grin. 'Believe me, I'd rather this was a simple disappearance and completely unrelated to my case, then I could be rid of her.'

But Palmer wasn't listening. She sat on the wall, tracing a finger across her notebook. She looked up, locking her gaze onto Kathy. 'Does *Charlie the Seahorse* mean anything to you?'

Kathy frowned, then took a deep breath. 'There's something you should see.'

# Nineteen

## *[17:03]*

Corcoran followed Kathy's Mondeo along what passed for a high street in Axminster, a gently curving road lined with soft white streetlights giving the place a magical, Christmassy feel. A chemist and a few other chains, but more local businesses than he'd expected. The big church on the right, maybe the minster of the town's name, was surrounded by sprawling trees already budding in March. 'Four hours from home but the seasons are a month or so earlier down here.'

Palmer was still staring at her notebook.

Kathy stopped and her arm popped out of her open window, gesturing at a hotel, presumably where Howard worked as a chef. A board on the pavement showed a menu, surrounded by neat chalk writing. Free-range eggs, locally sourced organic meat, extensive vegan options.

Kathy pulled out into traffic, then quickly parked outside a large stone building, three storeys and at least twenty windows wide, none of them looking like anything was going on behind them.

Palmer was tapping her pen off her notebook. 'Well, that seems to suggest that your animal cruelty angle doesn't apply to Howard.'

'Explain?'

'Even with meat on the menu, if someone attacked Sarah because she worked for a biotech firm that operated on animals, they'd surely pick a farmer or an abattoir, not a chef.'

'I suppose.' Corcoran found a space and got out. The numbness had faded into a dull ache. He followed Palmer across the road, limping slightly, and joined Kathy on the pavement. 'So what's this place?'

'Police station, closed down a couple of years ago.' Kathy walked up to the door and unlocked it. 'We reopened it last week.' She led inside, down a long corridor that stank of mushrooms and stale pizza, but she walked past the stairwell and out the back. Murky darkness, the sodium-yellow lights failing to illuminate the single vehicle parked out there. 'This is the old impound lot and that's Howard's van.' She pulled a lever and floodlights burst into life, shining on an ageing VW camper with a dark-grey paint job. 'There you go.'

'There we go what?'

Kathy rolled her eyes. 'The stickers!'

Corcoran squinted in the gloom until he saw it. The van was covered in them, with at least twenty of Charlie the Seahorse clustered to the side. Half of them were like the kids' cartoon, all summery and fun. But the other half were zany student humour, poor old Charlie either looking like he'd had a few too many or was smoking drugs.

Kathy tapped on one where Charlie sat in a squat, smoking his life away. 'This what you were getting at?'

Corcoran didn't know. Looked like Palmer didn't either. 'When we saw him in hospital, he kept singing the theme tune over and over.'

'That's pretty random.'

'You're telling me.'

Palmer had her phone out and was snapping shots, the flash whipping across the van's body. 'It's possible that who-ever abducted Howard saw these stickers.'

'Maybe.' Kathy clicked her tongue a few times. 'Probably a good idea for you to meet my boss.'

## [17:12]

The upstairs office that looked across the yard to Howard Ritchie's old van didn't seem too shabby. Freshly painted and decked out with decent-looking furniture.

Kathy was working at a laptop rather than a standard-issue desktop from the force's preferred supplier. So probably not on a network, meaning something hooky was going on. 'Here.' She shifted her laptop round for them to see. 'You look at this, I'll see where he's got to.' She left them to it.

Her screen was filled with a photo of a large bedroom. An unmade bed and clothes strewn across the floor. Stacks of CDs and DVDs. An Xbox and a PlayStation both sat in front of a monster TV. Dumb-bells and kettle bells. Drying wetsuits hanging from a trampoline. Drug paraphernalia filled the mantelpiece: a few bongs; some lighters; a pile of cigarette papers. A giant poster of Charlie the Seahorse hung on the wall, the poor guy sucking on a joint, with bloodshot eyes and a monster line of cocaine in front of him. It was unclear how he'd put the rolled-up banknote to his nostrils, or even if seahorses had them.

'Probably a million student rooms across the planet with that poster.' Corcoran stood up tall and stretched out. 'I'm struggling to see the connection here. So Howard likes a smoke, fine, but why would he be singing that song?' He closed the image and found a standard folder structure. There was a crime scene inventory, meaning some poor sod had been given the pleasure of cataloguing the CDs, DVDs and video games. He opened it and scanned the contents. 'No *Charlie the Seahorse* videos in here, but the contents of the PlayStation or the Xbox aren't listed. Possible Howard has them on either console, or he used the internet to watch it.'

'Or that Howard's interest in Charlie simply just extended to some ironic drug posters and stickers.' Palmer was writing notes again. 'No, there's got to be something in this.'

'Assuming, again.'

'Well, of course, but . . .' She looked over at the door.

'In here, sir.' Kathy reappeared. 'This is DS Corcoran. Dr Palmer.'

'Ah, the very man.' A broad grin and neat haircut stuffed into a Burton's off-the-rack suit. 'DI Patrick Magrane, pleasure's all mine.' Ultra-posh accent that could slice crystal from across the ballroom. And a firm handshake with some masonic flourish that Corcoran didn't dare return, not even as a wind-up. He gave Palmer a wide smile but she didn't shake his hand. 'So, what brings you two down here?'

Corcoran looked over at Kathy, but she wouldn't return his gaze. 'Aside from Howard Ritchie turning up in Rugby?'

'Good lord.' Magrane looked rattled, his forehead twitching. 'Knew some chaps at college who attended Rugby School.

Not the brightest, but not the worst.' His frown deepened. 'It's definitely him?'

'DC Pritzakis said his father is heading up there to confirm, but I'm pretty sure.'

Magrane nodded slowly. 'Please excuse me thinking it funny that Thames Valley are investigating something that happened in Warwickshire?'

'It's possibly related to another abduction.'

'Ah, the "Witney woman"?'

'That's what the press are calling her. Sarah Langton. Ring any bells?'

'Not to me.' Magrane frowned at Kathy, his eyelids flickering. 'DC Pritzakis?'

'Not come up in the case, sir.'

'Can you check?'

'Sir.' She grabbed her laptop and started working away.

Magrane perched on the edge of her desk, clasping his hands on his lap like he was posing for a portrait. 'I'm afraid there's not much else I can tell you. Howard's disappearance is a drop in the ocean compared with what else we're dealing with here.'

'And what would that be, sir?'

'This station was shut two years ago to save operational costs and maybe acquire a bit of capital in these troubled times. The powers-that-be arranged a deal to sell it off to property developers. However, completing on said deal was beyond them, so it's still on the books. Hence me requisitioning it for Operation Ilium.'

'That's an interesting name.'

'Ilium was the Trojan city in *The Iliad*.' Magrane did a

grimace-smile. 'And you know these are randomly allocated, but it fits spookily well. Ilium's a drugs investigation, if you must know.'

Corcoran walked over to the window and leaned back against the sill. 'So why is a big drugs sting looking at a disappearance?'

Magrane wagged a finger at him. 'You're a sharp one.' He smiled. 'Your accent's London?'

'What's your theory about Howard, sir?'

'We thought he'd done a Reggie Perrin. Swam out to sea and disappeared. That or suicide.'

'And why would he do either?'

Magrane cleared his throat.

'Come on, sir, this is—'

'I'm not at liberty to divulge that kind of information.'

Corcoran held his gaze. 'If you saw the state of Howard, you'd—'

'I just can't!'

Corcoran rubbed at his temples. 'Sir, my DI's going spare because she thinks this is connected to the Sarah Langton case.'

'But I see no reason why they should be. When DC Pritz—'

'Sir, Sarah and Howard were both kept in cells.'

Magrane stared into space, his mouth hanging open. 'I see.' His neck pulsed again.

Palmer snapped her notebook shut and leaned forward on her chair. 'We've driven a long way. It feels like you're obfuscating matters for some reason I can't quite ascertain.'

'I assure you, if I could share what's going on, I would.'

'Well, what's going on in my head is there's potentially a

serial abductor at work.' Palmer got up and stepped closer to Magrane. 'Someone who's tortured two seemingly innocent people before releasing them. Someone who might repeat the act. Who might even be doing so as we speak.'

Magrane huffed out a deep sigh and looked up. 'Listen, it's nice of you to join us down here, but my hands are tied.'

'Fine.' Corcoran buttoned up his jacket. 'I'll get my DI to ring you.' He walked off but stopped by the door. 'But if someone else goes missing or turns up in as bad a state as those two, just remember that you could've stopped this.'

Magrane took a few seconds, then gave another deep sigh. Still kept quiet, but the wall had cracked slightly.

Corcoran stepped towards Magrane. 'I'm also wondering why you've done a full crime scene analysis of a MisPer's bedroom.'

Kathy looked up from her laptop. 'Sir, there's no sign of Sarah Langton in the case file. No Sarahs at all, in fact. Checked without an H too.'

'Thanks, Constable.' Magrane sighed yet again and slumped down in his chair. 'Your theory broke apart when you said "innocent people". Mr Ritchie is the straw that broke the camel's back when it came to Operation Ilium.' He gestured at Kathy. 'When DC Pritzakis caught Howard's disappearance, one of those magical cases passed up from our uniformed brethren, she became extremely concerned about Howard's connection to the activities occurring where he was taken. So, she persuaded me to sign a search warrant for his property, which I gather you've seen the results of?'

Corcoran nodded.

'Well, we found several blocks of cocaine taped under his

mattress.' Magrane reached over for the laptop and pulled up a set of photos. Ten kilos, according to the caption. 'I was running Operation Ilium out of Exeter, but suddenly it all seemed to centre around here. Subsequent investigations revealed that Howard was dealing cocaine from the hotel he worked in. People travelled far and wide to buy from him.'

'And you think that explains his disappearance?'

'Our two theories are either that he fled, or that his drugs suppliers snatched him and . . .' Magrane tugged at his turkey-wattle neck. 'They could've offed him or kept him under lock and key. You name it. None of our suspects are speaking, though. We ask, of course, but they're keeping quiet. On the QT, we did receive word that Howard carried a sizeable drugs debt to a local drug lord, and our belief is this is retribution.'

Corcoran looked over at Palmer. 'What's your take on it?'

'It'd make our lives a hell of a lot easier.' She was standing by the window, the faint light catching her from behind. 'How sure are you, Inspector?'

'Not as sure as eggs is eggs.' Magrane chuckled. 'But I'm quietly confident these cases aren't related.'

# Twenty

## [Palmer, 19:30]

They drove towards another lit-up stretch, with a city glowing to the left. Could be anywhere. The satnav told Palmer it was Swindon.

Right hand clamped to the wheel, Corcoran took another sip of energy drink, smelling overly sweet and tangy, and returned the can to the drinks holder without looking. He kept his gaze on the road ahead.

Palmer had talked enough for both of them, about her worst fears come to life. He didn't talk, just drove. Silence was how he coped with his job. He compartmentalised everything, sticking all the trauma in a box, never to be opened.

Corcoran glanced over and caught her looking at him. 'You okay there?'

'Not really.' She went back to her page. 'I need to solve this puzzle.'

'You don't think Magrane's right?'

'Do you?'

Another glance at her, doubt twisting his lips. 'I mean, it's still possible these aren't linked but Magrane's drugs theory is pretty convincing.'

She set her pen down. 'Don't you think that it would be wiser to consider the alternative explanation?'

Corcoran stared hard at her, his baby-blue eyes catching the lights of oncoming cars. 'What, that there's a psychopath abducting people, torturing them, then letting them go?'

'Yes, Aidan. In fact, we should be looking at other abductions, historic unsolved ones. It's possible he's been trialling this with others. Maybe he's tried before, to see if he can get away with the abduction and release, but without the torture.'

'You're right.' Corcoran blew air up his face. He seemed exhausted. 'I should get Thompson to allocate some resources to that.' Another glance at her. 'In your heart of hearts, do you honestly think these are connected?'

'I'm saying that would make it ten times easier to find out who is doing it.'

'I know. Look, I see your point, I just don't necessarily think they *are* connected, that's all. I'm trying to be devil's advocate here. If we only focus on them being connected, then we might miss a clue that leads us to who kidnapped Sarah. It could be Klaus or her husband, even this Andy guy. Are you with me?'

'I totally see your point.' She looked right at him, then sighed. 'I don't like this, Aidan. The pressure . . .'

'Aren't you a psychologist? Don't you have to deal with stress and pressure on a daily basis?'

'Well, yes, but nothing like this. When Howard attacked me in the hospital? You saved me, Aidan.'

Corcoran gave her a casual shrug. 'All part and parcel of being a cop.'

'Well, *I'm* not a cop.' She sucked in a deep breath. 'How can you deal with this?'

'I'd ask the same of you. You speak to these psychopaths for days at a time, right?'

'Weeks in some cases.' Palmer took a few seconds, squinting at him through her glasses. 'As part of my PhD and my post-doc, I met with some of the most violent offenders in the UK prison system, patients with severe psychotic disorders, usually undiagnosed until it's way too late. You name them, I've met them.'

'Like who?'

'Raymond Burke?' That got a nod from him. 'Brutal murderer. Killed six prostitutes in London in the late nineties. He took out the anger he felt towards his wife and children on these prostitutes, acting out his psychotic behaviour. But he blamed it all on his own upbringing, on his violent father. Nothing was ever his fault, you see?'

'But you sat in the same room as him?'

'Well, only when he was on anti-psychotic meds, with a pair of twenty-stone guards to protect me. And they're being nice to me because they want something, say leveraging my influence for parole or a cell upgrade. Besides, you must've interviewed some murderers in your time. How do you cope?'

Corcoran looked over at her. 'Once I've finished, the Crown Prosecution Service takes over and they put them away, providing we've all done our jobs properly.'

Palmer had hit the nail on the head. Compartmentalisation. Relying on the system to deal with what he couldn't. 'Well, I have to hope they'll get better.'

'Raymond Burke getting better? Are you serious?'

'He's a painter now.'

'Bollocks he is.'

'I swear. Through his art, he's learnt to quell his violent urges. Even reunited with his wife last year and she visits him in prison. His kids are another story.'

'Bloody London.'

'This isn't just a London thing.' She frowned at him. 'You know Robert Carr from Edinburgh? The archetypal Scottish hard man. Again, psychotic behaviour bordering on psychopathy. Random assaults in the street, football hooliganism that didn't die with the Taylor Report. He was a Hibs fan, stabbed three Hearts fans on the same day in Edinburgh. Didn't register the fact he'd murdered three people. Couldn't even recognise the fact. Told the police it wasn't him. All three assaults were caught on CCTV. The knife was in his car when he was arrested and his football jersey was splattered with blood. And still he denied it.'

Corcoran shifted in his seat yet again, probably resetting his hip. 'You're going to tell me he's a sculptor?'

'He writes now.'

'You're just taking the piss now.'

'I'm serious. He writes romantic fiction. Very moving stuff, as it happens. We're trying to publish the books, with the proceeds going to the victims' families.'

'You really think someone like that can change?' Corcoran gave her a sour look. 'I've dealt with these people and there's absolutely no saving most of them. Good people might do bad things and people make mistakes. Sure, they can be treated. But someone who's born bad or raised to be evil? We could argue until the cows come home, but the Raymond Burkes and Robert Carrs of—'

'I hate pluralising.'

Corcoran let out a laugh. 'So do I.' He cleared his throat. 'But people like those two, true psychopaths or psychotics or whatever, we can only lock them up. That's it. They're broken beyond repair. They can't be treated, they can't be repatriated with society.'

She stared hard at him. 'I'm wondering how a Thames Valley detective has this kind of experience. You get many serial killers in the Cotswolds?'

Corcoran exhaled slowly. 'I moved here last November from the Met, where I . . . I saw evil with my own two eyes.' He sucked air through his nostrils, taking it deep into his lungs. 'Listen, I don't want to patronise you, but I've interviewed gang members. Took down a few of the Tottenham Mandem gang.'

'Oh, organised crime is *fascinating*. That hierarchical structure, that rigid top-to-bottom tree structure, where psychotic behaviour is entrenched into the culture, where to rise to the top you do so either through the force of your personality or through violence.'

'This all sounds like your PhD thesis. I'm struggling to see *how* any of these psychopaths can change. Practically. In the real world, not in the classroom.'

'With the right treatment, all violent offenders can be helped in some way.'

'Come on. "In some way" doesn't mean much.'

'It means everything, Aidan. Whether it's stopping them harming their family and their local communities, or whether it's them becoming fully functioning members of society, well that's down to the individual. But I can help them stop the violence. They all have triggers, those familiar surges of endorphins and adrenalin that spark before conscious thoughts can even form. Stop those and they can learn to control the rest of it.'

Corcoran shifted on his seat again as they ate up the carriageway. 'So somehow they all stop their violence, learn to control the triggers, feel remorse for their destruction. Yadda yadda yadda. If they do change, are they really different or are they just playing you for a better cell?'

'Back to that . . .' Palmer looked over again. 'Are you being deliberately obtuse?'

'No, I'm enjoying this discussion.'

'You have a funny way of showing it.'

'I'm jousting with an equal.'

She arched an eyebrow. 'An equal?'

'Equal and opposite.' Corcoran pulled into the right lane to overtake a lorry. 'Your approach is all theoretical, whereas—'

'Aidan, my work isn't just *academic*. I undertake therapy with these people. *On my own*.' She let the words sink in. 'I face them down, I get to know them as people. You just arrest them, compile evidence and, once they're out of your interview room, you wash your hands of them. Maybe see them in court for an hour while you give evidence. My work has seen *incredibly* positive results. When you get a psychopath to turn their anger into art or prose or just something that isn't extreme violence, it's . . . Well. I've helped them learn to control their rage. I've changed them.'

'I'd love to believe it, but a psychopath is always going to be a psychopath.'

'You really don't see my point?'

'No. Look, let's agree to disagree and keep an open mind here. Our priority is catching this guy, not helping him set up a business making Christmas cards.'

She shook her head. 'Very cute.' He sat back and he didn't seem to want to continue his jousting with an equal. Where did he get off?

Corcoran reached down for his drink but missed.

With a sigh, she held it out to him. 'There.'

'Thanks.' He slurped the cloying drink and passed it back to her. 'Why do you do this?'

She slotted the drink back in the holder. 'Do what?'

'Well, you think you can help or change these people, but . . .' Steel in his eyes, cold and hard. 'Why? Why do you think you can change them? How did you start thinking you could?'

Despite that hard glint in his eyes, she saw some deep trauma, some severe pain that had shaped him. Made her recognise someone similarly affected by the professional hell they put themselves through.

She took a deep breath and looked out of the car window. Here goes nothing. 'I grew up in Tewkesbury in Gloucestershire, in the shadow of a particularly sadistic killer. The local bogeyman. People's parents would say, "The Tewkesbury Man will get you." Then they caught him and locked him up. Years later, when I trained as a psychologist, I worked with a patient who was virtually catatonic. A male rape victim, wouldn't speak to anyone. But over time, I earned his trust. Then I got another patient, same symptoms, but through the therapy he revealed to me that he'd killed three people. The guilt and shame pushed him in on himself. I helped him open up, to accept what he'd done. Three families got closure for losing their loved ones. Then, as part of my postgraduate studies, I was asked to interview the Tewkesbury Man. I worked with him over a couple of years. It gave me personal closure about the horror that'd hung over my youth. He's still in prison, obviously, but he writes spy thrillers under an assumed name. He's learnt to channel that rage into something else.'

'Well, I still don't agree with you.' But the steel had softened in his eyes. 'What's our plan of attack when we get back?'

## [20:42]

Palmer stepped through the doorway into Sarah's room. Low lights, equipment hissing on both sides of her bed.

Dr Yadin tucked her hair behind her ear and leaned in to whisper, 'Sarah?'

Her eyes opened, clustered with sleep crystals and confusion. She looked even worse than earlier. Her face was shrunken in like a fruit dried in the sun. Parched lips. And just nothing behind the eyes, like she'd left her soul in the cell. She made a small grunting noise.

'Sarah, the police want to speak to you again. Are you able to?'

Sarah moved slightly, adjusting herself in the bed. Seemed

like she nodded, but even that took great effort. Her gaze shifted and she nodded again, definitely this time. 'I want to.'

Palmer took a chair beside the bed, but kept her distance. She gave a warm smile. 'Sarah, how are you feeling?'

'Worse than I look.'

Palmer fought the urge to laugh. Humour was a good sign. 'Sarah, there are a few things I need to ask you, okay? If you don't know, it's fine. Okay?'

She nodded.

'Does the name Howard Ritchie mean anything to you?'

Sarah thought about it for a few seconds, her forehead tightening. 'No.'

'You definitely don't know him?'

'Who is he?'

'What about all forms of the name? Howie?'

'No. Who is he?'

'What about Ward?'

'Is that a name?'

'It's a form of it, yes. You don't know him?'

'Who is he?' Sarah shifted uncomfortably. 'Did he do this to me?'

'No, Sarah.' Palmer looked over at Corcoran in the doorway and got a nod in return. 'Have you ever been to Axminster?'

'Where?'

'It's in Devon. What about Exmouth?'

'I know of it. Someone at college came from there.' Her fingers moved like she was trying to click. 'A friend of Christopher's. Can't remember her name.'

'Have you ever surfed?'

'What? No. I mean, I body-boarded on our honeymoon in Jamaica, but . . . No. I didn't like it.'

The next question was the hardest one. Palmer bit her lip, building up confidence. 'Sarah, have you ever taken drugs?'

Her teeth separated, thin lips forming a snarl. 'At university, I took an ecstasy tablet at a nightclub and . . .' She shut her eyes. 'I almost died.'

Palmer caught Corcoran's frown. The vaguest of links, but it didn't seem to help them in any way. She focused on Sarah again. 'What about Christopher?'

'Hardly.' Her nostrils flared. 'He drinks, but he's never taken drugs. Why are you asking?'

Palmer leaned forward. 'It's possible that somebody else has suffered the same fate as you.'

'Shit.' The word hissed out of her like the ventilator.

'When you were imprisoned, did you ever think there might be others being held?'

'I don't know . . .'

'You said you heard a rumble?'

'Maybe.' Sarah gasped. 'I mean, I was out of my mind in there. I couldn't think and I was so hungry and tired and thirsty.'

'But that rumble?'

'Just noises. I thought I was hallucinating. Like devils were singing to me.'

Corcoran stood up tall. 'What kind of singing?'

'I don't know.' Sarah picked at her eyes. 'Wait, when he opened the door and took me out of the cell, I think I could hear music playing. It was . . . It was like it was coming through a door?'

'From another room?'

'Maybe.'

'Can you sing it yourself? Or hum it?'

Sarah frowned. Then she started humming a jaunty tune, with the second phrase punctuated by a staccato rhythm. 'Something something and he's here for you.'

Corcoran was in the room now, his phone open. He tapped the screen and the *Charlie the Seahorse* theme tune blasted out.

Sarah's eyes bulged as much as her condition would allow. 'It was that, yeah.'

Palmer stared at Corcoran, could almost see similar thoughts racing through his head.

Sarah shut her eyes and tears slid down her face. 'Please find who did this to us.'

Corcoran led Palmer back out, that stupid tune still playing on his phone. He jabbed the screen a few times to get it to stop.

'Well.' Palmer's mind was racing now, churning through all the connections, inking in the pencilled-in joins in her diagrams. 'It's the same person.'

'You were right.' He looked at her. 'Hard as it is for me to admit.'

'I just want to find him and stop him. That's all.' She pulled out her notebook. 'We should head back to Rugby to speak to Howard.'

'You don't need to.' Yadin stood in the corridor. 'DI Thompson had Howard transferred over here.'

# *[21:14]*

Outside Howard's room, a tall man slicked back his grey hair. Salt-and-pepper stubble. Navy business suit. He frowned at them, his shifty eyes scanning for threats. 'What do you want?'

'Mr Ritchie.' Yadin's smile was fraying at the edges. 'These police officers are trying to find out who did this to your son.'

'Right.' He held out a hand. 'Name's Tommy Ritchie. I'd say it's a pleasure, but . . .' His reptilian tongue crept across his lips. 'You the ones giving me the runaround?'

Corcoran frowned at him. 'I'm not sure what you mean by that?'

'I got driven up to Rugby, then this copper said my boy was over here in bloody Oxford. What's that about? I just want to see my son.'

Corcoran gave him a wide smile. 'Sir, how about we have a little chat?'

'I've just got here and you're telling me I can't see my boy?'

'I'm sure Dr Yadin needs to run some tests?'

She took the cue, nodding vigorously. 'I'll need to borrow Dr Palmer for some psychiatric assistance?'

'This is bollocks!' Ritchie was fuming, fists clenched.

But Corcoran had his measure. 'Come on, mate.' He led him away. 'Let's get you a cuppa.'

Yadin took a deep breath and walked over to the door, but it was like she couldn't bring herself to look at Howard, like she was holding something back.

Palmer joined her. 'How's Howard been?'

'Asleep. He was so far out of it when he got here, I'm surprised that Rugby acceded to DI Thompson's request to co-locate them, but I've got a good team here and access to the best specialists.'

'Do you think Thompson jumped the gun?'

'That's not for me to say.' Yadin looked away with a slight nod. 'As far as I can tell, he's slept for over eight hours straight and could sleep for a whole week if we let him.' She looked at her patient again. 'I've administered caffeine. Sounds counterproductive, but if we let him continue to sleep, that could result in chronic insomnia lasting for years. This'll help him restore his circadian rhythms in the short term, then we can stabilise him into a standard sleep pattern. After that, we can focus on the longer-term trauma.'

'It's just sleep deprivation?'

'*Just?*' Yadin leaned in to whisper in Palmer's ear. 'Before this, I was in the Israeli army.' Her expression darkened. 'We . . . subjected prisoners to sleep deprivation for long periods of time. Blasting music at them was the favoured method. Which is exactly what seems to have happened to Howard. I think he's been denied sleep for twelve days.'

'Has he been starved like Sarah?'

'Howard is the exact same weight as when he was taken twelve days ago.' Yadin snorted. 'I'd also suggest they had him on a moderately high-protein diet to maintain muscle mass.'

'Okay.' Palmer snuck a look inside the room. Howard lay in the bed, groaning, lips moving. 'Is he still singing that song?'

'Won't shut up. As far as I can make out, he was subjected to it during all of that time.'

'Twelve days of "Charlie the Seahorse"?'

'You might be able to get more sense out of him than me.' Yadin motioned into the room. 'On you go, before his father returns.'

Palmer crept inside, wary of Howard and his sudden rage, even with Yadin's presence to guard her.

'It's time to play.' Howard shook his head. 'It's time to play.'

Palmer stood a good distance away. 'I'm here to help you, Howard.'

He frowned. 'Look, a few minutes ago, this cop came in and asked about my drugs.'

Palmer shook her head. Police officers seldom rested long enough for a patient's best interests. But at least he seemed more coherent. 'What drugs are those, Howard?'

'You tell me!'

'The local police near your home found cocaine under your mattress.'

'Shit. *Glyn*.'

'What does that mean?'

'My housemate. Glyn. He was selling drugs. Is he trying to pin this on me?' Howard jerked forward, knees digging into the bed. He was strong and muscled, with overdeveloped pectorals and biceps. 'I'm sorry about earlier. They said I attacked you.'

'Are you feeling better?'

'God, no. But . . . I'm sorry.'

'Do you want to talk me through what happened to you?'

'But I don't remember much. Just snatches, like it was all a dream.' Howard's eyes glazed over. 'Charlie! Oh, Charlie! Isn't life a dream?'

Palmer reached out and caressed the back of his hand.

He frowned at her, eyes flickering, back in the here and now. 'The doctor said it's only been two weeks, but it feels like years.' He snorted, rocking back and forth. 'I keep trying to play it back, but it's like my mind's a broken video tape. I can't tell what's real and what's a dream any more.'

'Just tell me what you remember. I'll help you process it.'

# Twenty-one

## *Howard*

The sun crawls up over the hills to the east, burning the clouds in the sky a bright orange. Dawn. Perfect timing.

Howard steps out of his van and sucks the bracing air deep into his lungs. Eyes shut, his body centring around where he is, when he is. No thoughts, no problems, just the here and now.

A deep breath in. One. Water hissing over the sand, gentle.

He lets the breath go. Two. The fading smell of diesel fumes from his van.

Another inward breath. Three. Seagulls screeching above his head.

Out. Four. A van pulling up a few spaces away, the engine rumbling.

In. Five. The slightly damp fabric of his wetsuit against his skin.

Out. Six. The low throb of a radio bleeding from the van.

In. Seven. A large wave rippling over the sand.

Out. Eight. Sharp stones digging into his feet.

In. Nine. A car door opening and shutting.

Howard lets the tenth breath go and opens his eyes. The

sky seems brighter and everything feels that much more alive. He looks south and the sea is swallowing up the beach, now nibbling away at the tidal defence wall, a stout row of grey holding back the fizzing waters. Each fresh wave looks bigger than the one before. An illusion, he knows, but it is just . . . perfect.

He reaches up onto the top of his van and finds the first strap securing his surfboard.

A strong arm wraps around his throat and a heavy body presses him against the van. Something jags at his neck and he tries to fight, tries to lash out, tries to—

Everything goes black.


Something cold splashes across his face.

Howard sucks in a breath, sits bolt upright and opens his eyes.

A room with a low ceiling. Brick, but darkened. The smell of mould. He is lying on a bed, a spring digging into his left thigh. Not much light, but enough to see the rest of the small room. Flagstones on the floor. The same brick on three walls, one of which has a desk.

A door shuts behind him.

He pushes up to sitting, which makes his head throb. Behind him is a closed door, covered in metal bars, rusted and thick. He tries to stand but has to brace himself against the bed. Everything swims in his vision.

He walks towards the desk, each step seeming to take hours, and slumps on the chair. He finds a desk light and clicks it on. No power cord, so battery. Some books on the desk, philosophy and . . . more philosophy. He picks one up and tries reading but he can't understand it. It seems to be in English, but the words aren't ones he uses every day.

Where the hell is he?

All he can remember is doing a brief mindfulness session in the car park at the beach, the waves kissing the sand; then another car or van turned up and he was taken.

Who? Why?

Could it be the police? Why would they do this to him?

A thump comes from behind him.

A paper bag lies in front of the door. He trudges over and spots a wide letterbox halfway up the door as it slides shut. He crouches but weaves around, so has to balance using his hands for support. The bag has a protein bar, not his usual brand, but twenty-three grams. A bottle of supermarket mineral water. And a banana, bright yellow and with just the right amount of green around the stalk.

He is so hungry. His belly rumbles, his mouth salivates as he tears at the banana and eats it in two goes. No bin or anywhere to put the skin, so he drops it back in the bag. He sits back on the bed and rips open the protein-bar wrapper, then chews it slowly. Saltiness cuts through the sweet. He takes a swig of water but leaves the rest of it for later. He has no idea how long he'll be here.

Then music blasts out of a speaker, ear-splittingly loud. A tinny piano and thumping drums. Deep bass like he's in a club. Then singing: 'He's Charlie the Seahorse and there's nothing he can't do!'

What the hell?

Howard covers his ears. He knows the song, but . . . What the hell?

'He's Charlie the Seahorse and he makes everything okay!'

Two speakers hang from the ceiling, aimed right at him.

'He's Charlie the Seahorse and he's here for you!'

Covering his ears, Howard walks over to the nearest speaker. While the ceiling is low, the speaker is just too high to reach.

'He's Charlie the Seahorse and it's time to play!'

He races back to the bed and tries lifting it. It doesn't shift. Bolted to the wall.

'Charlie! Oh, Charlie! Isn't this your sea?'

Then he tries the desk. Same story.

'Charlie! Oh, Charlie! Isn't life a dream?'

Even the chair is bolted to the floor. Some dust around the legs betrays fresh drilling. Meaning someone has designed this.

Howard eyes up the books. Seven thin paperbacks. They'd maybe give him three extra inches of reach at best, when he needs at least a foot. Even with a jump.

The music stops and he lets his hands go. His pulse is racing, thudding in his ears.

Then the piano starts again, jaunty and cheery, under-pinned by the drums. 'He's Charlie the Seahorse and there's nothing he can't do!'

Howard stares up at the same ceiling, counting each breath in and out. He is visualising catching a wave and coasting it all the way in, but he's chased by a seahorse. He doesn't know if he is awake or dreaming. Everything feels like a dream. He focuses on the sharp crack on the ceiling, tracing the line through to the wall, counting each breath.

'He's Charlie the Seahorse and there's nothing he can't do!'

He can hear it in his head now.

Or is the music playing?

No. The speaker cones aren't pulsing.

The door clicks and clatters open and he braces himself. Ice cold water splashes off his face, sluices down his body and soaks his bedding again.

'Please, just let me go.' Howard doesn't have the energy to get up. To even look over. 'Whatever you want, haven't I suffered enough?'

No reply. The door slams and clicks again.

Distorted piano blasts out of the speaker. 'He's Charlie the Seahorse and there's nothing he can't do!'

## *[21:33]*

Howard stared hard at her. Was she really there? The doctor with glasses, dark hair plaited. He knew she had a name, but he couldn't remember it.

He was in a room, like he was in a hospital. No brick walls, no locked doors, no music playing, except for inside his head.

She smiled at him. 'Howard, when you were released, do you remember how much time it took to travel there?'

'I saw a vicar.' Howard frowned. 'Did I just dream it?'

The doctor nodded at him. 'That happened. We have an eyewitness. Did you see anyone in your cell?'

Howard frowned again. A cell? Is that what it was? A prison cell? 'I didn't see anyone. Or hear anything other than . . .' The tune burnt into his brain again. He didn't have any control over the words, didn't have control over anything any more. 'It was a man, though, definitely. I didn't see enough of him to describe him.'

'That's okay, Howard. Just tell us what happened when you were let go.'

'I'm not sure if this actually happened.' He couldn't control his breathing. 'I was completely out of it and they'd bound and gagged me.'

She gave a nod of encouragement.

'It was still early, still dark. The dawn was cracking. Birds singing. Or that was in my head. I don't know, but when they went to release me, I almost got away. I managed to shake him. Tried biting him, but he stopped me. Was that the vicar?'

'We don't think so.'

Howard stared up at the sterile white ceiling, unblemished tiles so much more welcoming than burnt brick.

'Did you see anything else when you were released?'

'Nothing. I . . . I can't remember.'

She leaned forward on her chair, biting her lip. 'Did you speak to anyone when you were in captivity?'

'I didn't see anyone.'

'Did you hear anything?'

'Just Cha— That song.'

'What about when you were released, did you see any other cells?'

'No, sorry. I don't know. Maybe. I'd like to say yes, but I can't tell what's real any more. My brain feels like it's rotting away.'

'Well, I understand that.'

'Sarah?' Howard sat up in the bed. 'Was there a Sarah?'

The doctor smiled at him. Magic sparkled in her eyes.

'Last night, I saw another two doors there. One had Sarah written on it. Does that mean anything?'

'We're investigating the possibility that your case is connected to the disappearance of a Sarah Langton. Do you know her?'

All the hope he had about them finding and stopping this maniac deflated like a burst football. 'No.'

'But you said there was another door?'

'There was one, but the light was out this morning.' He scanned the ceiling, like that would remind him. 'But the light flickered. I saw it! There was a name on that door too. I think it said Matt.'

# Twenty-two

## [PC Wilkinson, 21:36]

Even on a Tuesday night, Brighton was jumping. The long row of hotel bars looking across the road to the Palace Pier was filled with drinkers. The smokers in the front yards laughed and joked and flirted. Just like any other Tuesday.

'Only another seven hours, then we get off, yeah?' PC Jason Wilkinson walked lockstep with his partner. Instinctively, he checked the crowd drinking outside for any troublemakers or known faces. Looked more like a football crowd than usual. The mixture of citrus and mint vape flavours instead of harsh tobacco was the only real difference from when he'd started this beat. 'I tell you, Ali, away days have become hell since Brighton got back into the top-flight, know what I mean?'

'Go on?'

He finally brought himself to look at her. PC Alison Davidson, almost the same height as him. The most-beautiful eyes Jason had ever seen, and those round cheeks . . . But she wasn't even looking at him. 'I mean, all those clowns from London, Manchester, Newcastle or Liverpool, man. Make a long weekend of it down here on the south coast.' He shook his head. Then stopped as he recognised a face. Turned out it was only half-recognised; the guy was about four inches too short. 'And when Palace come down from bloody London . . . Man. Fifty or so miles apart and the fans treat it like a local derby. I don't get it.'

'Something to do with two rival players managing them in the seventies or something.' Alison stopped alongside him and tucked her thumbs into her stab-proof vest. 'That or because one chants eagles and the other seagulls.'

'You a football expert now, yeah?'

'Every time the telly shows an Albion game, my old man keeps banging on about it. He's Croydon, born and bred.'

Three little words stung Jason's heart every time. *My old man*. And not her father, but Detective Sergeant Col Edwards. Her bloody fiancé. Absolute dickhead. And every time Jason caught the sparkle on her finger, the diamond that Col used to claim his territory, it was a full-on stab through the heart.

The only consolation was the slight snarl on Alison's face as she said those little words, the micro-gesture in the corner of her eye. Maybe the wedding plans would be abandoned. Maybe she'd leave the pillock. Maybe Jason would realise he was dreaming.

He looked at her now. And she looked back at him. And he didn't look away, for once. Neither did she. They stood like that, something unspoken passing between them. Felt like minutes, maybe hours.

'Control to PC Davidson, over.'

Alison shot him a wink, then pressed receive on her radio, all without breaking her look at him. 'Receiving. Safe to talk, over.'

'Got you on Marine Parade, that right?'

A row of cars swept past along the road lining the beach.

'That's right.' Alison rolled her eyes at Jason. 'Just outside the Charles Street Tap, over.'

The big hipster bar loomed above them, still open and still pouring high-strength fighting juice for the lumbering idiots inside.

'Got a report of someone standing on a taxi, throwing stuff around, about halfway up Charles Street.'

'On it.' Alison set off at a sprint, her feet slapping off the ground. 'Look lively, Jay!'

Jason raced after her, following her up the lane at the side of the boozer. Typical Brighton back street, narrow, long and lined with the sides of hotels. He tried to match her, but she was just too fast.

Up ahead, a red Vauxhall with taxi signage on top had pulled in. The streetlights caught the gaudy lime-green tiles on the front of the Mucky Duck pub. A man straddled the taxi's bonnet, naked as the day he was born and swaying like he'd been on the heavy sauce since noon, three days ago. He clambered up onto the roof and swung a long knife around, the serrated edge looking mean in the night glow. 'Get away from me!'

Jason slowed to match Alison's walking pace. 'Suspect is armed with a bread knife. Repeat: armed with a bread knife. Over.'

'Receiving. An ARU is en route. Approach with caution, over.'

Jason took a look at Alison, got a nod, then started a slow walk over, hands raised. The telltale *snikt* sound of her baton extending came from behind. He followed suit, holding the truncheon up behind his back to keep it hidden as they approached. 'Mate, we're here to help you, yeah?'

The man swung round, slashing the knife through the air in their general direction. 'Do you know my name?'

Jason stopped, frowning at Alison. Her confusion matched his. He raised his hand higher. 'Let's have a nice chat down at the station, get to the bottom of what this is about, yeah?'

The man jabbed the knife towards them, even though he was about twenty feet away. 'My name is Matt!' Another prod. 'Are you listening to me? I exist! Don't put me back in my cell! I don't want to float again!'

Alison mouthed: 'What the hell is he on about?'

'Mate, I'll swing for you!' Round the other side of the taxi, a polo-shirted hooligan type with a face as red as his cab's bonnet, meaty fists clenched. 'Get off my bleeding car!'

'You're not putting me back in my cage!' Matt aimed his rage and his knife at the cabbie now, turning his back and hairy buttocks to the cops. 'Do I exist?'

'You can fuck off!' The cabbie noticed them. 'Here, can you sort this prick out?'

'Mate, I need you to back off!' Jason shot him a hard look.

The cabbie was seasoned enough to comply.

Jason rounded the car, matching Alison's position like they were herding sheep. He focused on the naked lunatic on the car. Maybe he wasn't drunk, maybe it was hard drugs. Spice or PCP or God knows what else. Something new that made people strip off and do crazy shit. 'How about you put the knife down, yeah?'

'No!' Matt stuck the blade against his arm, right over the

wrist. 'If I don't exist, this won't hurt, will it?' And he started cutting.

Jason swung his baton through the air and connected with bone. Matt dropped the knife and Jason swept it away towards safety.

'I exist!' Matt stared at him, eyes bulging. 'You're not putting me back in the water!' Then he jumped down from the taxi onto Jason, pushing him over. They landed in a heap, Jason's shoulder cracking off the kerbstone in a blaze of furious agony. His baton clattered onto the cobbles, skittering under the idling taxi.

Something sharp dug into Jason's throat. 'Don't put me back in the water!' Matt was on top of him, pressing the same knife against his neck. How the hell had he got hold of that again? 'I exist! Tell me I don't or—'

A flash of metal and Matt slumped forward, his naked body rubbing across Jason's face.

Alison stood above them, clutching her baton like a golf club. She held out her right hand. 'I'd hate to see how far you'd go on a second date.'

Jason hauled himself up, trying not to laugh. But struggling. 'I'm anyone's on a first date, you know that.'

That got a smirk from her. Then her face tightened with a nod. 'You can do the honours.'

Jason walked over to Matt and snapped out his cuffs. 'I'm arresting you for assaulting a police officer. What's your full name?'

'If you put me back in a cell, I will kill you.'

# Twenty-three

## *[Corcoran, 21:45]*

Thompson stood in the hospital corridor, hands on hips. 'And have you found any Matts related to the case so far?'

Still fizzing with caffeine energy, Corcoran looked at Palmer, but just saw his uncertainty reflected back. He gave Thompson a slight shrug. 'Not to my knowledge. And certainly not in any of the chats we've had with Sarah or Howard.'

'So what does it mean?' Thompson's gaze was like a search-light, picking them out in the night sea. 'Another victim? The perpetrator?'

'It would appear to be another victim.' Corcoran felt his throat constrict. 'Up till now, I've been trying to treat these as separate, hoping that what happened to Sarah and Howard were unconnected. But that's bollocks. There are just too many connections now.'

Palmer twisted the loose ends of her plait in her fingers. 'I'm clutching at straws, looking for any way this isn't connected.' Her eyes were moist around the edges. 'I mean, Sarah told us about the "Charlie the Seahorse" noise terror that Howard was subjected to. He saw her nameplate.' She huffed out a breath. 'It's all connected, isn't it?'

Thompson focused on Palmer. 'Okay, doc, time to earn your corn. In layman's terms, what does this mean?'

'Well, an extra door points to someone else going through some torture, either at the same time as Sarah and Howard or at some future point. And aside from that, I just don't know.'

'And that's just not going to do, is it?' Thompson clapped Palmer on the shoulder, then gripped Corcoran's tight. 'You two have been up against it today. You've put in the miles and the hours. We've caught two cases, not one, which is far from ideal, but I need you to do your jobs. Tomorrow morning, focus on the connections between these cases. Palmer, I need a profile. Aidan, I need an identity on this Matt. Now get home and get yourselves a good night's sleep.'

'You say that like I can just click my fingers . . .' Corcoran ran a hand down his face. 'Fine, I'll do what I can.'

'Good man.' Thompson got out her phone and scowled at the screen. 'Ah, great. Your friend DI Magrane from Axminster has just arrived and is chomping at the bit to speak to Howard.'

'You heard about the drugs, right?'

Thompson nodded. 'I mean, it wouldn't be the first time a drug dealer lied, but God, this really is the least of our concerns.' She shook her head, then smiled at them both. 'Now, fresh as a daisy first thing tomorrow. Get some sleep, see if anything strikes you.'

Corcoran watched her slope off down the corridor, putting her phone to her skull. He looked over at Palmer. 'You okay?'

She shook her head. 'All along I'd hoped you were right, Aidan, that these were separate and the connections were just in my head. But they're connected, aren't they? This is one case. One offender. Two cases that might be three. Meaning a serial offender.' Her eyes bulged. 'And a parallel offender too. He's kept Sarah and Howard at the same time, mere feet away from each other. Add this Matt into the mix and . . . and . . . And if there's a serial offender at work here, they might escalate to murder. They might already have done so. Matt might already be dead.'

Corcoran didn't have the words for her. He could only offer a reassuring smile.

'This is my worst fear come to life, Aidan.' Her plait was at risk of untangling. 'How long will this go on for?'

Corcoran felt bad for his earlier aggression. But he'd just been doing his job, pushing the expert to help them look in the right place at the right time, to prove they weren't related. Now they knew they were, it was his job to help her find the sadistic animal before they could strike again. 'Marie, you've got this.' He gave her a smile. 'The best thing you can do is work your magic and get us a profile of the attacker.'

'Well, that sounds patronising.'

'I don't mean it to. I'm serious. And you look as tired as I feel, so do what Thompson suggests and get some sleep. Tomorrow's already feeling like a bastard of a day.'

She tied off her plait and tucked it behind her head. 'Well, I'll see you tomorrow.'

Corcoran waved her off, then watched her go down the corridor. His great white hope, with the hair of an eleven-year-old school swot.

179

# [23:46]

The janitor steered a floor cleaner around, the deep throb sounding like a street dealer's car with the windows down.

Corcoran yawned into his fist and the yawn took over, tugging at his throat and twisting his mouth wide, pinching his nose as the fatigue gripped him.

'You don't want the wind to change, Aidan.' Thompson was loitering by his desk. 'I could've sworn I sent you home two hours ago.'

'And yet here I am.' Corcoran looked around the quiet office, engulfed by another yawn. Over in Thompson's doorway, DI Magrane was on the phone, listening hard like he had yet another voicemail. Or was it one of *those* calls from a superior officer? 'How's it going with laughing boy?'

'Never even seen him smile, let alone laugh.' Thompson slumped down in the chair next to him. 'Give me it straight, Aidan. Why the hell do you think they are doing this?'

'Not my job, Alana.' Corcoran tried to stifle another yawn. 'Palmer will come up with the goods.'

Mischief twinkled in her eyes. 'You got a thing for her?'

'Don't.' Corcoran narrowed his eyes at Thompson. 'Seriously.'

She raised her hands. 'Smoke, fire.'

'I mean it.'

'Fine, fine. What are you up to?'

Corcoran waved a hand at his computer, not that he could really focus on it. 'I've been searching for abductions of anyone with the name Matt. I know Howard thought he saw it with two Ts, but I've included one T and Matthew. Found a few Frenchmen called Mathis and a German Mats.' He looked at his sheet of paper. 'I've got an alert for any new missing persons who meet my search criteria, but . . .'

'But what?'

'The problem is I've got so many results that it's going to be impossible to narrow it down without something else.'

Thompson winked at him. 'You mean some of Dr Palmer's special magic?'

Corcoran ignored her. 'I mean more biographical information. Age, hair colour, inside leg measurement.' He slapped the side of the monitor. 'And he might not even be on here.'

Thompson stood up tall and something clicked. Sounded mechanical. 'Anyway, I've got a meeting with the boss and with laughing boy first thing tomorrow, so I need you to lead the briefing.'

Nothing Corcoran could do to mask the sigh. 'Fine.' He checked his watch. 'Who needs sleep anyway?'

'Well, you will. After that, you need to stick to your doctor like glue.'

'You don't want me leading the investigation?'

'Nope. Focus on her. I've got another two sergeants for the real work.'

# Twenty-four

## *[Palmer, 00:44]*

Almost pitch darkness: just the faint outlines of light coming from the window.

Palmer lay in her bed and kicked her foot again. The case just wouldn't stop running through her head. Not that she could sleep anyway. Any time she almost drifted off, she got a flash of Corcoran's driving and snapped fully awake. 'Alexa, what's the time?'

The little puck glowed pale green and blue. 'It's twelve forty-five a.m.'

She turned over, facing away from the window. Too hot in here.

Sarah, Howard and Matt.

Three victims, assuming Matt existed. Starvation, sleep deprivation and . . . And what? What next? What had happened to Matt? Had it happened? Would it happen?

Somewhere, Matt was suffering. They needed to find him. *She* needed to find him.

'Alexa, bedroom lights on.'

Another blue-green glow, then the room lit up with dim spotlights. Palmer reached over for her phone, her dry eyes struggling to focus on the screen as she typed out a text: *You*

182

*up?* She regretted it as soon as she'd sent it. Shouldn't have to reach out like that.

The phone buzzed with a reply almost immediately: *Sure am. You need to meet up?*

## *[01:15]*

Palmer shivered as she walked through Oxford, her trainers sliding over the cobbles in a way her kitten heels couldn't. Arms swinging, her rucksack strapped on tight. Must make her look like a snail. The ancient winding streets, built so long ago but still standing, still holding sway over the rest of the country, casting a long shadow over London and the country's ruling class.

The bitter wind caught a stray hair, brushing it into her face. No time to re-plait her hair, just a ponytail hanging loose and swinging behind her like a lion's tail.

And she always forgot about that wind. Oxford seemed so idyllic in her head until she was here. She stopped outside her old college, the Lodge gates shut for the night, and rang the bell.

A pair of eyes appeared in the slot halfway up the tall door. 'Can I help?'

'Marie Palmer, here to see—'

'Ah, Marie, you're looking well.' The door creaked open and Dorothy stood there, a wide smile on her face, wearing the college porter's garb. Just a few more lines, a few more grey hairs, but she looked exactly the same as when Palmer had lived there fifteen years ago, though she'd somehow missed her on her subsequent trips back. 'Through you come.'

'How have you been?'

'Nothing changes here except the students. I hear you're a doctor now?'

'Something like that.'

Dorothy gave another smile, with just a hint of the malice you'd get if you crossed her. 'She's through there.' She thumbed behind her, then went back to her room.

Palmer took her time walking through to the quad. Despite the time, it was all lit up. Above, a few students looked down from their rooms, the sounds of illicit partying leaking out.

'I can smell your nerves, Marie.' A soft Scottish accent floated across the breeze. Professor Zoe Wilson was standing on the grass, smoking. Her dyed-red corkscrew curls hung free for once. A slight tan to her face betrayed her quarter-Algerian ancestry, a tale that changed every time she told it. Rings covered her fingers, all except the obvious one. She smiled. 'You're looking well.'

'Thanks.' Palmer felt her mouth twist in that way she'd tried to control, but . . . Being back there, with her, it was like she was an undergraduate again. 'Thanks for replying to my text.'

Zoe stubbed out her cigarette. 'Come on, you look like you need a cup of tea.'

## *[01:30]*

Zoe's office was much the same as fifteen years ago. Books everywhere. Everywhere. No room for anything else. Even her laptop rested on a stack of ancient hardbacks, her desk lost to an encroaching wave of books. The teapot rested on another stack, pouring a gentle mist into the air.

'So I take it you can't sleep?'

'Well, yes.' Palmer sipped her green tea, still too hot to glug, but pleasant enough. 'I mean, I'm *excited* about being involved in an active investigation, but this whole thing . . . There's no rest, and too much pressure.' She took another sip. 'And I'm terrified of messing it up, especially given Corcoran's attitude.'

'Corcoran?'

'The Thames Valley detective I'm working with.' Palmer brushed her arm through the air. 'I notice you didn't pick up on my concern about messing it up.'

'Because I trust you, Marie.' Zoe took a dainty sip of tea. 'And you suit your hair down.'

Palmer blushed. 'Thanks. I need to get it cut but—'

'—there's just never enough time?' Zoe arched her eyebrow. 'Never change, Marie. Never change.' She reached over to top up her cup, then splashed some into Palmer's cup without asking. 'This is a good opportunity for you to get out into the field. I've been there, but you've been stuck in that hospital for too long.' She looked around the four corners of her office. 'I know the feeling, stuck in here like a rat in a cage.'

'Don't talk about cages.' A shiver ran up Palmer's spine. 'Whenever I interview offenders, I have weeks and weeks with them and I'm working to a strategy I've spent *months* on, signed off with all relevant stakeholders. And the patients are already behind bars.' She held her cup to her lips but didn't drink, just felt the steam on her face. 'This time, though . . . Well. We're working against the clock. And all I can think about is what if they do it again? What if they keep doing it again and again?' She took that drink, swallowed it and felt the liquid burn down. 'How the hell do the police cope with the constant pressure without cracking?'

'What I wouldn't give to interview half the police officers in the country . . .' Zoe smirked. 'But their coping mechanisms are usually gallows humour, compartmentalisation and self-medication. Joking about it until it's not even funny. Not even thinking about it. Then when it does finally invade your thoughts, drinking yourself to sleep every night.'

Palmer nodded, depressed by the empathy she felt towards Corcoran's plight. And was it just empathy? She shook the unwelcome thought out of her head. 'Maybe I should've had some gin tonight. Might've helped me sleep.'

'But instead you turned to me for help.' Zoe raised both eyebrows, but it was like she was pleading rather than offering from a position of strength. Like she needed to help, rather than wanted to. 'How about we start by pulling together everything you know about both cases? Then we can tie up any links, no matter how trivial. That could help find out what's driving this. And we can look for anyone with a similar MO, see if that could help.'

Palmer sat back in the chair, the old wood creaking. 'Okay.' She looked for somewhere to rest her cup, but came up short again, so put it down on the small patch of floor by her feet and got out her notebook. She flicked through the pages. 'Well. All we've got so far is two victims kept in prison cells. Victim one for six weeks. Victim two for twelve days.'

Zoe seemed to shiver but didn't speak.

'Then both victims were released a day apart.'

'Released?'

'Well, set free. One in Oxfordshire, hence Thames Valley police. The other in Rugby, Warwickshire.' Palmer held up her notebook and showed all the pages of notes. 'But I can't figure out any connections between the victims.'

'How about we start with who they are?'

'Sarah is a project manager at a biotech company in Cambridge. A runner. Married. She was taken while running home from work. Then starved, almost until she died.'

'And victim two?'

'Howard, chef from Axminster in Devon. Single, sounds like a party boy. Taken while he surfed. And he was blasted with—'

'So both were taken during physical activity?'

'Well, we don't know Howard was.' Palmer felt her lips do an involuntary twitch again. 'The Devon cop who investigated said they couldn't tell if his wetsuit had been used that morning.' She frowned and scribbled a fresh note. 'Smell would tell us, wouldn't it?' A different flavour of frown now. 'But that assumes he washed it frequently. He surfed every day, so it's unlikely.'

Zoe filled her cup again, but Palmer covered hers. 'When were they released?'

'Sarah was let go yesterday morning. Howard, first thing this morning.'

'So, he or she had Sarah and Howard for some amount of overlapping time?'

'Well, the duration of Howard's imprisonment. And they think it's a he.'

'Okay. Did they see each other?'

'Not quite. They were vaguely aware of each other. Sarah thinks she heard this children's TV theme tune that Howard was subjected to. He saw her nameplate.'

'Nameplate?'

A shiver ran up Palmer's spine, crawling like spiders, then goosebumps prickled on her arms. 'Their cells were labelled. To remind him there's a person in there? To catalogue his collection? Either way, Howard saw another nameplate, marked for a Matt. And that's where we've got to.'

'Which could just be the confused memories of a man suffering from this extreme noise terror? Or it could be subterfuge? Could they be trying to rattle the police?'

'But it could be someone else suffering.'

'Right. But they were both released? Hmm.' Zoe finished her tea and set the cup down on the floor next to her chair. 'Has anyone tried to get in touch with you or the police?'

'No. And that's despite a news conference for Sarah's case on the TV and radio this morning. The newspapers will have it on their websites. I don't know, but I presume Howard's information will be released tomorrow.'

'That silence doesn't strike you as unusual?'

'How so?'

'With a case where people are released, wouldn't you expect some sort of message? Don't you think releasing live victims is unusual behaviour for this sort of perpetrator? Now, could it be he can't bring himself to take a life? Or is it possible he's building up to murder?'

'I'm here for answers, Zoe. Not more questions.'

'In some ways, what he's done to Sarah and to Howard, doesn't it sound like their torture is the end game? Maybe he doesn't want to kill them? Maybe their suffering is the message?'

'Well, I have thought of that.'

'Indeed.' Zoe was nodding to herself. 'In this sort of scenario, your perpetrator thinks of himself as the hero of his story, and he's righting some wrong. He has his own set of objectives and we are the obstacles. I mean you and the police are. I'd expect some tragedy in his life, where no-one helped him achieve a goal, or where he was disadvantaged by someone achieving their own senseless goal. That'll lead to a very black-and-white view of the world, his own moral code. It very likely precludes him from taking a life. But sending a message is his objective and the torture is the message.'

'But a message to who? Sarah has a husband but Howard's single, like I say.'

'Curious. Have they learnt anything from this ordeal?'

'Well, they're absolutely terrified. You should see what he's done to Sarah.' Palmer's mouth was dry. She reached down for her tea and took a still-scalding drink. 'As far as I can tell, there's no message.'

'Can you build a pattern?'

'Well, it just appears random to me. Senseless.' Palmer shook her head. 'No personal contact between the abductor and the victims, either.'

'Now *that* is curious.' Zoe clicked the fingers on both hands, rings clacking, eyes flickering. 'Okay, so talk to me. Freeform.'

'Well, Sarah and Howard were kidnapped. Sarah from near her home while she ran. Howard from a regular surfing site. As far as we can tell, both attacks were planned, and the adductor knew the optimal opportunities for taking them.

Meaning someone had been observing them and knew her life inside out.'

'Husband, wife, partners?'

'Doesn't fit. Sarah had an affair behind her husband's back, but can you think of a case where someone would do this as punishment?'

'Only in America.' Zoe moved her hands, chivvying Palmer along. 'And Howard?'

'Single, as far as I know.' She noticed a box on her diagram. 'Howard kept singing the theme tune to *Charlie the Seahorse*.'

'Oh, that?'

'You know it?'

'My niece does.' Zoe laughed. 'All the time, blasting it out on the iPad. Drives my sister potty.'

'Well, Howard kept singing it when we spoke to him. As far as I can decipher, he'd been subjected to it all day long, and at high volume.'

'Peculiar.' Zoe's lips twitched. 'Okay, let's go back to the abduction MO. Could be there's an elaborate fiction that's drawing these victims in. He talks to them, tells a story, then BANG, he takes them.'

'They were both attacked.'

'Attacked?'

'Sarah was tripped. Howard pinned to his van. Both were likely injected with something.'

'Likely?'

'They've been kept in a prison cell, Zoe. You of all people know how fragile human memory is at the best of times. And this is the worst.'

'Quite.' Zoe stood up and walked over to her window, over-looking the quad. 'Let's consider the offender journey. This is a complex operation, requiring much preparation and planning. Executing that plan is a whole different ball game. How did they train to do it? Have there been possible trials?'

Palmer felt a surge of vertigo, like she was on the top of a skyscraper and even the foundations wobbled beneath her feet. 'The police are investigating it, but nothing so far.'

'Okay. Well, I recommend geographic profiling.' Zoe turned back to face Palmer, outlined by the faint lights from the quad. Made her hair look like it was on fire. 'It's how I caught Ross Murray.'

Palmer folded her arms. She'd known coming here might be a mistake. Back to her role in Ross Murray's downfall, like always.

'In fact . . .' Zoe rushed forward to a stack of books, clicking her fingers again. She picked up a black notebook and sifted through it. 'Yes, here we go. Ross Murray had a similar MO to your guy. Serial rapist, who escalated to abduction by victim three, and to murder by victim six. I caught him after sixteen victims.'

'Sixteen?' Palmer took another drink of tea. Her hand was shaking. 'Whoever's doing this isn't a killer.'

'Yet.' Zoe looked up from her notebook. 'It's usually only a matter of time. And victims one and two could actually be victims seven and eight. It could be that those are the ones he's deemed to have been sufficiently punished or redeemed. This Matt could be the first murder.'

'You said he's sending a message to Sarah and Howard? That doesn't sound like someone on an escalation path.'

'I know, which is why you need to get inside this guy's head.' Zoe picked up her chair and put it next to Palmer's. She produced a shiny silver laptop from behind a tottering pile of books and woke it up. Her rings clacked as she typed. 'Here we go.' She rested the laptop on the wider pile of books and sat back. 'I'd put some popcorn on, but the microwave isn't working.'

A greyscale video filled the screen, the camera up high. Palmer knew the room. Interview suite B, Broadmoor. Zoe sat on one side of the desk, her hair in pigtails, offset by a pinstriped power suit, nothing like the earth mother sitting next to Palmer. The masks people wear.

The door opened and two hulking orderlies lumbered in, a mixture of power and observation, helping Ross Murray shuffle in, head bowed, shoulders rounded. He carried a notepad, cradling it like a child with a favourite toy, and sat side on to Zoe, only glancing at her in his peripheral vision.

She asked him a question which the laptop's speakers didn't quite reproduce.

'Page seven.' Murray's deep voice was crystal clear. His Essex accent twisting the syllables.

Zoe paused the video and passed over a stack of photocopied papers, neatly arranged and bound, but creased. At least two coffee rings on the front cover. 'This is the manuscript of his autobiography. It's the only way he communicates with the outside world. They photocopied it when he was asleep once.' She flicked through and passed it to Palmer.

All capitals, carefully written and with no crossing out or corrections.

You have to know who you're helping. Watch them, absorb their lives, until you know everything they'll do and see everything that's wrong with their lives. Then you'll see exactly how you can help. There will always be a gap where they will be open to receiving your assistance. In every hour of every day of every week, there will be a repeating window where they are almost begging for your help. It's just a case of looking hard enough. And being patient, biding your time. Remember how badly they need your help.

Palmer felt her gut tighten and clench. '*Help?*'

'At first, I thought he was being sarcastic.' Zoe reached over to tap the page. 'But he genuinely thinks he's helping his victims. He's an angel of mercy who sees his victims as injured parties at the side of the road and himself as the Good Samaritan.'

'Zoe, this isn't—'

'Marie, just go with this, okay?' Zoe tapped the document again. 'Page eighteen.'

A well-worn page, with some inscrutable notes in the margins on both sides and the back of the previous page.

The trick is to have somewhere nobody else knows, where you can come and go as you please. Cages are your friend. Like a dog, you need to show your friends who is boss. And just like with a dog, sometimes you need to put them in a cage to look after their needs. They will respect you more for it. And it comforts them. A human being needs constant care, constant attention. They will always try to escape, no matter how much love you give them. They're ungrateful for what you've done for them. I recommend a small cage, ideally seven foot by four. Enough for most people to lie down in. Whenever you go inside, make sure they're sedated, or in a state where they can show their love to you, their gratitude.

Zoe pointed at the highlighted section, a knobbly ring almost sliding off. 'Don't you think Sarah's starvation would make controlling her much easier?'

'Well, yes.' Palmer rested the document on her lap, starting to see some signal in the noise. 'Howard, though . . . Why not starve both victims?'

'Good question. You said Howard was missing for twelve days?'

'He's still the same weight as when he was taken.'

Zoe didn't seem to have the answer to that, except for turning the page. She had underlined and highlighted more than half of the text.

But sometimes you wonder if you're saving them from themselves. And if it's enough. It's the purest form of love I know. And perhaps you're the same? You will have done this once or twice, but you'll feel it deep in your soul. The voices, the stress, the pressure. You'll be thinking about who else you can help. And sometimes there's just too much love to give.

Zoe patted Palmer's knee. 'Whoever's doing this, they'll be experiencing so much stress and pressure. Absolute fear of getting caught. They're clearly psychopathic and don't feel anything for their victims, but they know the risk they're taking. They can feel the police closing in on them, which they get over by searching for their next victim. They focus their energies on the promise of the future, instead of fear over past deeds.'

'Meaning another victim is likely?'

Zoe just flipped the page.

As you get better at this, you'll want to help them for longer periods of time. It'll start with one short piece of attention, but soon you'll feel so much love and gratitude from them that you'll want to help more than one at a time. <u>Always</u> keep them separate. <u>Always</u>. Try to fight the urge to keep them together. I once tried helping two people in adjacent cages under my garage. Keeping two people alive is much harder than one. The emergent difficulties multiply in complexity. What's worse, when you turn your back, they start to think they can reject your help. They'll talk to each other and form a bond. They'll conspire against you. Other people are the poison, not you. I had to move one to the back of a van in my garage. Which is how the traitors found me. Don't make my mistake. Serially, never in parallel.

'If we're right, then my guy has mastered keeping two people. Maybe even three.'

Zoe nodded. 'Those two escaped. One bit his ear, the other kicked him, and they ran. Stole Murray's car and drove off. They handed themselves in at the police station in Thetford, but couldn't remember where he lived. All they knew is it was somewhere in rural Norfolk. We had a suspect in custody and had to release him. Weeks later, both victims were released from protective custody. We caught Murray killing the second.'

'Oh my god.'

'Want to know the worst part?' Zoe raised her eyebrows. 'Ross Murray had been seen in the vicinity of two abductions and was in our TIE logs. Trace, Interview, Eliminate. The useless police let him go.'

'Great. So I just have to wait until he does this again? Zoe, I can't. This is too much.'

'Marie, you'll likely need more than two victims to form a pattern. I was on the case from the second murder, his seventh overall victim, and even then we didn't get anything useful until victim nine. And we still had the wrong man in custody. But the important thing is we caught him. Ross Murray isn't doing this any more. If he was out there, he would still be murdering.'

Palmer got to her feet and stepped between tottering piles of books. 'I still have no idea how to catch him.'

'The police have brought you in because you're Dr Marie Palmer. You're an expert and you can do what they can't. You get inside the head of whoever is doing this. Can you do that?'

Palmer stopped her pacing. 'Zoe, I only do that once the police have done their job and the guy is under lock and key.' She was sounding like Corcoran now.

'Do your job, Marie. Build up a profile. Start wide, keep it unconstrained. There will be things you know for definite, so let the police know them. You never know, you might strike lucky. But you *know* the kind of man you're looking for, don't you?'

'A violent psychopath with sadistic tendencies, someone who enjoys seeing torment.'

'Weave those connections. Just because it might take six or ten victims to give you a concrete pattern doesn't mean you won't be able to infer anything from just two. He might be careless.'

'I've seen what he can do to people, Zoe. It's . . . it's horrible. And if he's doing it to someone else just now, if . . .' Palmer couldn't speak. She felt numb.

'You've got this, Marie. You know what you're doing. So do it.'

# Day three

# Twenty-five

## *[07:15]*

Palmer stopped on the staircase to steady herself. Her head was thumping and she couldn't decide if there was one police officer walking down the stairs towards her, or two. She stepped aside and let him – or them – past with a blast of metallic aftershave. Probably just one. She started climbing again, the banister resonating with each step, and opened the door to the Incident Room. A lone voice speaking, none of the usual hubbub. She stepped inside, letting the door shut behind her.

Corcoran stood at the front of the room, clean-shaven and wearing a navy suit with a red tie. He looked surprisingly presentable. Plainclothes and uniformed cops filled the room, more men than women but surprisingly balanced. He stopped and gave her a grin. 'Nice of you to join us, Doctor.'

But Palmer was scanning the room. 'Sorry, I needed a word but I see you're busy.'

'Won't be long.'

'I've got something that might prove crucial.'

'A profile, yeah?' A tall male officer near her snorted with laughter. 'Know your sort. Rather have a profile than solve the case.'

'DC Butcher.' Corcoran pointed at him. 'Have *you* solved the case?'

Butcher stood there, holding his gaze, sipping from a metal coffee mug. 'No, Sarge. Sorry.'

Corcoran folded his arms, teeth bared. 'Dr Palmer has spoken to many people with similar MOs, so I ask all of you to extend any and all assistance in helping her get inside our guy's head. Okay?' He raised his eyebrows and looked around the room again for any dissenting opinions. Then he rounded on Butcher again. 'Have you nailed down Christopher Langton's movements on the night of Sarah's disappearance?'

'Still a few avenues to chase down.'

Corcoran shook his head, a bitter smile on his face. 'That's your priority today, Constable. Not bullying Dr Palmer. Okay?'

'Sarge.' Butcher was still smirking.

Corcoran rested his notebook on the table and looked around at his officers. 'DI Thompson is meeting with Devon and Cornwall police about the ownership of Howard Ritchie's case which, as you all know, overlaps with a strategic drugs investigation. We obviously don't want to jeopardise that, but you've all seen what we've got on our hands.' He paused and looked around the room. 'Okay, we've still got a ton of witnesses to trace and eliminate. Get on with it.'

The crowd parted between them, letting Palmer get at him. Concern creased his forehead. 'You okay, Marie?'

'I didn't need saving.'

'No, but I needed to stamp authority on that rabble.'

Palmer rested her rucksack on the ground.

'You suit your hair down.'

Instinctively, she patted her head. 'Thanks. You look smart.'

'I feel like a large part of my brain died overnight. Not that three hours counts as sleep.' He yawned into his fist. 'I was up half the night looking through every Matt and Matthew who disappeared in the last six months between Penzance and Berwick-upon-Tweed. Wondering if I should search in Scotland and Northern Ireland. And that's assuming he's even been reported missing, or hasn't been gone longer than six months. Just way too many and no way to narrow it down without . . .' He looked at her with hope in his eyes.

'Well, I couldn't sleep last night. Had all that Matt stuff running though my head too. So I worked on the profile.'

'I could do with some hope.' Corcoran hefted up her rucksack for her. 'But I could do with some coffee more.'

## *[07:30]*

Palmer sat in the station's canteen, flicking through her notebook, refreshing her thoughts, but she was so tired and insights were elusive.

'Here we go.' Corcoran rested two steaming mugs on the table and sat opposite her, tucking his tie in. 'You said you took it black, right?'

'Correct. I'm lactose intolerant. And thanks.' She reached for a sachet and tipped the brown sugar into her cup, then stirred it in, all the while fighting off yet another yawn. 'You handled yourself well in the briefing.'

'I'll take that as a compliment.' Corcoran slurped at his coffee. Must have a mouth lined with asbestos. 'Taking briefings is the part of the job I like least, would you believe?'

'I would. I have to talk at conferences several times a year. Hundreds of bored academics is much harder than thirty wired cops.'

'Different crowds, I suppose.' Another sip and he rested his cup down. 'Not sure half of my lot know where to find the sinks in the bathroom, let alone someone who's kidnapped three people.'

Palmer stopped blowing on her tea and set it down. 'You definitely think it's three?'

'I was trying to keep Sarah and Howard separate, but you were right to be flexible.'

'This isn't about right or wrong.'

'No, it's not.' Corcoran nodded at her notebook. 'So what have you got for me?'

Palmer stared at the page, transfixed by the drawings.

'What's up?'

'I just don't know if I can do this, Aidan.' She looked up at him. 'Do you mind if I call you Aidan?'

'That's been fine so far. Do you prefer Marie or Dr Palmer?'

'I don't like Marie, but my parents didn't bless me with a middle name. And I've been letting you use it, so take that as a compliment.'

He smiled at that. 'Why don't you think you can do this?'

'As you've kept pointing out, usually when I speak to these people, I have a couple of twenty-stone guards next to me.'

Corcoran laughed this time. 'I promise you won't come a cropper, so long as you toe the line.'

'I'm not being funny, but you and your dodgy hip don't give me much reassurance that someone who's abducted and held two physically fit and strong people won't get at me too.'

'There's a whole squad here to protect us. Okay?' He picked up and sipped his coffee without flinching. 'We won't go in anywhere that's not completely under our control. Besides, we need to find this bastard first.'

'The hard part.'

He nodded. 'Anything that'll help with that?'

'I don't know. This is from first principles, okay? So please be patient.' Palmer traced her fingers over the page, deciding where best to start. There. 'Okay, so most of the serial killers I've had contact with—'

'This isn't a serial killer.'

'Correct, but the psychology is usually the same, it's just an escalation path.' She waited to see if he had any objections but he just took another sip. 'Most have been driven by fantasies of power and control, others by visions, and some by just pure lust. Disorganised psychopaths who pick their victims at random.'

Corcoran finished his coffee before she'd even started her tea. 'You mean like the Washington snipers?'

'You're well read.'

He shrugged. 'Two people who just shot at random people in car parks and on freeways.'

Palmer held up a finger. 'As far as I can tell, that isn't what we're dealing with here. While we don't have a clear MO, they're not just taking people willy nilly. There seems to be a method to this. Planning, striking at the most opportune moment. So I think we're looking for someone motivated by revenge and a desire to right a perceived wrong.'

'So, "mission-oriented", right?'

'Well, yes.'

A dark look flooded his face. 'Okay, so I'm with you so far. What's his message?'

'That's what I've been up half the night thinking through.' She took a tentative sip of tea. Still way too hot for a normal human to even touch. 'We need to listen to what he wants us to hear.'

He rolled his eyes at her.

'I'm serious. There's something that haunts him.' Palmer jabbed a finger on the page. 'We're dealing with a clever, precise individual, someone who may appear to be completely normal, but who won't stop until he's either apprehended or has completed his mission. But even then, he might just redefine the mission and keep going.'

'And what are you basing that on?'

'Well.' She turned the page back. 'Of the killers I mentioned last night, Burke was a mission killer who deflected failings in his home life by murdering random people. But there's someone much closer – Ross Murray.'

Corcoran flinched. 'What about him?'

'You know him?'

'Unlike most people these days, I still read the papers.'

'Well, you'll know he started out as a rapist, then became a killer. His mission was about helping people. I dug into the interviews when I couldn't sleep. He blamed it all on his ADHD, but the prevailing orthodoxy is he wanted to help his mother. See, when he was a small boy, his stepfather murdered her right in front of him. And he couldn't help her. So it all became twisted inside out. And he started thinking if he could help these women, he'd help his mother stay alive, but he just kept killing and killing until he was caught.'

Corcoran swallowed hard. 'You think our guy's similar?'

'Could be.' Palmer slurped tea and instantly regretted it. Her tongue was burnt. 'Or could be completely different. Ross Murray's first two were opportunistic rapes in parks. Our perpetrator . . .' Her tongue tingled. 'According to Sarah and Howard, our guy doesn't spend any time with his victims.'

'Meaning?'

'He doesn't appear to enjoy their suffering on an intimate level. He's seemingly more occupied with what the crime signifies than in any particular act.'

Palmer looked across the canteen. Thompson and Magrane were in the queue for coffee, laughing and joking like the best of friends. She couldn't figure out who'd won their turf war.

When she looked back, Corcoran was staring at her. 'So how do we catch him?'

'Well. Creating these cells or cages, wherever they may be, must require some degree of privacy and a knowledge of construction. He could own a piece of isolated land somewhere. Does that mean he's wealthy? And the engineering skills required to build the cells seems relatively advanced.'

'And how does that help?'

'It means we're probably looking for someone who doesn't live in a city. He can come and go as he pleases.' Using Ross Murray's words like that made her shiver. 'It starts to narrow it down.'

'Anything else?'

'For Sarah, he maintained a programme of calculated starvation, down to the day she would die. He's kept Howard at exactly the same weight . . .'

'So we're looking for a nutritionist who lives in the sticks?'

'Aidan, please.'

Corcoran held up his hands, but tilted his head like he hadn't conceded the point. 'I'm listening.'

'Our guy must've devoted significant time to his mission. Does that suggest he hasn't got a family? That he lives alone?'

Corcoran shrugged. 'So a single nutritionist who—'

'*Aidan.*'

'I'm joking.'

'It's how you cope, I get it.'

'Right.' He looked embarrassed for once. 'We've been hunting connections between Sarah and Howard, but I just can't see any.'

She scanned her notebook, stocking up her memory with facts rather than fanciful leaps. 'Both victims are from different parts of the country. Devon and Cambridge. Different backgrounds. One is a project manager, the other a chef. Seemingly different personalities and interests, different family lives.'

'Neither have children.'

'Correct, and they're both in their twenties, so that's maybe not unexpected.' She took a sip of tea. 'There doesn't appear to be any connection between where they were taken and where they were found. They both have secrets. Sarah's affair, Howard's drug sting. Beyond that, their lives seem perfectly ordinary. The only thing that seems to connect them is a rough age bracket and the ordeal they have been subjected to. I mean, Sarah runs and Howard surfs, but I can't divine anything from that.'

'How would Matt fit into this?'

'We just don't know.' She turned the page, just blank lines

filled with the three names and nothing much connecting them. 'Two data points isn't enough. We need to know more about Matt.' She circled the name with her finger, highlighting how little they knew about him. 'And it's possible he might have more people incarcerated than this Matt. He had Sarah and Howard. If we add in Matt as a third, parallel victim, then it's possible he could have a fourth or even a fifth now.'

Corcoran shut his eyes for a few seconds. 'Or Matt might not exist.' He reopened them. 'It could just be misdirection.'

'Well, quite. But I believe he's choosing to let them go rather than murder them. That greatly increases the risk of him being caught. So it's clear he wants the world to know they have suffered.'

'Back to your mission.'

'Precisely. It could be the connection is their actions are morally questionable, that someone's targeting people who have committed dubious acts.' Something sparked in her brain. She clicked her pen and scribbled a fresh connection between Howard and Sarah. 'This could be something, Aidan. He left philosophy textbooks for them to read.'

Corcoran twisted his lips. 'Her affair and his drug-dealing aren't public knowledge, though. We had to dig and dig to get that information.'

'So, it could be that it's not the connection, but it could also be how we strike lucky. There may be someone who is aware of the affair and the drug-dealing. Someone who wants them to pay.'

'Someone we need to find.' Corcoran took a deep breath, then nodded slowly. 'Okay, so I'm starting to—'

His phone barked out the *Charlie the Seahorse* theme tune.

'Aidan, really?'

'Sorry, I thought it'd help.' He checked the display. 'Got to take this.' He put the phone to his ear and turned away from her. Then straight back. 'My flag on the system has just been triggered. Someone by the name of Matt has turned up in Brighton saying he was abducted and kept in a prison cell.'

# Twenty-six

## *[Corcoran, 10:05]*

Hard to miss Brighton police station. A huge grey building like an IKEA store made from Lego. The oversized blue entrance was stamped with Brighton Police Station in the sort of font you'd see outside some east London web start-up. Most of the neighbouring buildings were stuck in the eighties, except for this office over the road, seemingly carved from blocks of glass.

Corcoran watched Palmer get out into the thin rain and jot down yet more notes. He sat back in his chair, trapped by his phone call.

'Aidan, what's your read on DI Magrane?' Thompson sounded cagey.

'He's angling to take over your case, right?'

'Maybe.'

'Look, if I was giving him the benefit of the doubt, I'd say he doesn't want to lose his drugs investigation. He's running a big operation down there, got someone for it and he won't let that go without a fight.'

'Aidan, be straight with me. Do you honestly think Howard was dealing drugs?'

'Couldn't say without spending a few hours going over their files in detail, then spending a day interviewing him.'

'But your gut feel?'

'Look, it doesn't matter to us whether Howard's guilty or not. Our case is about finding whoever did this to him.'

She grunted. 'Always the voice of reason, aren't you?'

'I try to be. Look, I'm in Brighton, I better—'

'*Brighton*? What the hell are—'

'I'll call you later. Bye.' Corcoran killed the call and waited for her to call him back in a fury. Nothing after ten seconds, so he got out and shuffled towards the police station.

Palmer tossed her long ponytail over her shoulder as he caught up with her. Now her hair was liberated from the plait, she looked more mature, like she meant business, and less like a disturbed schoolgirl. 'Two hours driving down from Kidlington and you've barely spoken.'

'Look.' Corcoran stopped beside her outside the front door, hands in pockets, smiling. 'We're both frazzled here. Both stayed up all night, pushing ourselves way too hard. Don't try and psychoanalyse me.'

'It's all part of the service, I'm afraid.'

Corcoran sighed as he shifted over to open the door, his suit jacket rumpling in the salty breeze. 'Come on.' He entered the building, warrant card already out.

An open space with a bored-looking desk sergeant staring at his mobile phone. He took one look at them, then whistled like he was out hiking on the South Downs and his dogs were straying a bit too far. 'Jase!'

'What?' A skinny uniform hauled himself up to standing. Spaghetti arms and chunky legs, dark skin, black hair shaved close and rounded off at the front. He offered a hand but winced as Corcoran shook it. 'PC Jason Wilkinson.'

'DS Corcoran. This is Dr Marie Palmer, who's working with me on this case.'

'Cool, cool, cool.' Jason led them through the station, yawning into his fist. 'Sorry. Been on since ten last night. Absolutely shattered.'

'Join the club. What happened?'

Jason stopped by the sign for the custody suite. 'Me and Ali.' He blew air up his face. 'That's my partner, Alison. PC Davidson, yeah? We were doing a walkabout last night, down the seafront, got a call about this geezer going mental outside a pub. We jogged round and . . .' He laughed, despite himself. 'Geezer was stark bollock naked, standing on a taxi, wielding this knife.' He was trying to keep his laughter under control. 'Not the first time we've seen that round here, know what I mean? But this geezer, he was trying to cut his arm off. I stopped him, but . . . mate . . .'

'Is your partner about?'

'She's not in.' Jason frowned, eyelids flickering. 'Meeting her wedding planner, yeah?'

'Can you call her? It's important we speak to her.'

Jason got out his phone and started tapping away. 'Sure thing.'

'The way I heard it, you were critical in taking him down, right?'

'Right.'

Corcoran opened the custody suite door. 'And he's definitely called Matt?'

'I mean . . .' Jason was focused on texting. 'That's what he was shouting. "I am Matt! I exist!" I took him down, but . . . crazy.'

'Strange.' Palmer had her notebook out again but wasn't writing anything. 'Was he drunk?'

'Didn't smell of it, but you never know, yeah? Could be spice. Could be anything. He kept mentioning cells. That's why I called you.' Jason was staring hard at Corcoran, open-mouthed. 'That Witney Woman case and that guy in Rugby. The press conference said they was in cells. Matt kept saying don't put me back in the cell. Didn't want to be drowned?'

Corcoran smiled. 'Did you get the impression he meant prison?'

'Nah, more like he'd been imprisoned. And that's why I called you.'

'Let us know when we can speak to your partner.' Corcoran let Palmer go first and followed her through.

The door to the cells squeaked open and a brute of a custody sergeant grunted through. 'Jason send you?'

'PC Wilkinson, yes.' Corcoran joined him by the doors. 'Here to—'

'He's been like that since they brought him in, I swear.' The sergeant shook his head and stepped out of the way. 'I mean, what do you take to get like that?'

In the cell Matt lay on the bed, almost perfectly still, just his chest heaving, like he was sleeping, but his eyes were wide open. Through his fuzzy ginger beard, in bad need of some grooming, his mouth hung open.

Corcoran grasped the metal bar. 'Is he meditating?'

'Don't know, mate.'

Matt looked underweight, slack skin on his arms, but that was still a step above the skeleton that Sarah had been reduced to.

'I exist.' Matt was now staring at Corcoran, huge dark bags under his eyes like someone had punched holes in his skull with a mining drill. His eyes were randomly moving as though he was following patterns that weren't there. A twitch. Then another one. Then he focused straight on Corcoran. 'Tell me I exist.' Then back to the random eye movement. 'Please, any of you?'

'You exist, as far as I can tell.' Corcoran entered the cell and crouched next to him, stabilising himself on the bed frame. 'What's your name, sir?'

'How can I know I exist?'

'Is it Matt?'

'Matthew, yes. Matt. That's me. That's my name.'

'Have you got a surname?'

Matt shut his eyes, his forehead screwed tight. 'I'm Matt . . .' He stared at Corcoran again. 'Is it Christmas?'

'Matt, it's the eleventh of March.'

'*March*?' He huffed out a sigh and his head sank deep into the pillow. 'How can it be *March*?'

'What's your surname, Matt?'

'Gladwin. My name is Matt Gladwin and I exist!'

'Okay, Matt.' Corcoran let go of the bed and held out his hands. 'It's fine, Matt. We're here to—'

'You've put me in a cell!' Matt swung up to sitting, fists clenched, teeth bared. 'Why have you put me in a cell! Don't drown me!'

'He was like this last night.' Jason was next to Corcoran, smiling at Matt. 'All the same—'

'Fuck you!' Matt lashed out, swinging a fist at Jason, who ducked like a boxer. Corcoran stepped forward.

Jason shimmied past Matt's windmilling fists and grabbing him in a half-nelson, then pushing him face first onto the bed. 'Declan, I could do with your help here!'

The custody sergeant wasn't so quick. He caught a kick from Matt in the knee and went down onto the floor. 'Christ on a bike!'

Jason took Matt's legs and stopped him donkey-kicking anyone else. The sergeant got in there and stood over Matt, holding him long enough to stop wriggling.

'I exist! Don't let me drown!'

Corcoran knew speaking to him wouldn't yield much that was useful, so he walked over to the custody desk and noticed the computer was unlocked. He switched to the Police National Computer window and searched for Matt Gladwin. IC1, with an age range 25 to 40, though he looked early thirties.

The system thought about it for a few seconds.

Palmer was scribbling away.

The computer came back with a Missing Persons report.

Matt Gladwin. Thirty-two, father of one. Went missing from east London on the ninth of October.

Palmer gasped. 'That's five *months*.'

# Twenty-seven

## *[10:08]*

Corcoran swallowed hard. Three victims now, held in parallel for almost a fortnight. Two of them for over five weeks. The multiplying complexities, the preparation, the stress. Christ.

He broke free of his thoughts and returned to the desk. 'Okay, can you get him taken to the Radcliffe in Oxford?'

'Oxford?' Declan frowned, exhaling slowly. 'That's hardly standard procedure. Can I ask why?'

'We have specialists there and I'm thinking this is related to two other cases.'

'Fine.' Declan cheeked his computer. 'I'll get a transport to take him. Be there by lunchtime.'

'Thanks. I'll call ahead to DI Thompson to let her know to expect him.' Corcoran focused on Palmer, scribbling furiously, then on Jason. 'Okay, Constable, I need you to show me where this happened.'

## *[10:24]*

Corcoran pulled up at the roundabout, indicating left, and waited for the traffic to clear. Up ahead, the pier glowed in the morning gloom, the Victorian-era clock out of place with the modern tat. The sea was a grey smudge, only differentiated from the sky by a thin line of blue on the horizon. Couldn't be France, could it?

'Five months . . .' Palmer leaned back, her pen resting for over a minute now. 'Can you imagine?'

'Can't even begin to. So, assuming Matt is a third known victim, he's managed to hold three victims simultaneously for almost two weeks.'

'That's all I can think about. The sheer horror of what they've gone through, and for what?' She looked round at him, eyes wide. 'I can't fathom a reason. In all this noise, I can start to see the how and the what, but I still don't have a why. We're still miles away from a victimology. And it terrifies me, Aidan, chilling me right down to the marrow. If I can get hold of a motive, we might be able to stop it, but there's just too much I don't know, too much I can't grasp.'

Corcoran cut into the traffic and set off along Marine Parade. 'It's just an assumption, though. Until we—'

'Come on, Aidan. He was held in a cell like the other two.'

She was right. Of course she was right. 'But there were only three cells, right? That's what Howard saw. Meaning they're all empty.'

'They might've been refilled.' Palmer shut her eyes. 'And he might have another site with more victims.'

Corcoran drove on, scanning the seafront bars and road signs. There. 'Could it be related to the sea? Howard was taken from a beach, Matt returned to near one.'

'It doesn't seem important to me, aside from potentially connecting some dots.'

Corcoran took the left between an old hotel and a refurbished pub, then trundled up a narrow street, the wheels rattling over the cobbles. 'But it could be, right?'

She went back to writing in her notebook. 'I need more data to do a geographic profile.'

'Assuming this is another case, is that enough of a pattern?'

'Well, possibly. They've all been abducted from somewhere near their homes, and dumped . . . Well. Sarah was left somewhere quiet and remote, but the other two have been in towns. But even Sarah's location wasn't so remote that someone wouldn't find her quickly enough to get medical attention or police assistance. The timings are all over the place, though. October, January, late February.' She sighed. 'Until Matt's awake and I can talk to him without danger, we won't be able to connect him definitely to the other two.'

'But in your heart of hearts?'

'Are you asking what my hunch is?'

Corcoran shrugged. 'I get a feeling deep in my gut. Maybe it's just Ockham's razor, you know—'

' "Entities should not be multiplied unnecessarily." ' She gave him a thin smile. 'That's the original text from William of Ockham, a Franciscan monk. But you're referring to "when presented with competing hypotheses that make the same predictions, one should select the solution with the fewest assumptions". Or do you mean—'

'You know exactly what I mean.' Corcoran pulled up

behind a squad car. 'But either way, we've got way too many assumptions.'

'Agreed.' Palmer got out onto the street, still clutching her notebook.

Corcoran locked the car and followed her. 'You getting much out of all that writing?'

She stopped outside a pub, eyebrows raised. 'I'm capturing raw data. I'll hopefully get some insights later.'

'Can I add my hope to your bonfire?'

A squad car pulled up. 'There you are.' Jason hopped out onto the street. 'This is my partner, yeah? Ali, this is DS Corcoran and Dr Palmer.'

A woman stood in the doorway of the Mucky Duck pub, wearing skin-tight jeans and a Public Enemy T-shirt. Her long hair hung loose. 'PC Alison Davidson.' She shook both of their hands, but looked as tired as the rest of them. 'You think this is connected to that case up in Witney?'

'That's what we're trying to ascertain.' Corcoran gave her a shrug. 'So, can you—'

'Supposed to be my day off. That man last night . . . Hasn't Jay told you?'

Corcoran saw some nerves in her eyes. 'PC Wilkinson said that, before he took him down, this Matt was—'

'Jay told you that?' She laughed, then shook her head at Jason. 'You're a sweetheart, Jay, but you're a lying git. I twatted the bloke with my baton. Poor Jay here got a face full of . . . Well.'

Jason was blushing. 'They didn't need to know that, Ali.'

But she was laughing, hand covering her face. 'Should've

seen his face. Geezer was naked as the day he was born.' She giggled. Her face was red and her eyes were filled with sleep.

Corcoran exhaled slowly. 'Did you hear him mention cages or cells?'

'Right. Something about how he didn't want to get put back in a cell. Stuff about drowning?'

'Did it seem like he'd been in prison?'

'No. It was like someone had trapped him.'

Jason was nodding. 'That's what I told them.'

'And you're not wrong.' She yawned again. 'I mean, the guy was in a *state*. No idea what the drowning was about, mind.'

'What happened after that?'

She puffed out her rosy cheeks and stared back down the street towards the pier. 'Well, we put him in the back of the car and Jay took him into custody.' She waved at the pub. 'I got a statement off some of the drinkers in there.'

'They see what happened before?'

'Never found the guy who called it in, if that's what you're getting at.' She frowned at the pub over the road, on the corner with a main road. 'The 999 call had someone outside for a smoke, saw this cab pull up. Then that naked geezer jumped up, got himself a knife from somewhere.'

'Any idea where?'

Alison frowned. 'Oh, wait a minute.' She reached into her pocket for her flip-top notebook and scanned through it. 'Far as I can make out, the geezer ran into that boozer there.' She waved at the Blue Man pub over the road. 'He ran around a bit, grabbed a bread knife off the counter where they, y'know, cut bread? Then he came back out before the bar staff could get at him. There was a taxi idling on the pavement there. Sounds like he tried to take the taxi, but the driver was having none of it.'

'You spoke to the driver?'

'Yeah, called him this morning, but he's taking a family up to Gatwick. Be back about lunchtime.' She frowned. 'He did say he'd been waiting for a few minutes, usual story when a fare isn't where they're supposed to be when they're supposed to be.' Her frown deepened. 'He said he saw a bloke lurking around the corner, like he was watching for someone. But he got into a big van and drove off.'

Palmer looked up, her eyes twitching.

Corcoran stepped close to her and spoke low. 'Could that be our guy?'

'I'm not sure.' She went back to her notes. 'But it's someone we need to tie.'

'To what?'

'T-I-E. Trace, Interview, Eliminate.'

'Right.' Corcoran chuckled, then turned to Alison. 'Are you back on duty?'

'I'm off to bed. I mean, if you need me, give me a call . . .'

'One of you.' Corcoran held out a business card. 'I need you to send me all of the CCTV from round here.'

Jason didn't take it; he rolled his eyes instead. 'Good luck with that.'

'Excuse me?'

'Few weeks back, this bunch of bloody students – *woke* as hell, anarchists or whatever – dismantled all the security cameras round here. Pending trial, but that doesn't help you, does it?'

Very fortunate. Or worse, that their guy knew and had used it to his advantage. 'What about banks? ATM machines have cameras that—'

'—have been hit with hammers every time they get fixed.' Jason tugged at his stab-proof. 'Ain't recording nothing. It's a bloody nightmare.'

'Was this in the news?'

'All over the local paper for days.'

Corcoran looked at Palmer. 'He's planned this. Knew there was a gap in the CCTV.'

Palmer nodded as she wrote. 'It's adding to the picture.'

Corcoran looked at Jason and Alison. Nothing more they knew, just needed to let them get on with their days until something else came up. 'Okay, you've been a great help. I'll be in touch.' He handed a card to each of them. 'And if you think of anything?'

'Sure thing, mate.' Jason pocketed it.

Alison shook her head at him as they walked off together.

Corcoran stared down the street towards the seafront. Cigarette smoke caught on the fresh breeze. 'So what now?'

'You're asking me?'

'This is your wheelhouse.'

Palmer smiled as she pocketed her notebook. 'Well, we have a few options, but I think we should visit London and speak to Matt's friends and family.'

Corcoran felt a jab in his hip, like it had just happened. The crunch and grind. The searing pain, the breath squeezed out of his lungs. 'You don't think we should focus our attention around here?'

She frowned. 'Aidan, are you okay?'

'Of course. I'm fine.'

'Well, it's just . . .' She was frowning at him. 'Aidan, we've got three *possibly* linked cases. Six sites. Three abductions, three releases. We've only seen five of them.'

He ran a hand down his face. 'Do you want to drive?'

# Twenty-eight

## *[Palmer, 11:31]*

Palmer kept it an even seventy, nothing above or below. She touched the gearstick to check it was still in sixth. The giant screen hanging above the motorway read *M25 1 mile.* No traffic warning, which was a blessed relief. 'Do I keep on the M23 or take the M25?'

No response.

She looked over at Corcoran, staring at his phone. 'Aidan?'

'A cold day in hell when you'd consider taking the M25.' He pocketed his phone and looked out of the passenger window. 'But that day is today. Three-car pile-up outside Croydon blocking the route north.'

'Okay, thanks.' She eased into the slip road for Heathrow.

'Wrong lane.' Corcoran waved ahead of them. 'Take the Dartford route.'

She didn't see any other lane until the road scissored and a second M25 lane appeared.

'Not so much *Driving Miss Daisy*, as Miss Daisy driving . . .'

She looked over at him as she traversed the chevrons into the east-bound lane. 'What's that supposed to mean?'

Corcoran let out a sigh and let go of the handle above the door. 'I'm just a crap passenger, that's all.'

'Is this about London?'

He paused, his lips twitching. 'Is what?'

'You don't want to go, do you?' She slowed up as the slip road doubled up, but kept to the left lane and followed the curve round, the oncoming road bending to almost meet them. 'As soon as we got the call about Rugby or Devon or even Brighton, you were off like a shot. Now it's London and you're very hesitant?'

He didn't say anything.

She kept an eye on the left wing mirror as another lane swept in, and she let a pimped-up Mini get ahead of her. 'Come on, what's going on?'

He looked over, then away. 'It might not be our Matt, that's all.'

'You're right, it might not be.' The three busy lanes of the M25 encroached on her view, a long red truck and a longer NHS lorry blocking her access to the road. She kicked down and hit eighty as she swept in ahead of the first, then let the engine slow them. 'But we've been erring on the side of a connection.'

Corcoran sighed.

'Aidan, something happened to you in London, didn't it?'

He looked over at her, nostrils wide, eyes narrow. 'Have you been checking up on me?'

'I want to help. Something's obviously bugging you.'

But he just shook his head and stared out of the window. 'We should get something to eat soon.'

# *[12:40]*

Palmer pulled up under the railway arches in east London. A train trundled east out to the Essex coast, another heading back into the city. She let her seatbelt ride up and looked over. 'So this is your old stomping ground?'

Corcoran took the last bite of his sandwich and stuffed the wrapper into the bag. 'You not hungry?'

'I'll have mine in a minute.' She got out into the street and the stale London rain. 'I did my undergraduate degree here. Well, other side of London was where I lived. White City, if you're being generous, Shepherd's Bush if you're not.'

'You know most people don't add "undergraduate" to differentiate.'

'Well, I do.' She led the way down the street, bustling with pubs, chain restaurants and upmarket shops. The old Spital-fields market on the right had been renovated, looking like it had been rebuilt from scratch. 'So much change.' She stopped outside the chip shop and soaked in the smell of vinegar and beef fat.

'Oi oi!' A squat man swaggered towards them, carrying the air of a Jack-the-lad, or at least someone who thought he was. A careful haircut, sharp suit and shiny shoes that had somehow avoided being splashed by rain. Might as well have had *London cop* tattooed to his forehead. 'Corky, as I live and breathe. Surprised to see you again so soon, matey boy. How's your bollocks?'

'They're both fine last I checked.'

'Yeah, in the shower this morning, you filthy bastard.' He

held out a hand for Palmer, accompanied with a wink. 'DS John Diamond. Real pleasure to meet you, darling.'

She shook it with a smile. 'So you two know each other?'

'We've had some dealings over the years, shall we say?' Diamond smirked at Corcoran. 'Yeah, let's just say that.'

Corcoran gritted his teeth. 'I just want to get down to basics, John. Find out what happened here.'

'You seriously think this is related to that naked bird out near Oxford?'

'Maybe.' Corcoran sighed. 'And that "bird" has a name. Sarah Langton.'

'Still a touchy git, then.' Diamond barked out a laugh. 'Have you really found Matt Gladwin alive and well?'

'We believe so. Turned up in Brighton, naked, trying to chop his arm off.'

'Christ, Corky, you sure get all the shit luck with shit cases.' Diamond sniffed and rubbed his nose. 'Anyway, I reacquainted myself with the case. I mean, I got my extra stripe not long after.'

'Congrats.'

'Should've been a DS years ago, but some pillock kept blocking it, didn't they?' Another sniff. 'Anyway, Matt's a husband and father, lives way out west in Hammersmith. Partner in an estate agent over that way. Kid's done well for himself. Plays Sunday league football with his old mates. His last known movement was leaving the pub. He'd played fives with the guys from the office one Wednesday night. Ninth of October. Third match back since his kid was born.' He pointed at a bar down the street. 'Few jars in there, then he called his wife on his way to the tube.' He pointed in the opposite direction. 'Only, she never heard from him again, did she? Called us.' He set off. 'Come on, mate, better if I show you.'

Palmer followed them, trying to add some notes despite the teeming rain. 'You said Hammersmith, and yet he was out here?'

'That estate agent business covers most of London, darling. Best fives pitches in all the boroughs are out here.' Diamond pointed at the new towers at the end of the road. 'Geezer was walking down to Aldgate East tube. District line takes him virtually door-to-door. We checked his Oyster card, his bank cards, you name it, but nothing belonging to him was swiped that night.' He stepped over to the traffic island in the middle of the road. 'Even looked at station CCTV in case he'd jumped the barrier. I mean, stranger things have happened, know what I mean?' He set off again. 'Again, no dice.' Over the other side of the road, he pointed back at the Ten Bells pub. 'This street was hell back then. Full of roadworks. Reckon that's how they did it.'

Palmer looked up from her sodden pages. 'Explain.'

'Hide in plain sight, darling. Whole road was blocked off from seven at night till six in the morning. Ton of vans and work gear around. No witnesses anywhere near the road. Least, nobody that came forward.' Diamond checked his watch with a frown. 'Soz, better take this.' He reached into his pocket for a swish smartphone and set off.

Corcoran watched him go, then looked round at Palmer. 'You got any ideas?'

Her notebook was a damp mess, and her head was worse. She traced the path from the pub down towards the tube station. A man walking alone at night, wearing a suit, his sweaty football gear in a bag, slightly tipsy but desperate to get home to his wife and his new son.

And someone took him. In plain sight. Enough pubs and restaurants to give a ton of witnesses now. The road being blocked off might change things, make it easier to snatch someone. Possibly the best opportunity to abduct someone in London, east or west.

'It fits our guy's MO.' She looked over at Corcoran. 'Coupled with Howard seeing his name, I think it's incredibly likely we have a third case.'

Diamond sauntered over, hands in his pockets. 'While you pair argue the toss, I'll take Matt's missus and his dear mum out to this hospital in Oxford. That okay with you?'

Corcoran looked relieved at the prospect of getting away from London.

# Twenty-nine

## [Corcoran, 14:45]

Corcoran powered along the hospital corridor, leaving Palmer trailing in his wake for once. Through another door and back into Dr Yadin's office.

And that prick Diamond had beaten them.

Corcoran knew they shouldn't have gone along the river, but would Palmer listen?

And God knows who'd approved Diamond's promotion to sergeant. Jesus wept.

He sat with a mid-twenties woman who cradled a screaming baby. Dark hair, an aggressive fringe skirting her eyebrows, but the terrorised look of someone struggling with a young baby and the trauma of a missing husband.

As ever, it looked more like Diamond was trying to pick her up than doing his job. He spotted Corcoran and came over with a cheeky grin. 'What kept you, Corky?'

'Take it that's Matt's wife?'

'Jen Gladwin. And that's baby Oscar screaming his head off.' Diamond shook his head. 'Why anyone would have kids, mate . . .' He grimaced. 'Oh, sorry. Touched a nerve?'

Corcoran barged past. 'Mrs Gladwin, I'm DS Aidan Corcoran and we're—'

'I know who you are.' Jen wrapped her son over her shoulder to burp him. Red lines crawled across her tired eyes, her expression switching between exhausted vacancy and outright aggression. 'Have you caught who did this to my husband?'

'We're working on it. Can I call you Jen?'

'That's fine.'

Corcoran took the seat next to her and kept his focus on her, trying to build trust. 'We think your husband's abduction is possibly linked to another two cases.'

'That woman in Witney?'

Corcoran nodded. 'And another in Rugby. I need to know—'

An older woman blustered through the door, carrying the air of royalty. Tall and elegant, though late fifties if a day, a Cruella de Vil streak through her hair worn like a badge of honour. She cast her gaze around the room and settled on Diamond. A nod and he was over, dealing with her every whim.

'That's Melissa.' Jen glared over at her. 'Matt's mother.' Her expression softened as she waved. Jen looked back at Corcoran. 'It's definitely him, you know. The doctor let me see him and . . .' She slumped back in the sofa. 'Jesus Christ.' Tears filled her eyes and she stared into space.

The baby started crying again, joining in with his mother.

Corcoran offered Jen a hand. 'Do you mind if I take him?'

She gave a slight shake of the head.

Corcoran took hold of the baby, rocking him gently, running a smooth hand down his back. 'He's a nice kid.'

Jen just raised her eyebrows.

'Oh, Jennifer . . .' Melissa swanned over and wrapped her daughter-in-law in a tight hug. She accepted Corcoran's offer of her grandson with a coy smile. 'How's my beautiful boy?'

She made cooing sounds. 'How's my ickle baby boo?' She stuck her nose against his belly. 'You're still my lovely smelly boy, aren't you?'

Jen gritted her teeth. 'Does he need changing?'

'No, he's fine, actually. For once.' Melissa cradled him and kissed his forehead. 'DC Diamond was going to take us to the cafe.'

'Don't you want to see your son?'

'Of course I do.' Melissa ran a reptilian tongue across her lips. 'But I'd rather see the police doing their jobs. I'll defer my full reconciliation until after you catch the vermin who's done this to my boy.'

Corcoran held her glare. 'Mrs Gladwin, it's been a long time. You should see your son. It might help us. Might open something up.'

Melissa seemed to consider it for a few seconds. 'Very well.' She walked over to the doorway, then stared up at the ceiling. 'Oh, Matthew.' A solitary tear slid down her cheek. She had to adjust Oscar as she nudged her cheek clear. 'I try to . . . All of his life, I've tried to give Matthew the best of things. To give him the best start in life. And these last few months have been beyond intolerable . . . There was *nothing* I could do. Nothing. He was out there, somewhere, with absolutely nothing I could do. Nobody I could speak to, or influence, or leverage or . . .' A deep sigh, her face filled with a mix of fury and fear. Then her expression settled back to her previous mask. She nodded at Diamond and marched off, tickling her grandson.

Jen struggled to haul herself up.

'You need a hand?'

'I'm *fine.*' Jen set off towards the doors, bouncing off the walls as she went. She gave Corcoran one final look. 'Find them.' And she was gone.

Palmer was talking to Dr Yadin, their voices low.

Corcoran joined them. 'It's okay, they've gone.'

'That woman will be the death of me . . .' Yadin snorted. 'As soon as she heard Matt was on his way here, she was on the phone to the trustees, trying to get him moved to her private hospital. Won't accept that this is the best place for him.'

'So how is Matt?'

'Come on.' Yadin led them to the room between Sarah's and Howard's, and looked through the window, criss-crossed with security wire.

Matt still looked at peace, his head on a crisp white pillow, the bedsheet tucked up to his armpits. He seemed sedated now. And the lights were off, just a faint blue glow from the side.

'We believe that Matt has been subjected to sensory deprivation.' She rubbed the glass to indicate his feet, raised up at an angle. The soles were puffed up and ragged. 'His feet are swollen in a way consistent with being immersed in water for a significant amount of time.'

'Water?' Palmer looked round at Corcoran, eyes wide. 'Is this what he means by drowning?'

'Has he been waterboarded?'

Yadin shook her head. 'I mean immersed in a tank of water. The way we've got the lights. He can't cope with anything brighter than a smartphone on the lowest light settings. He screamed on the way here as they drove through the midday light. The paramedics had to stick a mask on him.'

Corcoran held her glare. 'Sensory deprivation . . .'

Yadin brushed him aside, pushing herself between Corcoran and Palmer, and gestured at his arms. 'He has bonds on his wrists, much like Sarah's, but it looks like his have born weight. And while Howard was subjected to sleep deprivation and extreme noise torture for twenty-four hours a day, it was for a short period, but Matt . . . I genuinely think he could've been in a sensory deprivation tank for five months.'

'Has he been starved?'

'He's lost weight, certainly, but nothing like Sarah. He's lost enough to be weakened, making him easier to control.' Yadin inspected her tablet computer. 'From the biometric information in the MisPer report, I've calculated a diet of roughly thirteen hundred calories a day. But he's been drugged like Sarah.'

'You didn't tell us that.'

'I told DI Thompson and I assumed she'd tell you. Sarah had been administered a minor dose of Rohypnol, which doesn't persist in the blood, but we found traces on her skin where it must've spilled. Similarly with Matt, but in his hair, which appears not to have been truly immersed.'

Corcoran nodded slowly. 'Can we speak to him?'

'I need to check with the specialist. Just a sec . . .' She walked off.

Corcoran leaned against the wall and looked at Palmer. 'I'm so tired of waiting.'

'I'm just tired.'

'This seems like another victim, would you agree?'

She snorted. 'Look, Aidan, there's someone who can help us. We've got more data now to do a geographic profile.

Three discrete data points still might not allow for more of a connection, but it just could.'

Corcoran gave her a noncommittal nod.

'I'll need your help.'

He sighed. 'Why?'

'Because you're a cop and you might be able to throw some new light on the subject.'

Yadin returned with a sigh. 'Okay, you can speak to him, but watch out. He was very violent with the nurses when we brought him in.'

Palmer hung back, sucking in deep breaths.

Corcoran waited for eye contact. 'You okay?'

She nodded. 'After you.'

Corcoran opened the door and stepped into Matt's room. He stood at the end of the bed and his feet looked even worse up-close. Puffy purples mixed with dark reds, and they stank of the bitter tang of infection.

Matt looked up at him, dazed and confused, barely focusing. 'You're the cop, aren't you? Saw you in the other cell, didn't I?'

'That's correct.' Corcoran inched up the bed, but kept a good distance from him. 'Matt, I want to help find out who did this to you. Are you able to answer a few questions?'

A slight nod. 'You have no idea what I've been through. I can't . . .' He exhaled hard. 'I can barely remember who I am. But that's what he wants, isn't it?'

'Exactly.' Palmer was alongside Corcoran, but further away from Matt. Close enough that Corcoran could smell her shampoo. 'Matt, whoever did this to you probably wanted to send a message. Did they say anything to you?'

'Never.' Matt shook his head, his lank hair flopping against the pillow. 'I mean, one night I'm walking from the pub to the tube. Next thing I know, I wake up in this cell.' He rubbed his wrists, covered in bandages, fresh blood soaking the material and dying it red. 'These chains bit into my skin. You should see how deep the wounds go. How long was I gone?'

'How long do you think?'

'Weeks. Four, maybe five.'

'You've been gone for five months, Matt.'

'Christ.'

'Can you tell us what you remember?'

# Thirty

## *Matt*

Matt wakes up in pitch black. He is wet, soaked through. No sounds, other than the gentle lapping of water. He tries to move but something stops him, something sharp biting into his ankles and wrists. Water slips inside his mouth, tasting metallic. He wriggles but can't move far. The water dulls the sound, but it feels like metal. A chain?

What the hell?

And how the hell did he get here? He'd been playing football, had a beer after, and then what? All he can remember is heading to the tube, talking to Jen on the phone, then hanging up and . . .

What? It was all a blur.

A thumping sound comes from above. Bright light bursts at him, stinging his eyes. He closes them. Someone grabs his legs and he can kick free. A clanking sound and he comes up against another tension, not as tight but still limiting his movement. A shape moves in front of his eyes, and his hands come free. He tries to swing but they're held firm.

Then he is lifted up. Water sloshes and he's carried through the air, splashing and dripping, until he rests on a bed. Still far too bright and he can't open his eyes.

'Who are you?'

No response, just slightly heavy breathing and some more clanking.

'Why are you doing this to me?'

Strong fingers clasp his mouth and pry it open. Liquid hits his tongue, thick, sweet and salty. His gag reflex kicks in but the flow stops. His lips are pushed shut and he fights against swallowing but something closes his nostrils and he can't help but swallow. Then his mouth is forced open again and more liquid pours in. He doesn't fight it this time, just swallows it down.

Then he is let go and rested down on the bed. His eyes are adjusting to the harsh light, but he can only discern the outline of the man leaving the room. The door clangs shut and it sounds like a lock is turned.

Matt tries to sit up, but he's still so woozy. His head feels like it's going to burst. God knows what was in that drink, but—

He convulses. It keeps happening. Some side effect to whatever that bastard is doing to him? Or the desired reaction? Matt doesn't know either way. He takes his time sitting up and takes another look at the deprivation tank. He's seen one before, in a client's dug-out basement in Kensington, but this one isn't high-end Californian technology. It looks homemade; he can see the welding marks.

He tries to move but he is chained down, his ankle and wrist restraints attached to a post in the middle of the room. A few tugs at the chain and he figures out how far he can move, how far the chains will stretch. So he stands up and inches over to the desk, the chains stretching as he goes. He has to brace himself on the tank and take deep breaths. Even through the hellish birth, through helping Jen home, through setting up Oscar in the nursery, he'd kept fit yet here he is, breathing like his old man in his dying days. He goes over to the desk and slumps in the chair.

He finds a thin pile of books. Philosophy. Descartes, Kant, Hume, Bentham, Singer. All writers he knows from college. Moral philosophy. Is someone making a point?

Who's doing this? Someone he's screwed on a property deal? He can't figure it out. All is fair in love and war, even in property conveyancing. Everyone he's done over, they've done it back to him. And all of his clients are happy.

Aren't they?

He picks up the first book and opens it. *Utilitarianism* by John Stuart Mill. He should know what that means, but his brain is all fuzzy. Something to do with maximising happiness, even if it causes misery to a small minority.

Is that what was happening here? His suffering is for the greater good? How the hell is that right?

The door clicks and clunks open. He tries to turn to look but he's too slow. Those meaty hands grab him again and lift him clean off his feet. He is as weak as a kitten and can't fight back.

*Splash* and he is back underwater, bobbing in the tank, gasping for breath. A firm grip on his left leg, then he is pulled back. A chain tightens on his left ankle, then the right. He tries slapping out, but his arms are locked in place.

He reaches some sort of equilibrium, floating in the tank. Then the lid shuts and he is back in darkness.

Matt is dropped on the bed. Can barely move now. Been so long. He doesn't even fight as the thick liquid is poured into his mouth, sucking like a newborn on a bottle, like when he stayed up playing games on his Nintendo Switch, while he bottle fed—

He lies back on the bed and lets out a frustrated sigh. He's forgotten his son's name.

Isaac?

Scott?

Ollie?

Aaron?

What the hell is it? He can remember all the options, just not the decision they made.

He struggles to see his face now. How long has he been trapped here? Weeks? He'll be—

How old is he?

He hears music playing somewhere. A TV theme tune, one he'd put on to help his son go to sleep. *Charlie the Seahorse.* Christ, he can remember a stupid TV show but not his own son's name.

The door clanks shut.

Matt knows he needs to stop this. And he knows how.

He pushes up to standing. His knees ache but he gets there. His muscles have atrophied from inactivity. But weakness is there to be overcome. He shuffles over to the tank and braces himself against it for the final time. The dank water swills around, smells like an open sewer. He dunks his head in through the opening.

The chains pull tight and jerk him back. He pushes against them but he can only put his chin in the water.

Can't even drink it to poison himself.

Can't even drown himself.

# Thirty-one

## *[Corcoran, 15:05]*

Corcoran shifted forward in his seat. 'Were you like that all the time?'

'No. For the first . . . I don't know. Three months? I was in a room. Had a bed. A desk. These books. I mean, I read them. Philosophy. Weird stuff. I did law at uni, but I was always into that stuff. But it made me question my own exist-ence. Kant will melt your head if you let him. But the last while, I was in the tank all the time. Until just at the end.' A tear slid down his cheek. 'I . . . I can't remember who I am.'

'Did you see anything else of him?'

'I was facing away from the door so I never saw him arrive, but . . . every day at the same time, he forced me to drink something. He blindfolded me.'

'That was it? No food?'

'Right.' A frown twitched on his forehead, then spread to his eyes and nose. 'The water tasted funny, like off milk. It was thick, like sea water.'

'You said you heard music coming through the wall.' Cor-coran stepped closer to Matt, praying he was right. 'Do you know what it was?'

'*Charlie the Seahorse.*'

Corcoran looked round at Palmer. Another link in the chain connecting the cases. Definitely a third, shared victim. Probably in the cell next to Howard.

'My niece loves the tune. Jen's brother's kid. Every time me and Jen babysat Chelsea, she'd insist on watching it. This was before . . .' He frowned deeply, paining himself. 'Before we had . . .' Another frown. 'What's my boy's name?'

'Oscar.'

'God, I forgot my son's name.' A mangled cry crept out of his lips, stuck between panic and despair. 'I tried to recite it, but somehow it became Ollie or Aaron. I'd never call my boy either of those names and I got so angry with Jen for calling him that.'

A sharp pain dug into Corcoran's wrist.

Matt had hold of him, twisting, bending Corcoran's arm against the way it should go, pushing him down to his knees. 'Why did you do this to me?!'

The door clattered open and a huge male nurse burst in. He grabbed Matt's shoulders and got him to release his grip.

Corcoran stood up again, clutching his aching arm.

Dr Yadin was in the room now, a syringe primed and ready.

Corcoran got in her way. 'Wait.' He focused on Matt, fresh pain jabbing at his wrist. 'Did you see any other cells in there?'

Matt looked hard at him for a few seconds, then seemed to recover himself. 'Can't remember. Heard lots of noise.'

'Hammering?'

'Charlie the fucking Seahorse!'

'Did you see any other doors?'

'One.' Matt scowled. 'Howard?'

Palmer was nodding. 'What about any others?'

'Nothing.'

Yadin pressed the syringe into his upper arm.

Matt watched her inject, all the violence draining out of him, then he swung round to look right at Corcoran. 'Wait . . . As I was taken from the place, I was out of it, my head was swimming. But I saw the other doors. One had Howard on it, but the one in the middle . . .'

Corcoran nodded. 'Go on?'

'The name had been removed.'

# Thirty-two

## [Palmer, 15:45]

Palmer pulled up and let out a groan.

Up ahead, a crowd had built up round an anti-austerity protest, blocking the road towards her old college. Upended boxes formed a makeshift stage, bookended by giant portable speakers just about louder than the diesel generator belching out fumes, the harsh stink mixing with the smell of falafels from a stall and marijuana from half of the crowd. A man and a woman were singing on the stage, her strumming a guitar, him hitting a tambourine almost in time. 'Which side are you on, boy? Which side are you on?' That old anti-war standard, Palmer's uncle's favourite song, now used to protest the war on the poor.

'What's the groan for?' Corcoran was in the passenger seat, texting someone on his phone. 'Thought you'd be against austerity?'

'I am, it's just . . . Come on.' She got out onto the street, the stiff breeze as firm as an embrace.

Corcoran took about thirty seconds to haul himself out of the car.

'Are you sure you're okay?'

'It's my bloody hip.' He grimaced, letting her see through his mask for once. 'It's giving me no end of hassle today.'

Palmer set off, dropping a fiver into a bucket, and pushed her way through the throng towards the college entrance. 'What happened?'

'Long story.'

'Aren't they all?' Palmer stopped by the lodge.

Dorothy the porter had a colleague with her and they were backed up by some rented security goons who looked like the sort Palmer would usually have helping her in a secure hospital. She flashed her ID and Dorothy waved them through without a second look, her attention focused on the dreadlocked couple dancing a few feet away, taking turns to bite each other's lips.

Inside, the quad was lined high on all sides, the patchy lawn not quite surviving through the harsh winter. And right in the middle of the grass, stretching out like she was basking in Mediterranean sun rather than in the darkness of an Oxford quad, was Professor Zoe Wilson. Eyes shut, meditating.

'What the fuck?' Corcoran stopped dead, jaw clenched, nostrils wide.

'Aidan, she's just meditating.'

'It's not that, it's . . .' He took another look at Palmer, then set off. 'I'm leaving.'

Palmer raced off after him and grabbed him just by the lodge door. 'Aidan, what's up? Are you okay?'

Corcoran wouldn't look at her. He just stood there, fists clenched, shaking his head. Couldn't even speak.

Palmer had seen a hidden side of him, the impossible drive to save people, to pile pressure on himself so that he could catch the villains. The hero complex that seemed to weigh him down.

But there was something else to this, something about Zoe. 'Do you know her?'

Corcoran glanced back into the quad; Zoe was still unaware of their presence.

'Aidan, she's the foremost expert in the field. She can help us find whoever's doing this.'

'Anyone but her.' He flashed a smile. 'I'll wait in the car. Good luck.'

She grabbed his jacket sleeve and held him there. 'Aidan, I need *your* help as much as hers.'

He took his time turning round, still bowing his head. 'You don't understand.'

'Try me.'

But he either didn't want to or couldn't.

'Aidan, I've taken a back seat until now. You've driven this case so far, while I've just collected data. Now it's time to turn that data into intelligence.'

'I'm not stopping you.'

'Aidan, if it's just me in there, we could miss something. Your brain isn't wired like mine. There's usually something us academics either ignore or overlook, something trivially obvious. You know we need help tying our shoelaces.'

That made him laugh.

'So help me tie my shoelaces. Please.'

Corcoran took a deep breath and let it go slowly. 'Marie, I can't be in the same room as her.'

'Tell me why. Help me understand.'

He looked right at her, fragile and broken. 'We worked together. I was a lead detective on a serial abduction case, not a million miles from this one. She was the profiler.'

'Oh no.' Palmer felt a stab in her gut. 'Ross Murray?'

'Him.' Corcoran stared up at the arched ceiling above them. 'Murray picked up and raped women, then progressed to killing them. I had a suspect and I was sure it was him. But Prof Wilson, she fucked up royally. She argued against me, went behind my back to the SIO, my boss, got him to listen to her theory.'

'You were a DI?'

'Took a demotion to come out here. Can do without all the hassle.' Corcoran leaned back against the wall and laughed. 'Frying pan into the fire, though, and I don't even get compensated for this bullshit.' He stared through at Zoe, still cross-legged, fingers steepled in front of her. 'So *her* geographic profile showed a home location of Brixton. My boss made us focus on that as a base of operations. Trouble is, Ross Murray lived in fucking Norfolk and commuted to south London every morning for work, where he committed the crimes.'

'Was he on your radar?'

'Interviewed him myself. He gave us fake alibis, which I didn't believe but they checked out. Your mate and my DCI had a different suspect who lived in Brixton, so Murray was kicked to the side. Then two women turned up in Norfolk, walked into Thetford nick, claiming they'd been captured and had escaped. Their timelines were all over the place, and Ross Murray's alibi still covered it. So they released him.' He bit a nail. 'Trouble was, Murray waited until they were released from protective custody and killed them. I found the first in Islington, dead. Then I caught him murdering the second out in Mile End.' He rubbed at his side. 'Got into a stupid chase with him and injured my hip. That's the least of it, though.' Another glare back at Zoe. 'She caused the deaths of two innocent people. If my boss had listened to me instead of her, they'd both still be alive.'

Palmer took her time digesting the story. 'Thanks for sharing with me.' She gave him a warm smile. 'I know how hard that must be.'

He nodded without looking at her.

'But you can't punish yourself for not saving everyone, Aidan.'

'No . . .' Another long sigh, one that didn't take much pushing. 'But I can punish myself for letting myself get fooled into trusting the wrong person.'

'Doesn't mean you shouldn't trust anyone.' Palmer stepped closer to him, trying to make it impossible for him to avoid her gaze. Even so, he still managed to. 'Look, I know what Zoe can be like. She was my PhD supervisor. We've had our run-ins, don't get me wrong, but I don't see any choice here.' She waited for him to look at her again. 'I've got your back, Aidan. I don't play games. I want the same thing as you, to catch whoever's doing this to those poor people. I need to stop him, bring him to justice. Then I'll help him.'

Finally, he smiled. 'Back to that?'

'I'll never let go of it. But we need to work with Zoe. Play devil's advocate all you want, Aidan, but at least play.'

Corcoran looked at her, a hard edge in his eyes, then he walked over to Zoe. He stood on the grass a few feet away.

Zoe looked up at Corcoran, blinking in the light, her red hair glowing. 'Aidan?' She raised herself up without using her hands, in one fluid movement. 'Aidan Corcoran?'

He grimaced. 'Not often you see a professor meditating in the open.'

## [16:03]

Palmer took a seat in the office. 'Well, at least you've tidied.'

Overnight, Zoe had cleared her floor of books and filed them away, though there were still several stacks around the floor near the door. While it freed up a lot of space, the room still needed a deep clean. Dust danced around in the light breeze from the open window.

'After your midnight visit, Marie, I decided the mess was obstructing my flow. But it takes so much time. I kept having to pick up and examine every second book. Half of them I've either not read or just dipped into, so I've got a *lot* of reading to catch up on this summer. I simply had to meditate to clear my head.'

Corcoran stayed standing. 'Can we get started?'

'Ah, of course.' Zoe walked over to a giant map of the south of England pinned to the wall. Contoured, with colour-coding marking out cities, rivers, forests, long dashes separating the counties. She stuck a sheet of paper to the wall, filled with chunky handwriting, then started sticking red pins into the map. 'These are our abduction sites.'

Devon in the south-west, Cambridge in the north-east, then east London almost due south.

She stood back, hands on hips. 'Do you see anything?'

Corcoran shrugged. 'Pretty far from a straight line.'

'I don't see a pattern.' Palmer grimaced. 'Unless we're missing other victims.'

Zoe nodded slowly. 'As it stands, that's a random distribution. Cambridge to Exmouth is over two hundred miles, right?'

Corcoran's turn to nod. 'I checked it last night. Two hundred and twenty-seven miles by road.'

'Okay, well that very randomness implies that he's probably targeting his victims by some non-geographical means.'

Corcoran narrowed his eyes. 'Explain?'

'He isn't luring people into a trap. Instead, he's attacking them. Your lack of obvious connections implies there's a deeper one, which we just don't see yet.' Zoe looked back to her sheet of handwritten notes. 'Marie's assumption is that these abductions are precisely navigated points in the flow of the victims' days. For example, the spot where Sarah was taken is a CCTV blindspot.'

'Same story in Brighton.' Palmer checked her notebook again. 'The release site was in an area of damaged CCTV cameras. Well publicised, so it was common knowledge. Also the abduction site in London was during night-time roadworks.'

'We're getting ahead of ourselves here.' Zoe gave a curt smile. 'The varying torture methods suggest meticulous planning.' She took another set of pins from a tub on her desk. 'And there's a long gap of time between abductions. Matt in October, Sarah in January, Howard in late February.' She paused, frowning. 'But the releases . . . There's no cooling-off period like you would expect with a serial killer. He's released all three over three days. Monday morning, early Tuesday morning, then Tuesday night just before ten. Thirty-four hours apart, give or take.'

Corcoran stared at his watch. 'What does that mean?'

'As per Marie's second assumption, this is someone working to a mission. Like the abductions, his release schedule is clearly planned. Evenly spaced and drawing attention to what he's doing, yet he hasn't taken credit for it. Don't you think that's curious?'

'Look, this is all stuff I could get from Dr Palmer. You're not adding anything to our case.'

Zoe ignored him and started sticking blue pins in for the release sites: Witney over in the west, Rugby further north and closer to the middle, then Brighton down on the south coast and south of London. 'Again, quiet locations, correct? No eyewitnesses?'

'Almost.' Palmer joined her by the map and pointed at Brighton. 'A drinker spotted someone here.' Then up at Rugby. 'A man attacked Howard when he was released. In both cases, there was a van.'

Zoe wasted no time in going on the attack, looking over at Corcoran with *that* look. 'Have you got detailed witness statements?'

'Not from Brighton yet.' Corcoran kept his cool, training his focus on the map. 'These things take time. The Rugby one was a kid.'

Zoe's smile showed she was taking that one as a victory. 'Looking at the release shape, it's possibly a diamond centred around Buckinghamshire.' She swept her finger across the map, hovering over the county. 'That could be his home.' She looked around the area, her smile broadening. 'It gives a sufficient geographical scale over which he could operate. Or it could be a moving location.'

Corcoran stepped away, yawning as he checked his phone.

'Well, I'm doubtful of that.' Palmer looked at the shape again, trying to have faith in Zoe's method. She pressed her finger into the area south of London, the chunk of M25 they'd sped around earlier. 'Assuming it's a diamond, the fourth point would be somewhere between Croydon and Sevenoaks.'

Zoe was nodding vigorously. 'That's a possible release site for another victim. It'd fill the right side of the diamond.'

Corcoran looked up, rolling his eyes. 'But it could be a kite shape. Or the first few prongs of a trident . . . Or whatever a twelve-side . . . thing is called.'

'A twelve-sided polygon is a dodecagon.' Zoe beamed wide. 'And you're talking about a regular one.'

'Whatever. This feels far too cute.'

'*Cute*?' Zoe chuckled. 'I could point out seven cases where that *cuteness* is the exact scenario. People are unimaginative and follow unheeded biases in these situations.'

Corcoran pocketed his phone and folded his arms. 'We've still got nothing, though.'

'No.' Zoe's eye twitched. 'The map shows that he's a commuter.'

'He's doing this for work?'

She held up a finger. 'A commuter is the technical term for someone who travels into the area they're targeting. In a German study, they showed that abductors who drove tended to travel six times as far from their home sites as those who walked.'

'They're hundreds of miles apart! Even I could've told you

our guy's driving!' Corcoran laughed. Then his forehead tightened and he frowned at the map for a few seconds. 'The car . . .'

Palmer joined him, trying to follow his gaze as it darted across the map.

He tapped on the map on the eastern edge of Buckinghamshire. 'Yesterday morning, I visited a site where the SUV possibly used to release Sarah was found. A VW Tiguan. Thing had been stolen and was burnt out.' He tapped the map again. 'It was just outside Amersham in Buckinghamshire.'

'That lends more credence to Bucks being a possible home base.' Zoe stuck a pin in and stared at it for a few long seconds. 'And if it's there, then he's either got an accomplice to collect him or he walked from that site.'

'Meaning he's left a trail.' Corcoran set off towards the door but stopped. He turned and nodded at Zoe. 'Thanks.' Then he left.

Zoe's shoulders slouched.

'It's okay.' Palmer gave her an encouraging smile. 'Him even being here means a lot. And that could be the lead we need.'

'Part of me hopes I'm wrong, and your guy isn't kidnapping someone else from Buckinghamshire. But that part still wants you to catch him.'

# Thirty-three

## *Dawn*

The train's rhythm is a familiar sound now, the repeating loop of the wheels against the tracks just like the *Doctor Who* theme. It weaves round a bend and I chance another glance at him. Big guy, muscly arms, almost a whole carriage away. He stands up and slips on his black biker jacket, then heads over to the door.

I get out my phone and hit dial. 'Hey, Caz, it's me. I'm starving. Could you stick the oven on?'

'Sure thing. You just about home?'

I look out of the window and see the familiar sights of home. Sure enough, the announcement speaker chimes. 'The next stop is Princes Risborough. Next stop, Princes Risborough. Thank you for—' The rest of it is lost to the hubbub of people packing up and getting ready to leave. Stowing away laptops and designer headphones.

'I'll see you soon. Bye!' I put the phone away and swap my second high-heeled shoe for a trainer, then get up and walk over to the door. Another glance at him, phone out, texting someone, listening to his headphones. Music? A podcast? Maybe an audiobook?

My cheeks flush with the wine after work and I'm feeling a bit weak. Too much sugar in that wine.

The train slows, the force tugging at me as I brace myself. Outside, the darkness gives way to a long platform and the train slows to a halt. The door chimes and I release it, then hop off and set off along the platform, following the crowd up and over the bridge to idling cars and taxis.

I power on past, weaving in and out, still not at the front yet but not far. Up and round the bend, past the shop.

He's not there today. Michael, that friendly homeless guy. I hope he's okay, that he's getting whatever help he needs, but part of me wonders if he died during the night.

Jesus.

I set off again and the crowd thins out, people taking side streets and I can't help but think about Michael. What the hell is wrong with me? I should find out where he is. He's sat there every day for the last six or seven months, his little dog at his feet. Took me a week to speak to him at first, but it soon became every day. He told me about his time in Iraq, his difficulties afterwards. I never let him get too close, but I still worry about the guy.

I turn into my street and stop dead. There's a burst water main, foamy liquid sluicing everywhere. Men in yellow jackets and hard hats out working. Vans and lorries parked up. The road's blocked off, a uniformed cop stopping traffic.

Someone bumps into me from behind. 'Sorry, love.' The fit guy from the train powers past, his phone to his ear. 'Steve, mate, what's up?'

I follow him along my street, watching his bum in those tight jeans.

'Yeah, mate, sure thing. It's not a problem. No, it's cool. All fine, all good.' He stops to speak to the cop, pointing at a house past mine. 'Live along there, mate.' He gets a nod and the baby policeman gives him a smile and a thumbs up, then he charges off.

The cop barely looks at me. 'On you go, love.' He's more interested in the cars.

I set off after him, absolutely powering home, eating up the distance and listening to his call.

'Yeah, mate. Has to be this evening, though. Can't do tomorrow.' He slips down a side street and I lose him.

At the corner, a workman in a digger blocks the path to home. All the upper floors are dark, the lower ones mostly blocked by curtains. The workmen are focused on controlling the chaos. I nod down the street and the workie keeps a gap wide enough for me to pass through. I close in on my house, keys out. A wave of relief hits me as I put the key in the lock.

Then an arm snaps around my throat, something covers my mouth and I'm pulled off my feet. Someone hauls open a van door. My knees hit something wooden and I go down, face against metal. I try screaming but my mouth's still covered.

The van door slides shut and my arms are pinned to my back. Something jabs my neck and I kick and scream and try to lash out but everything's going numb. I hit the wooden floor and can't get up.

The door slides open then shut again. Seconds later, the engine growls into life and I try to scream again but everything goes black.

# Thirty-four

## *[Corcoran, 16:24]*

Corcoran stood outside the college, clutching his phone. 'Alana, if you let me—'

'Aidan, I—'

The protest band were dismantling their stage but the crowd still lingered, trying to keep their message alive for as long as they could. The local cops in standard formation didn't look too impressed with the delay.

He tried to put some distance between him and the clattering. 'Ma'am, I just can't hear you.'

'Aidan, I've told you, call me Alana.' He could hear the smile in Thompson's voice.

'That's better.' Corcoran leaned against the wall. The austere colleges seemed to be closing in on him.

Palmer walked out of the college, looking as though she wanted to talk.

Corcoran held up a finger to Palmer, one minute, then turned away. 'We're working on the assumption there could be another victim. We've done some geographic profiling, giving a possible location of Buckinghamshire.'

A few seconds of muffled speech. 'Why there?'

Corcoran felt himself shrug. Involuntary. 'I'm not the

biggest fan of profiling, as you well know, but there's a pattern to the map that . . . Well, it could be anywhere, but it's convincing. Their theory is that him burning the car was a mistake and he's let slip the fact he's based in that area.'

'And what do you think?'

Corcoran blew air up his face. 'This is mostly based on some arcane mumbo jumbo, but I'll give Palmer the benefit of the doubt on this. Until now, we've been focusing on there being no pattern, just a series of senseless, random acts. But the more of them we find, the more we can potentially draw information from. We might be able to find the next victim in Buckinghamshire, I don't know.'

'Christ, you almost sound convinced.'

'That burnt-out SUV was the clincher. It's possible he walked home from there or went somewhere he could easily get home from. Where are we with that?'

Thompson muttered loudly to someone in the background. 'You think it's near where he lives?'

'Assuming he burnt the car, yes.'

'Or he could have an accomplice.'

'Either way, it's information. Do I need to follow up with the local taxi firms in Amersham to find out if someone stinking of smoke got a lift?'

Thompson sighed. 'I'll have to call you back.' Click and she was gone. Always the same with her.

Corcoran took in the sights and smells, trying to process everything before he faced Palmer. The more he thought about it, though, the more it fit together. Or was that just him hoping it did? Making him as guilty of seeing patterns in the fog?

'You okay there, Aidan?'

Corcoran looked round at Palmer and let out a breath he didn't remember holding. 'Thanks.'

Her forehead creased. 'What for?'

'That was the right thing to do.' He waved up at Zoe's office. 'We're searching where we dropped our keys rather than where the light is.'

She smiled, but soon the frown was back. 'I know how hard it was for you to trust Professor Wilson.'

'I still don't.' His turn to smile. 'But I appreciate that she might be useful. This could help us. Could be a disaster, too, but you were right to try it.'

'Aidan, about that case. If you want to talk to someone about your experiences, then—'

His phone blasted out. Thompson.

'Better take this.' He put it to his ear. 'What's up?'

'Oh, Aidan, I swear I sent your not-so-little mate Butcher to visit Amersham looking for the taxi companies, but Pete can't find an update on HOLMES. Got seven there and three in Chalfont St Giles, just down the road.'

Corcoran ran a hand through his hair. 'We'll head there now.'

'Wait a minute, Mr Postman. Are you and your crazy doctor actually going to do some proper work?'

He spoke quietly. 'You brought her on the case in the first place.'

# [17:25]

Vic's Cabs had clearly seen better days, but whether anyone alive could remember them was doubtful. The place made run-down seem like a lofty aspiration: a front door that didn't seem to shut, a bell on the counter that clunked instead of ringing, and a disgusting odour of decay that hung in the air.

Palmer hit the bell and it clunked again. They could barely hear it themselves, so how could anyone through the back? 'How many is this?'

'Third of seven cab firms.' Corcoran looked for a gap in the partition, but it wasn't obvious how you got through. A phone started ringing on the desk. 'Then there's Chalfont St Giles. Isn't that slang for—'

'Checking taxi firms is just us validating an assumption.' Her expression brightened. 'And excluding them is critically important to our mission. It can add grist to our mill.'

'Add what to—'

The door juddered open and a middle-aged man in a cardigan darted through, chewing a bacon roll, a half-smoked cigarette wedged behind his left ear. He scowled at them as he answered the phone. 'Vic's Cabs, Vic speaking.' He mouthed: 'How can I help?'

Corcoran showed his warrant card.

Vic groaned. 'Sorry, love, he should be there any minute. Give me a call back if he's not there in five minutes, yeah? Cheers!' He hung up and rested against the partition. 'What?'

'Charming. I need to—'

The bell above the door chimed and a cabbie slouched in,

slurping through his own bacon roll. 'Vic.' He eyed them suspiciously.

'Trev.' Vic leaned forward, eyes on Palmer. 'What's this about, then? Pair of coppers coming in here. I ain't done nothing.'

'Then I'm very pleased for you, sir. I just need to know if any of your guys had a passenger on Monday night who smelled of smoke.'

Vic stood up tall and took a deep breath, like he was inhaling mountain air. 'There was that one fella, now you mention him. You had him, Trev?'

But Trev was gone, the front door slowly swinging shut. The bell rang.

Corcoran followed, racing across the car park and catching Trev as he got into his cab. 'Sir, need a word.'

Trev stood up tall and picked at his teeth with his tongue. Fraying jeans, lime-green T-shirt that'd seen more than its fair share of washes, and the overpowering stink of breath mints. 'What about?'

'What he said in there that made you try to run away from us.'

'You're imagining things, mate.'

'Sure about that? Vic seemed pretty sure you had a fare who stank of smoke.'

Trev let out a deep sigh. 'Mate, I've got a code of conduct, okay?'

'A code of conduct?'

'I never talk to the police about a fare.'

'I wonder if your code of conduct might be waived for a case where this guy abducted three people.'

Didn't seem to be. Trev went back to picking bacon from his teeth.

'Of course, I could start looking into your background. Maybe *you* burnt the car. Maybe you're just helping who did.'

'Desperate, ain't you?' Trev laughed. 'You can look all you like, mate, I ain't done nothing.'

'We just need to find out what we can about your fare on Monday night. That's it. You tell us, you can go about your day. Get another fare.'

'And how am I supposed to know this is legit? Could be this fella just looked at one of you all funny, and you want to throw him down some stairs or whatever.'

Corcoran stepped forward. 'Sir, let's have this word down the nearest station, shall we?'

'I ain't going nowhere without you arresting me. I know my rights.'

Corcoran's phone blasted out again. He reached into his pocket for it. Thompson.

Trev laughed. 'Saved by the bell?'

Corcoran bounced the call, then took a slow breath while he tried to calm the hell down.

But that let Palmer jump in. 'Sir, I'm a criminal psychologist working with DS Corcoran on a serial abduction case and I assure you this is all above board.' All it did was make Trev fold his arms. 'Sarah Langton was starved until she almost died. Howard Ritchie was subjected to sleep deprivation and extreme noise torture. Matt Langton was kept in a solitary confinement tank for over five months.'

It seemed to pierce Trev's bubble a touch. But he looked away. 'Code of conduct, love. Sorry.'

Corcoran shared a look with Palmer, caught sight of an inner rage boiling away in there. She dealt with psychopaths and psychotics and whatever else the terminology was, but this Trev was something else. He stared hard at him. 'Listen to me. It's very possible that—'

'Whatever.'

'Don't you whatever me. Are you telling me that you're happy for a serial abductor to kidnap and torture people?'

Trev sniffed.

'We'll strip you of your licence. You know as well as I do that it's conditional on you having a duty to report—'

'Fine, fine, fine. I had a geezer stinking of smoke. Can't remember much about him. It was all dark.'

'Where did you drop him?'

'Princes Risborough, if memory serves. I've got a note of it in my cab.'

'On you go.'

Trev huffed out a sigh and got in.

Corcoran kept a watch on him in case he shot off. 'Think that's our guy?'

'Princes Risborough would certainly fit.'

'I should call—'

Corcoran's phone rang. Thompson again. 'I'd better take this. Keep an eye on him.' He walked off and answered it. 'Boss, sorry but I'm—'

'Aidan, shut up.' She was running, her heavy feet slapping off concrete. 'I've just received report of an abduction in Princes Risborough. Right in the middle of Buckinghamshire.'

# Thirty-five

## *Dawn*

My mouth is gagged, tight. I can't move it. I feel like I've died. My head is thumping, worse than the worst hangover, worse than when I forget to—

My vision swims in front of me. I see two of everything, then four, then back to two. I blink hard and see one thing. Finally.

And I have no idea where I am.

In a van, maybe. The rumble of the engine drowns out the radio playing quietly in the front. There's a mesh panel separating the front and back. Enough to see through, but I can't breach it. Outside, the yellow glow from the streetlights catches an urban fox rooting through a bin. Whoever is driving is wearing a mask, I think.

We've stopped.

I push up to standing. Looks like we're in an industrial estate. He gets out and leaves the van idling.

I try to budge the door but it's locked. Or the mechanism isn't working, or it's blocked from the outside.

The door slides open and a bitter wind rattles through me, making me shiver as the cold crawls all over me. A man stands there, dark eyes scowling through the holes in a balaclava. I have no idea who he is.

His giant hands grab my arms. He lifts me off my feet and puts me over his shoulder but I'm too weak to punch or kick, even to slap. He keeps hold with one hand as he opens a tall gate. A piercing shriek calls out into the night and he walks through. No other nearby lights, no cars, nobody around to hear the banshee cry. No hope. He shuts the gate behind us and powers on, his footsteps virtually silent, carrying me like I don't weigh nine stone. We pass stacks of ruined cars piled high and I realise we're in a scrapyard. Across the way, his van sits next to a pile, looking to the untrained eye like it's going to be stripped for parts.

In the distance, the gentle curve of the hills is caught in the harsh moonlight, the stars in the sky almost lost in a town's glow. A full moon, but I don't know what hills they are. Could be a million miles away; could be just outside town.

He stops by a hut and puts me down. Looks empty; not even a puff of woodsmoke. A tarpaulin flaps in the breeze. A car passes on the road, a few hundred metres away and too far to hear me, even if I could make a noise. He opens the cabin's door with a clang and lights flicker on. He steps inside and closes the door with a resonating metallic clunk, then carries me over to a concrete ramp and down a spiral into a basement.

He sets me down, but he's behind me and I can't see him in the soft light. 'Do you know where you are?'

Three doors, all open. Inside, harsh lights, brick walls, low ceilings, stripped beds. Cells. Prison cells.

I shake my head. I'm starting to hope this is a mistake, that he's got the wrong person.

He nudges the middle door shut. Midway up, there's a nameplate: DAWN.

Panic hits me like a wall. No mistake. It's me he's after. The gag puffs as my breath speeds up.

He pushes me over the threshold into the cell and I topple onto a bed. Whatever he injected me with, it's *brutal*. He tears my gag off.

I roar out a scream. 'You sick fuck! Why are you doing this?'

He just stands there, listening to my scream. Doesn't even laugh at me.

'I'm diabetic!'

No reaction from him. No acknowledgement, even.

'You hear me? I'm diabetic! I'll die if I don't get my insulin!'

He runs his fingers against his palms, licking his lips. 'I know, Dawn. The clock's ticking.' And he slams the door.

# Thirty-six

## *[Palmer, 17:54]*

Corcoran drove, one hand casually resting on the wheel, most of his concentration on the case rather than the road. The first knockings of Princes Risborough hurtled towards them, worn-out houses stealing the countryside's scrubby fields.

Spiders crawled up Palmer's forearms, puckering the flesh. 'This can't be another victim, can it?'

'Of course it can.' He looked over at her, then back out of the window at the town centre, upmarket boutique shops lining the streets. 'Whether it is or not is another matter. Princes bloody Risborough . . . bang in the middle of Wilson's diamond. Hate to admit it, but this location fits with the others. This could be his home, or near it. And it could be a million miles away.'

'Don't you think picking his home town to enact another crime is strange?'

'You mean, "Don't shit where you eat"?' Corcoran looked over, blushing. 'Sorry, force of—'

'It's okay, Aidan, I can swear with the best of them.' She smiled to reassure him. Kind of touching, in a way. 'But you're right, assuming you mean he's thus far put off committing a crime here because it's close to where he lives.'

'Why make that shape with his release patterns, though? Seems like a rookie error.'

'People are people. They make mistakes.'

'You think this is his?'

She held up both hands, her fingers crossed.

Grinning, Corcoran pulled into a street engulfed in absolute bedlam. Workmen struggled to fight a raging torrent foaming up from a burst water main. A squad of police officers got in their way, moving the traffic away.

Corcoran parked and got out of the car, charging over before Palmer could remove her seatbelt.

She caught up with him, speaking to a tall woman with horse-riding hips, dark hair tied in a chunky ponytail.

Corcoran was putting away his warrant card. 'Dr Palmer, this is Sergeant Broadribb.'

She held out a hand. 'Call me Steph.'

'Palmer.' She shook it. 'Marie.'

'Okay, so I was just telling your partner here' – Steph thumbed at Corcoran, but neither he nor Palmer corrected her assumption – 'that one of the emergency workers saw a man abducting a young woman.' She put her fingers round Corcoran's neck. 'He attacked her, grabbed her by the throat and shoved her in the back of his van.' She let go of Corcoran and waved at a narrow lane set between some post-war houses, lit up by arc lights. 'He reversed down that lane and that's the last they saw of him.'

Corcoran nodded slowly. 'You need to identify the victim and find that van.'

Steph shot him a glare. 'You think I don't know that?'

She shook her head. 'Got half of Thames Valley out knocking on doors.'

'And?'

'Well. We've drawn a blank so far, but . . .' Steph walked over to a squad car. She pulled out a rugged laptop and rested it on the roof. 'I'll check CCTV.'

'A good plan.' Corcoran gave her a warm smile, but Palmer saw his impatience, his fingers drumming his trouser legs. He focused on her. 'Snap judgement?'

'Well, it might be the right place but, assuming it's him, he's changed his MO.'

'You mean letting himself be seen?'

'Right. I mean, Sarah and Matt were abducted in similar locations.'

'Hoi!' Steph was waving at them, beckoning them over. 'Okay, so I've got access to the local CCTV feed. Two of my guys are scouring through this back at base, but I suppose I could show you, if you ask nicely?'

Corcoran rolled his eyes. 'Pretty please with sugar on the top and chocolate diamonds.'

Steph smiled, then let them see the screen and hit play.

The camera had views along another street, probably the one backing on to this. The sky was lighter and the flood of water was a lot worse, with yellow-vested workmen fighting a seemingly losing battle. A van slipped out of the side lane and drove along the street, before disappearing out of shot.

Corcoran's shoulders slumped. 'That's it?'

'Don't know what you expect?' Steph shrugged. 'We can't find it arriving and my lads have been through hours of footage already.'

'Can you run the plates?'

'Oh shit, why didn't I think of that?' Steph rolled her eyes at him. 'There's something masking the plates, some sort of reflective coating.'

Corcoran groaned. 'Can I ask you to get your lads on CCTV duty to focus on other cameras in town? Cash machines, shops, red-light cameras, anything. Start at this time and this location, then fan out. There might be a shot where we can read the plates.'

'I'll get them to have a look, but only if you stop being such a dickhead.'

Palmer left them to have their power play and walked over to the lane.

Assuming it was their guy's van, which seemed likely given the plate obfuscation, then it was very similar to the other three. And the CCTV search hadn't been entirely futile. The absence of the van's arrival indicated that it'd been waiting to whisk the victim away. To where, though? And to do what with her?

And who the hell was she?

'You think it's him?'

Palmer turned to nod at Corcoran. 'Well, I'm certainly beginning to suspect that. But it's incredibly unlikely he'd use his own van for this, don't you think?'

'Agreed. But it bears all the hallmarks.' Corcoran sighed. 'Most of them, anyway. Let's take it a step at a time, okay? Do the basics and see where that takes us?'

'Hoi!' Steph jogged over to them, her ponytail dancing behind her. 'One of my lads has identified her. Dawn Crossley.' She pointed at a house behind her. 'Lives in a flat upstairs.'

# [18:07]

Exactly like Corcoran expected any young woman's shared flat to be. Beige paintwork, neutral furniture, and the oppressive smell of perfume. A red velvet sofa covered in pillows and throws, and two fully stocked wine racks, mostly supermarket whites.

'You think she's been kidnapped?' Dawn's flatmate, Caroline, wouldn't sit down. Couldn't sit, by the looks of it, her wiry frame fizzing with energy. She ruffled her spiky hair. 'I mean, really?'

'Well, we have a witness statement suggesting someone was abducted.' Palmer raised her hands. 'But whether it's Dawn is an assumption.'

'Jesus.' Caroline bit her lip, then set off again, walking around the small living room, shaking her head. 'Jesus Christ.'

'It might not be her.' Corcoran joined Palmer on the sofa, easing himself down slowly. 'Can you take us through the last time you heard from her?'

Caroline stopped her frantic pacing. 'Okay, so she called me on the train, asking me to put the oven on for her.' She put a hand to her forehead. 'But she never showed up. And I've been going frantic since.'

Palmer got up and patted the sofa. 'It might help if you sit down?'

'There's no way . . .' Instead of sitting, Caroline leaned against the window, looking out at the chaotic mix of workmen and police officers. 'I mean, if someone's taken her . . . Dawn? Why?'

'Well, it might be something entirely unrelated.' Palmer rested a hand on Caroline's forearm. 'She likes a drink, right?'

Caroline cast a guilty look at the wine racks. 'Who doesn't?'

'I'm asking if it's possible she could've met someone after work?'

'She did. Went for a glass of wine with some girls she works with.'

'Locally?'

'Dawn works in London, commutes in by train.' Caroline finally sat, perching on the edge of the sofa. 'Goes out with them every Thursday. Wine o'clock, they call it. Usually ends up on the last train, hammered. It's a struggle to get her up at six on a Friday, I tell you.'

'But it's Wednesday?'

'Right. She said they had a swift half after work tonight. Not unusual, if that's what you're getting at.'

'How well do you know her?'

'Went to school together. She grew up in Princes Ris. My parents moved us here from Birmingham when I was twelve. Dawn was a good friend to me, helped me settle in and, you know, we've been mates ever since.'

'Caroline, can you think of any reason why someone would do this? Ex-boyfriend, maybe? Stalker? Anyone angry with her?'

'Not really.' Caroline got up again and started stomping around, her heavy footsteps thudding off the bare floorboards. 'Feels like there's something you're not telling me. What is it?'

'Well, it's just if there were any secrets she had. A reason someone might think she had a "hidden" life?'

'What?' Caroline stabbed a finger in the air at her. 'You can't come in here, you know, and . . . and . . .' She collapsed onto the sofa and started sobbing.

Palmer shared a look with Corcoran. She waited for Caroline to meet her eyes. Took almost a minute. 'Is there something?'

'We . . .' Caroline brushed at her eyes. 'We're not just housemates. We're girlfriends. Lovers. In love.' She shut her eyes. 'I mean, she still flirts with guys and . . . guys flirt with her, but she says it's just sport. She's playing with them. Or so she says . . .'

Palmer tried it on for size. A secret lesbian. In 2019? It was hardly a motive. 'Who knows about you?'

'My folks do. Her mum.'

Corcoran frowned. 'And her dad?'

'He's . . . a difficult guy. Hard to talk to. Set in his ways and all that. I mean, we can legally get married and have children and it's really none of his business, but . . . he could never accept his only daughter being gay.'

Palmer still didn't buy it as a motive. 'Have either of you ever had any hassle about your sexuality?'

'What do you mean?'

'You know there have been a spate of hate crimes, right? That couple assaulted on the night bus in London, that kind of thing.'

'Princes Ris isn't that sort of place. I mean, it's a bit fuddy-duddy, but they don't lynch people here any more.'

'Has Dawn ever mentioned a Sarah, a Howard or a Matt?'

'Not that I can think of. I mean, she works with a Sara, but that's without the h, you know. Sah-rah, not Say-rah. Howard or Matt?' She exhaled slowly. 'Nope.'

'You're sure?'

'Positive.'

'Is there any other reason that someone could target Dawn?'

'Not that I can think of.' Caroline bit her lip again, cracking her ruby lipstick. 'The thing is, Dawn's diabetic. Type one, from childhood. If she doesn't get her insulin tonight, she'll *die*.'

# Thirty-seven

## *[Thompson, 18:29]*

Thompson parked her Passat outside the Crossley house. One of those houses you'd get anywhere in England. So normal, so average, so beige. She could see right into their living room from the road. Another normal evening, him in his La-Z-Boy clone recliner, legs up on the footstool, reading glasses plonked on his forehead. She was on her sofa, the other side of the room. Glass of wine in their hands, the half-empty bottle on the coffee table between them, acting like a demili-tarised zone. TV blasting out, rotting their brains.

David and Lesley Crossley, with no idea what was just about to hit them.

Thompson opened her door just as the local police car arrived. The uniforms got out into the thin rain. Both tall, but the lad was all skin and bones, his chunky partner about ten years older.

'Well done, lads.' Thompson led them towards the house. 'I've driven from Oxford and I still beat you.'

The older one spoke. 'Sorry, ma'am. It's Alfie Stringer.'

'Well, Alfie, you can call me Ala—. No, actually, ma'am's fine.' She opened the garden gate and set off down the path.

Lesley was in the window, looking out at the commotion,

cupping her wineglass in her hands. Frowning, squinting, wondering why the police were outside her home at half past six. She set the glass on the windowsill and started fussing with her hair.

Thompson stopped by the door. 'You want me to deliver the news?'

'I'll do it.' Alfie the alpha cop puffed out his chest and gave the standard policeman's knock. 'Show Kieron here how it's done.' He waited, steeling himself, adjusting his hat until it sat perfectly. The thin rustle of distant traffic whispered over them.

The door opened and Lesley frowned out. 'Can I help?'

'Sorry to call so late, Mrs Crossley, but—'

Lesley slapped a hand to her mouth. 'Oh, my heavens. What's happened? Has my mother had another fall?'

'We better do this inside.'

'Okay.' Her frown deepened but she let them in.

Nice place, every inch of decor considered and carefully implemented.

Lesley showed the cops into the living room. David rocked forward on his chair, turning off the television and sinking the last of his wine. Alfie was holding his hat respectfully now, though Kieron wasn't, and he politely nodded at David. 'I'm afraid we've got some bad news about your daughter, Dawn.'

The news dropped like a bomb. David stared at the floor, dumbfounded, confused. Lesley got up and paced the room, looking like she urgently needed to clean or cook or something.

Thompson tried to blend into the background, staking out the room as they talked and soaked up the news.

The wood-burning stove pumped out heat below a mantelpiece dotted with tasteful picture frames, bookended by digital ones, both cycling different sets of shots. She stepped over to the window and the rain hammering the glass.

A car sat there, two spaces away from Thompson's car. A man behind the wheel, glancing at the house, lost in a phone call. Another car shot along the street, driving way too fast, and parked opposite.

Corcoran got out first, followed by Dr Palmer, arguing about something. Some theory they'd got, some nonsense she was *positing* but he was disagreeing with. Like an old married couple already. So sweet.

The other car drove off slowly.

Thompson pulled the curtains.

# Thirty-eight

## *[Corcoran, 18:36]*

Corcoran pressed the bell and waited, peering through the fracture-patterned glass but seeing only a dark hallway. 'Surely they're still in?'

'There's a light on.' Palmer stepped onto the gravel drive and inspected the bottle of insulin Caroline had given them. Half-full, but it looked enough to Corcoran's untrained eye. 'I thought your colleagues were supposed to be here?'

A car drove off, something dark and low-slung.

Palmer pocketed the drug and reached over to press the bell again. 'I've been thinking. If this is our guy,' – she held up a finger – 'and that's still a big if, then your "don't shit where you eat" theory could mean he's getting closer to home.' She looked round, fear in her eyes. 'Making it possible this is the last one, the victim he's worked up to.'

Corcoran thought it through but didn't take much hope from it. 'Diabetes is my big worry right now. We've probably got just hours before Dawn slips into a coma. We need to find her and soon.'

A light glowed through the glass and seconds later the door opened.

'DS Aidan Corcoran.' He shoved his warrant card in the

279

young beat cop's face and charged past, his footsteps clunking off the hallway's tiled floor. 'Have you broken the news?'

The lad nodded, struggling to keep up. 'Alfie's just briefing them now, but your boss looks like she wants to take over.'

Corcoran got his sigh out of the way before entering the living room with a curt smile, friendly but trying for reassuring and confident.

Dawn's parents sat on the sprawling sofa, beige and stuffed with cushions. David and Lesley Crossley, according to the file. Mid-fifties, but he was a silver fox. His wife must have borne the brunt of raising their daughter, looking a good ten years older. Maybe she was.

A hook-nosed uniform stood by the ornate fireplace, his gear at least a size too small for his bulky frame.

Thompson leaned against the windowsill, the curtains scrunched up behind her. She gave Corcoran a look that read, *I'm very interested in seeing you make a pig's arse of this.*

'I'm Aidan.' He smiled at the parents. 'I'm here to help find your daughter. We have a large team out combing the area for her. I gather my colleagues have briefed you?'

David got up and charged over, his face distorted, eyebrows twisted up in the middle. 'You should've found her by now. This is unacceptable!'

'David, you should—'

'I'll do nothing of the sort!' He jabbed a finger in Corcoran's face, not far off making contact, then over at the uniform by the fireplace. 'This one says she's been taken by a serial abductor. Is he right?'

Corcoran glared at the uniform, then looked back at David Crossley with a calming smile. 'That's an avenue we're investigating, but it's entirely possible Dawn has just dropped off the radar. Happens all the time.'

'Say it like you mean it, then.'

'Sir, I understand you're distraught, but this isn't helping us find your daughter.'

David stared him down. Then the violent energy stopped sparking and he slumped next to his wife. 'If anything happens to her . . .'

'I understand, sir. The things we wouldn't do for our children, right?'

He looked up at Corcoran, took his measure, then nodded. 'Right.'

'Now, I understand Dawn has diabetes.'

David nodded slowly, exhaling. 'Diagnosed when she was a kid. Absolutely terrified us at the time. It's a genetic thing. I've suffered all my life.'

'How does she get her insulin?'

'They tried fitting a pump, but it didn't take, so she has her jag every night.' David looked over at the mantelpiece and the brass carriage clock. 'She should've had it by now. Christ.'

'It's possible she has had it and she's out with friends.'

'So who the hell are these friends, eh? And why isn't she answering her bloody phone?'

'Sir, I want to do everything in my power to save her. It's important that we speak to anyone who knows her, okay? Now, is there anyone that springs to mind?'

David looked at his wife, then shrugged. 'I don't know. Sorry.'

'We've already spoken to Caroline.'

David cleared his throat. 'She knows our daughter better than we ever will.'

'I understand.' Palmer perched on an armchair by the window, almost blocking Corcoran's view of Thompson. 'Do you know if Dawn has any friends called Sarah, Howard, or Matt?'

A look passed between Dawn's parents, then they both shook their heads.

Palmer held up her phone, showing Sarah's before photograph, her round cheeks smiling. 'Her?'

More shaking.

Then she showed Howard's photo, him grinning in a wetsuit, carrying his surfboard under his right arm. 'What about him?'

'No.'

Finally, Matt's LinkedIn profile photo, taken at a slight angle, a professional smile plastered over his face. 'And what about him?'

Lesley took the phone from her and stared at it. 'Wasn't he on that property programme on the TV?' She showed it to her husband. 'You know, the one with the woman who's always pregnant?'

'It's not him.' David took the phone and handed it back. 'Sorry. I don't recognise any of these people. Is this who has her?'

'No, sir, these are—' Corcoran's phone thrummed in his pocket. He got it out and checked the display. DS Sortwell. 'Sorry, I better take this.' He smiled at Palmer to take over and left the room. The hallway was lined with old books. First-edition hardback novels, and enough gardening books to cover the average lawn. He put the phone to his ear. 'Alright, Pete?'

'Aidan, mate. I can't find your overtime from last month.'

Corcoran clenched his teeth. 'I'm in the middle of a—' He sighed. 'Are you taking the piss?'

'Yeah, I am.' Sortwell laughed. 'Sorry, the boss asked for an update on your van but she's not answering her phone.'

Corcoran made eye contact with Thompson through in the living room. 'Right, I'll pass it to her.'

'Okay, so my old mate Steph spoke to some curtain twitcher in that street that girl's gone missing from. Mad old coot who looks for strange cars and writes down their plates. Called in this van yesterday morning, but nobody did anything about it.'

'Yesterday?'

'It was in the lane next to Dawn's house.'

Something tingled on Corcoran's neck. 'Take it you've run the plates?'

'That's where it gets weirder. Reported stolen from Buckingham last week. Owner's heading to the station up there to give a statement, but it looks kosher.'

The hairs on the back of Corcoran's neck stood on end. 'The owner probably isn't our guy, but check if he saw anyone around the time. Cheers, Pete.' Corcoran put his phone away but didn't go back through straight away.

That news definitely meant something. A stolen Tiguan and now a stolen van. Someone covering their tracks, someone who had parked the van there, knowing they'd search CCTV for it arriving and not find anything. Masked the plates, even though the van was nicked. More and more, it looked like their guy.

A fourth victim.

He walked back through the living room. The older

uniform stood next to David in the window, the curtains open again, and they looked out onto the street.

Palmer was with Lesley and Thompson by the fireplace, looking at framed photos. 'That's a lovely shot.'

'Oh, David's the photographer, though I'm quite good at framing, I have to say.'

Corcoran joined them.

Lesley flipped open the back of a picture frame and shuffled out a snap of Dawn at her college graduation. 'Oh, that was such a lovely day.' She wiped a tear from her eye and passed the photo to Palmer.

Corcoran looked at the other shots, mostly family photos of the three of them in various locations, ranging from a hike in what looked like the Peak District to a Greek taverna at night. At either side, the electronic photo frames cycled through older shots, snapshots from their youth in the eighties. David in a long greatcoat in the middle of summer, Lesley all Bananarama hair and dresses.

The one on the left shifted to a snap of Dawn's father on his last day of school, big hair flying as he and a group of other teenagers did a collective leap.

Corcoran frowned at it, his neck tingling again. He recognised something in it . . . some connection . . .

THERE.

Next to David was Sally Norton.

Sarah Langton's mother.

# Thirty-nine

## *[Palmer, 18:48]*

'Here.' Corcoran handed Palmer a digital photo frame.

She stared at the screen, showing a grainy and faded photo. Twelve kids jumping in the air, holding hands, loving life.

And it was gone, replaced with a moody photo of David outside a university quad, all floppy-fringed and intense.

Corcoran grabbed the device and found the controls on the back. He flicked back to the previous photo. 'Recognise anyone?'

Palmer immediately spotted David. But next to him . . . A lot older now, but it was very clearly the same person. The same eyes, physique, same intense look. 'Oh my god.'

Corcoran took it over to the window and passed the photo to David, tapping at the screen. 'Who is this?'

David took the frame and held it out at arm's length. 'Her?' He swallowed. 'Oh that's . . .' He clicked his fingers. 'Sally Burford.'

'You know her?'

'*Knew* her.' Another hard swallow. 'We were friends at school. Haven't seen her since . . . Oh, good heavens. 2001? 2002? Something like that. School reunion. Like in that Pulp song. *Let's all meet up in the year 2000.* We missed it by a couple of years, but we still did it.'

'Until now, we haven't found a connection between the victims.' Corcoran pointed at Sally on the photo. 'She is the mother of Sarah Langton, the first victim.'

'My god.' David tightened his grip on the photo frame. 'Sweet Jesus.'

Corcoran got out his phone and walked away from them, back to the fireplace. 'Hi Pete, you still at your desk?' He paused. 'I need the names of Howard Ritchie's parents.'

Palmer joined him.

Lesley stood over her husband. 'David, what the hell's going on?'

'I don't know, love.'

Corcoran turned to Palmer. 'Turns out Tommy Ritchie is Howard's stepfather. Howard changed his surname when his mother remarried.' He looked over at David. 'Does Nathan Barnes mean anything to you?'

David scanned the photo again, then tapped at a kid on the far right, the only one whose legs hadn't cleared the ground when the photo was taken. Wild goth hair like that guy from The Cure.

Anticipation gnawed at Palmer's gut. 'What about Melissa Gladwin?'

'That's Melissa Perry.' David pointed at the woman next to Nathan Barnes, holding his hand as she jumped. 'Does this mean you can find Dawn?'

'Maybe.' Corcoran walked over to Palmer. 'That's our link. One parent of each victim knew each other as teenagers. They may have since moved away, or married and changed names, but they all lived in Princes Risborough at the same time.'

The connection she'd been looking for. Knowing the answer now, it was so obvious. Impersonal torture, followed by release. Indirect attacks that made the parents suffer as much as the victims. Their worst fears coming to life – their children, badly harmed.

All the victims had a parent in this group of friends. Did that mean there were another eight possible victims? Another eight children who had already suffered?

'Who could be doing this?' Palmer handed the photo frame to David Crossley. 'Who would want to take revenge against you all?'

David shook his head. 'I have no idea. I mean, we were just kids there. Bunch of dickheads who thought they knew everything, but in reality knew nothing. Then we went to uni, drifted apart and that was it. Nothing more to say.'

'Are you sure?' Palmer saw guilt in his eyes. She just needed to coax it out. 'Someone has tormented three of these people's children and now they've taken Dawn. And I think you know why.'

David grabbed the half-empty bottle of red and tipped out a glass.

Corcoran snatched it out of his hands before he could finish, splashing some onto the red carpet. 'There are twelve people on here. So far, three of these people's children have been taken, tortured and released. Your daughter was abducted tonight. Do I need to get the other eight's families into protective custody?'

David clammed up, his eyes locked on the wineglass in Corcoran's hands. 'No.'

'Is there something specific connecting you four?'

'David?' Lesley shook his arm. 'David, what the hell is going on?'

He ran a hand across his face. 'Good Christ . . .'

'David, tell them everything you know. *Now.*'

He collapsed onto the sofa, pushed his head into the rest and stared up at the ceiling. Then the tears started, his throat locking, his face screwing tight. 'Oh, Dawnie-Dawn . . .'

'What *have* you done?' Lesley kneeled on the sofa and punched him on the arm. 'What the hell have you *done*!?' Another punch.

Thompson eased her aside, holding her and stopping her from attacking her husband. She collapsed into her arms, sobbing into her shoulder.

Which let Palmer in. 'Mr Crossley, it's important that you talk to us. I know how hard this is, but we need to do everything we can to find your daughter.'

David looked up at her, tears streaming down his face. He dug the heels of his hands into his eye sockets, then blew air out of his lungs, years of guilt or shame erupting in one go. 'Okay.'

Palmer took the wineglass from the table and handed it back. 'Here.'

David sank the glass in one go, then rested it between his fingers, spinning it slowly. 'Sally, Melissa, Nate and I used to hang out as teenagers. We drank and listened to music. Then we started smoking dope. Hash, marijuana, whatever they call it nowadays. The state we'd get into . . .' He laughed, lost to some flight of nostalgia. 'We were all from good homes, good grades and all that.' He gave his wife a nervous look, but really she was the least of his worries. 'One evening, in 1986. August, not long before we all went to uni, we . . .'

Lesley cried in Thompson's arms.

'What happened that night?'

David looked over at Palmer, like he'd just remembered what was happening. That his daughter was missing and it was all tracing back to his youth. 'Where do I start?'

# Forty

## *David*

David sat there, cross-legged, the burning sun on the back
of his neck. Bobbing his head in time to his Walkman as
'The Cutter' reached its beautiful crescendo, his fingers
working double time as he tipped the contents of the cigarette onto the skins, stuck together with saliva. He sparked
his lighter and put the cube of dope into the flame, then
crumbled a good chunk into the joint as the song faded out.
Then the Arabic guitars of 'The Killing Moon' kicked in. He
finished skinning up, closing the joint with another lick. Perfect, even if he did say so himself.

He put it behind his ear and hopped up to standing, shrugging up the collar of his army greatcoat. He caught a glimpse
of himself in a broken van wing mirror, and sang along with
the music, every inch Ian McCulloch on *Top of the Pops*.

Sweat trickled down his back. His shirt was soaked. Wearing a coat like that in August, but he wouldn't listen to his
mother, would he?

Someone tapped his shoulder and he spun round, tearing
his headphones away.

Nate stood there, grinning from ear to ear, looking like a
jumble sale version of Robert Smith from The Cure. His dark

hair stood up, blow-dried and backcombed to within an inch of its life. 'You having fun there?'

'I'm okay.' David cleared his throat. 'What the hell are you doing with your hair?'

No nervous patting or anything. Nate just stood there, shrugging. 'Thought I'd give it a go.'

'Mel seen it?'

'It's my hair.'

David reached up for the joint, but it wasn't there.

Nate reached up to the other ear and produced it like a trick. 'Ta-da!'

'Very funny.' David snatched it back. 'You want first toke?'

'Better if we wait, yeah?' Nate took out a cigarette instead, cupping his hands like a rock star in an *NME* spread as he lit it. 'Should get some grass instead of that crap next time.'

'Can't afford it. I'm saving up to buy a bass.'

'A bass?' Nate exhaled smoke out of the side of his mouth. 'Stop buying those stupid coats then.'

'Says goth boy.'

Nate grinned. 'And here's goth girl.'

Melissa strutted through the scrapyard towards them, thin to the point of skinny. Long black dress, her dark hair wild and flowing.

David let out a sigh. 'I want what you've got with her.'

'Well, hands off.'

'You know what I mean.'

Nate nodded, exhaling again. 'Going to ask Sally tonight?'

David glanced at him, but couldn't hold his look. 'If she turns up.'

'You get nervous, I understand.' Nate clamped his shoulder. 'Just think what would Bowie do? Or Ian McCulloch.'

'Like I'd know *that*.'

'What are you two talking about?' Mel took the cigarette out of Nate's mouth and took a deep puff. 'Where's the joint?'

Nate swiped it out of David's hands and gave it to her. 'You want first toke?'

'Only if you haven't spiked it with something.'

'As if I would.' Nate smirked, and lit the joint for her.

Mel took the first toke, her expression souring. She coughed. 'That's *harsh*, Dave. Where did you get it?'

'Big Mixu.'

'Keep telling Nate we should get some grass. This stuff will rot our brains. We'll be lucky to have kids.'

David muttered, 'Like anyone's interested in having mine.'

Mel nodded at him, as if to ask what he'd said. 'Sally is coming, isn't she?'

David shrugged. 'Not sure.'

'Well, let's go downstairs, shall we? I don't want to get caught with this.' Mel took another smoke and passed the joint to Nate.

David stepped over to the front door of the squat one-storey building. Derelict and out of time. But he spotted Sally walking through the scrapyard. He skipped back down the steps and checked his haircut in the broken mirror. Sweating like a pig now.

Mel laughed. 'Just ask her, you dimwit. She likes you.'

'Okay.' David turned to Sally with a broad grin.

But Sally wasn't alone. A big lumbering idiot walked behind her.

Mel put a hand to her mouth. 'Oh.'

Nate was frowning. 'Who the hell is that?'

'Don't you remember?'

'No.'

'What about you, Dave?'

He spotted the guy. Massive, at least six five and strong like he could tear cars apart with his bare hands. He shook his head. 'Oh no.'

'It's Terry Beane.' Mel prodded Nate's chest. 'That loser everyone made fun of at school. Someone called him Frankenstein's monster.'

David recognised him. The dunce who'd moved to town at the start of lower sixth, who'd spent that year staring out of the window in class. He used to be a streak of piss but he'd filled out a lot since he last saw him. 'Mel, even the teachers used to pick on him.'

'That's probably why he dropped out.'

Terry wore black jeans tucked into those stupid white Hi-Tec basketball boots. A Megadeth T-shirt under a blue denim jacket, covered in Iron Maiden patches.

David's mouth was dry, so he took the joint off Mel and sucked deep. 'What the hell is he doing with her?'

Terry grabbed Sally's hand, and she held it as they approached, only breaking off to hug Mel. 'How are you doing? Haven't seen you in *ages*.'

'Yeah, I'm alright. And it's only been like a week?' Mel frowned at Terry. 'Hi, I'm Mel.'

'Eh, Terry. Terry Beane.'

'Right.' Mel gave Sally a puzzled look. 'Nice to meet you, Terry.'

'Em, I sat next to you in Geography in lower sixth?'

'Did you?' Mel took the spliff back from Nate and passed it to Sally. 'Here you go, you're playing catch up.'

Sally took a toke and sucked smoke deep into her lungs. Then she grabbed Terry in a kiss and blew smoke into his mouth. But she was staring at David all the time.

His sweating increased. Like his heart rate. 'You got kicked out of school, didn't you?'

Terry took the joint and inhaled like a pro. 'I hated it, so I left, mate.'

David took a long hit, struggling not to cough.

Sally took it from him. 'Shall we go downstairs to smoke this?'

Terry frowned at her. 'Em . . .'

'What's up?'

'I'd rather not.'

Sensing weakness, David stepped closer. 'Come on, you can head down there first.'

Terry's eyes widened. 'No way.'

David clapped Terry's shoulder. 'Come on, mate, go down there. It's cool. Used to be a prison in the war or something.'

Terry brushed his hand away. 'Fuck off.'

Nate stepped forward, hands raised. 'Come on, Tez. Just head down there. It's easy. We all go down there.'

'I ain't stopping you, and never call me Tez.'

'What, so you are chicken?'

Sally sighed. 'Nate, back off.'

Nate made a chicken noise.

'Look, I've got a phobia of the dark.' Terry swallowed,

then turned to Sally. 'If you'd told me we were going down into somewhere like that . . .'

She gripped his hand tight. 'It's okay, we can—'

'Mate . . .' Nate spun round, his stupid haircut catching the breeze. 'Oh, come on, Tez, it's a piece of piss. Just go down there, stop anyone smelling that joint.'

Sally pushed Nate away. Maybe being sensitive was the way to her heart.

But Nate kept up his assault. 'Tez, you are such a chicken!' He made squawking noises, jigging his arms like a hen. 'Chicken!'

Mel started laughing, her stoned eyes showing she didn't care about Terry's feelings.

David stayed back, letting it all play out, ready to jump either way, depending on how Sally seemed.

Terry was staring at his shoes, shaking his head. 'Fine.'

'No.' Sally ran a hand across his back. 'It's okay, Terry, we can go to the pub or something.'

'No, I'm fine.' Terry brushed her off and stomped up to the door. He stood there for a few seconds, staring up at the sky. Then grabbed the handle and yanked the door fully open. A long, deep breath, and he stepped inside.

Nate followed him up and stood by the door, blocking his exit. 'Over there.'

David joined him and peered inside.

Terry was over by the ramp, the concrete all cracked, almost hidden in the gloom. He looked round at David with the expression of a scared child. 'This'll do, right?' His deep voice was thin and shrill now.

David looked round at Sally and got an eye roll from her. He saw then that he never had a chance with her. Sod it. He turned back. 'Not even close to being done.'

Terry stared at him, almost pleading. Then he shook his head with a snort and set off down the ramp.

David shut the door and locked it.

Sally raced over and pounded his arm. 'David!'

He let out a hollow breath. 'It's just a joke.'

'This isn't funny! You heard what he said!'

'It's just a joke.' David took the key out of the lock and walked away.

Sally followed, her fists pounding his back.

A thump on the door from inside. Then another. 'Let me out!'

Sally ran over. 'It's okay, Terry.' She tried the handle. 'Wait a minute.'

'Nooooo!' A loud moan roared out. Then a scream. 'Let me out, you fuckers!' Terry's fists pounded the wood, harder and harder.

Nate was in a different sort of hysterics, his face screwed up tight. Mel struggled to keep a straight face as she took another toke of the joint.

'David, for fuck's sake, you've taken this way, way too far!' Sally tried to slap David again but he caught her hand. And held it. 'Let me go!'

He complied. 'Sorry, it's just a joke.'

'No, it fucking isn't. You heard him. Now, give me the key.'

'Okay, okay!' He held up the key, ready to give it back to her.

'HOOOOYYY!' A loud voice tore out, rattling around the area. 'YOU BASTARDS! GET AWAY FROM THERE!'

A wild-looking man raced over from a truck idling by the entrance. Big thick beard, long hair, checked shirt and jeans tucked into muddy boots. 'This is my bastard property and you're trespassing! Clear off!'

'Sir, my boyfriend's down there and—'

'You're smoking them drugs here?' The yokel snarled at them, nostrils twitching. 'I'll call your bastard parents and the police!'

Nate walked over, hands up. 'It's cool, mate. We thought this was a public space and we'll just leave as soon as—'

'Stop it, you little bastard.' He grabbed the joint out of Mel's hand. 'Smoking this filth here?'

The guy backed off, then charged over to his truck. A dog started barking. Maybe even a couple of them. He reached into the back and pulled out a big fuck-off shotgun. 'I have a way with trespassers.'

Even Sally ran, brushing past the raving owner.

Nobody told him that Terry was still in the bunker.

# Forty-one

David pounded through the wood, snapping broken twigs, nettles stinging his hands. Lungs burning, gasping for breath, his coat feeling like it weighed several tons. He stopped and looked back. Mel and Sally ran alongside each other. Nate was last, his face a deep purple. In the distance, lights glowed in the scrapyard. The dogs were barking, the sound carrying all this way.

Terry was still down there and, no matter how much of a prick David thought he was, he didn't deserve that. Nobody did.

Mel and Sally reached him, their faces like thunder. Then lightning flashed behind them, like their emotions controlled the weather. Seconds later rain poured down, thick and heavy.

Nate stopped just behind, then threw up onto his shoes.

'You stupid arseholes.' Sally charged over to David and dug her finger into his chest. 'You're such a selfish dickhead.'

'Come on, this isn't—'

'Shut up!' She pushed him hard and his back hit a tree. 'Have you still got the key?'

David opened his hand and the rusty brass caught the light.

'Right, well you and your fucking arsehole *mate* there are going back to let Terry out.'

'We shouldn't be here.' Nate stopped and pulled his coat over his head. Didn't make much difference – his long hair was plastered down with sweat and rain. 'Let's just tell them we let him go and he ran off.'

'No way Sally's going to buy that.' David peered across the country lane heading back into town, almost flooded in the rain, trying to spot the building. 'Shit.'

The scrapyard owner laughed at something. Another couple of vans were parked next to his, blocking the gate, and two of his mates stood there with shotguns and their own packs of dogs.

David walked over to the fence and tried to spot a way in. 'What the hell do we do?'

'We just leave it. Got to, mate. They've got *guns*.'

'We should call the cops. Get them to free Terry.'

'Yeah, and they'll grass us up.' Nate looked hard at him. 'Mate, Mel and I are going to Oxford in October. No way am I giving that up.'

'This isn't right, Nate. We need to get him out of there.'

'You got a plan?'

'They've not got the key and they'll get bored, right? I mean, eventually. Then we can get him out of there.'

'Are you saying we wait here overnight?'

David shrugged. 'I don't see any other option, do you?'

'Right. Stay here. I'll get something to keep the rain off.'

\*    \*    \*

A nudge in the arm woke David. 'Not sleeping!'

'You are, mate.' Nate yawned as he sucked on the joint. 'Jesus, this *is* harsh.'

David blinked away his tiredness. They were lying in a ditch a few hundred yards from the scrapyard, their umbrellas sodden and the mat soaked through. The darkness was receding, the sun climbing up into the sky, burning through the morning rain, still pouring down. So much for August. 'Anything?'

'Nope.' Nate handed over the joint. 'Here.'

'How can you smoke at a time like this?'

'One, it's keeping me awake. Two, it's keeping me from freaking out about what the hell is happening here. I can't lose my place at Hertford, mate. Dad's been banging on at me since I was five to get into Oxford. He'll kick me out!'

David took a long drag and let the drug work its magic. He stood up and squinted over. The other two vans started up and drove off with a honk each, slightly out of time. 'Nate, look.'

'What?'

The owner walked over to his truck and hopped in, following them off down the road.

'Come on, then.' David led him off, taking it slow, trying to blink away the tiredness, and stopped.

A giant padlock was tied to the gate.

David shook it but it was a forlorn hope.

Through the fence, six huge dogs patrolled the grounds. Dobermans or Rottweilers. Massive snarling beasts, and they still had their balls.

\* \* \*

David knocked on the door and brushed his hair flat as he waited. The number of times he'd imagined doing this, but not under these circumstances. Under this pressure.

The door opened and Sally's mother looked out, her half-moon glasses dangling from her neck. 'Can I help?'

'Hi, Mrs Burford, is Sally in?'

'Sally?' She frowned. 'Well, it's a bit early, but in you come.' She held the door open for him to enter, then looked up the stairs. 'Sally! You've got a guest!' She smiled at David. 'Sally will be but a moment.'

David stood in the hallway, checking out the family portraits. A very stiff family, formal and almost Victorian. And that shot Mr Foster had taken of them all jumping on the last day of school, where Nate missed the cue and was caught on the ground.

Footsteps pounded down the staircase from above, then stopped. 'Oh.' Sally skipped down the rest of the steps and grabbed a hold of his sleeve, dragging him outside into the heavy downpour. 'Where is he?'

David couldn't bring himself to look at her. His mouth was dry despite the rain and he was exhausted from sleeping rough, his adrenaline replaced by hash fatigue.

'Oh my god, you just left him in there, didn't you?'

'You've got to understand!' David looked at her, pleading, but he just felt guilty. 'The gate's padlocked and there are—'

'You're a selfish prick. I should tell your parents.'

'Sally . . .'

'You're such a dickhead. You and Nate. Forget your parents, I'll let the police do that.'

'If the cops . . .'

She raised her eyebrows. 'Oh I know, it'll jeopardise your university places. Pair of spoilt brats.'

'We . . .' She was right. David took a deep breath. 'I'll find a way in.'

'You better.'

David yawned as he pedalled hard, leading Nate down the road towards the scrapyard. Monday morning, still pitch black but at least the rain had stopped. And they were trapped in this impossible dilemma of their own making.

What David wouldn't give to go back to Friday night and not trap Terry in there.

He slowed to a halt and got off the bike. Didn't look like anything had changed. His dad's binoculars dangled around his neck. He put them to his eyes and scanned the scrapyard.

Nate walked towards him, pushing his bike. He dumped his sports bag on the ground. 'You got anything?'

David handed him the binoculars. 'Those snarling mutts are still there.'

'Shit.' Nate tugged at his hair, staring over at the scrapyard prison. 'What are we going to do, mate?'

'I don't know.' David genuinely didn't. It was Monday. He had to work in that bloody factory for eight hours and he hadn't slept since Thursday and Sally was going to the cops and—

'Dave.' Nate nudged him and handed over the binoculars. 'Check that.'

David put them to his eyes. Through the wire mesh, the scrapyard owner got into his van and drove off. David scanned the area again. No sign of the dogs. 'Holy shit, Batman, we're in!'

The owner stopped by the gate and redid the padlock, then they hid low as the van trundled down the lane, accompanied by a cacophony of barking dogs.

'Come on.' Nate reached into his bag and produced a pair of bolt-cutters. 'My old man will go spare if I lose these.' He jogged over to the gate and snapped the padlock. 'Help me.'

It took both of them to open the gate, an almighty screech tearing out into the dawn gloom.

David scanned around in case anyone had heard them. No sign of it, at least. He led Nate, still struggling with his heavy bolt-cutters, and shot over to the building. The front door was still locked, so he slotted the key in. And it turned. One last look round and they opened the door.

No sign of anyone, save Terry.

'What if the owner has found him and taken him away? Like in *Deliverance* or *Scum* . . . but worse?'

'Forget that. Let's search the place. Okay?'

'Right. Right.' Nate clicked on his dad's torch and it lit up the entire room. Their favourite smoking room seemed a lot scarier now, even with torchlight.

David headed over to the ramp and peered down, but his shadow blocked out the light. He started down and it seemed to get darker with each step.

Nate's light scanned around the room, but no sign of Terry.

David's foot splashed in a puddle. He grabbed the light off Nate and shone it around. The entire basement was flooded and he was up to his ankles in silty water.

And still no sign of Terry.

Just the three cells, the doors all shut.

David waded over to them and tried the middle door. It opened.

Terry lay in a ball, sobbing and moaning. He looked up at them and shut his eyes.

# Forty-two

## *[Corcoran, 19:05]*

'By the time we helped Terry out, the kid had been in the dark for over sixty hours.' David stared at Corcoran, his guilty eyes glazed over and not entirely from the wine. 'He was exhausted, dehydrated, starving, cramped, cold, alone, soaking, terrified.' He ran a hand down his face. 'The worst part was his silence. Never said a word.'

'You . . .' Lesley had broken free of Thompson, rage burning in her eyes, fists raised and ready to strike. '*You* . . .'

'It was a joke.' David had his arms raised, ready to block another barrage of punches from his wife. 'Just a joke.' His voice was a whimper.

Corcoran played it through and it all fit together.

Starvation.

Exhaustion.

Solitude.

'Nate and I . . . We said sorry to Terry, begged him not to say anything to the school or police or his parents . . . but he didn't even seem to hear us. He just followed us out and . . . man, the kid was just . . . empty. No other way to describe it.'

'What happened next?'

'Sally didn't forgive us, but she didn't report us either. Probably figured she was complicit. She ran, rather than getting that yokel to let him out.'

'What happened to Terry?'

David shrugged. 'Never really saw him again.'

'Never?'

'Occasionally, he'd be spotted in town. Seemed to be drinking heavily with the wrong sorts. Bikers, skinhead football hooligans, you name it . . . Sometimes just on his own, staggering around town with a bag full of strong cider bottles.'

'Nobody who stayed in touch?'

'Only Sally was ever really in touch with him.' David shook his head. 'But I honestly haven't thought much about him since I left town for university.'

'You sick bastard!' Lesley held out a hand like she was going to slap him. 'He's taken our daughter and it's all your fault!' After a moment she let her arm go. 'I can't believe you.' She rushed out of the room, slamming the door behind her.

'I'll get hold of Sally Norton.' Thompson stabbed her finger on her phone screen as she left the room.

Palmer narrowed her eyes. 'This bunker would be the ideal holding place. The ideal prison. What do you know about it?'

'Other side of town, in the grounds of a scrapyard. It's inside the town now, of course. Nate reckoned the place was a POW camp in the war. Bunch of freaky cages downstairs, which made me believe him.'

'We need to find Terry.' Corcoran had his phone out, dialling. He stared at David. 'Where did you say this bunker is?'

# [19:16]

Still holding his phone, Corcoran got in the car and hit the ignition button. 'Pete, can you really not find a Terry Beane?'

'That's what I said.' Sortwell sighed down the line. 'And you getting angry isn't going to help. Might make me hang up on you.'

The dashboard woke up and Corcoran stabbed the scrapyard postcode into the satnav. Pretty much a straight line. He put his seatbelt on, swapping his phone to his right hand halfway through. Bloody thing wasn't pairing with the dashboard. 'Have you tried Terence?'

'Obviously...' Sortwell sighed again. 'Mate, I've been doing this as long as you have. There are just way too many. Do you have a middle name or anything to narrow it down? His age, maybe?'

'Afraid not. That's all we have. Terry Beane. Terence Beane. Look, dig into it and call me when you find him. I don't care if he's in Timbuktu or Outer Mongolia, I just need you to find him for me, okay?'

'I'll try. Oh, just got a text. Sergeant Broadribb has found the owner of that place and she's heading over there.'

'That was quick.' Corcoran stuck the car in reverse.

Something thunked off the passenger window.

Palmer stood there, face like thunder. She jabbed a finger at him.

Corcoran put it in park and wound down the passenger window. 'I can get someone to—'

'You're not leaving here without me, Aidan.'

'Seriously, Marie.'

She shook her head. 'Where are you going?'

He let out a breath. 'I'm going to check out that old scrap-yard. Turns out it's still standing. Sold off for development, but no work's started yet.'

She tore open the door and sat in the passenger seat, wrapped the belt around her purple coat, dumped her bag in the foot-well. 'Well, I'm coming with you.'

He looked over, but there was no arguing with her. 'Okay, but just stay in the car? Take your notes. Whatever. You're a civilian and I need you to stay out of danger. Deal?'

'Deal.'

He put the car back in reverse and eased back a touch, then swung out onto the street. A few curtains twitched as they rumbled past suburban homes. No doubt about it, there was something going on inside the Crossleys'. Usually the rumours were ten times worse than the truth, but in this case . . .

'Talk to me, Aidan.'

He glanced at her as he pulled up at the junction. 'This is . . .' He felt it in his chest, the tightness, the stress, the pressure. 'You've been talking about your worst fear come to life . . . This is mine. It's so obvious now. How the hell did we not know?'

'You don't think I'm asking myself the same questions? I've got one job and that's building a profile. And it was completely wrong.'

'It's not your job to find the guy, though.' Corcoran pulled off from the junction, merging into the lane the satnav told him, less than a mile to go. 'That's on me.'

'It's on both of us.'

He shrugged. 'Maybe you're right. You can have half the blame.'

She shook her head. 'What are you planning to do at this scrapyard?'

Corcoran hadn't thought that far ahead. His brain was only occupied with immediate tasks. He needed to zoom out, think about it strategically. But where the hell had strategic thinking got them? Nowhere.

He pulled up behind a long line of traffic queuing outside a supermarket. 'Ideally, getting a lead on Terry Beane.'

'He's taking his teenage trauma out on the children of the people who did that to him. Reflecting his torture on their children. Possibly even been watching them, enjoying their torment. The news conferences where Sarah's parents and Howard's father sat next to DI Thompson . . . Feeding off their torment like a psychic vampire.'

'A psychic *vampire*?'

'It's a psychological term, Aidan. Instead of blood, they feed on anguish and sorrow.'

Corcoran sat there, the engine idling. Not far from here, Terry Beane had Dawn Crossley. 'Sod this.' He flicked the siren on and pulled out into the oncoming lane, getting a clear run on the road. 'Makes me wonder who the bad guys are sometimes.'

'The world is nothing but grey, Aidan. And that's my whole point.'

'You think I see things as black and white?'

'Don't you?'

He didn't have anything for that.

'You heard what David Crossley said. The cages in that

bunker. Assuming it's still there, assuming they're still there, that sounds exactly like where he's been keeping them. And if Terry Beane isn't there, then investigating the scene of his isolation will help me with the profile.'

'Is there anything else we can do?'

'We could get them all together. Nathan, Sally, Melissa, David. One of them might know something about Terry, some additional information that four old friends talking can bring out into the open.'

Corcoran swung out to overtake a parked bus swallowing up a queue of passengers. 'They've got, what, thirty-three, thirty-four years of history built up around them. We need to break that down.' He glanced at her. 'Sounds a lot like a job for you.'

'It'll take time to get them together. I don't think there's much more I can get out of David just now. You saw the state of him.'

'But I also saw how well you worked him.'

'I want to wait until DI Thompson has brought Sally Norton over.'

'Fine.'

'What do you expect us to find there?'

In truth, he didn't know. He hoped they could descend into the villain's lair and save Dawn.

# Forty-three

## *[Palmer, 19:31]*

Corcoran's police radio buzzed on the dashboard. 'Sergeant Broadribb to DS Corcoran, over.'

Palmer answered it for him, holding it up to his lips as he drove.

'Receiving.' He glanced over at Palmer with a smile and a wink. 'Safe to talk.'

'Aidan, we're en route to this scrapyard. Two minutes away.'

'Okay. Did you seriously track down the owner?'

But she was gone.

Corcoran parked a few hundred metres away, hugging the shadows. 'We'll wait for backup, okay?'

'Fine by me.' Palmer took in the site.

The dark scrapyard was surrounded by a chainlink fence, three or four metres high, with nasty-looking wire spiralling at the top. Next to impossible to climb. Probably easier to snip away a section. The huge wrought-iron gates were maybe a better bet, assuming you could get them open. All she could make out from the road was piles of rusting cars, stacked five or six high. A crane caught the light further in, but there was no sign of any building work taking place.

A car swooshed past in the rain and lit up the billboards advertising a forthcoming property development. Artist's impressions of happy families enjoying their fictional life in beige boxes yet to be built. In stark contrast to the torment Terry Beane suffered in there, trapped underground as he faced his greatest fear.

What doesn't kill you can only make you stronger.

Or it can break you, smash your brittle psyche into a million pieces.

Palmer let out a slow breath. 'An episode like that is exactly the kind of thing that could motivate someone to . . . to do this.'

'But?'

She looked round at him, frowning, doubt itching her scalp like an ant crawling over her skin. 'But the problem is, what little we know of Terry, he doesn't fit my profile. It's . . .' She tried to get her thoughts in a row. Felt next to impossible without the crutch of a spread-out notebook, two virgin pages to scrawl over, all the items joined with cold, hard logic. 'All the evidence suggests we're dealing with a supremely organised individual, someone who has meticulously planned this entire operation. He's tortured three people and is doing God knows what to Dawn now.'

'But?'

'Well. You heard the state Terry was in when David and Nathan rescued him. Dehydrated, starved, exhausted, freezing cold from lying in the wet. Those matched with what he's done to their children.' She tried to swallow her doubts, but they caught in her throat. 'The trauma seemed to drive him to alcoholism. Drinking with Hell's Angels, lugging bottles of super-strength cider around. Does our profile sound like a middle-aged alcoholic?'

Corcoran looked away. 'People change.'

'They tend to get worse over time, less organised.'

'Second law of thermodynamics, yeah?' He looked back at her, eyebrows raised. 'The total entropy of an isolated system can never decrease over time. Meaning everything slides into chaos.'

'Is mansplaining another of your hidden shallows?'

A shrug, but hiding a grin. 'I dropped out of a physics degree. That's pretty much all I remember except how much I hated it.' His nostrils flared, another hidden torment revealing itself.

'But you see my point, Aidan. People get more chaotic as they get older. Everything slides into abject chaos, leaving a mess for their kids to stuff into bin bags when they go.'

'Sounds like something you need to talk about.'

'It just rankles with me, that's all.'

'You heard David's story. He was the ringleader, the one who locked the door on Terry. The others could've been trials leading up to this final act.'

Before she could dive into a response, a police car pulled up outside the heavy gates with a flash of headlights.

'Stay here.' Corcoran got out first, pounding along the road as fast as his hip would allow.

Palmer ignored his advice and got out, and followed him at a distance.

Up ahead, Steph went round the car to open the passenger-side back door and helped an old man out.

A saggy mess in a red-and-blue tracksuit, long greasy hair

and a nicotine-stained beard almost down to his sagging belly. He wore a patch over his left eye. David Crossley's yokel, reduced to this state in his old age.

Broadribb helped him stay standing and nodded at them. 'This is Carl Taylor, the owner.'

'Thanks for tracking him down, Sergeant.' Corcoran gave a smile to the old man. 'Some place you've got here.'

Taylor snorted at him. 'She's saying some bastard's been using my land?'

'That's possible, sir. How long have you owned the place?'

'Since the sixties, son. My father, God rest his soul, passed away in his sleep. I were but a lad. He showed me the ropes, still, showed me how to work the crusher when I was knee-high to a bastard. All my life's gone into turning other people's cars into lumps of metal that I can get a pitiful income from.' Taylor snarled, like he didn't square his life with success. 'Sold up, not that my bastard kids will appreciate the money. Just more for them to squander on bastard iPads and those fancy bastard headphones.' He shuffled to the gate. The keys jangled as he stuck the first one in the lock. 'Lucky first time. Not lost my mojo, I tell you.'

Corcoran helped Steph open the right-side gate, making it squeal like a banshee.

Palmer caught up with them and linked in with Taylor's right arm, feeling his weight press on her as he limped through the scrapyard. Every ten metres, another security light flicked on. Either they were alone in there, or someone else hadn't moved for a while.

Taylor looked round, spitting whisky breath over Palmer's face. 'Why are you so interested in this old building, my sweet?'

'It's a scene of interest in a case. That's all.'

'Had some archaeologists come out a few years back to look over it, from that TV show with that bloke. You know the one?'

She nodded like she had the foggiest idea what he was on about.

'They was interested in the war stuff. Used to house Germans here. Prisoners of war. Bastards. Not many of them at a time, either.' Taylor chuckled. 'The bastards got what was coming to them.' He pulled up short, sucking in deep breaths, then set off again. 'When I sold it to the developers, those bastards in the local trust made them preserve it as a museum. Why anyone would want to visit a place where some bastard Germans had electrodes shoved up their—' His eyes bulged as Steph tripped the next set of lights. 'What the hell is that?'

A van sat outside a brick building. Exactly the same model and colour as the CCTV feed. Stolen from Buckingham, used to abduct Dawn, and left here.

Corcoran got in Taylor's face. 'Is that your van?'

'Don't recognise it, son.' He shuffled towards the door.

Corcoran snatched the keys off him and nodded at Steph. 'Keep him here.' He stepped over to the door, his gaze darting around for threats, his free hand dampening the jangle of the keys. He stopped to listen.

'What's the bastard doing?'

Steph motioned for her constable. 'Ed, can you take him?'

The constable took over babysitting Taylor, leading him back towards the car.

Corcoran gave Steph a nod as she snapped out her baton,

then tried the other key in the padlock. 'Bloody thing doesn't even fit.'

'The builder must've changed the locks.' Steph looked round. 'Back in a sec.' She jogged back to her car and stomped back, lugging a pair of heavy-duty bolt-cutters. She eased past Corcoran and cut into the padlock, gritting her teeth and pushing and pushing. The metal landed on the ground, tinkling as it rolled away.

Corcoran snapped out his police baton and nodded for Steph to go first. She opened the door, took a look around, then stepped inside with her torch sweeping the interior.

Corcoran entered and a strip light flickered on inside, dull and faint, but getting brighter with each passing second.

'Clear!'

Palmer swallowed hard and followed Corcoran in.

A bare room, the walls daubed with graffiti. Slogans and initials, mostly crude drawings. But there was power. A brand-new circuitboard hung on the wall just inside the door, humming away.

Steph opened a door, revealing a ramp leading down. Where the cells were.

Palmer followed Corcoran down into a low-ceilinged room. Three doors to jail cells in rusting metal. Two were open. The one on the right was mostly filled by a giant steel contraption.

The middle one was closed and marked 'DAWN'.

Corcoran sucked in a deep breath and raised his baton, then opened it.

# Forty-four

## *[Corcoran, 19:38]*

Empty.

Empty?

'He should be here.' Corcoran collapsed back against the brick wall and let out a deep sigh. 'She was here, wasn't she?'

'We're too late, Aidan.' Palmer was next to him, cradling her arms around herself. 'He's taken her elsewhere. We're too late.'

He kicked the door, made it bounce off the wall and snap back shut.

'DAWN'. Her label, etched into polished wood with a chisel. Some level of artistry to it. Care taken, even though it's only for his use. Why the hell would he do that? To remind himself there was a human being in there? Or was she just a step on the path, another milestone on the journey?

'What the hell was he doing to her down here?' Palmer bit her bottom lip. 'She's going to die, isn't she? A diabetic coma and she'll . . .' Her thoughts were running away. 'With Sarah, he let her go before she died. What if he's . . .'

'Hey, hey.' Corcoran grabbed her shoulders, held her steady and stared deep into her eyes. 'We're on to him, okay?'

'You know the risks of diabetes, Aidan. And it's bad

enough what he did to the others when he had complete control, but he's under pressure now.'

'Marie, we're chasing him. We know who he is. Sortwell has an APB out on him.'

Palmer looked around her surroundings and seemed to shiver. 'But he'll feel like a rat in a cage.'

Corcoran found Steph crouching in the left-hand cell. Speakers were mounted into the ceiling, explaining the cables running down in the main room. Where Howard was tortured. Thicker walls than the other two, to insulate the noise terror from the others. He cleared his throat, made her look up. 'Can you get forensics in here? Comb the building and that van. If this Terry guy's on the system, I want us to place him here.'

'Will do.' Steph got up and talked into her radio.

Corcoran walked back to Palmer, standing outside the other room. A hose hung from the ceiling, filling directly into the giant sensory deprivation tank where Matt's sanity had been stolen away from him.

'This is . . .' Palmer exhaled slowly. 'It's barbaric. How can someone do this to people? No matter what their parents did to him, this is . . . How? How, Aidan?'

'You're the expert, Marie.'

'Are you being facetious?'

'Sorry to butt in.' Steph ran her tongue over her teeth. 'Just got word that the van upstairs matches the one on the CCTV of Dawn's abduction. The stuff they've sprayed on the plates . . . Blocks the cameras from reading it. I know places in Germany where you can get it.'

'Germany?'

'It's highly illegal, but round here we get boy racers treating the M40 as an autobahn and getting away with it because they've masked their plates. So we're checking for it using speed cameras. Spot one and we despatch a pair of BMWs at full speed, catch them.'

Palmer frowned. 'Meaning he'd get pulled over?'

'He'd have to go past one of our stops, but yeah.'

Palmer looked at Corcoran. 'That means he hasn't driven the van very often.'

'Right.' Steph took one last look around the place. 'This place gives me the creeps. I'll see you upstairs.'

Corcoran knew the feeling. He put his hands in his pockets. 'So he burnt the Tiguan, then stole that van and masked the plates to give a double bluff. That fit your profile?'

'I can't tell. I mean, this place has obvious significance for Terry Beane. He's making their children suffer for what happened to him. I get why he's done it, but why not pick on the parents? Or their spouses? Why choose their children?'

Corcoran shrugged. 'Remember that we're dealing with a complete nutter here.'

'You shouldn't trivialise him as a "nutter", Aidan. He's been subjected to a severely traumatic incident.'

He could only shrug. 'It just has to be logical to him, is all I'm saying.'

She went back to her notebook, scribbling away and updating her theories and whatever else.

'I'll see you upstairs.' Corcoran walked up the concrete ramp and outside into the cold air. The moon was out, lighting up their surroundings, and the rain had stopped. Rotting metal piled high, husks of vehicles left to decay. A crane sat a distance away.

Steph was helping Carl Taylor in to her car.

Corcoran walked over and caught his attention. 'Have you seen anyone here recently?'

'Not been here for months.'

Corcoran nodded. 'Matt Gladwin was held down there for over five months.'

'What?'

'Terry Beane abducted him from a street in east London.' Corcoran stepped closer, fists clenched. 'He transported him here, and made him stand up. He was here for months, under your nose.'

'Son, I'm in a home.' Taylor's lips twitched. 'I can't even look after my bastard self. Tonight's the first time I've been here since I signed the contract with those bastard developers.'

'They own the place?'

'Changes hands when the bastards get round to paying me. Don't get to dig into the ground until then, though they had cranes and God knows what else here. Bastards. Don't get to start until I get my money. My son, he's a good lad, he's on top of them.'

'You sure you don't know a Terry Beane?'

'Should I?'

Corcoran had to give up. 'When were you last here?'

'Six months ago. Middle of September, it was. Son was in Majorca with his family. Had to let this engineer in, said he was strengthening the place ahead of the development.'

Palmer appeared, frowning. 'An engineer? How old was he?'

'Can't remember. My eyes aren't so good these days.'

'Was he old? Young?'

'Not sure. One of those fellas could be anything from thirty to sixty, you know?'

Palmer snorted. 'His motive is enacting revenge against the children of the people who trapped him down there back in 1986.'

'What?'

'Come on.' Corcoran grabbed Palmer's arm and led her away. 'He doesn't remember anything, Marie. He's an old man.'

'He . . .' She shut her eyes. 'You're right.'

She's losing it, thought Corcoran. All this time, she's talked about pressure and I've let it build up a head of steam, using it to my advantage, but now she's crumbling under the weight of it all.

Corcoran's phone rang. He fished it out of his pocket. 'Sorry, it's the boss.' He put it to his ear. 'Alana, what's up?'

'Aidan, uniform have picked up Sarah's mother and they're five minutes away from Dawn's father's house. Get yourself over there now.'

# Forty-five

## *[Palmer, 19:55]*

Corcoran held up his warrant card for the shivering uniformed officer at the roadblock. 'Cheers.' He stuffed it away as the window slid back up and he drove off. 'You know, I was expecting to rush into that bunker, catch the bad guy and save Dawn.'

'I know.'

'What do you mean, you know?'

'You wanted to carry her out in your arms and bask in the glory to make up for what happened with Murray Ross.'

'Quit psychoanalysing me, Marie.'

'You don't think this impacts your ability to do your job?'

'No. I don't. And it doesn't.' Corcoran pulled up at a roundabout and scanned the other exits, drumming his fingers on the wheel. 'I'm not one of your patients.'

'You're not that different, Aidan.'

Corcoran laughed. 'Marie, you shouldn't have come down there with me. I warned you.' He stared at her again, softer this time, like he was on the edge. Of what, she didn't know. He set off across the roundabout and cut onto a dual carriageway heading south.

She let him have the victory. 'Sorry.'

'Good.'

# *[20:02]*

Palmer stopped on the threshold into the living room and took stock of the scene.

Thompson and Corcoran were in a huddled conference by the mantelpiece. No sign of Lesley Crossley, but David stood in the middle of the room, next to Sally Norton. Old lovers, reunited. Or just old friends. Seemed like the thirty-odd years hadn't passed and they were in someone's parents' living room. Painfully uncomfortable, avoiding looking at each other, but they clearly had a strong bond.

And yet Sally was still livid with him, her jaw set tight. 'David, I'm truly sorry about what you're going through with Dawn, but my Sarah . . . she's in a really bad way . . .' She brushed a tear away. 'She might die, David. Or she could be disabled for the rest of her life. And it's all thanks to what we did. What *you* did.'

'You don't know how sorry I am.' David hung his head low, eyes closed. 'I hold myself responsible for this. The whole thing, it's all my fault. It was my stupid idea. I mean, we were kids and I was a complete arsehole. You know that thing where the male brain isn't fully developed until it's twenty-one?'

'That's the only excuse you can cling to?'

'I mean, I've changed, but . . . I can't change what we did. We fucked him up, Sally. We broke him and . . .'

'You were showing off.'

David went quiet.

Thompson beckoned Palmer over. 'This going according to plan?'

323

'I'd rather have been here at the start, but yes. Them processing what happened may yield further clues. Now we know the link and his reasoning – the who and the why – this can validate our hypothesis.'

'But it might open up other possibilities.'

'Well, yes.' Palmer looked at her. 'But our priority has to be saving Dawn. Arresting Terry Beane is secondary. Agreed?'

Thompson snarled. 'I'd rather have them both, but I'll settle for rescuing Dawn.'

Car headlights glared in the window. DS John Diamond helped Melissa Gladwin out of a Mondeo like he was her chauffeur. Matt's mother certainly acted that way, taking his hand as her dark-pink dress exploded out of the car, and letting him lead her up to the house. Her footsteps clicked in the hallway, but seemed to stop outside the living room, like she was waiting to make her grand entrance. Then she flounced in with a frosty face.

'You're looking well.' David examined Melissa closely. 'I'm really sorry for what you're going through with Matt.'

She closed her eyes. 'David. I hold you directly responsible for this. What you did has caught up with us.'

'Mel, I'm sorry, but it was Nate who—'

'Yes, yes. Nathan might well have been the instigator, might've guilted him into going down there, but you locked the door. You trapped him in there. And you were the first to run when the owner appeared.' Her west London accent was slipping, letting the rural Bucks back out. 'You let this happen to our children.'

'Believe me, Mel, nobody's suffering as much as I am right now.'

Melissa slumped onto the sofa, her dress splayed around her, tears glistening in her eyes. 'Your actions did this to my boy.'

Palmer took the seat next to Melissa, carefully shifting the dress material aside. 'Are any of you still in touch with Howard's father?'

'Nate . . .' Melissa looked at Palmer, her eyes misting over. 'As you know, Nathan and I went out together at school and for a while afterwards, but . . . I moved to London. To Imperial College.'

'What happened?'

'It's a long story.' Melissa gritted her teeth. 'As far as I know, Nathan went to Devon to teach surfing. That's the kind of man he was.'

'Was?'

'He died last year. A heart attack. From what I gather, things didn't work out in Devon. He married and divorced years ago, when Howard was still young. He moved to Spain, but said he deeply regretted what happened.'

'To?'

'To his son.' Melissa snorted. 'Howard grew up without his father. I gather his mother died a few years ago?'

'Correct, but his stepfather seems to love him.'

'That's good.' Melissa let go of Palmer's hand to rub her eye, but took hold again. 'We did talk about Terry Beane, about what happened that night, that weekend. 'Nathan used to bring it up when we were drunk. Or high. Then he'd clam up. Once it made him cry and he wouldn't talk about it again.' She gestured at the other two ex-friends. 'It splintered us as a group and drove us apart. We were such good friends until what we did.'

'What do you remember about Terry Beane?'

'Very little.' Melissa glanced at Sally. 'I mean, he was *her* boyfriend, wasn't he?' She spat out the word.

'He was hardly my boyfriend, Mel.'

She snarled. 'You brought him along that night to make David jealous, if I recall. Some big lump of rough, trying—'

'Shut up!'

'Why? Does the truth hurt?'

Sally had nothing to say.

'If you must know, I did get jealous.' David looked over at Sally. 'You brought him along and I . . .'

Sally blew air up her face. 'I'd been trying to encourage you to make a move, but . . . but you didn't have to do that to him!'

David shook his head. 'I wish I could've stopped what happened.'

'These two . . .' Melissa folded her arms. 'They were always this "will they, won't they" thing all through school. It was so wearing. I don't blame Sally for bringing some big idiot from work along.'

Palmer frowned. 'You worked together?'

'In the local supermarket.' Melissa unfolded her arms, resting her hands on her lap. 'That's right, isn't it? Sally and I worked on the tills, and Terry stacked shelves and sometimes filled bags for us. He used to flirt with her in the canteen.'

'I saw another side to him in there.' Sally looked out of the window. 'He was like a different person away from school. And he was okay, actually. Funny, kind, generous.' Her face lost its steel. 'But that night, we broke him. He stopped speaking to me, stopped speaking to the other people in the shop. He became an alcoholic, barely functioning, while we all went on to our degrees and our glittering careers.'

'This isn't getting us anywhere.' David started pacing the room. 'You're digging up long-dead history while my daughter is out there somewhere, dying. You've got your kids back, for better or worse, but my Dawn . . . She'll *die*.'

Sally walked over and took his hand, holding it tight.

Corcoran sniffed. 'He's right. We need to find Terry Beane. He's got Dawn and we need to get medication to her.'

Melissa looked down her nose at him. 'Are you telling me you can't find him?'

'That's right. We've searched. It's possible he's changed his name. You're absolutely sure his name was Terence Beane?'

'Of course I am.' David snorted again.

'Wait.' Sally broke free from David's grasp. 'Remember at school, Terry used to get picked on by Geoff Andrews and Michael Richardson? What did they call him?'

Melissa frowned. 'Wait a second.' The facade of the middle-class businesswoman slipped, letting the dope-smoking schoolgirl back out. 'Didn't they find out that Terry was his middle name?'

'God, that was it. Kept calling him "fifth", right?' Sally clicked her fingers. 'It was his full name. Something Terence Beane the fifth?'

David groaned. 'John Terence Beane the fifth.'

Corcoran stormed out of the room, brandishing his mobile like he could do some serious damage with it.

Palmer joined him in the hallway.

Corcoran looked round at her and nodded. He put his call on speaker. 'You getting anything, Pete?'

'Hold your bloody horses, mate.' Whoever was down the other end of the line was taking their sweet time. 'Hmm. That's not what I expected.'

'Pete, what is it?'

'I've found your John Terence Beane.' A sigh rasped out of the speaker. 'Thing is, he killed himself ten years ago . . .'

# Forty-six

## *[Corcoran, 20:11]*

'Say that again?' Corcoran held the phone in front of him, hands shaking. Couldn't bring himself to look at Palmer. Couldn't begin to process what it meant.

Sortwell sighed down the line again. 'Like I told you . . . he died in September 2010.'

Corcoran finally looked at Palmer. Their suspect was dead. 'Was there a post mortem?'

Clicking keys. 'Sure was. Suicide. Shot himself, too. Not the full Kurt Cobain either. Pistol to the temple, enough left for a positive ID. Definitely him.'

'Who identified the body?'

'That's the thing. The writing on the form is even worse than your last overtime form. He wasn't married, had no siblings, both parents are dead. Haven't found a living next of kin.'

'Thanks, Pete.' Corcoran stabbed the button. 'Penny for them?'

'I . . . This . . .' Palmer leaned against the kitchen table, staring into space, a blank, emotionless frown plastered all over her face. 'What do you think?'

'It fitted so well. A solid revenge motive.' Corcoran put his phone away. 'How can he be dead?'

'I did say he wasn't a perfect match, Aidan.' Palmer looked him straight in the eyes. 'Believe me, I want to find him as much as you do.'

'But it's not him. Terry Beane.' He walked over to the sink and poured himself a glass of water. 'You thought it didn't add up. I didn't listen. You were right. I was clutching at straws.' He downed the glass and refilled it. 'Where do we go from here?'

'We need to stay flexible, in case we've missed something crucial. In the Ross Murray case, like you say, if Zoe had been on the ball, you *could've* caught him before he'd murdered, while it was still serial rape. This case can still end that way. We can save Dawn. We can stop him from killing.'

'I'm now looking for a who, though.'

'Well, all roads still lead to Terry Beane.'

'John Terence Beane the fifth.' Corcoran played the name around in his head. What kind of person controlled their children like that? Enforced their own name on their first-born son, like they could continue their own lives after death? 'But how can a dead man be doing this?'

'Not existing is the perfect cover, right? Assume a new identity and you're much harder to track. This is the man who's stolen cars and masked the plates.'

'But you heard what Pete said, Marie. He didn't fake his suicide. There was a post mortem. It was him.'

'It's worth me looking at the detailed report and speaking to the pathologist.'

'Maybe, but focusing on him isn't exactly keeping this flexible, is it?'

'There's something I'm not quite getting here and this might be the best possibility of—'

'—validating our assumptions.' Corcoran felt himself grin. 'Gotcha.'

'At the moment, we've got the possibility that Terry faked his suicide. Outlandish, but it's the simplest explanation. The primary alternative is somebody else has used his ordeal as a motivation.' Palmer looked like she was running out of straws to clutch at. 'Other than that, there could be some other connection. Now we know these people grew up together, maybe there's someone else with a beef against them. Maybe they lied to each other to cover up what they did to Terry. Who's to say he's the only one?'

It all made sense to Corcoran. Perfect sense.

And yet, it was all supposition and assumption.

No next logical step that would save Dawn from whatever fresh hell she was experiencing.

## *[20:15]*

Back in the living room, David, Sally and Melissa had spread out, sitting apart from each other. Melissa was on the sofa, her back to the other two. Sally sat with her head in her hands, quietly sobbing. David stood by the window.

'Okay, I need to know everything you do about Terry Beane.'

Melissa narrowed her eyes at Corcoran. 'Have you not got any leads on him?'

'He killed himself ten years ago.'

Her hand shot to her open mouth. 'Oh my god.'

Sally put her knuckles to her lips, gasping like she was going to be sick.

'Jesus.' David turned round and leaned back against the window frame. 'So, who the hell is doing this to our kids?'

'That's what I'm trying to discover. When was the last you heard of Terry Beane?'

David shrugged. 'I moved back here after uni and, like Mel told you earlier, I'd see him around town. After what we'd done, I didn't even want to think about him. I'd messed up his life and I could see it in the way he walked. The one time I know he saw me, he ran away. And the guy's twice my size.'

David sat between his old friends on the sofa. 'The time he saw me, I was on a pub crawl with lads from work. Ended up in some rum boozers. Terry was in The Crown with some metal warriors. You know the type, Metallica and Megadeth patches on their denim jackets. Stars and stripes headscarves. Hard nuts, bikers. I thought he might speak to me, fuelled by booze and backed up by his hard mates. But no, he backed away.'

'The Crown?'

'Right. Closed down when the Wetherspoon opened. Think it's someone's house now.'

'That was the last time you saw him?'

'Right.'

'What about you two?'

Melissa looked up at Corcoran. 'I've avoided coming home. My parents died so I stopped having the need.'

'When was the last time?'

'Okay, when Dad was in the hospice, I was clearing out my parents' house. So that was eleven years ago, maybe twelve? I popped into the supermarket to get some wine and dinner. Place had hardly changed. And he took one look at me and ran back into the stockroom.'

'Used to see him every time I came home to visit.' Sally swallowed hard. 'In the shop, like Mel said. And he blanked me too.'

'I saw him there too. Did our weekly shop in there.' David splayed his hands on his lap. 'Ten years ago seems about right.'

'Is there anything else, anyone who he was friends with from school or work?'

'Well, I kept in touch with someone who worked there.' Sally looked out of the window. 'Helen Smith. She said he was the store man. You know, organising all the deliveries and putting the stock out onto the shelves. Recycling the boxes. Stuck in the back room, avoiding much human contact. Just did his job, then went home. Didn't answer a question unless it came from the store manager. They only kept him on because he worked twice as hard as anyone else.'

## [20:35]

Princes Risborough had one of the strangest supermarkets Corcoran had seen. Made of brick, the pillars inset with rough stone, it looked more like a country farm shop than a chain supermarket.

He waited for the trolley lad to pass, his extra-thick glasses warning that he'd struggle to see anything further than three inches from his face, and might batter twenty trolleys off your car.

Corcoran checked Palmer was following, then slipped through the front door into the chilled interior. He walked up to the customer service desk and unfolded his warrant card. 'Supposed to meet a Jack Edwards here?'

The woman smiled, then reached for a microphone. Her voice boomed throughout the store. 'Manager required at the kiosk. Manager required at the kiosk. Thanks.' Another smile, then she looked at the old lady behind them. 'Lottery ticket, June?'

Corcoran stepped aside and looked around. The shop seemed smaller than it should've done, the low ceiling and tight aisles squishing everything in.

'DS Corcoran?' A corporate suit swaggered towards them: flame-red hair, a broad grin and a firm handshake. 'Jack Edwards.' He looked like he'd only just started shaving. 'Good to meet you. How can I help?'

'We're looking for anyone who would've worked with a Terence Beane, maybe known as Terry. Full name John Terence Beane.'

'Doesn't ring any bells.'

'This will be from the mid-eighties until about ten years ago.' As he said it, Corcoran knew it would be futile, given the guy's age.

'Ah. I'm afraid I won't be able to help.' The store manager raised a bushy eyebrow. 'I would've still been at school when he left.'

Corcoran didn't ask if he meant primary or secondary. 'Look, is there anyone who would've been here then?'

'Maybe.' He set off towards the greengrocery section. 'Manfred?'

A beanpole appeared, with the longest arms Corcoran had ever seen. Like tentacles, and thick with the kind of muscle you got from hard work rather than disco weight exercises in the gym. He grunted at Edwards and it sounded like a question.

'Manfred, mate, do you remember a Terry Beane?'

Another grunt, full-throated and deep. 'Worked for him, yeah. Why?'

'The police here are . . .' Edwards frowned. 'What exactly is it you're—'

'We want to speak to anyone who knew him.'

'Why?'

'That's a confidential matter, sir. Did you know him well?'

'Solid worker. Never spoke. Just got on with it. Only told me what I was doing wrong. Never took a day off.' Manfred bared his teeth. 'Tragic, though. Didn't turn up one day. Shot himself.' He shook his head. 'I identified him. Me. Nobody else in his life. And I barely knew him.'

'It was definitely him?'

Manfred tugged at his nose. 'Not that there was much left of his head.' He put a finger-pistol to his head and made an explosive sound. 'Definitely him.'

'Did he have any friends?'

'Nope.'

'No colleagues here, or people who'd speak to him when he was working? Maybe someone who met him after work?'

'No idea. Sorry. Never used to even come out front when there were people in the shop. Soon as the place shut, he'd be out front making sure everything was okay. Just the way he was.'

'So there's nobody you can think of? No wife or girlfriend? Boyfriend?'

'Nope. Wasn't the full shilling. Don't mean disabled like young Johnny on the trolleys. Had his demons. Know a few lads who were out in Iraq. That kind of thing.'

'Okay, thanks for your time.' Corcoran gave him a final nod, then led Palmer out of the supermarket. His brain was fizzing with possibilities, but all of them showed their lack of progress. 'So what the hell do we do now?'

'I'm struggling, Aidan.'

'Me too. I mean . . .' He stopped by the car and breathed out slowly. 'I don't know what I mean.'

'So in lieu of tracking down some drinkers from the late eighties and nineties, we're stuck.'

'Right. Doesn't sound like Terry could've faked his suicide.' Corcoran stopped by his car, head bowed. 'I was clinging to that hope.'

'Officers!' Manfred was jogging over to them, his arms waving wildly. 'Heard about Hayley, right?'

'Hayley?'

'Terry met her a couple of times. Saw him sneaking off. Young Hayley Mitchell.' Manfred thumbed inside the store. 'Worked the cigarette kiosk. Flirted with him. He wasn't any good at it. Saw them in The Crown once. Bottles of wine. Pints of bitter. All over each other.'

'They were an item?'

'Don't know. Sorry. I identified his body. You'd think if they were together . . .'

'Any idea if she's still in Princes Risborough?'

Manfred shrugged. 'She died.'

# Forty-seven

## *[Palmer, 20:48]*

'Thing is, I've got six Hayley Mitchells in Princes Risborough.' Sortwell's voice echoed out of the dashboard speakers as they drove. 'You need to help me narrow it down.'

'Let's see if I can. Cheers, Pete.' Corcoran killed the call and kept driving. '*Smashing.*'

Palmer sagged back in her seat. 'So what do we do?'

Corcoran followed the satnav's directions and pulled in. 'Have we got any other options?'

The brick building seemed to house a few businesses as well as the local GP surgery.

'Well, there are still lights on.' Palmer checked her watch. Nearly nine o'clock. You never knew. She got out and set off across the car park. Still a few other cars parked there, high-end models that a doctor would drive. She knocked on the door and waited.

'Marie, this is a waste of time.' Corcoran was out of breath as he caught up with her. 'We should . . . I don't know.' He rubbed a hand across the fresh stubble on his chin. 'Dawn's going to die, isn't she?'

He'd imploded into despair and negative thinking. Maybe

his usual casual, confident manner was a bluff, his way of dealing with failure.

She took another look at the lights and figured it was just an automated system to deter burglars. Her turn to sigh. 'You're right. We should regroup tomorrow and—'

The door clattered open. 'Elsie, we'll just have to see, won't we?' A male nurse stood there, one hand holding the door, the other gripping the handle of a wheelchair, an ancient lady slumped in it. As he saw Corcoran's warrant card, hope diminished in his eyes. The prospect of a quiet drink in front of the television was slipping away, replaced with questions from the police. 'We're shut, I'm afraid.'

'Police.' Corcoran shook his warrant card in the man's face. 'I know it's late, but there's an emergency situation. A woman was—'

'David Crossley's girl.' The old woman shook her head, glazed eyes like she'd had a healthy dose of morphine. 'Is she okay?'

Corcoran didn't seem to take any notice of her. 'Sir, we need to access some medical records and desperately need your help here.'

'And I can't give you it.' The nurse scowled. 'I'm the only member of staff here. After his last appointment, Dr Lindsay was out of the door like a shot. Of course, that's when Elsie here had her little fall and cracked her hip. It really shouldn't take three hours for an ambulance to come here, should it?'

'There's a burst water main in town.' Palmer elbowed Corcoran out of the way. 'And there are police surveillance checks all over the place after the abduction.'

'Lord save us . . .'

Corcoran took another step towards him. 'We really need to see records relating to a couple of your patients. It's crucial.'

'As much as I'd love to help, there's just no way. The standard procedure is for you to request a warrant, then present it to a doctor. I'm not a doctor, so I can't help, even if I wanted to. Now, if you come back in the morning with all the paperwork, then you can see what any of our doctors think. They can help you. I can't.'

Palmer tilted her head to the side and spoke in an undertone. 'Listen, I'm not a police officer. I'm a criminal psychologist working for the NHS.' She dug into her purse for her own ID, wrapped in a navy lanyard. 'And I am a medical doctor, so I can have access to records as I see fit. Now, I can call your supervisor or you can help me find a serial abductor and maybe save a woman's life.'

The nurse took a hard look at her, then patted his patient's arm. 'Come on, Elsie, looks like we've got time for another cup of tea.' He wheeled her back into the surgery, all pine cladding and green-felt chairs. 'Do you two want one?'

'Lifesaver.' Corcoran flashed a smile. 'Just milk, cheers.'

'And you, love?'

'If you've got green, otherwise I'm fine.' Palmer looked around. 'Where are the records kept?'

The nurse wagged a finger. 'I don't want him going in there, okay?'

Corcoran held up his hands. 'I'll keep Elsie company.' But he reached into his pocket for his phone.

Palmer followed the nurse into a long corridor. Office doors for the staff, with even the nurses getting one each. He unlocked one marked *Records* and held the door for her. 'I'll come help you in a minute, once I've put a brew on.'

'Thanks for this. I really do appreciate it.' Palmer opened the door and got the musty smell of any filing room. 'I'll put in a good word for you about Elsie, okay?'

He rolled his eyes. 'She's a nightmare. I can't feel anything wrong with her, but I've got to err on the side of caution. Her son's a lawyer who's got a rep for suing us.'

'Like I say, anything I can do.' She winked.

'Thanks.' He sashayed off into the kitchen, a beat in his step.

Leaving Palmer with the records. Mac—Mc filled a whole cabinet on the far wall. Next was Ma—Me, meaning Mitchell was in the next one, Mi—Mo. She rifled through it. Four dead Hayley Mitchells, two living. Great.

Manfred the storeman had intimated that Hayley was younger than Terry, who would've been eighteen in 1986, so born in 1968. 1973 to 1983 seemed a reasonable starting point.

She flicked through them. First, born September 1923. Second, born June 1981. Unlikely, but possible. She set it aside. Third, born November 1973.

Possible to likely.

She pulled out the hefty file and started reading. This Hayley Mitchell died of alcohol-related liver failure last April. Becoming probable . . . A short life filled with so many tragedies and traumas. Self-harming, depression, treatment for alcohol abuse. Had her stomach pumped three times as a teenager, then her body seemed to cope with it as she got older. The doctor's notes referred to her suffering aching feet and back from standing all day while working at a supermarket. Bingo.

Palmer headed back through to reception. 'Got a possible date of birth for you.' She held up the cover sheet. 'See what you can get.'

Corcoran started calling someone. 'How did she go?'

'Assuming this is who we're after, she died of liver disease. Possibly caused by all that drinking.'

'What a way to go.' Corcoran whistled and walked off, phone to his ear.

Palmer went back to the file, flicking through pages and pages of notes. One of the first patients in the UK on Prozac, not that it seemed to have done her much good. Referrals to depression clinics, to alcohol clinics, to a hospital specialist for a cough that wouldn't go away.

Wait a second.

Pages bundled together, water damage tying them at the edges.

Referral to a maternity ward.

A copy birth certificate for a son. DOB 10th January 1994. John Terence Mitchell.

No father's name on the birth certificate.

Born when she was twenty, and he was twenty-five when she died. Sixteen when Terry killed himself.

But that name . . . Surely he would be John Terence Beane the sixth?

Surely he was Terry's child?

# Forty-eight

## *[Corcoran, 20:59]*

Corcoran killed the engine but didn't get out. He nodded at the block of flats. 'So he still lives in Princes Risborough.'

Palmer looked over from her notebook. 'Terry's son abducting and torturing the children of his father's tormentors back in the eighties. Does that fit?'

'I can certainly buy it. Are you saying you can't?'

'No. I do, but that's the problem. This is a perfect fit. I just don't want us to have all our eggs in one basket.'

'Sometimes that's just how it works.' Corcoran stepped out onto the parking bay, the zigzag brick patterns soaked through. He waited for her to get out before charging over to the address. 'Want to lead here?'

'That's not my job.'

'You could've fooled me back at the doctor's.'

'We were desperate. I did what we needed to do.'

'How Machiavellian.' Corcoran knocked on the door and waited, listening for any movement inside. Or out the back. Assuming this was their guy, he'd possibly make a break for it. Then again, the kind of person who can do this to people, their psychology leads them to be charming and manipulative. The kind of person who can talk themselves out of any situation, who can offer any explanation for every outcome.

And there was that word again. Assumption.

They were assuming it was John Mitchell because of some old stories. Desperate parents clutching at straws. A desperate cop looking for simple answers. Revenge for what they did to his old man. A father not even on his birth certificate. Who was clutching at straws now?

The door slid open and a young man stood there, tie tucked over his left shoulder, shirtsleeves rolled up to his elbows, forearms damp with soap suds. 'Can I help?'

Corcoran showed his warrant card. 'Looking for a John Mitchell.'

'Sorry, but he doesn't live here.'

'We've got this as his address.'

'Very pleased for you, mate. He doesn't live here.'

'But he did live here?'

'Last tenant, I think. Keep getting his sodding mail.'

Corcoran tried to keep faith that they were on the right track. 'Mind if I have a look at it?'

'Fine.' The door slammed in their faces.

'This isn't looking good, Aidan.'

'You're telling me.'

The door slid open and the current tenant handed them a pile of old letters. 'That's all the stuff I've got. Now, I've got to head out, so if you don't mind?' And he was gone.

Corcoran flicked through the post. Pizza adverts, loyalty cards, a credit card statement, and a payslip from last July.

Unopened, the tear strip still intact.

# *[21:10]*

For an architectural firm, BEV Associates took surprisingly little care with its own building. A strange extension between two old stone buildings, bricks painted dark blue with yellow metal piping. The mismatched windows were all still brightly lit, even at this time, and the bottom floor had a long single-paned window, showing a plush reception area and four offices, all filled with busy workers. A billboard stood in the lawn just outside, an advert for a development at the scrapyard.

Corcoran stopped. 'Shit, it's him. Isn't it? This is how he got access to that building.'

'Makes sense.'

He looked over at Palmer. 'Not, I told you so?'

'I told you I don't play games, Aidan. I just want to find Dawn.' She gave him a narrow-eyed look. 'Shouldn't we wait for backup?'

'We've got a ticking clock. Dawn's diabetes.' Corcoran pushed into the building and the bleary-eyed security guard looked up from a laptop, easing off his headphones to let excited football commentary bleed out. 'Need to speak to a John Terence Mitchell.'

The guard typed something into a keyboard. 'Just a sec.'

'What did you just do?'

'Sent a Slack message.'

'A what?'

The door behind them opened and a tall man eased through. Hands stuffed into shiny grey slacks. Navy cardigan, hiking boots, his curly mullet glistening with hair product. 'Thanks, Jordan.'

'Mr Mitchell?'

'Afraid not.' He held out a hand for Corcoran to shake. 'Mark Vaughn. I'm the V in BEV.' He beckoned them through into an office and gestured at seats in front of a giant draughtsman's table, pitched up at an angle. Looked like he still kept up the drawing despite having an initial above the door. 'John's on leave just now and I'm—'

'DS Aidan Corcoran.' He held out his warrant card. 'We really need to speak to a John Mitchell.'

'Can this wait until the morning? I'm up to here.' Vaughn raised his hand way above his head.

'We need to speak to Mr Mitchell.'

'What's he done?'

'I'm not at liberty to divulge that, sir.'

'Shit.' Vaughn set his pencil back down again. 'Look, John is an employee in the firm but he's on leave.' He cracked his knuckles. 'You've got to understand . . .' But he bit his tongue.

Palmer stood over him, leaning against the board. 'Help me understand.'

'Been a hellish few months for all of us here, getting this development through planning, then the funding drying up. And the current owner of the scrapyard, well it's his son, but he isn't exactly a willing seller. Every single thing is a complete nightmare. And John, bless his soul, was leading on the development. He took it all to heart, so he's taking some time out just now.'

'Taken what to heart?'

'The development's stalled. Not usually our problem but the builder's not the most orthodox firm. Made us take on more of a project management role. Trouble is, we're short of a few instalments of our seven-figure fee because of things we can't control.'

'And John was leading this?'

'Right. Don't get me wrong, he's a great worker. Give him a few words and he'll come up with something magnificent. And he's a whizz on the computer programs. I can use them, have to, but I much prefer pencil and paper. But John's had a difficult life. Takes things a bit too personally at times.'

'You seem close?'

'Totally. I took him under my wing when he started here, see him as a protégé. He's a good guy. I thought he was. But . . .' Vaughn laid the pencil down on his board.

'Sir.' Palmer waited for him to look up. 'We need to know—'

'You need to tell me what he's done?'

She looked over at Corcoran.

He took over. 'We believe he's abducted and tortured three people.'

Vaughn slowly placed a hand on his mouth. A calm but measured reaction, but his eyes betrayed the sheer shock. 'Listen to me, John was taken into care at a young age. Didn't know his dad and his mum was an alcoholic, a complete mess. He went through foster homes, always getting into trouble. His fifth foster family, John lucked out and connected with the father. Guy was a hero, had the patience to turn John round and ended up adopting him. Got him back on track and he went to university, which is how he ended up here.'

'Are you trying to defend him?'

'No, I just can't believe he's capable of even contemplating something like this.'

'Sarah Langton. Howard Ritchie. Matt Gladwin. We also believe he has abducted a Dawn Crossley this evening. She's diabetic and if she—'

'Good heavens.' Vaughn sprang up from his board and found a sheet of paper. 'John's just moved house. Place he built himself, just outside town.'

## *[21:35]*

Corcoran took the corner way too fast, but still managed to stick to his side of the road. He got the speedo over ninety on the street, then slowed to seventy for the next bend, slaloming round as a car swept past them. The town's streetlights gave way to countryside darkness.

The dashboard lit up and his ringtone blasted out. Unknown caller. 'Yep?'

'Why's your Airwave off?' A woman's voice.

'Because I'm driving. Who is this?'

'Sergeant Broadribb.'

Corcoran hit the floor and blasted past a pair of cars. 'Are you on your way?'

'Is this going to be a total waste of effort like last time?'

'It might be, but it's called doing our jobs, Sergeant. Just get there with a gang of knuckle-draggers, okay?'

Steph sighed down the line. 'Fine. We'll be waiting.' And she was gone.

Palmer was staring out of the window at the passing darkness, trees and sleeping cows lit up by the moon's glow. Didn't even have her notebook out.

'You okay?'

She didn't reply immediately. 'The pressure's getting to us both, Aidan. I just can't stop thinking about Dawn and . . . You know, John Mitchell fits my profile in so many ways. He's in his twenties and he's built his own house, hence being capable of adapting the cells and creating the torture devices. But there are other details I was missing, such as having access to the scrapyard through his job.'

'And how could you have got that from a profile?' He looked over but got a shrug. 'He's a loner with a troubled upbringing. Sure that's in there?'

'Well, yes, but . . .'

The satnav indicated the next turning, so Corcoran hit the brakes, trying to gauge his speed with the turning, then hared up a barren backroad winding up a gentle hill. Up ahead, torchlight shone outside a dark house, a modern building looking like it was built from a kit.

Corcoran parked behind two squad cars and traced the four torch beams back to the uniformed officers searching the vicinity. Steph Broadribb was one of them, shouting orders and instructions. He got out and jogged over as fast as his hip would let him, his own beam dancing across the rough ground.

Steph swung round, shining the beam straight into his face, then back at two of her guys. 'Robert, Dennis, need you to circle round the back.'

And off they went, leaving her and another female officer. Steph waited for them, hands on hips, looking up at the sky. 'I always wondered what David Bowie meant about serious moonlight, but that looks pretty serious to me.'

She was right. The full moon was partially obscured by a thin patch of clouds, lit up from behind.

'Any sign of him?'

'Nope.' Steph walked up to the house. 'Looks like it cost a pretty penny. You sure this is right?'

'He built it himself. The only expensive bit will be the land.' Corcoran stopped by the front door and shone his torch inside the nearest room. A kitchen, well equipped but no signs of life. The floor was bare: no tables and chairs, just boxes. On the other side of the door was a bare living room, empty and cold. 'No sign of anyone inside. You okay to lead?'

'It is my job, after all.' Steph knocked on the door.

No answer. No sounds of anyone rushing to answer, but no sounds of someone hiding either, no creaking floorboards or shutting doors.

'Hit it, Jess.'

The uniform walked up to the door and braced herself, ready to launch shoulder first.

# Forty-nine

## *[Palmer, 21:46]*

The house lights flashed on inside.

Palmer made to step over the discarded door, glowing blue under the house lights.

Corcoran put a hand out to stop her. 'Let them do their job.'

'Aidan, I need to see inside.'

'And you will. Just let them do their jobs.'

'I'm . . .' He was right, of course. Palmer took in their immediate vicinity. Remote and wild. Over the nearby hills, Princes Risborough lit up the sections of the night sky not glowing in moonlight. No obvious places where he could hide Dawn.

Crashing came from inside as Steph's team rooted around inside the house, their torches swapped for side lamps and overhead lights. No sign of anyone, so Steph beckoned them in.

'Careful, okay?' Corcoran went in first. It still had that new-house smell: fresh carpets, glue, paint.

Steph joined them in the hallway, blowing out her cheeks. 'We'll do a sweep upstairs, but nobody's down here.'

Palmer met her eye. 'Search for hidden doors.'

'This isn't a haunted house . . .' Steph shook her head but followed one of her team up the carpeted staircase.

Palmer went into the living room, just an empty space

waiting to start living. Plush carpets, unmarked by furniture and unworn. The window took in all three cars and looked back right down the hill to the main road.

If he'd been here, maybe he'd seen their approach and fled. But they had people out the back and he'd have to carry Dawn. Assuming he hadn't left her somewhere.

A second door led off the side, wooden floorboards leading into what would be a dining room if there was any furniture. Another door connected with the kitchen at the other side. Patio doors looked across bare earth at the back to a slight dip, then three low hilltops, their covering trees cast in moonlight and swaying in the wind. A long garden led up to a stone wall.

Nowhere to run, nowhere to hide.

Palmer tried the patio doors. Locked. She grabbed Corcoran's torch and examined the glass.

'You got something there?'

'Not sure.' Palmer squatted down to examine the door. It looked workshop perfect, a sheet of plastic still attached to the glass. 'No fingerprints or marks of any kind.' She looked up at him. 'I haven't seen any signs that anyone's even been in this room before us.'

'Agreed.' Corcoran opened the kitchen door and left her alone. Strong lights cast a second-hand glow across the perfect floorboards, drowning out the room's subtle glow.

Palmer stood up tall and tried to process everything. Just a sterile house. No psychopaths hiding in the cupboards, no victims tied up in the spare bedroom. But if he had built it himself, then maybe there was a trapdoor somewhere, leading down into a hidden room in the foundations. And if that was the case, why would he use the old POW camp?

Footsteps thundered down the stairs, the echoes amplified by the bare walls and floors.

Steph walked through to the kitchen to meet Corcoran. 'Nothing up there. No secret panels or trapdoors. And believe me, we've looked.'

Palmer followed her in. Shiny and showroom perfect, white and grey. All of John Mitchell's possessions were piled up against one wall, a life in a few cardboard boxes.

Corcoran was rooting around in empty cupboards. 'You're sure?'

'No, he's hiding under the bed.' Steph rested her hands on her hips. 'Except there isn't even a bed.'

'Has he been living here?'

'There's an inflatable mattress in the master bedroom. Towel on the en suite radiator. Bone dry.'

Palmer spotted just one box that looked opened, the torn tape almost hidden by the other boxes. She shifted them aside, lighter than they looked, and eased it out. Inside, some towels on the top, then a layer of folded clothes. He had been here. Right at the bottom was a set of old photograph wallets from various print bureaus, bound together by rubber bands.

She took them out and pried off the bands. The first packet was tattered and frayed at the edges. Printed by Boots, with the shop address on a sticker, an illegible home address scrawled in blue biro.

Inside, photographs of a young man at a party, his dark hair yanked back in a severe ponytail. Denim jeans and jacket, covered in Iron Maiden and Metallica patches. Terry Beane, looking much older than the sole photo David Crossley had provided, though the dates were a year apart. Two other men were visible through the fug of smoke, their drunk faces and eyes glowing red in the harsh light.

She flicked through the rest. It looked like a roll of film had been taken in one night, documenting a party in the early nineties judging by the Pearl Jam and Nirvana T-shirts. Most focused on the man as he drank and smoked drugs. Then later, topless with his ponytail out so he could mosh, his hair splaying wide as he banged his head. Several shots of people talking, but Terry stood to the side, withdrawn from the group. He only came alive with his music.

A string of arty black-and-white photos showed him at a cliffside, unclear where it was, with Terry staring down into the brine.

Near the end of the packet, another shot of him dancing, reaching out a hand to the person behind the camera. A woman's bare arm, weighed down by wristbands. Hayley Mitchell, presumably.

Palmer put them away and got out the next packet. Photos of Terry and Hayley out and about, some more in the same room the party had been in, then a series outside a country cottage. Even though they should be young, free and happy, they seemed to be withdrawn from their friends, lost in their own world. They both smiled in one photo, seemingly drunk.

She set that packet back in the box. 'This is our John, that's for sure.'

Corcoran was by the slim wine-rack spacer unit, the criss-cross grid waiting for bottles. 'So where the hell is he?'

'Good question.' Palmer flicked through another packet of photos, more recent than the other shots.

Baby photos: an exhausted mother and a distracted father.

Hayley looked young, barely sixteen even though she was over twenty. Some photos in hospital, then back home posing with their baby. Terry's happiness at his son didn't seem to spread to his eyes, betraying a fear and anxiety. Later, the stresses and strains started appearing on their faces, even as they hugged the kid. Would only be days or weeks before John Mitchell was put into care.

Did he remember? Was there some level of trauma he soaked up as a baby, with two warring parents, his mother still a child herself, his father way out of his depth? Both lost and empty, the only solace found in alcohol rather than family. Neither had the tools to cope with life.

Or perhaps John was scarred by his subsequent ordeals? Shunted from foster family to foster family. No matter how hard they tried, they couldn't cope with him.

Either way, he seemed to blame his tough start in life on the mental strains his father had suffered down in that bunker, where his fractured psyche finally broke and shattered. Unable to look after the child he had with another child, unable to commit.

'You getting anywhere, Marie?'

Palmer looked over at Corcoran. 'Not really.' She put the photos back in the box. 'It's possible he has another cell for Dawn.'

'Which is why we're going to check the garage.'

'Okay, yes. Good idea.' She shivered. 'That's like—'

'—Ross Murray's cages under his garage.' Corcoran led her through the house, back out onto the drive and its crunching pebbles.

A stand-alone garage sat in darkness to the side, the house's lights not quite stretching that far over. Steph's other two uniforms were making a mess of using her bolt-cutter to get inside. She snatched it off them and snapped the padlock in half herself.

Just a concrete floor, pristine if rough. No tyre tracks or footsteps, no obvious signs anyone had been in here since it was poured.

Palmer looked for any way down into a hidden underground room. Nothing. 'We're screwed, aren't we?'

Corcoran looked round at her, eyes narrow. 'It's not . . .'

'Where is he, Aidan? And where's Dawn?'

'The mattress, the towel. We know he's been here. He's got to be nearby. Right?'

'Not so sure.' Palmer stood in the cold and dark, shivering. 'But he isn't here, Aidan. We've lost his trail. He's not been here in hours, maybe days. He could be anywhere.'

'I don't like giving up.'

'Neither do I.' She looked back at the house, a thought floating around in her head, rattling around like a marble in a maze. 'Aidan, I think I've got a hunch.'

# Fifty

## *[Corcoran, 21:57]*

Corcoran drove, wedged between squad cars, blaring sirens hurting his ears, but curtailing his speed. He looked over at Palmer, strobing lights covering her face. 'Thought you didn't believe in hunches?'

She rolled her eyes at him. 'Keep focused on the road, please. But, in lieu of any other leads, this might—'

'Terry Beane died years ago. There's no chance John Mitchell still owns that cottage.'

'I wouldn't say no chance . . .'

His phone rang. The dashboard read *Sortwell calling* . . .

Corcoran hit the accept call button on the wheel controls. 'Pete, you got anything?'

'Something, maybe, but not sure what it means. Turns out that property is owned by a John Mitchell.'

'You're sure?'

'Inherited it in September 2010.'

Corcoran played it through as they weaved around a slow-moving tractor. John inherited a house from Terry when he died. Meaning a connection at his death. 'Can you check the previous purchases?'

'Let me see.' Typing sounds clattered out of the speakers.

'Okay. In 1989, a John Terence Beane inherited it from . . . What the hell?'

'What is it?'

'He inherited it from himself. John Terence Beane.'

'Right. That's fifth getting it from fourth.'

'With you now. Looks like fourth died in a car crash. And I've got a divorce settlement in 1984. He got the house, she got the pension.'

So much tragedy in one family.

Up ahead, Steph indicated left down a winding lane cut between two fields.

'Okay, Pete, cheers. Better go.' Corcoran killed the call.

'So Terry got the house when his dad died.' Palmer was nodding. 'That divorce tallies with what David and Sally told us, how Terry came to their school late. Some kids settle, Terry clearly didn't. A messy divorce shattered his confidence.'

'Sounds like it.' Corcoran slowed as they approached a house, Steph's headlights illuminating a crumbling cottage surrounded by an out of control woodland. 'I don't know if he's here, but I need you to take care.'

'I don't plan on doing anything different.'

Corcoran got out and checked his baton was ready. He snapped it out and swiped it through the air.

Steph nodded at him, then at her sidekick.

Corcoran followed them in silence, stepping slowly across mossed-up flagstones to the quaint cottage door.

Steph's torch flashed across the front of the house. Looked as empty as John's house.

Corcoran felt a rage in the pit of his stomach. Another swell of hope dashed. He thought through the options, struggling for anything that could lead them to Dawn Crossley being alive. Sod it. The door was old wood, splintered and damaged.

Here goes nothing.

He stepped back, then pushed his shoulder against the cracked paint, driving through the wood. It toppled in, crashing against the wall.

Corcoran stepped into the hallway, baton out and raised high. The place reeked of mildew and mould. Three doors led off. He pointed at Steph and the first door, her mate the second, then took the third himself.

A farmhouse kitchen, with Shaker-style cabinets. Half-empty whisky bottles covered the small table in the middle. Just one chair. The home of a lonely man, desperate and ready to die. A back door, locked and no sign of a key.

Back in the hallway he almost bumped into Steph's colleague. All she'd found in her room was a folded-up rug. Corcoran peered past her into a bedroom. An old-fashioned bed, with a wrought-iron frame and a patterned quilt instead of a duvet. A fireplace on the wall. Shuttered windows for a shuttered life.

Steph's room was clearly where Terry's topless head-banging had taken place. More shutters, but a sofa in front of a portable telly. Steph was sifting through a tall wardrobe, filled with old clothes. A wide desk sat against the back wall, mounted with a vintage typewriter and piled high with neat pages.

Corcoran checked the title page. *The Darkness Within* by Chuck Shepherd. A pseudonym? He slipped some gloves on and flicked through the pages. Looked like a novel, and a stream of consciousness too. One for Palmer.

Corcoran opened the only door. A bathroom: the most modern room in the house, but that wasn't saying much. An avocado suite with a bidet and shower hose running off the taps. 'Nobody here, anyway.'

Steph nodded. 'It's not like it's been empty for years, either. Rented out until three months ago.'

Corcoran felt himself shiver. 'Get a team in and go through everything. Same as the other house. And speak to the neighbours in both places. Should be farms and cottages in the vicinity. I want to find out who's been here and when.'

'On it.' Steph tapped her Airwave and spoke in a quiet voice.

Corcoran left her to it, savouring the cold night air as he walked back to the car.

No sign of Palmer.

Shit.

He jogged on, getting a stab in his hip. She was crouched by his car, waving her phone near the ground like that was normal.

'Christ, Marie, you scared me half to death.'

She looked up, frowning. 'Mm?'

'I worried he'd taken you.'

'I got bored sitting in your car.' She pointed at the damp earth. 'I spotted some fresh-looking tyre tracks.'

'What?' Corcoran clicked on his stronger torch and traced the trail through the field neighbouring the cottage, over to some woodland. He got out his Airwave and dialled Steph's badge number. Engaged. He let it ring but she bounced him. He tried again and got her. 'Steph, we've got a trail into the woods. Stay there and secure the house.'

'You sure?'

'It's probably nothing.' Corcoran was already walking, keeping to the side of the track. 'Just wanted you to know where we were heading. I'll call you if we need backup. Over.' He ended the call and continued into the forest, the trees opening out and letting them in. He had his baton primed and ready, with his torch shining ahead.

The beam caught something metal. He jogged over. A Ford Mondeo, with chunky off-road tyres.

Palmer's eyes were white with fear. 'Is he here?'

'I don't know.' Corcoran spotted footprints leading away. Just one set. Short and wide steps, though, like he wasn't walking at pace, but . . . Shit, carrying something. He set off again, slow and steady, and tried Steph again. 'Get over here.'

'Just be a minute.'

Up ahead, the wood had almost swallowed up a building, brick and low-slung. Maybe a shepherd's hut or an old dairy. Looked sound though, with an intact roof and solid door.

Corcoran gripped his baton tight and nudged the door open. Looked empty, just a straw-covered floor. He stepped back and tried Steph again. Got her this time. 'Dead end, by the looks of it. We'll head back.'

'Okay.' Click and she was gone.

'Aidan, are you sure? Those footprints look—'

'—like he'd been carrying someone. I know.' Corcoran scratched at his stubble. 'There's no easy way past here, the wood's thick as hell.'

'Come on.' Palmer led inside and started kicking at the straw. 'There's got to be something.'

Corcoran scanned his torch across the floor. It all looked

level. Except. Over there, in the middle of the back wall, it was all bunched up. 'Now, wait, okay?' He took it slow as he crossed over. Beside the rucked-up straw, a wooden hatch lay in the floor, with a single metal handle. Corcoran reached for his Airwave.

Someone screamed, 'HELP!'

Palmer stepped back and let Corcoran rest the hatch against the heaped-up straw. A weak light source down there, probably a battery-powered lantern.

And Dawn lay on the floor, eyes open wide, screaming for help. Distressed, exhausted and terrified.

'Stay there.' Corcoran stepped onto the ladder, reassuringly solid, but the light barely reached down there. 'I mean it.' He eased himself down, one step at a time, until his foot touched the bottom. The light didn't reach into the corners and the room seemed bigger than the space upstairs, certainly a lot wider. He took one look at Dawn, then back up at Palmer. 'Need you to check her.'

Palmer clambered down with much more grace than he'd managed. She pressed her head to Dawn's chest to take a pulse, counting to ten against her watch. 'Her heart rate's dangerously low. She needs urgent medical help.'

'We can't wait for an ambulance. I'll carry her up.'

'With your hip?'

Corcoran gritted his teeth and got out his police radio. 'I'll call Broadribb and—'

A man stepped out of the gloom and pointed a gun at Corcoran's head.

# Fifty-one

## *[Palmer, 22:08]*

'You first.' The gun told Palmer more than the man could. He wore a balaclava, though the light barely touched his face.

'What do you want, John?'

He didn't flinch at the mention of his name. 'I told you, up there.' He pointed with the gun. 'Go.'

She looked at Corcoran. That steely glint in his eyes, switching his gaze between the pistol and the man. The things he'd do to him. Smashing his brain into a pulp not the least.

She looked up at the top of the ladder. She could get up there and run. But Dawn was ill and needed medical attention. 'I need to help her.'

'You're not listening to me. Get up there.'

'She'll die!'

'Up there. And don't think about running or I'll put Dawn out of her misery now, followed by him and then you.'

'You're not a killer.'

'Yet.' Another flick of the gun. 'Now, go.'

Palmer hauled herself up the ladder, taking it slow, pretending she'd never climbed one before, but soon enough she was up the top and out.

She could run for it. Get to Corcoran's car, get his phone or hers. Call it in. Get backup.

But John would have Corcoran and Dawn. Two lives. And he had a gun . . .

Corcoran was crunching up the ladder. His hip didn't look right, each step causing severe pain.

Palmer looked down into the gloom at Dawn, spread-eagled on the floor, lying there, dying. A casualty of his stupid war. Palmer knew she should try and save her, but he had all of the power.

Corcoran pulled himself up to her level and flopped over, whispering, 'Let's bide our time. I'll attack him, you get the gun, we can save Dawn.'

'Are you sure?'

Before Corcoran could do anything other than nod confirmation, John appeared, training the gun on Palmer. 'Steady.' One step at a time, then he cleared the top, aiming the gun right at her, flicking between her stomach and her heart as he stepped onto the straw. On his knees, then standing up. 'Okay, here's what's going to happen. We're going to—'

'You can't just leave her down there!' Palmer stepped closer to him. If she could push him back down . . . 'She'll die!'

'That's the whole point.'

'You haven't killed so far, John. You don't have to cross the line.'

'Stop appealing to my better nature. I don't have one.'

'This isn't you—'

'It is.' John shoved the gun against her chest, then wrapped an arm round her neck. Up close, she could appreciate his sheer size. At least a foot taller than her and built. He pushed her outside, the pistol now digging into her back, and he led them to his car. 'Get in, passenger side.'

Corcoran followed at a distance, looking around for anything he could use to overpower their captor.

'Spoiler, but there's nothing.' John aimed the gun at him. 'Phone and police radio. Now.'

Corcoran dropped them both on the ground.

John sighed. 'Kick them over.'

Corcoran did, but only to halfway.

'I'm losing my patience with you.' John bent down to pick them up, keeping the gun trained on him, then he slipped them in his pocket. 'Which one's your sore hip?'

Corcoran frowned at Palmer, then back at John. 'The left.'

'Thanks.' John aimed the gun at Corcoran's right leg and shot into his thigh.

'No!' Palmer jolted forward but John held her back.

Corcoran stumbled backwards, screaming.

John shifted the gun to Palmer, the mechanism grinding as he reloaded. 'I told you to get in!'

Her breathing came hard and fast. 'You, you—'

'Get in the fucking car or so help me God I will shoot you in the fucking face.'

Palmer stared at him. She didn't have a choice. Corcoran was screaming, Dawn was dying and there was nothing she could do to help either of them. She opened the passenger door and got in.

John got into the driver's side and twisted the key in the ignition. The car burst to life and he pulled off, easing round the tight circle to head back towards the cottage. Lights off, one hand steering, the other pointing the gun at her.

Palmer looked in the wing mirrors but Corcoran was lost to the darkness now. Just lying there, shot and bleeding. A leg wound shouldn't bleed out, but he would need medical attention. She looked over at John. 'You've done well.'

John drove past the cottage and turned into the lane, taking it slow. 'What do you mean?'

'Everything. You've planned this out well and executed it expertly. We had no idea it was you until we spoke to Dawn's father and even then I—'

'I know you're judging me for this but I really don't care.'

Palmer focused on the gun, flinching slightly, then she looked out again. 'Why are you doing this?'

John turned right at the main road, hitting the floor until the needle hit seventy, the automatic grunting through the gears. 'I thought you knew.'

'I get why you think you're doing this. Those people tormented your father, ruined his life. He blamed them for everything, for the destructive spiral that led to your birth, to him and your mother not being able to keep you. But you can't bring either of them back into your life.'

'No, but I can make those fuckers suffer for what they did. My father was a good man. Troubled, damaged, but good in his heart. And they broke him. I should never have been born. I know every angry teenager thinks that, but I genuinely mean it. If he hadn't been so badly damaged, he wouldn't have met my mother when she was so young, wouldn't have made her pregnant. She was a *child*.'

'Have you talked to anyone about this?'

They entered civilisation, the first little houses of Princes Risborough.

He reached up to rub his chin with the back of his hands, shifting his balaclava up to reveal a couple of inches of precisely trimmed goatee. 'None of your psychobabble, please.'

'It's called therapy. All this rage, it's possible to channel it into some—'

'I'm channelling it into this.' John wound down his window and chucked Corcoran's phone and radio out. Palmer watched them bounce and roll across the carriageway as they raced away. 'I was taken away from my parents because they were incapable of caring for me. I had so many terrible experiences that you wouldn't believe, denied a basic family life until I met my dad.' He tore his balaclava off and his face was twisted into a smile. 'Stuart. He was a good guy. Him and Mum adopted me. Turned my life around. He died three years ago. Complications from his diabetes.'

'Is that why you're doing this to Dawn?'

'That's a happy coincidence.' John sighed. 'When I was sixteen, my father, my real father, he came to see me.'

'Terry.'

'Right. He was drunk, dishevelled, pathetic. In tears, apologising for being such a bad father.' John snorted as he slowed to the thirty limit, passing normal people and their normal lives. 'You know that Nirvana song, where it goes "I tried hard to have a father, but instead I had a dad"? I totally get that. Stuart was my *dad*, Terry was my *father*. When Terry's parents divorced and his mum stayed in Birmingham, his own father used to lock him in that milk shed overnight . . . That building back there. Downstairs. Made him scared of the dark. And school was hell for a kid going through that.

Then he got a flicker of hope. There was this girl, see, not my mother. Someone else.'

'Sally.'

'Get you.' A snarl escaped his thin lips. 'That *harpy* . . . Her and her *friends*. Those pricks locked my father in a bunker for sixty hours. Almost three whole days. To most people, it would've been tough. Damaging. But to him? It broke him. "It was like being in hell, son. I didn't even know if I was dead or alive." Those four pricks all went off to university, and my father . . . He suffered what people like you would identify as PTSD. He never slept properly again, had flashbacks, became withdrawn, hallucinated, grew dependent on alcohol . . .'

'He could've sought help.'

'Nobody would've given him it. Not back then. But you seem to know all about his disastrous relationship with my mother, Hayley. That night Terry came to see me, he apologised for never being good enough for her, blamed himself for everything that happened to me and to her, then he stumbled off . . . But I followed him. Wanted to get to know him, the *real* him, not the fuck-up I saw. In time, I was able to forgive him for what had happened and I tried to help him get back on track. Then a few weeks later, Terry killed himself. At that cottage.' John held up his pistol. 'Shot himself with this gun.'

Something crawled up Palmer's spine.

'It changes you, doesn't it? Something like that. Made me determined not to let my early trauma affect my life the way it had my father. So I worked hard to get ahead. Stuart helped, of course, and I did okay. Not the best university, but I studied architecture. My dream job. Things were going well. But then my mother found me. She'd left town when I was young, when she was still young. She lived in France for a bit, then America. She came home, but she was broken too. Her father used to abuse her, sexually. She wanted to be all grown up, to take control of her body, which is why she met my father, why she hooked up with this guy who could buy her drink, who got drunk all the time.'

John flew across a roundabout. No sign of the police road-blocks now. 'She was in a hospice outside of town, dying of ovarian cancer. Hard not to blame myself for that. If I hadn't been born, maybe everything ... inside her would've been fine. She died two weeks later, but I got to know her a bit. This skeleton, only forty-five. No age at all. If she hadn't had me, hadn't met my father, she'd still be alive. Maybe she'd get peace for what happened to her, I don't know. But standing by the side of her grave, I just couldn't let it go. My entire life, my mother's and my father's ... Three lives ruined by the selfishness of those entitled teenagers who tortured him, because they didn't want to risk their own futures. I promised I'd get revenge.'

'Listen to me, John. What you've gone through, what your parents went through ... I understand. Believe me. I know what's going on in your head, all the blame and shame and guilt and fear and anger and despair. You only wanted to do the right thing for your father. But you've given these people your message. Let me get out here.' She kept her focus on him. 'And you can just disappear, become someone new. Live a life for all three of you.'

'Don't you think I've considered that? And I know what you're trying to do. It won't work.'

'John, you can choose to stop this. We can still save Dawn.'

'But I can't be saved. I need to do this.'

'That's not true. I can work with you and we can help you. We spoke to your boss. You were running a property development. That's huge.'

'I made a complete mess of that.' He pulled up at the side of the road.

She saw where they were. Outside Dawn's parents' house. And the cops had all gone.

'Those people inside already have one death on their conscience.' John reached across her and got out a fresh set of bullets, then started loading them into the gun. 'They deserve more.'

# Fifty-two

## [Corcoran, 22:18]

Corcoran lay in the damp mud, his thigh on fire. Pain screamed out all over his body, from kneecap to hip. Everything burned.

They'd lost. John had Palmer now.

And that hit him hardest of all. Forget about the victims and their tragedies, as devoted as he was to saving them and helping them through their traumas; John had Palmer.

He felt a thickness in the back of his throat, a fluttering deep in his gut. Jesus, there was something there. The case forcing them together, binding them tight in its shared horror. But she was inside his head. He could feel her thoughts in his head, beneath his skin, see her face when he closed his eyes.

And that bastard had her and there wasn't a thing Corcoran could do to stop him. No telling where he could've gone. Would probably use her as insurance to escape. Flee the country or just go to ground.

He hauled himself up to his knees and the pain flared again. Then up to standing, both sides broken and buckled.

What the hell could he do? He was shot, bleeding and broken. His car was back at the house, assuming John hadn't done anything to it. He just needed to go over and—

DAWN.

Save her first.

Corcoran set off, step then slide. Step then slide. He got into a groove, then rested against the shed's front wall, clutching the door as he eased his way in. His trouser leg was soaked through. He step-slid over, each movement a sharp rasp of burning agony, leaving a bloody trail in the straw.

The trapdoor was still hanging open and she lay on the floor, eyes shut. She opened them and looked right through him. 'Help.' Her voice was a weak plea, rather than the loud shout that had alerted them.

'It's okay, Dawn, I'm coming for you.' Corcoran put the foot of his shot leg onto the ladder first, got it stable, then his other foot. Slowly does it. Another step with the shot foot, and he slipped, the bloody sole of his shoe falling away. His fingers clutched at the ladder, then were torn free and he crashed down, his right knee clattering off a step, his coccyx crunching off the stone floor. A new flavour of agony swept over his body. 'FUCK!'

'Help me. Please.'

He sucked in deep breaths, battling against the surging waves of agony coursing across his body. He forced himself up, his vision swimming. He braced himself against the dresser and stood up.

Dawn lay on the bed, looking over at him, her eyes barely opening now.

Corcoran tried to steady himself, breathing deeply. Completely out of his depth here. How could he save her?

She looked at him again, her arm ever so slightly raised, pointing at the dresser. 'Sugar. Pill.'

Corcoran swung round and opened the drawer. It was

stuffed with pills and syringes and vials. He got one of the pills and took it over to her. 'Is this what you want?'

She peered at it, then nodded.

He held it out in front of her.

She ate it from his hand like horse, swallowing it straight down. 'Syringe. Please.'

He staggered back to the dresser and got a needle. And a vial of insulin. He held them up to her and got a nod. 'We're going to get you out of here, okay?'

She seemed to have got better remarkably quickly. She gave him the up and down. 'You don't look so good yourself.'

Corcoran stared down at his leg and got a fresh blast of pain. His trousers were ripped and soaked a deep red. He slumped back against the dresser, deep pain shooting up his torso, up his neck. He pushed out a deep breath, gasping and moaning.

Dawn snatched the syringe out of his hand and tore off the cap. 'Are you police?'

He nodded. 'DS Aidan Corcoran.'

She plunged the needle into the vial and sucked it up into the chamber. 'Who is he?'

'He didn't speak to you?'

'Not a word.' She pulled up her skirt and pinched a chunk of flesh on her tummy, then jabbed herself with the needle. Didn't even flinch. She held it there, counting silently. 'I doubted it was even a man.' She pulled the needle out and tossed it to the side. 'I need to get you to a hospital.'

'He's got her. I can't . . . I can't lose her.'

'Got who?'

'Come on.' Corcoran hauled himself up and step-slid over

to the ladder, fresh pain tearing at his thigh. He rested his head against the metal of the ladder. 'We've got to . . . Get up there, then find my car. Then we're going to stop him.'

'You're losing a ton of blood. You're in no fit state to drive.'

He looked round at her. 'Can you?'

'I can. Are you sure you don't—'

'We need to stop him.' He passed her his car keys.

'And where is he?'

Corcoran gripped the ladder tighter. He didn't know. 'No idea.'

'I want to bring him down. He doesn't get to do this to me. Do you hear?'

'I hear you.'

And Dawn was the answer.

The parents, all of John's anger directed against their children. For his father's torment in the bunker, the cause of his tragic life. The start of John's own tortured existence.

Corcoran put a foot on the ladder. 'I've got an idea where he is.'

# Fifty-three

## *[Palmer, 22:36]*

'Well done getting them all here. Saves me a job.' John trained the gun on her, still in the car. 'All those people who left my father to rot in that cell. I've made their children suffer, now it's their turn.'

Palmer tried to keep calm. Let him feel like he was in control.

'Should I start with Dawn's father, David? He was the ringleader, wasn't he? But it was Nathan who forced my father into that bunker. Maybe I'll leave David till last. Maybe his wife's there, maybe she—'

'Let me go. Give yourself up.'

John smiled at her. 'Not going to happen.' He pressed the gun into Palmer's side, pinching her flesh and tapping bone. 'Now, get out. Nice and slowly.'

Hands up, Palmer opened the door wide and put her foot on the ground. She got out, wobbling, and rested against the car door.

And he was already out, aiming the gun across the roof at her. 'Steady now.' He waved the pistol. 'Come on, let's get going.'

Palmer set off across the road, her legs like jelly. 'Did you know we'd get them all together?'

John followed her close, pressing the gun against her spine. 'I didn't think you'd be this quick. I'm impressed.' He reached round to open the front door. Unlocked. 'Then again, you found me, so you have some skills. Go on.'

Palmer entered and walked along the hall. Raised voices came from the living room, echoing through. David, Sally and Melissa stood in the living room, arguing. They saw her and stopped.

John brushed past and stormed into the room, marching right up to David. He pushed the gun against his head. 'This is loaded, in case you're wondering. More than enough bullets left to kill everyone in this room.'

Palmer stayed on the threshold, frozen to the spot. She had no training for this. No experience. No nothing.

'Stop!' Thompson charged through. Too late. She spotted the gun, watched it swivel round to point at her head, then put her hands to her head, clutching her mobile.

'Drop the phone.'

It clattered to the ground. John stepped on it, crunching it beneath his boot.

'John.' Palmer stepped into the room. 'John, don't kill anyone. Please.'

Her turn to face the barrel. 'Shut your mouth.'

'You're a cornered rat.' Thompson was inching closer. 'Nowhere for you to go. You know that. Was this your plan all along?'

'You don't know anything.'

'I've called in backup, so you should just give up now.' Another step from Thompson. 'Okay?'

John pointed the gun at her chest. 'This is the only important thing in my life. I could've run away, could've left this godforsaken place, but I haven't.'

'Don't do this.'

John swung the gun round to aim at Melissa. 'Do you know how much torment you put my father through?' He pointed the gun at Sally. 'Do you?' Then David. 'Where's Nathan?'

'He's dead. Died in Spain.' David kept his focus on the gun. 'Where is my daughter?'

John stepped closer, pointing the gun at David's head. 'She's dead.'

'You fucking *animal*!' David lurched forward, reaching for the gun, but John kicked him, cracking his heel into soft knee. David went down, hard.

John kicked him in the groin, again and again until he squealed. 'You wish I was an animal.' He crouched and pressed the barrel against David's temple. 'None of this affects anything. It doesn't change what you did, or the life my father lived. The shit I've been through. But it's a consolation to be able to do this to you.'

'I can help you, John.' Palmer tried to distract him, but he didn't move away. She caught Thompson's look of surprise out of the corner of her eye. 'I've worked with people like you, John. I've helped them control this. You need help and I can give you it.'

'Shut up. Shut up!'

'Your father should've been helped through his ordeal. He

shouldn't have suffered alone, shouldn't have had to lose himself in drink and drugs. You don't need to do the same. Stop now.'

'Bullshit.' John charged over, aiming the gun at Thompson's head. 'She is your fault, isn't she? Thought you'd be smart bringing someone like her in to help you and your thick bastard squad.'

'She shouldn't be here.'

'It's all bullshit. You let the real villains get away with crimes.' John swung the weapon round to aim at Melissa again. 'These people, they're all to blame. They're all guilty.' Then Sally. 'My father told me about you. You were the tease, weren't you? Lured him along so you could play your games with him.'

'It wasn't like that.'

'Wasn't it? You were interested in this punk here.' John aimed the gun at David. 'You liked him. Wanted him to make the first move, but he didn't, so you used my father.' He pressed the gun right at her forehead. 'And. You. Ruined. His. Fucking. Life.'

Palmer spotted movement outside. A car pulling up, headlights off. The passenger door opened and Corcoran got out, limping and grimacing. She gasped. If John saw him, he would shoot them all. No question, no hesitation. 'John, they were just kids.' That got his attention, made him aim the gun at her. 'They were kids. I detest what happened to your father, but I don't think they knew what they were doing.'

'Shut up!'

'I think every one of them was tortured by what they did. It's haunted them throughout their lives. Haven't you done enough to their children?'

That hit him, her words like a clenched fist in the teeth.

'They've suffered, John. Their children . . . You starved Sarah to the point where her liver and kidneys won't function properly. Howard will always hear that song and will likely suffer permanent hearing damage. Matt will never sleep again without nightmares. They'll all carry physical and mental injuries. And you've killed Dawn. You've crossed that line.'

'Shut up!' John pulled the hammer back. 'Shut up!'

Corcoran stumbled into the living room, limping and bleeding everywhere.

John aimed at him. 'Stop!'

Corcoran forced himself across the room, stepping with his bad-hip foot, sliding with the other, leaving a trail of blood on the red carpet. He put his head against the gun barrel. 'Give yourself up, John.' He was breathing heavily. 'There's nowhere to go.'

Palmer didn't know where to look. 'Aidan!'

John pulled the gun away from Corcoran slightly. Panic in his eyes, like he knew he'd lost control over the situation.

'You've done enough.' Corcoran narrowed his eyes, shifted his head closer, daring him to shoot. 'Go on! Kill me! I already died! DO IT!'

John held his gaze for a long time, his emotionless eyes focusing right on Corcoran. Then he put the gun against his own head and the noise was deafening.

# Fifty-four

## [Corcoran, 23:21]

Corcoran lay on a gurney in the back of the ambulance, two paramedics injecting and examining and doing God knows what else they did with a gunshot wound. Outside, Steph and the other police controlled the crime scene, stopping the journalists and rubberneckers getting through.

The second ambulance lights danced on the glistening pavement, the siren silent, as the paramedic helped Dawn into the back.

Palmer gave a thumbs up as she walked over. 'She's looking good, Aidan.'

'That's a relief.' Corcoran gritted his teeth and sucked in a breath. 'This is absolute agony. Can I have any more morphine?'

His paramedic shook his head. 'You'll overdose.'

'That feels like a good idea right now.'

Palmer hugged her arms tight. 'Don't even joke about it.'

'Well, well, well.' Thompson appeared next to Palmer, hands in pockets, blowing air up her face. 'The dream team took him down, eh?'

'He took himself down.' Corcoran grimaced. 'I should've stopped him earlier.'

'Come on, you didn't know until—'

'—I burst into that basement like an idiot.' He grunted as the paramedic stuck something in his leg. 'Doing that let him get away. Let him confront all those people . . .'

A shake of the head from Thompson. 'Get over yourself.'

Palmer laughed. But she recovered before Thompson noticed. 'John was going to kill them all, you know? That was his plan. He targeted the kids to torture the parents. He wanted them to suffer horrifically before he killed them.'

'But this was his endgame. Making them all suffer for what they did. Your work was crucial in there, Dr Palmer. Better keep it to yourself, don't want the powers that be kicking out us lowly cops in favour of your type.' Thompson gave her a wink. 'Okay, well, I'll leave you two lovebirds.'

Corcoran couldn't look at Palmer. 'Alana, there's nothing going on here.'

'Keep telling yourself that.' She strolled off, laughing.

They sat in embarrassed silence while the paramedics worked at Corcoran's injuries.

He looked up at Palmer. 'There is nothing going on here, right?'

Palmer was blushing. 'I mean, you're a nice guy but you've got so much baggage.'

'You're one to talk.' Corcoran looked at her. Two days ago, she was an obstacle, someone getting in his way, bringing her psychobabble mumbo jumbo with her, preventing him doing his police work.

But now . . .

She was a friend, someone he'd been through a horrific ordeal with. That sting in his gut when he realised John had her . . .

Maybe in time . . .

No.

'Look, Marie, I've got a wife and kid. Back in London.'

'Oh.' She tucked her hair behind her ear, avoiding his gaze. 'I didn't know.'

'I didn't tell you.' Corcoran winced as something really bloody sore was rubbed into his thigh. 'We're separated. It's over. Lucy kicked me out, put in a restraining order. Won't let me see Adam.'

Her eyebrows danced up and she looked at him. 'What the hell did you do, Aidan?'

'Nothing.' Now Corcoran couldn't look at her, though this time it was because of shame. 'After we caught *him*, I got depressed.'

'Ross Murray?'

'Right, him. I fell onto train tracks and injured my hip. Forced to take time off work and of course I was too stubborn to get surgery. But I'd let Zoe Wilson get in my head, let her fuck up that case. Let two people die.'

'But *you* caught him, Aidan.'

'I did. And at great cost.' He could only shake his head, like it'd blow away the cobwebs. But it all stayed the same. 'I went back to work, but . . . A long time ago I made a decision to never talk about my private life at work. You know how we need to compartmentalise? Well, I did. What happened at work, stayed at work. Only . . .'

'It followed you home?'

'Right. And I couldn't open up at home. The stress got to me, exploding after we put him away. I was off for months, a zombie. For seven months. All I did was lie in bed or sit at the breakfast table. Even taking Adam to school was beyond me. I just kept thinking about what Ross Murray had done to all those women. About how I could've stopped them. The last two victims. Kate Pearson and Alison Gray. I could've stopped them. Two people died because of me. How do you . . .?'

Palmer reached over to touch his arm, gentle and soft. 'Aidan, I deal with the other side of the coin. People like Murray Ross and' – she swallowed hard – 'John Mitchell. I try to rehabilitate them. I tell myself I can do that, that there's still an essence of humanity in there.' She reached for his hand and he let her take it. 'But seeing you like this? That's the hardest part. You didn't do anything wrong. In fact, you caught a serial killer and now you've stopped a serial abductor, and yet you blame yourself.' She squeezed his hand, sending a pulse of life up his forearm. 'You can't change the past, but you can accept what you are.'

He looked over at her, frowning. 'What am I?'

'You're a hero, Aidan. And you're suffering survivor's guilt. But I've told you not to blame yourself. I know you didn't stop him killing Kate or Alison, but you did allow all the families of those victims to grieve. You gave them closure and you helped them start to heal. You need to do that yourself.'

He looked at her again, saw reflected light sparkling in her dark eyes. And he almost let her have it, to admit she was right, but that would be too easy. 'I wish I'd caught John Mitchell rather than . . .' He shut his eyes.

All he could see was John Mitchell's brains exploding, blood spraying across David Crossley and Sally Norton.

'And now there's no chance for you to help him.'

'I could have, you know? It would've been hard, but . . . I don't believe he was past helping. He wasn't the worst person I've been in a room with.'

'That'll be me?' Corcoran tried a smile and she actually laughed. 'You know, a wise person told me "you can't punish yourself for not saving everyone".'

That got a smile out of her. 'We saved Dawn, we saved their parents. It's all we could've hoped for.'

A gust of wind blew into the back of the ambulance. 'I know. I just wish we . . .'

'Aidan, stop!' She ran a hand through her hair. 'You put yourself at serious risk there. Pressing your head against his gun. That was stupid. We didn't know he wasn't going to kill. You saw what he did to David Crossley. And he just left Dawn to die.'

'But you really think he'd have killed me? An innocent man?'

'I thought you were guilty of not catching all these killers at the right time?'

That hit him like a punch in the guts, forcing a laugh from his throat. Not the right time, maybe, but God it was what he needed. 'You can always do something earlier, right?'

'Exactly. Focus on what you have done.' She bit her lip. 'I'm sorry about what happened with you and your wife, Aidan. I really am.'

'One of those things.' He shrugged. 'Maybe you're right, maybe I need saving. Learn to control my impulses and stop repeating the same cycles.' He grinned at her. 'Do you know a good psychologist?'

One year later

# Fifty-five

## *Palmer*

The black cat crawled round Palmer's legs, forcing himself onto his back and raking against her shoes. Cute as hell, but such a little sod. She reached down to tickle his tummy but he raced off through the flat, ears up. 'Must be good being back with him?'

The communal gardens bloomed outside, lush cottage garden plants under a sprawling hawthorn in full blossom.

Sarah Langton took a sip from her coffee. 'Good old Milhouse.' She was almost back to her previous weight, but her pallor was like she'd died a year ago. Pale, yellowy skin stretched too tight. 'They're saying I might be able to go back to work next month.'

'That's good. But you should take your time, Sarah.' Palmer wrapped her hands around her mug, her green tea left in too long, but she didn't want to say anything. 'You're looking healthier but your ordeal—'

'I wish Christopher was here to help, but . . .' Sarah sighed. 'He's back home with his parents. This was all too much for him.'

'It's a lot to go through for anyone.'

'You know we were childhood sweethearts, right? It stopped

being so sweet. That's why I slept with Klaus. Why I kept on sleeping with Klaus.' Sarah shut her eyes. 'What a bloody mess.'

'It's okay to think that, you know? To put emotional distance between yourself and your situation. To describe it, to colour it with words. Helps you say what you really mean, helps you see where you need to change the most.'

'It's messed up, that's all it means.' Sarah's phone rang. She reached over to the breakfast bar and picked it up. Her smile looked genuine and warm. 'It's Howie.' She let it ring out.

'Howie?'

'Howard Ritchie.'

Palmer nodded, gave her a warm smile. 'You can answer it.'

'I'll call him back later.'

Palmer took a sip of her tea. Definitely way too strong for her. 'So you're still in touch with the other three?'

'Just Howie. I mean, they're okay. It's weird. For a fortnight, myself, Howie and Matt . . . the three of us were just metres away from each other, but we didn't even know anyone else was there. I was in there just over six weeks and Matt was there all that time. We couldn't help each other.'

'But you can help each other now?'

Sarah's face lit up with a broad grin. 'And we are. Howie's back surfing and cooking. Matt's talking about going back to work, but he's found it hardest of all of us. He's not right in the head. And Dawn was a hero. Even though she was only in his grip for hours, she was there with us through those sessions. Kept calling us, arranging meetings. Made us talk about it. Can't believe what he—' She caught herself.

'What *John* put us through. All because of our fucking parents.' She picked up Milhouse and cradled him in her lap, stroking his luxurious fur. 'I mean, you grow up thinking your folks are these heroes, that they know everything. They remind you of the sacrifices they made for you and . . . Then you find out what they did. I mean, Mum wasn't the worst of them, but Christ, if she hadn't brought him along, none of it would've happened.'

Her phone rang again.

'Take it. Please.' Palmer got up. 'I'll see myself out, okay?'

'Okay.' Sarah bit her lip as she answered the phone. 'Hey, Howie, guess who I'm with?'

'Say hi from me.' Palmer walked out of the flat and skipped down the steps, pleased to help victims instead of villains, for once.

Outside, a black Golf had boxed her car into the car park. She stopped with a groan.

Corcoran stood by the Golf, smiling at her. 'Only way to get your attention.' He looked frayed, tired, but in control. Moving a lot freer too as he came over to kiss her cheek.

'My god, you can walk?'

He laughed. 'Finally got my hip resurfaced. Took me so long to face up to reality. Couple of months off work but I feel like a new man now.'

'I'm impressed. But how did you find me?'

'I spoke to Sarah this morning. She said you were meeting her.'

'Right.'

He stared at her. 'Thanks for listening to me. I didn't thank you before. Things have been . . . well.'

'I'm here for you, Aidan. I just wish I'd seen you in the last, what, five months?'

'Sorry, I can blow hot and cold.'

'So why now?'

He gave her a dark look. 'There's another case, and it's even worse than the last one . . .'

# THRILLINGLY GOOD BOOKS
# FROM CRIMINALLY
# GOOD WRITERS

CRIME FILES BRINGS YOU THE LATEST RELEASES FROM
TOP CRIME AND THRILLER AUTHORS.

SIGN UP ONLINE FOR OUR MONTHLY NEWSLETTER AND BE THE FIRST
TO KNOW ABOUT OUR COMPETITIONS, NEW BOOKS AND MORE.